The Life of Bea

I0635341

A Sequel to 'Don't Look Behind the Fridge'

By
Julian Lechmus

ISBN 9780648821670

Editor Dana McCown

Copyright © 2023 Julian Lechmus

First printing 2023

StoryBridge Press
Brisbane, Queensland, Australia
2023

Cover design Dana McCown

PREFACE

With only his white rat left, Jules proceeded to bury his wife, sister and friend who did not want to continue to be injected with the life prolonging peptide. They had said, "Jules, we've had a very, very long life but it's time to depart. Do you want to join us? We have four fast-acting cyanide pills."

Jules didn't join them on their path to self-destruction, but for a while he wished he had, and he looked for that 4th cyanide pill. But he had droped it and couldn't find it on the sandy beach. Then, suddenly, one of those new silent helicopters landed on the sand by the sea and out steps Bea, a member of *Pi5* (an ASIO type Polish organization, like *Ai5*, that also hired agents out for more unscrupulous activities than just spying). She was accompanied by two burly accomplices. Bea forced Jules to fly to Poland with her and start the manufacture of the peptide, as she had depleted the stock she had stolen from Jules 100 years ago and was now getting wrinkles.

And so, a new adventure starts with many twists and interesting characters who all have complex and slightly troubling stories, but all manage to save each other and live funny and never dull lives. It's a fast-moving, pretty crazy story, but on the serious side, it does address issues society faces at the moment, the rich striving to get richer but not realising you can't take it with you to an 'after-life', and burgeoning issues like AI and androids (human-looking robots) which even now are being developed to be more human-looking. The future could be very interesting and make more sense if logical-thinking androids enter the political system rather than the human self-seeking, glory narcissists we have governing countries around the world.

"Life of Bea" is the sequel to "Don't Look Behind the Fridge" (Amazon) The stories are connected but are mainly independent, except for the explanations of some of the relationships between the characters, so you don't have to read the first. "Ana, Ana Conda" is a prequel to the first book and will be available soon.

Chapter One

"Jules, the world can't support this growing population, and we've done more than our fair share of time on this planet due to you injecting us when we were asleep with that thing you call the life-prolonging peptide. Jules, you have to say goodbye sometime. Come with us," Smithy said before swallowing his cyanide pill.

I should have followed Smithy's advice, but then that was an initial evaluation. I chickened out. I look around at the ten cabins in a horseshoe arrangement, facing a BBQ area near the beach where we all had our meals and had such a good time, but I chickened out; I feel like a coward and slap my face. I didn't swallow the cyanide pill even though Melissa, my partner, Charmaine, my transgender brother who became my sister and Smithy, her partner and my friend, all did, and they used newly purchased pills, unlike the old ones I from serving with *Ai5*. Their deaths were quick, and now I'm trying to dig holes to bury them on our North Queensland Island.

Chloe4, the great-granddaughter of the original white rat is sitting on my shoulder as I dig and uncontrollably sob shedding copious tears. I briefly go back into our cabin complex and inject Chloe4 and myself with another dose of the life-prolonging peptide; I can't die of old age before I finish the burials. I will miss my partner, sister and friend so much. I give the little white rat a kiss. She's the only companion I got left, and as the mental darkness descends, I start to venture into that PTSD state again.

Just as I'm stepping out from my cabin with a big knife and contemplating hari-kari, a speedboat arrives at the island jetty. Out steps Bea. She looks the same as when we had a very brief unsuccessful fling 90yrs ago before I met Melissa. She has short blond hair, a roundish face, not thin, about 165cm in height and a huge smile. She used to laugh at my jokes, maybe because she couldn't understand them. No English-speaking person had ever laughed at my jokes, so I was instantly attracted to her, but she was baiting me and digging for information. Later I found out that she worked for the Polish spy agency called *Pi5* while I had worked for the equivalent OZ agency called *Ai5*.

"Hello, Jules, you look so bright or is the word white?" Her English has not improved despite doing all those English-speaking courses at a TAFE college. Polish was my first language, so I am translating her speech from Polish as best as I can when she is stuck for a word to say in English.

"Actually, you look terrible, like you have seen a ghost," she says after taking off her sunglasses. She continues, "That peptide formula I stole from you 90 years ago does not work for people over 130 yrs of age. It is possible it was an earlier version. I need you back in the laboratory to manufacture a new version of the peptide as I have lost count of the wrinkles on my face, which no current cosmetic moisturiser can fix."

"Bea, my memory has come back. About 90 yrs ago, you tried to shoot me but missed and put a hole through my favourite painting."

"I did not know that handgun was loaded, and I am sorry about your painting, but this laser gun I am holding now is fully charged, and I have since had shooting lessons and can hit a cow's eyeball, so are you coming back with me to Poland to start work? I have got a laboratory organized and lots of white rats to test a new version of your life-prolonging peptide on."

Chloe4, my pet white rat cringes. I pat and reassure her that she's not going to be an experimental rat, and in a way, it's a relief to see Bea even though she's pointing that gun at me. It takes my mind off the deaths of my wife and friends, and besides, Bea would never shoot me. I was wrong. She's fiddling with the laser gun controls and accidentally fires it. The laser beam disintegrates my favourite pawpaw plant. I think Bea should demand her money back for those shooting lessons.

"Put down that gun. I'll come with you but first, help me finish digging these graves for my friends."

"Polish women do not dig; we just cook wonderful healthy cabbage-based meals; *Pierogi, Golabki,* lots of *Kapusta,* so our men always have healthy bowel movements due to all the cabbage they ingest. No need for that over 50s bowel cancer testing kit you have in this country."

The rat looks despondent. I give it a kiss. "Chloe4, I will be back soon. There is plenty of food in the fridge, and you know how to open it."

"Marek, Jurek, come help me," Bea yells in Polish.

Two large, not particularly friendly-looking guys hop out of the speedboat and come walking down the jetty towards us.

"Marek, Jurek, you have plenty of experience at digging graves. Help Jules to dig. There are three graves to dig and bury the bodies. He will get more shovels."

"We like burying people," the lads say as they smile and rub their hands in anticipation.

Bea follows me to the garden shed, her laser aimed, and escorts me back after I gather two more shovels.

We carry the bodies well above the high tide zone and start digging but keep hitting tree roots. I run back to the garden shed, without Bea, and grab an axe. Four hours later, my wife and friends are buried, and the three of us diggers are sweaty and exhausted. Then I feel a prick on my shoulder and look up at Bea, who is holding an empty syringe.

"Don't look so miserable, Jules. We may let you escape eventually."

Seeing Bea made me briefly forget the tragedy of my wife and friends dying, but consciousness is quickly fading, and another adventure or nightmare is about to begin.

Chapter Two

We're somewhere in Poland, as I can smell Golabki, the now Polish national food which is full of minced meat and rice wrapped in a cabbage roll, which is good for maintaining bowel health. I must have been drugged, as have no recollection of how I got here. I look out of a small window in the little bare room I'm in. All I see is a tall barbed-wire fence and armed guards with their dogs patrolling this compound. It certainly doesn't look like any lab that I worked in before, and it's super cold here. I'm shivering, and my teeth are chattering. The door opens and in walks Bea, followed by a security guard. "This is going to be your bedroom. We will find a mattress, blankets, and possibly even some instant coffee and a jug. This is your new home, but it has no toilet, but there is a potty in the corner and some newspapers to do the wiping with."

I look around the tiny stark room. I'm sure the highest security prison cells in OZ are better equipped. I check my pockets for the cyanide pill, but my pockets are empty. Why didn't I listen to Smithy? If I was religious and believed in heaven and hell, then this is definitely hell.

"I'm taking you down to the biochemistry laboratory; it is next to the nuclear fusion reactor and is quite warm. If you prefer to sleep in the laboratory, I can have a mattress deposited there. The laboratory also has a toilet and shower. You will be able to do more hours of productive work, and we will not have to defrost you in the mornings."

The choices aren't great, but the lab seems far better than ending up an icicle each morning. I say yes to the lab living quarters, and Bea and the guard take me to the elevator. It must have plunged at least 30 floors in 10 seconds as I felt very floaty on the descent, like in free-fall. It must be a deep underground facility. Every country has those to house political leaders in the event of a nuclear war. We enter the lab.

"This is your equipment, the latest. Mass spectrometers, electron microscopes and gene editing devices, far more advanced than that CRISPR technology."

I look around. It's certainly more impressive than what I worked with over 100 years ago. Then the lab door slides open, and a female enters. My eyes must have lit up.

"This is Pleborska, but she prefers to be called Pleb. She speaks reasonable English and will be your research assistant but do not even think of any hanky-panky business because you have work to do, and you will be closely monitored."

I look at her and try to maintain my composure. Pleborska has long blond hair. She is on the thin side, malnourished, which is unusual for a Pol, and maybe 175cm in height, a bit taller than me, just as Melissa was. And in fact, if I believed in reincarnation, she is very much the spitting image of Melissa, but I don't believe that the spirit of Melissa is stalking me. She is rather attractive and could become a distraction. A brief daydream flashes in my mind of Pleborska and me running through a forest in slow motion, her hair fluttering in the breeze whilst we hold test tubes filled with green liquid and glancing at each other, well, until I hit a tree, face first, and that's when the fantasy ended. She could definitely be a distraction.

"Bea, Pleb will have to wear a tight rubber swimming hat. I can't have blond hair dropping into test tubes and beakers and contaminating our research."

"I do not shed," Pleb indignantly says in a husky voice.

Bea continues, "This is actually a fusion nuclear research facility. The peptide is my pet project and not related to the other work we do here. You will both be covered in disposable clothing and be sprayed with the Polish version of Dettol before entry. It is not corrosive or carcinogenic, so do not believe those articles posted on the Internet about people who used it and had contracted melanomas and hideous scars on their skins. Now move your backsides. You need to shower first and put on special clothing so you will not contaminate this facility. Quick, quick, start moving; there is work to be done."

In some Eastern block and Scandinavian countries, men and women often shower together purely to conserve natural resources. Fortunately, I have developed a slight erectile dysfunction, which was being treated. I can maintain my scientific professionalism, but only as I hold both hands across the lower parts. We get out of the shower and go into the blow-dry room with fans. Her wet head hair is fluttering around, so attractive. Luckily, I still remember some of that Transcendental Yogi Meditation I once watched on MeTube. I start muttering the *Hmmm, I'm dumb* mantra and maintain my below-the-groin composure, but only just. We finally put on disposable plastic costumes and masks and enter the sterile laboratory through the airlock. The thought again crosses my mind, Smithy's last words; This planet won't survive if we all get to live forever.

"Jules, how does this peptide substance of yours work? Can it keep me forever young? I want to be forever young."

"Pleb, I'm not a geneticist, so I don't fully understand it myself. But I'll explain it the best that I can with the knowledge I learned over 100 years ago. I haven't tried to keep up with the latest knowledge, so my explanation may be out of date. Still, our chromosomes, inside every cell of our body, apart from red blood cells, carry the instructions to manufacture peptides, proteins, and our body shape and replicate cells that make up our bodies. But the ends of chromosomes contain markers called telomeres. The easiest way to think about it is that every time a cell replicates, the marker in its chromosomes moves down a notch until it hits a type of stop sign, and then your organ tissue cells cannot replicate anymore and so cannot replace dying tissue cells. That marker is like a time clock. The peptide is just a string of 4 amino acids, simple organic molecules. It sticks onto the marker like chewing gum and stops the marker from moving so the cells can continue to replicate."

"But Jules, does not cancer work in a similar way. Cancer cells uncontrollably replicate."

"Pleb, there may be similarities in the way the peptide functions to cancer cells, but the three of us whom I injected, and me as well, never had any cancerous growths."

"I understand it is a form of gambling with your life at stake; we do not have legal gambling in Poland, so some of our compatriots have discovered a way to get unlimited gambling on foreign website slot machines. They use a software chewing gum to place bets, but that also stops their credit from diminishing if they lose. The concept is similar to your peptide. Jules, you better start working or appear to be working, as this is not a desk job. We have to appear to be active and solving the peptide production problems."

"It's not that simple, Pleb. The amino acids that make up the peptide are isomers, mirror images of normal amino acids that make up human proteins; they are not normally found in nature even though they have the same chemical formula as the natural amino acids. I think I might have destroyed the documents containing the instructions on how to manufacture the isomers that make up the peptide, but I remember that there were many steps involved."

"Did not your father first manufacture the peptide? He might have a copy of the instructions in his coffin."

"Pleb, I don't know. He was a chemist, whereas I was initially a pharmacologist, two very different disciplines before I was recruited into the sort of work that Bea does, but in a different country. My knowledge of chemistry was never that good. I just followed the instructions in the documents he left before he got cremated, so any documents are just ashes floating in the bay."

"Jules, Bea can employ a chemist, and we have mass spectrometers and other equipment in this lab that can separate isotopes and even amino acid isomers; now start thinking clearly."

It's hard to think clearly when looking at the attractive Pleb, but Bea is ruthless, so we have to appear as working on this peptide project.

"We need cans of Soya beans. They are the starting ingredient, rich in protein which is the source of amino acids, and fibre as well. But we don't need the fibre for the peptide. You have security clearance, so can you get out of that costume and preferably put on some normal, streetwise clothing? Find a supermarket and purchase 20 or more cans of Soya beans."

"Jules, Polish people like meat. We are not into that vegetarian food in Poland. I do not think supermarkets sell Soya beans here. What about cabbage?"

"Yes, yes, we can try that. Go now. There's a trolley in the foyer."

Pleb leaves on the shopping assignment, and I'm stripping off the plastic garments. I have to escape from here, but then Bea walks in, and that looks like one of those electro-stunners in her hand, aimed at me. "You are not going anywhere," she says. The choices aren't great. It's an iron-curtain stun gun capable of producing myocardial infarctions (heart attacks). I sit and wait by the computer terminal until Pleb gets back from the shopping. I try to think. There are only 20 different amino acids that constitute all the proteins in our body, but how do you produce a mirror image, called an isomer, of those amino acids to make the peptide? The life-prolonging peptide molecule consists of only four amino acid isomers, but I forgot how to manufacture it but think I may have the formula and manufacturing process back on my island in the underground laboratory. I Doogle life-prolonging peptides. *Disgraced scientist Jules Lemos* appears on the screen. I nervously look around before pulling the power plug to the computer. Pleb comes back and is struggling to hold the shopping bags. "I have purchased 10 kgs of minced meat and three cabbages. It will have to do. There was a shortage of tuna and no Soya beans." I give Pleb a hand to get the mince into a fridge.

"You start working now," says Bea, whilst pointing her stun gun at me as she sniffs the shopping bags. "I be come back in two hours to see what progress you have made."

Chapter Three

"Pleb, we have to appear to be working. Put some of that mince in ten test tubes and some in those beakers."

"Jules, do you know what you are doing?"

"No, I haven't a clue, but it will buy me time. The *Pi5* organization makes the Ruski, *Ri5* appear like tame pigeons or pussycats. *Pi5s* are ruthless. I have to escape."

"I cannot let you escape. I will not have a job as a research assistant if you escape."

"Pleb, you can come with me back to OZ. I leased a tropical island just off the coast of a town called Townsville in Australia, and I'll purchase some really vicious pit bull terriers to protect us if Bea should follow."

"I will think about your offer, but now I am very hungry; I haven't eaten for 4 hours. I also bought some rice to mix with that mince and cabbage leaves to wrap the mixture. I am going to do some cooking and make Golabki. That experimental nuclear fusion reactor down the corridor should cook them very quickly as it can produce temperatures of several million degrees Celsius."

"OK, cook. I'm peckish myself."

Shivering certainly makes a person hungry, plus it burns dietary calories; that's why I still have a stomach two-pack, though it once used to be a six-pack. Two stomach muscles were still highly visible. I was proud to parade them when my transgender sister/brother psychologist ran her therapy classes on the island that involved nude dancing and drinking magic mushroom soup. I used to spend an hour a day in the solar-powered freezer shed, with the fish and vegetables just so I could shiver and keep off the flab from my two-pack.

Pleb comes back with the cooked cabbage rolls. "Jules, are you having convulsions?"

"No, no, it's all OK. I'm just shivering. I was just checking our food supplies in the freezer."

Those cabbage rolls, or Golabki, as they are called, taste good, better than a pie with tomato sauce, the staple food of Ozzies but then Bea enters the lab followed by two-armed security guards. "That smells good," she says whilst sniffing around.

"Yes, this batch of Golabki is made of mincemeat and amino-acid isomers, those needed to make the peptide. Our bodies cannot absorb them. You can eat as many as you like because you will not put on weight, but they will keep you forever young," Pleb says.

Bea grabs one of the Golabki, then another and another and another." Mm, we may have another job for you when you finish this assignment; manufacturing calorie-free Golabki." She pinches her waistline and smiles before leaving with the guards.

"She ate ten of those Golabkis. If she puts on weight, our scientific credibility will be ruined, and our lives will be very limited. There were no isomer peptides in that minced meat protein. We are doomed if she puts on weight."

"It is all right, Jules. I put one of your socks into the blender when I did the cooking as I forgot to buy spices. Polish love the pheromones. I'm sure Bea is now having some very healthy bowel movements and oral excretions, so she will not put on any weight; she will probably lose some weight."

I rush to the toilet, trying not to vomit. Pleb follows me.

"Jules, your rarely washed socks and underwear and your pheromones could make us millionaires in the diet food industry, that is if we escape, which is a possibility as I have some friends who own large drones. They may be able to lift us out of this facility."

Chapter Four

We catch the lift to ground level using Pleb's security pass, and I sneak outside behind her. We hide behind a shed and watch the security guards.

"Jules, it is their Vodka and smoko break, they will not be functional for at least 6 hours, and the drones are nearly here."

"But, Pleb, what about their German Shepherd dogs? They'll make mince out of us."

"Jules, the dogs are given Vodka in their water bowl and fall asleep by the side of their carer guard. They snore as well, so it gets very noisy out there. Many of those dogs and their keepers end up together in an alcohol detoxification clinic."

Let me say that holding on to the pads of a drone is not a pleasant experience. My arms are stretched to the limit, and I must look like a chimpanzee holding onto a monkey bar. If only I had done those stretching exercises at the gym. My arm tendons and joints are aching after the 10 minute flight.

"Pleb, which way do we go?"

"I am not sure; the battery on my mobile phone device is flat, so I have no GPS."

"Pleb, I can see a light over there; it must be a cottage. Press that red button to make the drone descend."

After later research, I learnt that the red button would only be used if a drone's Lithium-ion batteries were on fire. Luckily it was only a 4-metre drop into a peat moss bog. We crawl out, covered in brown slime, and make our way to the cottage. We knock on the door, both suffering from severe hypothermia and in dire need of a shower and a washing machine for our clothes.

"Come in and sit by the fire. Do I know you from somewhere, the female, that is?"

"Papa, it's me, Pleborska, and I'll never forgive you for giving me that name."

"It is you! My darling, we were far from a hospital and quite distressed when your mother went into labour. That name just came into our heads, the name of a weed killer we used in our garden. It always did a good job. I was spraying the garden that day, and between sprays, I held your mother's hands whilst she was contorting during childbirth. You were a difficult one to extract. I had to cut your umbilical cord with garden trimming shears."

"Why didn't you just use a sterilised knife or nail clippers?"

"My darling, I have no medical knowledge. I thought that is how it is done, and it was very successful from what I see of you."

Pleb would later have cosmetic surgery on her obtrusive belly button and make it presentable when wearing skimpy swimwear on the beach but back to the story.

"Father, this is Jules. We are not connected by umbilical cords or in any other way. But we need some brief accommodation to take a bath and wash our clothes. We may also be being chased by a Polish spy agency."

"Come over here, my daughter. I told you once before never to have anything to do with the *i5* organisations and never go swimming in the peat bog. I will find you some clothing and put your clothes in the washing machine. I am the washing machine, and it is good exercise to use your arm muscles to wash clothes since strangling enemy spies was banned and only laser rifles are now allowed."

Later I would find out that Pleb's father, Wadek, had once been in charge of *Pi5*; what a coincidence. I wonder if he knows Bea, but it's probably better not to ask, and Pleb and I are too tired for long conversations.

I wake up on a couch near an open fireplace. Pleb comes down the stairs looking refreshed, dressed in sheepskin. She must have got the spare bedroom whilst I tossed and turned on a very uncomfortable couch all night. Wadek wanders in. "I've just messaged your last known coordinates to *Pi5*, false coordinates far from here. You will have time to escape. Your clothes are washed, dried and ironed to look presentable; you must maintain the good Polish culture appearance."

"Papa, we need passports to escape Poland and enter another country. Can you still make them?"

"I still have my machine to make false passports, but these days, the passports need a SIM card, the type found in those smartphones. Information about you has to be encoded into the chip, including a photo and your thumb fingerprint, but it is all right; I have the machinery to do that. It will take about two hours, but first, I must photograph you both and take your thumbprints."

"Papa, I have a smartphone with a SIM card, but Jules has not."

"You have to get another one, my darling."

"Papa, we are fugitives. We have no Zloty Polish currency. Can we use the SIM card from your phone? You could come to Australia with us. Jules has a tropical island,

and eventually, he might remember how to manufacture an anti-ageing substance so you will never die."

"Dear Pleborska, you can have my phone SIM card, but I am happy here though I miss your mother very much. I have a small vial of her DNA, collected when she had stomach motions after drinking too much Vodka. Take the sample. If you can bring her back, I will find a way to join you. There is also some Zloty credit on this sim card that I will put into your passport; enough to buy your airfares and other expenses. The microchip data has to include where you and your partner have recently travelled. I can create a list of legitimate tourist destinations and download them to the sim card."

"Thank you, papa, but it is not like that. We are not in a relationship. He is over 140 yrs old, and my limit is 30 for a partner."

Wadek gets busy and has a smile on his face. It looks like he is enjoying the feeling of being useful again and being temporarily out of retirement. Pleb and I pace the floor but do stop to look at photos hanging on the walls of Wadek and his deceased wife Greta and all the other collected historical items, which are mainly weapons and electronic spy devices.

"Jules, there is a warning written on each of these weapons and devices, it says in Polish Property of *Pi5*. If you find and you do not return this item, you will spend the rest of your life in the Artic with the polar bears chewing your remains."

"Pleb, I'm sure your dad knows what he's doing, plus I can read the dates of manufacture. They are over 50 yrs old and probably obsolete museum pieces."

"It is done. Here are your passports. I will now drive you to the nearest international airport. It is not a luxury airport like the ones you have in the West, but there are many traders selling fine food there from their trolleys in the departure lounge., Find Krzystof; he makes the best Bigos stew, even better than your mother used to make."

"Thank you, papa," Pleb says as tears flow down her face.

I thank him too and wave before he drives back to his home, but not before he whispers in my ear, "Look after my daughter. I can tell she likes you very much and that you also like her very much. I can read body language and taught body language science to all *Pi5* operatives. She will not assassinate you."

Wadek gives me a wink, a smile, and the phone number of his spare phone. "Keep me informed," he says and then drives away.

"What did Papa say to you, Jules? He was whispering, so I could not hear him."

"He said you are not a good shot with a gun, so I should have no fear of being assassinated."

"I will ring him when he purchases a new sim card for his phone. How dare he spread rumours that I am not a good shooter?"

"Pleb, calm down, I lied. That's not what he really told me at all. He told me he taught *Pi5* agents to read body language. I was just embarrassed because he read me so well and possibly read you well too."

"What did he say? Tell me!"

"Pleb, I promise I will tell you, but not just yet. I must learn to read the signs before I compromise myself."

"I know, he said. I am making eyebrows at you and want you to be my lover before I assassinate you."

"Yes, no, let's just forget about it for the moment." If looks could kill, Pleb doesn't need a gun.

We walk through the body scanner at the airport, not that the attendants were watching the screen, neither were we asked for our newly created passports. We have no luggage to be scanned, so we just enter the departure lounge. The flight is delayed, so we have time to enjoy Krzystof's Bigos stew which is full of cabbage, potatoes, spices and meat. It tastes so good, and I don't care that the meat may have been sourced from the bodies of deceased Russian soldiers still fighting in the Ukraine. We must have consumed three bowls each.

"Let me do the maths," says Krzystof, "You had six bowls in total. We have a special discount offer today, so one bowl is only 9 zloty which means you owe me 58 zloty; cash or credit?"

"Excuse me, but 9 times 6 is 54, not 58."

"Sir, the cost includes the nightly surcharge. I cook all day while looking after my young kids, who are probably playing computer games and not doing their school homework or practising how to make Bigos stew. I am both a cook and a nanny," Krzystof pleads.

"Pleb, what have we got?"

"Jules, I managed to get your wallet out of Bea's office, but there is no Zloty in there, and I do not think this guy takes a credit card. I will pay."

"Madam, this is a 200-zloty currency token you are giving me, and it is ten times the fee for the meal. Is this some kind of financial mistake?"

"No, but this is my email address, and you should email me your recipe for that

Bigos you make. We will be on opposite sides of the world, so we will not compete in who makes the best Bigos."

"Madam, I thank you so very much. I will now walk home, confront my children and force them to cook Bigos. I will use a whip to keep them in line and not online, but I will also tell them that they will inherit a fortune when I depart this planet."

Finally, we board a Polish airline. We are the only passengers.

"Where do you want to fly to?" the burly pilot asks in Polish.

"I thought you'd know. The sign says 'Australia: This Way to Plane'."

"Ahh, those signs are always wrong. One time two signs were pointing to two different boarding gates for Australia. One sign said 'To Heaven' and the other 'To Hell'. There was a big queue for the 'To Hell' flight that offered unlimited sexual experiences whilst roasting, but the pilot never turned up. No airport authority checks the signs, so if I get some passengers, I fly them wherever they want to go as I get paid by the kilometre of flight, and this plane can do vertical descents and vertical takeoffs, so it does not need an airport runway."

"Townsville, it's a city in Queensland, Australia," I reply, "Can you land us on a little island just off the coast of Townsville?"

"Rufus, look up the coordinates of a town called Townsville in Australia and set a flight course. Now Rufus, now!"

"Who is Rufus?"

"Rufus is an android pilot, and I am supervising his practical, hands-on pilot training. I am like a teacher, an instructor, and a supervisor. And I get bonus pay for my supervision duties. Now let us enjoy some duty-free Vodka; Rufus does not drink but is a very good pilot despite that flaw in his Polish character."

Planes fly faster these days at hypersonic speeds. It only takes 4 hours to get to Townsville airport in OZ though the quality of onboard movies hasn't improved much. Pleb is asleep, leaning on my shoulder, so I have no one to talk to. I politely ask the flight attendant, the pilot's wife, for a Tas Bitter beer.

"Sir, the company that manufactured that beer liquidated many years ago, but I can offer you a glass of our traditional Beetroot Bitter; it's high in alcohol and tastes very sweet. The colour compound in Beetroot is not metabolized by our gut, so do not panic if tomorrow your anal expulsions look red." I would later find out that many flight attendants, even the married ones, are androids who don't mince their words and say it how it is, which I rather like.

I sip the Beetroot Bitter. Yum, I ask the flight attendant for another and reflect on the recent past. The Polish *Pi5* organization is definitely alive and possibly infiltrating OZ, and they must be stopped. I ask the flight attendant for a phone and call my great-great grandkids, who once headed the family business *Ai5*, the more-for-profit spy agency in OZ. Sultana answers the call.

"Great, great, great granddad, we closed down *Ai5* years ago. The offices are closed; too much pressure on us; it was too stressful. We now run a Miracle Flower and Cannabis shop in Byron Bay and doing great business. It keeps us high and very busy. We have also financially sponsored training of our former agents to be wildlife photographers. Some are working for that 'National Demographic' magazine and spying on wildlife animals. Their photos are great, and I'm just looking at one now; it's of a guy who went swimming in that crocodile-infested Darwin River. There's definitely beetroot or carrot juice in that river."

"You put too many greats in when referring to me. I'm only a great, great granddad. Go easy with the Cannabis."

"Sure, 3-G dad, stay cool and like, come visit sometime for a puff."

It looks like we can't count on my Byron Bay relatives for any help or useful advice.

"Sir, we are approaching Townsville. Which island should I deposit you on?"

"That one! It's low tide, so that you can land on the sandy beach."

"Sir, will you fill in this online document to rate my performance as a trainee pilot?"

"Yes, yes of cause. You did a great job," I say whilst filling in the questionnaire.

The pilot and his wife are snoring away, so Rufus helps me carry the sleeping Pleb off the plane, something he'll have to repeat when he has to carry the pilot and his wife off the plane when they arrive back in Poland.

"Pleb, wake up, wake up."

"Don't slap my face, or I will slap yours, and it will not be just a hand as I am highly trained in Karate."

Pleb then marches off and sits under a palm tree overlooking the water, her head down low and her hands holding her cheeks. I guess Pleb has never experienced the type of action we had endured in the last 48 hours; there's a lot of information and emotion to mentally process. I look around; weeds grow quickly in a tropical environment, then Chloe4 jumps on my shoulder and starts licking my face. "Chloe,

I missed you too, but now we may have another rat," I say to Chloe4, who then hisses at Pleb. Pleb must have heard the conversation and comes alive.

"You implied I am an art, or is it a rat? I am not either or both. I want to go back to Poland."

"Pleb, calm down. I was just trying to say to Chloe4 that she might now have competition for hugs and kisses. Forgive me; I made a very poor choice of words."

Pleb can sure pack a powerful slap to the cheek, my cheek, and then marches off and sits under the palm tree again. She reminds me so much of Melissa, same style of behaviour. She is like a reincarnation of Melissa, so it makes me feel good and not despondent at Melissa's passover to another world; she is still here, embodied in Pleb. Time for some Sav Blanc. It may ease the tension. I grab a couple of bottles from the fridge and two wine glasses and march over to where Pleb is sitting. We sit staring at the ocean, not saying a word until Polly slivers near Pleb's legs.

"What is it? Is it a poisonous viper snake?"

"Yes, keep absolutely still. I will risk my life for you and subdue it."

I grab Polly, a harmless Python we purchased at a pet shop many years ago to keep mice and other rodents under control on the island. Polly had come to an understanding that Chloe4 and all white rats are out of bounds, and she probably just smelt the Sav Blanc and wants a sip. Smithy always let Polly sip from his glass when she brought back a mouse or rat in her mouth as proof of capture. The snake is very used to humans, and we have a symbiotic relationship; she captures the rodents and gets rewarded with some sips of Sav Blanc. Polly raises her torso, and I grab her by the neck very gently. I whisper to Polly, "Didn't Chloe4 teach you how to pretend to be dead? Now pretend to be dead, else no more Sav Blanc for you."

The snake seems to understand what is at stake, so drops her head and becomes limp.

"Jules, you killed that venomous snake to save me, but what were you muttering to the snake as you strangled it?"

"I was listening to the snake's final confession and comforting it before it departed. The snake was a Catholic, so it needed to make a final confession."

"Jules, are you an animal whisperer?"

"Yes, Pleb, I've been blessed with the gift of whispering."

Whispering was what we always did when working for *i5* organizations, but Pleb doesn't need to know that.

"Pleb, stay here, don't follow. I have to bury that venomous viper; it's a short emotional ceremony that only animal whisperers can participate in. I'll be back soon, so have another glass of the Sav."

We're out of hearing range. I stop at my cabin, get another bottle of Sav Blanc, and place it 100m from the cabin. "Polly, here's a bottle of Sav, top removed so you can sip it, but we both may have to do one of those AA courses at some stage. Anyway, I will convince my possible future partner that you are harmless but stay away from the BBQ area and our cabins for the next few weeks." Polly nods her head and sips the Sav. I never knew that Pythons could burp. I go back to join Pleb.

"Jules, you saved me from that dangerous reptile. We have none of those reptiles in Poland. I forgive you. You are like that ancient TV hero 'Polona Jones', who wrestled with snakes and crocodiles. They were my favourite movies on TV when I was young, but they were not in 3-D."

"Pleb, you can use *Cabin01*. It's next to my cabin, which is *Cabin02*; let's go."

"Jules, this *Cabin01* is so messy; men's and women's clothing, towels and underwear are scattered on the floor and furniture. Who could live in such a mess?"

"Pleb, I'll tell you the full story later, but they were a married couple who I knew very well and are now deceased. Let's put all the clothing in the second bedroom and find clean bed sheets and towels for you."

"Jules, like most Polish people, I am a practising Catholic, and I believe in ghosts. The ghosts will be upset if I take their cabin, so I will sleep outside on the grass."

"Pleb, you can't sleep outside because I'm out of mosquito and viper spray."

"Jules, apart from ghosts, I am feeling very fragile after all that has happened recently. Can I sleep in your *Cabin02* as well? We can toss a coin to see who gets the couch and who gets the bed."

"Pleb, if you thought *Cabin01* was messy, well, you'll get a shock when you see the inside of my cabin."

"Jules, as long it has no ghosts, I can handle the mess.

Chapter Five

I open the solar-powered fridge in the basement laboratory. There are still 12 vials of the peptide left. I need a syringe, so wander off to the beach. The island must have been visited by the mainland druggies as there are many syringes lying around by the BBQ area. I pick them up and dispose of them, except for one that I wash with bleach and soap and let it dry.

Pleb wanders into my kitchen, rubbing her eyes.

"What are you doing?"

I turn to her and conceal the syringe. "Just some cleaning; we have a lot more cleaning to do outside. Will you help?"

"I will, Jules, but I have a secret to tell, which you may not like."

"I'm used to secrets; tell me."

"Jules, I have a daughter. She is in an orphanage in Poland and is ten years old, and the result of an indiscretion I committed with my professor after my university graduation ceremony. I would like her brought here to live with us on this island. I have not seen her for three years. You could become her de facto father."

I am stunned by Pleb's admission. I pause and hold my head. The same scenario is repeating as when I was involved with my second wife, Melissa. I was a de facto father then as well.

She continues. "I had checked your fridge when you were outside. You have enough of your peptide to last you six years. By then, my daughter, who is called Mystca, will be 16 years old and able to survive with only her mother and the legal inheritance of this island which I will convert to a thriving resort for the local Polish community."

My head is spinning. Is Pleb still working for Bea, and is this some ploy to get me working on the peptide again? I'm not sure I trust her, but then a ferry arrives at the jetty and distracts me from my sceptical thoughts.

A buxom woman dressed in colourful Polish clothing gets off holding the hand of a small child who must be Pleb's daughter. So much for Pleb first asking me if it would be all right to bring her here. I'm too old for this, but give the kid a peck on her cheek. The kid smiles and laughs. It's like when you go to an animal rescue centre to adopt an abandoned dog. Every dog is smiling and wagging its tail, trying to make an impression, hoping it will be the one. You wish you could adopt them all. Anyway, there is only one feral kid here to adopt. The delivery woman is standing there with her arms crossed. "I have not been paid yet; 20,000 zloty is the delivery fee, with the first adopters' 50% discount. If your wife or you are infertile, we have many more children that need adoption."

I rush down to the basement of my cabin and open the safe. I have no idea what the currency conversation rate is now, but grab 200 of those $100 plastic currency notes, which have our current president, Alf Doser, on them. I definitely preferred the ones with British monarchs. I believe the currency is still legal tender and probably worth a lot more to collectors who like currency you can actually touch and not that crypto stuff. She counts the plastic notes whilst examining, with a magnifying glass, the holographic codes on the notes. "That will do. I cannot stay; I have many other delivery assignments today."

I should have checked the exchange rate. I had just paid enough for two Mystcas. The delivery woman leaves with a smile, and I look at the stumbling 10-year-old who can barely walk. She must have some mental deficiency. That initial evaluation would prove so very, very wrong.

"Jules, will you help me look after her? I think she has a bright future. I was not ready to be a mother, so she lived in an orphanage for most of her ten years. I recently Doogled that orphanage and found out that it has a terrible reputation. The kids were not allowed to play outside and had little access to education. Most of them became fragile and feral. They are like wild monkeys."

I look at Mystca again. She's behaving differently from the first impression. She snarls at me and then pokes her tongue out. She definitively needs a bath, a haircut and an attitude change. It's not dark, so no ghosts. I grab some scissors and shampoo and walk Pleb and Mystca to *Cabin01* so that Pleb can do the bathing and hair trimming to make the monkey presentable in our society. Pleb, you should also wash her clothes as they don't smell that good."

Three hours later, Pleb and Mystca knock on my cabin door. They both look bathed and very unusually elegant like they are about to go to a fancy-dress party. I sort of recognise the clothing.

"Jules, there was much clothing and cosmetics left behind in *Cabin01* and even a sewing machine. Mystca and I have been busy cutting, slicing, spicing and sewing."

Mystca starts fiddling with all my electronic gizmos. "Don't press that! It's the destruct button! Pleb, she can stay, but you have to constrain her curiosity. And can you do your best to keep her looking presentable, else she'll have to be led around like a dog on a leash? You can have *Cabin01* for as long as you like." Chloe4 nods her head in approval. She has a new friend to play with. "Pleb, we also have to take Mystca into town and enrol her in a primary school."

"Jules, she needs to improve her English language skills first, else the other children will tease her. Let us go to your Townsville town and purchase some books for her to read, and we can tutor her at home until she catches up with her English skills."

The motorboat starts first turn of the ignition key, and we're off with sea spray and wind on our faces and hair. From the joyful looks on Pleb's and Mystca's faces, this must be their first motorboat trip. Twenty minutes later, we've docked at a jetty and march to the shopping precinct. A bookshop next to the supermarket is the first stop.

"Madam, sir, there are 15 paper-bound Mathematics and Chemistry books in this trolley, and paper-bound books are the rage at the moment if you are sitting by a pool or at the beach and wish to look intellectual. The Web books are not that popular anymore. Can you pay for those books?"

"Yes, sure, but could we have drone delivery services for the books. We have to do food shopping as well."

"That will be $3000 for the books and $40 for delivery."

"That's ridiculous! That's $200 per book, and some of those books are very thin!"

"Sir, there is a worldwide paper shortage because we don't have many trees left on Earth. That is also why toilet paper is so expensive and why you can now buy medicinal tablets at a Pharmacy to induce constipation and reduce your dependence on paper."

"OK, OK, I'll pay. Here's my credit card."

"Sir, this credit card expired nearly 100 years ago. It is a historical relic and should be donated to a museum."

Pleb interrupts. "Put the bill on my credit card; my card is still acceptable."

"Madam, I will have a drone deliver the books to your abode. Please write your address on this electronic pad."

"Pleb, I'll pay you half the expense in cash when we get back to the island."

"Jules, does that mean you are willing to be Mystca's stepfather?"

"Yes, yes, yes, I've been a stepfather before, and it's a pain, but I will."

Most days, we drive the motorboat to a netted beach in Townsville. Both Pleb and Mystca are learning to swim on a beach protected from sharks and crocodiles. Afterwards, we buy lunch and watch the ocean as we eat. Three years pass so quickly. We have dinners beside the BBQ and then watch the news on the 3-D projection TV and then wrestling matches before bedtime. Both Pleb and Mystca get hyper-excited watching and try to kick and throw coconuts at the 3-D villains in the 3-D wrestling ring. I sort of like it too. Sure, I could tell them that the wrestling matches are all fake, but she and Mystca enjoy it, and so do I. After the wrestling, we recede to our cabins for sleep. Pleb and I maintain our distance, but then Mystca enters my cabin. "I think I know how to make that peptide thing that keeps you alive for so long. I do not want you to die just yet. There is a way to flip those amino acids and produce mirror images."

My initial assessment was so wrong; another super, super smart kid. I hate kids who are smarter than me – just joking. Pleb comes back and grabs her. "Jules, can Mystca and I spend the night with you? I would prefer that to spending the night with all the rat progeny your friend Chloe4 has produced. They have taken over *Cabin01* and are very noisy at night."

Chapter Six

"Jules, I like elderly gentlemen, and you fit well into the elderly category. Would you like to make love?"

I shiver and remove her hand from my shoulder and turn around.

"Pleb, you're still working for Bea, I know it. I won't compromise myself. I will not, not ever!"

"Relax, Jules; this is not some kind of plan to acquire your peptide. You just remind me of my great-grandfather, who was kind to me. He had a large aristocratic nose like you have, and he worked for Chanel as a perfume sniffer. His nose was very valued, and after his death, it was amputated and now sits in a glass jar, dipped in preservative at the Chanel headquarters in London. If you ever need a job, I have contacts at Chanel."

I was about to reply, but then I hear and see a helicopter about to land on the island.

"Pleb, get Mystca and quickly pack all your belongings in your suitcases. We have to get out of here and hide. These heat-reflecting aluminium blankets will block any infrared radiation we give off, so we'll be invisible to their sensors, but we have to cover ourselves."

We're hiding in the bushes. Out steps Bea, followed by two-armed military-looking guys, each holding a doggy lead to a German shepherd tracker dog. "Check all the cabins and do not shoot anyone, not just yet."

"Stop looking at her, Jules. I can see a bulge in your pants."

"I have a secret cellar on the other side of the island; well it's actually my lab. Take your suitcases, Polish clothes and those shopping bags. The cellar has a powerful negative ion generator that neutralises smells, so the tracker dogs won't pick up that we're hiding there. Pleb, we have to run to the other side of the island. Let's go."

"Jules, why cannot we hide in your cabin cellar? I checked. You have a negative ion generator in there as well."

"Pleb, that's only to sterilize my socks and underwear as I hate doing clothes washing, and I haven't as yet soiled any underwear."

She looks at me and makes me melt, "Jules, I will wash your socks and underwear;

us Polish women are good at that."

"Pleb, you and Mystca must have sampled all the perfumes at that David Moans store. The negative ion generator in my cabin wouldn't cope. We have to go to my laboratory, it's 3 metres underground and has a very powerful negative ion generator, now let's go. The dogs won't pick our scent in there."

"Jules, cannot you invent a positive ion generator? I may not cope with all this negativity."

Chloe4 is sitting on my shoulder. "This way, but Pleb, did you leave any evidence that we're back on this island."

"Only my makeup kit; I left it behind. It has my fingerprints, but it will be Vodka break soon for Bea's staff so we may be able to retrieve it."

"Keep moving, but first we have to get into the ocean to wash away the smell that their tracker dogs may be following. Hide your luggage behind those bushes and run into the ocean."

"Jules this costume I bought cost you a lot of money, it could be ruined."

"I don't care about the money. Just move, I'll buy you a new one."

Chloe4 is running along the beach, followed by the tracker dogs, whilst we, Pleb, Mystca and I take deep breaths and then duck our heads in the ocean. Chloe4 is distracting them and climbs up a tree. The dogs are barking and trying to jump up the trunk of the tree. Their guard handlers grab the dogs and eventually manage to get the dogs focused again.

"Jules, I hope your rat friend makes it out alive."

"She will; she's a very smart rat."

"Jules, are you painting an allegory between your rat and me?"

"That's not how we use the English language. Now stay quiet, duck again and hold your breath."

Bea catches up. "They must be on the island. I could smell that Dom Pérignon perfume in *Cabin01*."

"Madam Bea, I think that perfume smell was Christian Dior, I once bought a 10ml vial for my girlfriend who is now my wife," one of the guards comments.

"Kowalski, you will stay here on the island while Kosciuszki and I will make a brief journey to the mainland and search for them there. We will be back tonight."

Kowalski and his dog start marching back to the resort cabins.

"What shall we do Jules? We cannot stay out here in the open. We have no mosquito spray, and I am being drained of blood."

"Stop slapping your arms and legs. We have to keep quiet and I'm out of ideas. I don't know what to do. The cellar lab is not designed for sleeping and we have no food with us."

"Jules, have you got any *i5* standard cyanide tablets? You should have. All *i5* agents had to carry them along with their personal belongings. We could slip one into the guard's food ration and also one into his dog's food."

"I have an idea, but we have to go back to *Cabin01* to get some things. We can do that after the guard and his dog have their afternoon Vodka break," whispers Mystca.

Chapter Seven

We sneak back into the resort BBQ area. Kowalski and his dog seem to be fast asleep since Polish dogs enjoy Vodka just as much as their human carers.

"Mr Jules, have you got fairy lights, some headdress to cover my face and a white dress?" asks Mystca.

"Just call me Jules, kid. Yes, I have LED fairy lights, and they're battery-powered. My deceased wife has a white dress, but it's way too big for you."

"Have you got scissors and some safety pins and hairpins as well?"

I sneak back to *Cabin02* and bring back the items Mystca requested.

Pleb and I stay hidden but watch as Mystca approaches the snoozing Kowalski. His dog wakes up and starts barking and snarling. Kowalski rubs his eyes and looks up in disbelief. They are speaking in Polish.

"Helena, what are you doing here? Why are you not at school, and why is your hair a different colour?"

"Dada, I am astral travelling in my sleep, and hair changes colour when astral travelling. Now, Dada, you have to go back to Poland. Mother and I are having serious problems with our neighbours, and we are so very, very frightened. They threatened to kill us. You have to come back and save us and take your dog back as well. I have floated around the whole island, and there are no humans here but plenty of rats. Tell Miss Bea that the people she is after are stranded in the Antarctic after their ship got stuck between icebergs and some whales as well."

"Come here, Helena and let me cuddle you."

"I cannot, Dada, I am just a ghost, an apparition, and I am fading; come back home soon and save us otherwise, you will only be able to visit our gravestones in a cemetery."

"I am leaving on the first flight I can get. I will be back to our Polish home tonight, I promise, and I will use whatever it takes to solve the problem with the neighbours."

Kowalski furiously packs his backpack, and he and the dog march off to the jetty just as Bea and Kosciuszki return. We can see Kowalski gesticulating and arguing with Bea . Eventually, all five of them (3 humans and two dogs) go to the copter pad and take off.

I'm dancing around in joy and grab Mystca. "That was brilliant, I can't believe it. You did it. Kid, you can use my credit card again but stick to the $200 limit, no extra zeros."

I hug Pleb. "You can try on that clothing you bought and my deceased wife's clothing as well."

Mystca comes over again. "I did explore your lab in the cellar when we first came here. You have sticky notes plastered on the walls. I put them together in order, step by step, to make that life-prolonging molecule that you call the twisted amino peptide. I would like it if you could still be alive and attend my university graduation ceremony, so I hope you will make some more of your peptide and inject it."

I give the kid another hug, and then, after a very long, tumultuous day, we all return to our bedrooms. Pleb puts her arm around my shoulder. I shudder as I think of Melissa.

"Jules, do you think it is over? Can we lead a normal life here?"

"I don't know what normal is anymore, but for the moment, we're safe, but Bea will come back. She doesn't give up easily."

"Jules, I looked it up on the dark web, the *Pi5* website. Bea was supposed to be on a scientific expedition investigating and tasting whether seals and penguins could satisfy the meat appetites of *Pi5* agents who apparently are malnourished and only have access to those canned baked beans for nutrition and do not have access to toilet paper or a bidet. Jules, there was no mention of Bea visiting this island. She is using *Pi5* resources for her own benefit. She will be in big trouble if *Pi5* find out."

"Pleb, that's something we can use against her if she comes back and causes us trouble."

"Jules, have you got a Taser or a laser gun?"

"No, Charmaine put all my *Ai5* weaponry in the BBQ fusion reactor. She was into the revival of the Hippy era of the 1970s: Make love, not war, was her motto. I think she had a pretty good success rate from all the thankful emails she received, including one that said, 'thank you'," I have discovered other uses for my penis apart from urinating."

"Jules, we should purchase some weapons for self-protection against Bea if she comes back. I have read that if you go to a place called a Bikie Pub, you will be served by angels, and you can purchase any weapon you like, but all transactions are cash only."

"Pleb, I'll give it some thought, but I really don't think Bea would shoot us except by pure accident as she has not got a steady hand."

"You do still like her, I can tell."

"Pleb, I am very cautious in her presence though I do think she is what we call *all talk but no action when it comes to any act of violence.* Even when she was on this island with her armed men and dogs, I could barely stop myself from laughing as we watched their incompetence. Pleb, I had no dispute with *Pi5*, and they probably have no idea that Bea used their resources to take me to Poland and then come looking for us on this island. Just in case I shall draft an encrypted letter using that Social Media app called InCaseIdie where I'll post everything I know about Bea and have it forwarded to all *i5* agencies."

"Jules, but how will *Pi5* agency receive the decryption key?"

"I will email the key to them."

"But what if Bea shoots me too, and I cannot make it to the keyboard to press the SEND button?"

"OK, good point Pleb, we'll have to formulate a plan B, but not tonight. It's been a busy day; let's just go to sleep and think about it in the morning."

"Jules, your life does not make much sense to me, and I have a psychology degree. You would qualify as a case study if I should resume my studies and focus on what you call *anomalous, psychotic behaviours.*"

"Pleb, there's nothing anomalous about me. I said before that I was never cut out for i5s. I don't even kill spiders."

"Jules, stay very still, do not move or speak."

I hear a swish and feel a wack on my shoulder.

"It was just a mosquito. Your spiders are safe."

Chapter Eight

A few uneventful months pass except for the ceaseless downpours of rain. La Nina is making our life a misery, and the high humidity is causing mould to form on our clothes and the few leather shoes we possess. Fortunately, we had enrolled Mystca in online education. She insisted on the year ten online course, not the year 7. I help Mystca with some of her homework, only English, not Maths, Physics or Chemistry, subjects she doesn't need any help in. Pleb often watches and has her hand on my shoulder.

The rain finally stops. El Nino must have pushed La Nina out away from the coast. I suppose the good thing is that our three 100,000-litre water tanks are overflowing, and it's nice to have a short shower in freshwater rather than bathe in the sea.

I nearly forgot; it's time for the six-monthly jab of the peptide. When Pleb and Mystca are asleep, I call Chloe4 and we descend to the cellar beneath our cabin, where I keep the peptide vials in a small fridge. What a shock! The basement must have flooded. It never flooded before. The fridge is not working, and the vials of peptide are covered in mould and at room temperature. They have to be kept at or below -4 Celsius else the peptide degrades unless it's attached to chromosomes.

I sneak out from *Cabin02* and run to the underground lab entrance and climb down the ladder. Chloe4 follows. The lab entrance is on top of our only hill, and the entrance is well sealed. I find my notes which Mystca had sorted, and make a list of ingredients needed which don't include cabbage or rice; only need acetone, pure ethanol and Soya beans. I also find the notes I took when Mystca came up with her prepubescent brain on how to manufacture the isomer amino acids needed for the peptide.

"Wake up, Pleb. we have to go to Townsville to enrol Mystca into the local high school, and then I got to do some shopping."

"Jules, you were gone all night. I thought you were oldnapped or is it kidnapped, and I was worried. I do not want to be a single mother, not just yet."

"I was reading my notes and Mystca's suggestions on how to manufacture the isomers to make the peptide. Now move, Pleb, as today is the last day for school enrolments."

"Jules, I do not have her academic credentials from Poland. I do not even have her Birth Certificate."

"That's OK, we're former *i5s*; you know we can manufacture those and Mystca seems to have mastered how to use the technology that I have here to print almost anything."

Both Pleb and I help. Mystca Lemos is printed on a new Birth Certificate, a perfect replica of one we found online except for the name. I spill some beer on it and rub my foot into it. It has to appear aged and genuine. No microchip identification is required for people under 17 yrs. of age.

"Pleb, she's only 13 years old yet according to this Birth Certificate, she was born 16 and a half years ago. At that age, kids in our high schools are usually in year 11 classes."

"Jules, she will pull it off. Our standard of education in maths and science is far higher than in this country, and she loves Maths, especially solving simultaneous equations. The children in the orphanage she attended may have been feral, but they did have a school run by unusual people, eccentric you would call them that followed that ancient Greek teacher called Archimedes.

Jules, can you pull it off as they say, I mean at the school interview?"

"I've done it before, over 90 years ago."

"Mystca, you cannot wear that sack at the interview. Wear that Polish dress you have."

I let Mystca drive the motorboat into town. She was thrilled and parked perfectly at the jetty by the school.

"Mr Lemos, I hope that is your name as we had two girls attend this high school over 90 years ago with the same surname and same address, that island resort. Their father's firstname and lastname was Jules Lemos as well," the principal of the school says.

"Do I look like a really old guy? That must have been my great-great grandfather. My father named me after him to honour his name."

The principal does not reply but has a sceptical look on her face. "Do you have academic results, or report cards, from her previous school?"

"No, our daughter was educated in a convent in Poland. My wife Pleb and I planned that she would become a Catholic nun and spread out faith to all pagans but the convent burnt down and all academic records were destroyed. The convent did not believe in off-line storage, so we have no evidence of her academic achievements."

"Does she speak English? Our lessons are in English, not Polish or ancient Greek."

"I'll be right mate," Mystca comments in an OZ accent while trying not to laugh. The principal has a stern look on her face and is not impressed.

"You have no academic records and yet you are enrolling her in year 11, our next to final school academic year. She will have to do the entrance exam under my supervision, no phones or any electronic devices allowed. So, she wants to study English, Maths1, Maths2, Physics, Chemistry and Biology, hmm, they were my year 11 subjects when I was a student many, many years ago. The test is done on-line, at the school, and supervised as I said before; one hour for each subject. Mystca, you have 15 minutes for any preparations and you parents can come back in 5 hours or I will call them on your phone if you find it too stressful and wish to terminate the tests."

Mystca is rubbing her hands as if eager for the start. "I will do good Miss Principal. Fire away as they say in this OZ country."

"We will be back in 5 hours," yells Pleb.

"Mother, be back in 2 hours else the school principal may take me down to the school cafeteria which may not have seaweed and sea snails, the food I have gotten used to."

"Jules, I hope she is successful in the tests and goes to school. I am not a schoolteacher and I find it tiring trying to answer all her questions most of which I cannot. Yesterday she asked me what is Dark Matter? I replied that it is the coating on the BBQ plate when Jules does not scrub it."

"Enough Pleb, I need to do some shopping for the peptide ingredients. Let's go," I whisper in Pleb's ear.

"We will be back soon my darling; we have some food shopping to do. Strive and be challenged else you will be living with us forever eating seaweed and sea snails. You have to expand your taste buds."

I'm holding three one-litre bottles each of acetone and ethanol and 48 disposable syringes. I drop them at the cash register at the discount pharmacy.

"Sir, these solvents are often used to make illicit drug substances and you also wish to purchase 48 disposable syringes. I need to record all your contact details as it is the law."

"I only make nail-polisher remover and Botox injections for my wife, that's all they'll be used for, isn't that right my darling wife?"

"No, that is not correct. He uses these solvents to sterilize unsightly infections and inject his festering moles with that disinfectant mouth cleanser that he makes. He can pull his pants down to show you what I mean."

"Madam, that won't be necessary. I need to maintain sanitary standards so no pulling down the pants, but sir, I need your car license and record your address details. That is our protocol."

I comply and then we trudge to the supermarket to get 20 cans of Soya beans. I also tell Pleb that she was brilliant at the pharmacy.

"Sir, I am a vegetarian myself. These Soya beans are very good for encouraging your bowel activity."

"Thank you but we have to rush. I'm going to have a Soya bean movement soon."

We get outside the supermarket, our large backpacks full of solvents and Soya Beans cans, and then the phone buzzes. Pleb pulls out my phone from a trouser pocket.

"Jules, there is a text message from the principal of the school and she wants us to come back to the school as soon as possible. Could it be that Mystca had some sort of physical injury? We have to run; it is not far to get back to the school."

Carrying kilograms of beans and solvents and doing a dash is not easy and we arrive panting and very sweaty.

"I am not happy. Your daughter completed the tests 20 minutes quicker than I ever did. She has a talent for the sciences."

"Is she accepted?"

"She is enrolled but needs a school uniform and sports uniforms. You can purchase them from the school tuck shop."

Just as we're about to depart the principal's office, a tall, athletic, muscular woman dressed in a tee-shirt and short, shorts enters.

"This is Miss Maya. she is the physical education teacher."

"And who are you?" Miss Maya bends down and looks at Mystca.

"I am new, but I would like to be a runner, and I would also like to do weight training to get muscles like you have."

"We have a gym at the school, and a few students train during the lunchtime break. We also have a running group that trains after school. You are most welcome to join us in both activities."

Mystca jumps up in joy and gives Miss Maya a hug.

The shop assistant beckons Mystca and takes her height, chest and waist measurements. "My, my, my! You should feed this girl more food. She is very skinny almost anorexic compared to our other Townsville lasses," says the burly, elderly woman shop assistant.

"That is because we do not feed her junk food, and she exercises a lot," Pleb comments.

"Right madam/sir, that will be $800 for the school uniform and another $1000 for the sports uniforms and sports gear. I'll send her dimensions to the dressmakers as we don't have small uniforms her size in store. You can pick them up in 3 days. The Chinese dressmakers are quick."

"OK, that's fine but tell your dressmakers to allow for her growth, 2 or 3 sizes oversize. I don't want to be paying for more uniforms if she has a growth spurt."

"Pleb, can you pay with your credit card as I forgot to bring cash? I will pay you back."

"Jules, you are such a scrooge bagel," Pleb whispers.

I whisper to Mystca, "I can't help you with the Maths that much but we can all take up running and swimming so we can justify those expensive sports uniforms."

"I don't need any help with the Maths, and I can beat you running anytime. I will race you to the wharf. It is only 400 metres away."

"Mystca, we have all these heavy bags and backpacks of food to carry. We cannot run now."

"I will carry half the shopping while we both run."

And so, we sort of ran to the wharf, but it was more like stumbled. I'm bent down trying to catch my breath back. Pleb is 5 minutes behind though she is wearing high-heel shoes that will need to be discarded as both heels broke.

"Jules, are you having a heart attack, are you?" asks Pleb. "We need you now more than ever; can you save the heart attack for another day?"

"Old man, are you well?" asks Mystca.

"I am not an old man and don't you ever call me that again!"

"Is not old man another word for father in OZ? There is a funny song I heard on the radio called 'My Old Man's a Dustman'. That is where I learned the word."

"I'm fine, just out of breath. I just have to take up running again. No way is a 13-year-old going to beat me in a 400m race. I will prove that I am not an old man."

After many tries and many more trips to the discount pharmacy and interrogations by their staff, I finally manufacture what I believe is the peptide. It must be right; it's

3-D image is the same as the last remaining sample of the original peptide. I inject a dose in my arm and a 10th of a dose into Chloe4.

I should have never challenged Mystca in running. The next two years began with a daily morning run, on the beach sand around our island with Pleb, me and Chloe4 running way behind Mystca who usually does two more laps whilst Pleb and I wait panting, whilst sitting on the sand. Mystca completed year 11 and achieved very good academic and athletic results under the guidance and encouragement from Miss Maya. In the final year of school, she was elected school captain and invited to many parties. Pleb and I stayed awake till she returned home by motorboat. Luckily Mystca is not a late-nighter and she also didn't want to have a party on our island or have friends visiting. Pleb thinks she is embarrassed to have her friends visit as our non-luxurious lifestyle did not match that of the other students. Pleb and I talked to her about that and finally convinced her that it's not the material possessions but the deeper things like values that you possess that are important. That could have been a mistake because after our conversation, every second or third Saturday Mystca would take the motorboat and pick up her six close friends and they'd eat drone-delivered pizza's and stare at the sky whilst lying on the beach.

"Jules, what is that smell? What are they smoking?"

"Pleb, it smells like cannabis. Let's go and join them. It's over 100 years since I've had a puff."

"No, Jules. There is a thunderstorm predicted and heavy rain. We have to phone their parents and use the motorboat to drive them back to Townsville."

"Pleb, I have phoned Mystca's friends parents. None of the parents have answered their phone; I think they may be glad to have a night of peace."

"Jules, let us guide Mystca's friends to *Cabin03*. It has 3 double beds. They can all sleep there."

We eventually get all the girls to *Cabin03* and position them on the beds.

"Pleb, this cannabis seems like 1000 times more potent than what I had as an early adult. I don't know the answers or where to start, but we may have to have a talk to Mystca and maybe her friends about using cannabis."

"Jules, they seemed drunk, but they did not consume all those calories from alcoholic beverages. This type of behaviour has been happening for thousands of years; people used mind-altering substances; the Vikings did that before going to war and Jules, they only have their smoko sessions once or twice a month. I prefer they do that here rather than in some risky, unsafe environment and also, I read some of your diaries. Your psychologist sister, her clients and you spent quite a bit of time doing Omm chanting after indulging in those magic mushrooms."

"OK, OK, you're right. We'll allow them some indulgences."

There were also many interstate trips where Mystca represented Townsville and won the 800m races. Miss Maya had a big influence in her success. Mystca was also asked to compete in the Junior World Championships in Poland this year, but Pleb and I finally convinced her it would not be a good idea to go back. I had to buy her the most expensive runners to keep her from throwing a teenage tantrum.

Pleb and I approach Miss Maya during the valedictory function and thank her for the encouragement she gave Mystca.

"We are sorry that we did not bring you a gift apart from this card, but you are welcome to stay on our island anytime you wish. We have spare, furnished cabins you and friends can use at no cost."

"That is so kind of you; let me give you both a hug. Your daughter is very talented, and it was a pleasure to teach and inspire her. We cannot take up your offer now since my boyfriend and I both applied for and were granted sporting jobs in Mexico. Michale, my boyfriend, achieved the bronze medal in rifle shooting at the last Olympics, so he had many offers for teaching shooting, whereas I have a job in a Mexican secondary school. We are both studying Spanish at the moment, "Parlez-vous Spanish?""

Pleb and I look at each other. "Miss Maya, the offer is always there and thank you again. We hope you come back safely."

Mystca joins in the hugging.

"Jules, Mystca has nearly perfect scores in all her year 12 subjects, but she wants to be a psychologist instead of a physicist. With her scores, the world is her prawn; she would be accepted into any university course she wanted."

"Pleb, the first year of psychology includes mainly science subjects. She can change her course when she acquires some practical common sense."

The next day, there is much noise, and the sky is covered in airborne sand and leaves. A helicopter lands outside the resort. In storms Bea, without her security guards and looking very dishevelled and cold, "Have you got a sauna?" She asks.

"No, we don't need one on this tropical island. Where have you been?"

"I have spent three years searching for you in Antarctica and it was colder there than Poland in winter, that is where I have been. It was my punishment for letting you escape."

"Well, your English has definitely improved so it wasn't a total waste of time."

"I need to eat before we talk business. All I ate for those three years were penguins. The supply ships couldn't get in because of the ice." She looks up and notices Pleb. "So, you stole my research assistant as well. I hope you are not fornicating with her."

Pleb interrupts. "He is too old to do that sort of activity."

I'm tempted to refute that comment by Pleb, after all, the painter Picasso was still into it in his 90s certainly fornicated and he had no peptide. I refrain. I have to be logical. Pleb and I do like each other and sleep in the same bed but as attractive as she is, she worked for *Pi5* and I'm a suspicious guy. We just cuddle at this stage of the relationship.

"Bea, where's the pilot of that chopper, he may want a cup of tea or coffee or something stronger?"

"I am the pilot, and I have learnt to fly it, and I have only crashed once. I borrowed it. It has long-range fuel tanks, and I just made it here; only 5 litres of fuel is left."

"Bea, we have an outdoor solar-powered hot spa. I suggest you jump into it to defrost. We'll talk afterwards."

I get a towel for Bea and guide her to the spa. When I'm back Pleb looks at me. "Jules, this is going to get very complicated, she stole a helicopter, and we could get implicated in the theft."

"Pleb, she implied the copter is virtually out of fuel. If we could fly it back to Townville and just abandon it in a park, the authorities probably wouldn't come looking for us."

"Jules, can you fly a copter? I cannot, plus we need fuel. For the moment, we have to hide the copter."

"How are you going to hide a large copter? I don't have a copter garage?"

"Jules, I think I know how."

Chapter Nine

I had never, ever ventured into the large shed behind the cabins. Apparently, it just contains very large trawler fishing nets and a winch, according to Pleb, who must have done a lot of exploring. When Bea steps out of the spa, I give her an old tracksuit of mine. "We've got work to do."

It took four hours for the four of us, Pleb, Bea, Mystca and me, to drag the net from the shed and then use the winch to drop in on the copter. It took many tries. Then we collected palm fronds and threw them up onto the net to cover the copter.

"It will not work," says Bea. "The copter has a homing beacon, which sends out radio signals every 12 hours with its location coordinates."

"Do you know where the beacon is?"

"I think I do. I will tell you."

I crawl underneath the canopy we have created and pull out the beacon from under the copter.

"I have to get to the motorboat. I'll drive the beacon far out to sea. No, on second thought, there's this guy who owns the next island 6km away, and I don't particularly like him. I'll dump the beacon on his island."

Job done. The beacon is gone. Now we have to work out the sleeping arrangements.

"Jules, I don't feel comfortable with this. Put her up in *Cabin06*, far away from us," Pleb says. "And can you stop putting a zero in front of a cabin number when you speak? It makes you sound like, what do you call it in OZ, a nerd? Please stop being a nerd!"

"I happen to very much like the number zero," I reply, and then Bea comes trudging in looking worst for wear. "I need that peptide of yours. I'm feeling very tired and old."

"Bea, I haven't started manufacturing a new batch just yet. I had forgotten the manufacturing process." OK, I lied to her.

Bea falls in my arms, her hands held upwards, her head flung back, and her eyeballs rolling.

"Jules, give her an injection of the peptide. We can manufacture more of it, and we do not want to have to cover up her death as well as the missing copter."

"Pleb move away from Bea," I whisper. "Pleb, don't tell her about my lab inside the hill. I'm manufacturing and storing the peptide there for now. It doesn't flood."

I run up the hill to the entrance of the underground laboratory and descend the ladder. The fridge is chugging away. Six full vials and eight coffee jars full of the peptide. I grab one vial and one packeted syringe.

"Jules, you hit the sweet spot first shot, perfect shot in the artery near her wrist. Have you got some disinfectant?"

"Pleb, the puncture mark is minuscule and will not bleed. We can just wipe it with dishwashing liquid to wipe off any germs."

Thirty minutes later, Bea springs back to life. "You are coming back with me to Poland," she says rather loudly.

"No, I'm not Bea, I'm staying here, and if you try to get me again, I'll destroy the notes on the complex manufacturing process of the peptide. The new variant of the peptide protects the telomeres in your chromosomes better than the first version, and the protection lasts longer. I will post a vial to you in Poland every year but don't even consider trying to get your researchers to reverse-engineer it. I've designed the peptide to know when it is being probed by X-rays and other means. If it is probed, it will turn into a rapid aging-enhancing compound, only good for people who want to get the old age pension early. Bea, think about it, if you manufactured and sold the peptide, you'd be rich, but the planet would die. It couldn't sustain all the people who live past their natural use-by date."

"Sure, you can talk. You are a total hypocrite."

"Bea, I'm helping Pleb bring up her daughter. I have to be around for at least another ten years."

"Well, my pet South Ecuadorian turtle Castro needs me as well to feed him and take him for walks. They live up to 200 years, and he is only young. He sleeps for long periods but will wake soon."

I thought it was only in the USA that you could purchase exotic species of wildlife, but apparently, you now can in Poland.

"I'm taking you back to Townsville, and I'll purchase a plane ticket for you to get back to Poland and feed Castro."

"Mystca, could you use my 3D printer and produce a passport for Bea?"

"It will take 30 minutes, and she needs to tell me some personal details."

Bea follows Mystca, so Pleb and I are left in peace. "Jules, that was a convincing presentation, but was it the truth?"

"No, mostly lies, but it may give us peace for a while till she departs."

"Jules, in the Eastern European block, we used neurotoxins to dispose of people just as the *i5* organizations did, but we did not use cyanide as it is too easily detected. It would appear like a natural death; just a little undetectable pin prick is all it takes with the neurotoxins."

"Can you order these neurotoxins online?"

"I'm just logging in now. Yes, Novichok from a Ruski website. I'll order some now."

"OK, just one dose, one dose only."

"What, do you suspect that I would use it on you as well as Bea? You are currently useful Jules, as you encourage my daughter, but you are no substitute for my vibrating battery-powered device in bed. I will use some of my *Nitcoin* cryptocurrency to pay."

"I'll pay you back in OZ dollars."

"It should take only three hours to deliver. They use supersonic jet drones."

My slightly fragile ego has been shattered. I will have to conduct a scientific test to determine if I'm better than a battery-powered, penile-looking device. It's time to take a chance, plus I do like the cuddles. I look out the window, and there are Mystca and Bea walking along the beach, both laughing.

"Pleb, I can't do it, and like you said before, we'd have to cover up her death. This island has too many buried bodies in it already. I'll start the motorboat and take her to the airport tonight. I checked on my device, and there's a flight to Singapore and then a connecting flight to Warsaw in Poland. The flight leaves Townville at 8 pm. Oh bugger, the flight to Singapore is booked out. She has to stay the night, and don't use that Novichok on her just yet."

"It sounds like you're very concerned about her."

"I'm concerned about all humans who have a tinge of goodness in them."

"I will not prick her, but she has to stay in *Cabin06*. I don't want her crawling into our bed at night."

Bea would end up staying more than one night due to pleas from Mystca. I have no idea if Bea is using Mystca as a ploy but then again, maybe not. Bea never had kids, and maybe she's just trying to enjoy the harrowing experience of having a kid around.

"Pleb, can you use more of that Nitcoin to get Bea's pet turtle delivered here."

"Jules, that is highly illegal and goes against your country's pet importation laws."

"Pleb, everything we've done, even though it hasn't hurt anyone except those trying to kill us, is highly illegal. Now can you get back on the web and get the turtle over here. I'll pay you back."

Chapter Ten

And so, Castro, the turtle, gets dropped off by a drone device, and Bea grabs and hugs him but the large turtle seems less than responsive. He just looks around and around. I'm sure he's thinking what the f... am I doing here? Then a grasshopper flies by, and Castro, within a microsecond, flings his tongue out, captures it and starts chewing. Castro may be useful as my recent efforts at growing vegetables have proven futile due to insects devouring them first. Meanwhile, Bea and the turtle walk back to *Cabin06*. Chloe4 sits on my shoulder, swaying her head as if worried and thinking that Castro will now get all the pats, attention, and leftover food. I reassure the rat by giving her one of the walnuts I'm holding. She scuttles away and is trying to break the hard shell.

"Jules, you are looking at Bea, not the turtle. We could try making love. I bought this attachment that you can hook on if your appendage does not rise to the occasion."

"I think I may have forgotten what to do, it's been so long."

"I will give you instructions or you can watch some educational videos on the WEB," says Pleb.

For a moment, I cringe. I remember how Melissa got stuck into me for watching those educational sexual training videos. Anyway, no need for videos as my memory miraculously came back. We didn't get much sleep that night, and Pleb and I are exhausted and sweaty. I have to put under-arm deodorant on the shopping list as she doesn't seem to shave her under-arm hair, which is like a jungle and a breeding ground for odorous bacteria. If I ever go bold on the scalp, I know that she could donate her hair under-arm jungle for my scalp hair transplant.

I stroke her lips, "Are you sure you're postmenopausal?"

"I have missed a period or two, so I must be."

Memories of Melissa come flooding back when she said the same thing, and yet we had a kid together. I must have a terrified look on my face. I don't really want to be a great, great granddaddy.

"It is fine, Jules. I am on the contraceptive pill. I thought it was a waste of time and resources taking that pill, but it does prevent facial pimples."

And so the romance resumes, a long, long night with clean socks in our mouths so our groaning doesn't wake anyone; we might have broken a record and are exhausted and dripping sweat on each other.

"Your performance was an A+. I am glad you watched those licking videos. I will report the statistics to *Pi5*," she giggles.

Chapter Eleven

Next morning there's a knock on the door. It's Bea.

"Castro is missing! You all have to help me find him," she frantically yells and gesticulates whilst thumping her feet and looking like a petulant child.

"Bea, comb your hair and put some clothes on."

"But I thought this was a nudist colony."

"It sort of was once, but for adults only. We have Mystca, a child, staying here.

I throw her a towel and some safety pins. Pleb helps Bea to secure the towel.

"Ouch," yells Bea . I just hope Pleb hadn't dipped that safety pin in Novichok.

We're all scouring the island and yelling 'Castro, Castro', but no sign of the turtle. Then Mystca, whose hearing is quite acute because of her age, says she knows where he is.

"Your rat stood up on her hind feet and pointed to the helicopter blades. I can hear the turtle munching. He's sitting on top of those palm-covered helicopter blades."

"How on earth did he climb up there?" I yell to Bea.

"He must have levitated. He is a very gifted turtle."

And who do you think had to get Castro down? I fall four meters down, landing on my back with Castro, who lands on my chest. Fortunately, the sand was soft.

"Jules is your brain injured?" asks Pleb.

"I don't think so, Pleb. I am now an Ozzie, and if you look at the performance of our politicians, we only need one functional neuron, but I may have a few broken ribs. Help me get Castro off my chest. I can hardly breathe. I'm also going to trim Castro's claws. My only good shirt is covered in my blood."

I find a whiteboard in the cellar and some water-soluble whiteboard markers. We have to do some serious brainstorming.

"Pleb, Bea and Mystca, we've got to get rid of this copter. We can't leave it here. It would take hundreds of years to rot away. Any suggestions?"

"We could blow it up and scatter it into little pieces." The kid must have watched too much TV.

"Not a good idea, Mystca. I have no explosives."

"You can buy them from bikie gangs. They sell anything."

"Any other ideas that don't involve blowing things up?" I ask.

Bea puts up her hand. "You could hire a digger and a big winch so we could bury it."

"You know how hard that would be? There could be water and sewerage pipes lying underneath this sand."

Then Pleb responds. "Jules, let's just report it to the authorities, but we have to have a consistent story of how it got here. Bea's name does not have to be mentioned. We will just say we found it here, on our island, all covered up with our netting, and ask them if they can come and pick it up as it is spoiling our view of the ocean."

"Sounds good, but Pleb, we got to come up with a good story, and we all have to stick to it. When we have the perfect well-rehearsed story, I will guide you through my psychic meditation and hypnosis, something I learnt when falsely imprisoned 120 yrs. ago, that way, you won't panic when questioned."

I find another whiteboard in the cellar and some more water-soluble whiteboard markers. We all start writing the story, and I put a summary on the whiteboard. Six hours later, we perfected it, at least, I think.

"Bea, you have to dye your hair black, and I've got some skin-coloured putty. We'll make your nose look bigger, and Mystca will create you a birth certificate, an OZ driver's license, and a new passport. You'll be my sister if we get interviewed."

"I do not want my nose to look like yours, I am a communist at heart, and I do not want a big aristocratic-looking nose."

"It's only temporary. Once the copter is removed, you can take the nose enhancement off."

"Now, I'll be Jules the 5th, I don't want to tell them my age and why I still look so young."

"You have some grey hairs, I can see them," says Bea.

"Mystca, you'll have to fake some more birth certificates and passports. Pleb and I will help you."

I ring the Townsville police. "We discovered this covered-up vehicle, which appears to be a helicopter on our island. We don't know how it got here as we had been camping on the other side of our island for the last week. Can you come over and pick it up?"

"Sir, we'll be there soon. A long-range helicopter was reported stolen from the Australian scientific base in Antarctica. We'll be there soon."

Two hours later, two motorboats dock at our island jetty. Four policemen and two officious-looking guys walk out. The police officers pull off their bulletproof vests, and one of the guys puts on a monocle eyepiece and inspects the copter. He is elderly, tall and seems to be the head of the investigation.

"It is definitely our missing copter, and it has set a world record for flying all this way on a single load of fuel. I designed it." He claps his hands in joy. "Our copter may make the Guinness Book of Records."

Bea whispers to me. "There was a strong northerly wind. Wind-assisted records do not count."

"Now, madams and sir, we have a just few questions to ask, and we have to take your fingerprints," the monocled guy says after giving the copter another kiss.

Bea, Pleb, Mystica and I nervously glance at each other with pretend smiles.

Chapter Twelve

"So, can I get some details, your identification documents? It's just protocol, and we have to follow the rules. This conversation will be recorded. Do you consent?"

"Yes, of course."

We rush back to our cabin and bring the identification materials that Mystca had created.

"Mm, they smell freshly of acetone."

"It's our monthly cleaning day, and we sprayed everything with Doorek. It's got acetone and lots of other hydrocarbons, plus it kills noxious mould and bacteria."

"Now, madams and sir, where were you on the night the copter arrived?"

"We didn't notice it first. It was covered up, but before that, we were doing a spiritual retreat on the other side of the island. We were camping and praying."

"Are you members of that Hedonist religion? If so, I'd like to join."

"No sir, we just study the stars with our telescopes and look for a god - any god will do."

"Now, who is this lass? She must be your sister. She has the same distinctive nose that you have."

"Yes, she is my sister. Aneather is her name. We just had similar accidents when roller-skating and hitting a pole nose first."

"And who is this attractive young-looking lady?"

I lower my face and rub my eyes. "Her name is Pleborska, an abandoned kid who became pregnant at an early age, and this young girl is her feral daughter. I'm doing my community service, and these poor, emotionally shattered people live on my island for free. It's my contribution to the community and god. It's all I can do to be of service."

"I hope you're not taking advantage of their vulnerable condition."

"Sir, it could be the other way around. I'm just doing my best to contribute to the welfare of poor unfortunate people."

"You're cleared, your story makes sense. Now I have to order some fuel for this copter and get the boys in blue to remove all that netting on the rotor blades. Now have you got a beer? I'm thirsty."

"It's only home brew."

"Anything will do. I just need a drink."

A police boat arrives with many metal containers filled with copter fuel. Four hours have passed, and the Police and their expert are about to leave by boat and copter. Then the other non-uniformed guy yells out in a panic state. We all cringe.

"There's this white marsupial sitting on my shoe."

"Flangers, it's just a white rat licking up the remains of the pie you had for lunch and obviously dropped some remains on your shoe," the monocled guy assures the other officious-looking guy.

"Have you got a licence for pets on this island?" the monocled guy asks.

"No, not yet. We saw the rat in an animal homeless shelter in Townsville. The rat must have escaped and followed us back in our motorboat. I promise I'll get it registered."

The Police motorboats and the helicopter depart. We wave goodbye and then walk back to *Cabin02*, where we jump up and down in joy. We pulled it off.

Chapter Thirteen

We're all sitting on my balcony enjoying a beetroot juice beer, except for Mystca, who is given a coconut and furiously drilling with my solar rechargeable drill to open it.

"Jules, let us go into town. I would like a real meal for once. What do you call it, a pub meal?" asks Pleb. Chloe4 and Castro stand up on their back feet, expecting that we'll bring home the leftovers. I'm so glad Pleb didn't suggest that French restaurant where the cheapest meals start at $100.

"OK, let's get dressed up. The pets aren't coming. We'll bring back yummy food for them in rat and turtle bags."

We're all getting dressed after showering to maintain personal hygiene, though in this humid environment, you must shower every hour if going out in public.

Bea knocks on our door. "Bea, you cannot look like you have just come from the Swiss Alps. Pleb will find a costume for you that is more appropriate for OZ conditions.

"I would like to join you for a meal that is not just seaweed and clams."

"Jules, I do not like these short pants and tee shirts. They make me look fat. Have you got a kaftan?"

"No Bea, we don't have any kaftans, and besides, it's a really hot and humid night, so you have to let your body breathe."

Eventually, the ladies, after 2 hours, find some clothing they like. Mystca decides to join us. We arrive at an Irish pub close to the ferry terminal. There's Sid standing next to the counter, drinking an ale. Sid owns a motorboat repair business and has recently retired. In the past, he showed me how to service my motorboat by myself, an activity I rarely perform.

"Jules, is this lady your sister? You have the same nasal features."

Bea quickly removes the putty from her nose. "We were rehearsing for a play called Macbeth, so I had to appear evil," Bea says.

"You look beautiful; what's your name again?

"It is Bea "

"Well, Bea, you look like an A to me," Sid says as he stares at her and forgets about the rest of us. He finally comes to his senses.

"Let me buy you all a beer and coconut juice for the junior."

Pleb whispers in my ear, "Jules, your friend Sid is entranced by Bea. Maybe she will move in with him and take that annoying turtle with her."

"Yes, Pleb, they are certainly having a verbal and non-verbal connection and are totally oblivious of us."

Mystca comes over to Pleb and me. "I don't want Bea to move out. I can see into the past, present and future. Bea will move out and live with that guy, and I will not have a friend on the island."

"Mystca, you may be psychic or psychotic, but it's best that Bea leaves. We'll find you another friend."

"It will not be the same." Mystca starts crying and buries her head in Pleb's armpit; then a young guy comes marching in from the toilet block, pulling up the zip on his pants.

"This is my son, Sid Junior or Sid2, depending on how formal you want to be. He's turning 18 tomorrow, and he and my ex-wife are in Townsville for the week," says Sid.

Sid2 looks at Mystca. There are fireworks as they look into each other's eyes.

"Dad, I don't want to go back to Melbourne to live with Mum again. I've done that for nearly 18 years," says Sid2.

"Mum, I also want to stay here in OZ. I like the climate," says Mystca reversing her previous inclination to move back to Poland. The kids wander off to do some exploring.

Sid asks, "What do I buy an 18-year-old son for his birthday? I was an orphan, so I never got any birthday presents, so I need some ideas."

We four adults are talking about birthday present ideas, then I have to go to relieve myself in the toilets, and then I notice; Mystca and Sid2 are engaging in unhygienic oral activities; Yuk, they're tongue kissing in a corner.

"Sid, has your son got any germs or diagnosed medical condition?"

"I wouldn't know. Why do you ask?"

"Your son and my sort of stepdaughter are exchanging a lot of saliva just outside the toilets."

"I'll be back soon," says Sid.

Pleb puts her hand on my shoulder, "Jules, all teens do that, didn't you when you were young?"

"No, of course not. I didn't know any girls when I was young. I went to an all-boys Catholic school and was very conservative."

Sid comes back, holding the two teens by the scruff of their necks. "You sit here where I can see you both, and Sid2, if you make this young lass pregnant, you'll have to get a job in a coal mine because I'm not paying for any medical expenses."

The two teenagers nervously exchange glances and sip their coconut juice. Sid buys the meals. We all have a burger special except for Mystca, who has a veggie burger special. Mystca reminds me of my first stepdaughter, a vegetarian, who has long been deceased because she wouldn't take the life-prolonging peptide. Sid, like most males in this part of OZ, is rather loud. "Bea, would you like to go out to dinner with me tomorrow, just you and me only?"

Bea looks down and answers, "I would like to. Can you pick me up from the island where I am staying?"

"I sure can. I got the latest speedboat, and it is super fast. I'll pick you up at 6 pm."

We walk out of the hotel. Bea looks back at Sid and trips over due to a missing paving stone on the pathway. Sid comes rushing over and hugs Bea. "Are you hurt? I'll call an ambulance."

"It is only a bruised knee. I am not fatally injured. I will meet you tomorrow."

Pleb yells out to Mystca, who is looking back at Sid2 whilst following Pleb and me, "Watch where you step, and look at the ground as we do not have health insurance in case you fall."

Chapter Fourteen

Two weeks pass in a flash. Apart from boating Mystca to University in Townsville, we're not doing very much. Bea has moved out and now lives with Sid in his harbourside mansion. Mystca was initially very upset till she discovered that Sid2 is now participating as a human guinea pig in a psychological case study at her university. Bea also took Castro, and I think Chloe4 is quite upset as well. She got used to having the turtle around and engaging in some jousting. I'll have to find out from Bea how to order a turtle-like Castro online.

I ring Sid. "Sid, your son, Sid2, is now going to the same Uni as my stepdaughter. I thought you said he was only staying in Townsville for a week."

"I thought so too, but my ex has moved back to Townsville and enrolled Sid2 in some sort of educational programme for not well-mentally endowed students. Got to go, Jules and enlist a lawyer. My ex is chasing me for supposedly unpaid alimony payments."

"Pleb, they start early these days. Can you do the sex education with Mystca and maybe get her the contraceptive pill?"

"Jules, I got her a packet of condoms. She can instruct Sid2 how to use them because, as you say, in this country, he is not the sharpest kid on the block."

I feel relieved but not for long. A motorboat arrives at our jetty and out steps the monocled government official with his officious-looking assistant.

"We're trying to find an explanation. The iFinger device, which we fingerprinted you with and then downloaded the data to our database, came up with a match. A Jules who moved to this island over 100 years ago; we have to do another test. Stick out your digit."

"Humanoids have lived on this planet since we walked upright, about a million years. It's highly likely some of us will have the same fingerprints."

Pleb walks in. "He is a young and frisky 40-year-old. He is not the man you are looking for, but Jules, get scanned. It will prove their device is malfunctioning."

I get scanned. "Sir, this is a positive match. His name was Jules Lemos as well."

"Well, I'm Jules Lemos, the fifth. All my past relatives lacked imagination when naming progeny. All boys in the family were named Jules".

"Sir, that still doesn't explain the anomaly that your fingerprints are the same."

"That's pure chance, as I previously explained. Look up probability theory in a stats course if you don't understand what I'm talking about."

"The original Jules had a car parking fine in Townsville. With the accumulated interest, it's now $30,000. Now can you pay up?" Says the monocled government official.

"No, I'm not him, and besides, that parking zone sign was covered by a tree branch."

"Sir, you're coming with us. The iFinger device may be wrong, but we have a DNA sample, on ice, from the original Jules. If the two are the same, you have some explaining to do, and you'll have to pay that parking fine."

I look back at Pleb as I'm led away to the police motorboat then Pleb yells out.

"He had a thumb transplant after he stopped working for the *i5* agencies. You know what they are, don't you?"

"Burly, lookup *i5* on Doogle."

"Nothing, sir."

"Try the dark web," yells Pleb.

"Sir, there are over 20,000 entries concerning *i5*, and they are very long and will take weeks to read."

"You have a reprieve for the moment," the monocled guy says, "But I'll be back."

Chapter Fifteen

"Jules, you will have to tell him the truth," says Pleb after the guys depart.

"Pleb, I don't want to be the world's oldest person. I'd get bombarded by emails from those rich IT guys wanting to know the formula and live forever young. This has to be kept private."

"Come over here, Jules. When you are deceased, I may write a story about my relationship with the longest living Homo Sapien."

"Pleb, you definitely know how to comfort a guy. Now I have to think. Maybe you can help me. That guy will be back, and I don't want to pay $30,000 for an overdue parking fine. We have to be creative."

"Jules, we could just eliminate him, like they do in *Pi5*."

"You still work for them?"

"No, not officially anymore, well, not much."

"Think of something more creative."

"Ask your friend Bea . She might have some ideas. She's been on this planet much longer than I have."

I ring Bea . "Jules, I'm very, very sad. I am crying, and the bucket is nearly full of my tears. I have broken up with Sid, or he has broken up with me. He and Sid2 have relocated to another town, not on the coast, called Mount Isa. Jules, I am very upset Jules. Is he mounting Isa? I have a friend back in Poland called Isa. Was Sid cheating on me? We are broken up, but I have met this new guy called Harry. He is very high up in the Townsville city council."

"Bea, I feel your grief, but this guy Harry, has he got influence and connections."

"He has with me when we are together."

"Bea, focus, I have an outstanding parking fine from over a hundred years ago, and it's accumulated, after interest, to $30,000. Can you get Harry to exert his influence and get my parking fine cancelled? Can you do that?"

"I will, Jules, but you will have to buy me a steak. Harry is a vegetarian, but I need some meat like all Polish girls do."

"I will. I'll buy you a whole meat pack if my fine is wavered. You can cook your steaks on the BBQ when Harry is at work and not around."

"I will try, Jules," she says sobbingly. "Now, have you started production of your life-prolonging and cosmetic-enhancing peptide?"

"I'm working on it, Bea, the enhanced version. You'll get a dose when the latest version is finished."

"Jules, I do not want to be a genuine pig. You take the first dose from the batch you produce. If you live, I will try it."

Whatever Bea did to influence Harry, well, it worked. My parking fine must have been wavered, and two months have passed. The monocle guy and his assistant haven't been back. Bea must have been successful, but then a surprise. She arrives on the ferry carrying Castro. Chloe4 jumps up in joy. She has her turtle friend back.

"Jules, I need some accommodation, else I will be homeless and sleeping on the streets with rats, dogs, cats and kangaroos. I have broken up with Harry, and I have nowhere to go. Can I use *Cabin06* again?"

Mystca must have overheard, "Stepdaddy, let her stay; she is my friend."

"Mystca, I'm not your stepdaddy, but yes, OK, she can stay and get her some tissues to wipe her eyes."

"Oh, Jules, you are so kind. If you ever come back to Poland, you can stay at one of my opulent houses in Warsaw and not that underground laboratory where I kept you locked up the first time." Mystca walks Bea over to *Cabin06*.

"Jules," Pleb says, "I did some research on Bea. She is a wanted person by *Pi5* because of her failures, and we could be in danger by housing her on this island. She also took some documents that could be an embarrassment to the Polish government, and she is on their hit list as well. We have to be very careful. I still have the Novichok, so we could dispose of her and send her body parts back to Poland."

"No, Pleb, we got to do some of that up and down thinking, or is it called lateral thinking, side to side."

"Jules, we could just cut off her thumb and say she got eaten up by a, a, a Platypus. *Pi5* must have her fingerprints and would believe that explanation."

"No, not yet; no amputating bodily parts just yet, as I vomit at the sight of blood. Let's try to come up with another solution."

"Jules, you still like her, I can tell."

"Pleb, I've known her for over 100 years. She's like my sister, so don't even think about Novichoking her."

I grab Pleb, hug her and give her a kiss. She seems to have relaxed.

Chapter Sixteen

"Pleb, Bea, Mystca, come help me. There was a king tide last night, and it uncovered the deceased skeletal remains of my wife, Smithy, and my transgender sister. The remains of their foam-covered bodies are floating off to sea, and we have to retrieve them else will be in even bigger trouble with the authorities than a $30,000 parking fine. "

"Jules, Polish women are not good swimmers. The water was too cold to learn to swim amongst icebergs," says Bea .

"Why did not the bones sink? Why are their white skeletons floating?" asks Pleb.

"I sprayed polystyrene foam all over each body. It's all I had. I wanted to turn the bodies into mummies."

"Jules, has the motorboat got fuel?" Pleb asks.

"Not much, just enough to get to Townsville and purchase some more fuel."

"Get that canoe you have in the shed," Pleb says.

I'm exhausted from paddling and towing. It took almost three hours to retrieve the semi-skeletal foam-covered bodies.

"Jules, we should cremate the remains unless you have some religious problem with that."

"No, I don't Pleb, but we'd have to find lots of dry leaves and timber, and we can't generate too much smoke, else there will be a fire brigade boat arriving from the mainland. We'll try the cremation tomorrow. For the moment, let's dig three shallow graves and cover the bodies with sand."

That night there must have been another king tide as much of the sand covering the bodies had been swept away.

"Jules, the bodily remains of your previous wife are exposed. There is still a gold diamond ring on your wife's skeletal finger. Can I have it? It would save you money if we should ever get married."

"Yes, take it, Pleb."

I kiss what remains of Melissa's skeleton and shed a few tears.

"Jules, you just kissed the bones of that male friend of yours. Your wife's bones are over here. Women have different pelvic structures from men."

"Oh yuk, yuk." Embarrassingly I wander over to Melissa's bones and give them a hug and kiss.

"There's a wheel burrow in your shed. We can take these bones to the other side of the island and do the cremation there. It won't be visible to the Townsville folk."

It must be 4 am. We couldn't find any dry combustible material, so the four of us used rocks to grind the bones to a fine powder and added it to the soil to enrich its calcium content. The plants will be grateful.

We're all walking back and emotionally moved. Lots of tears are flowing. I have some bone grindings of Melissa in a little vial that I have taken with me. I hope it's Melissa's grindings and not Smithy's.

"Jules, let us have lots of coffee and perform a wake with candles to honour your friends," Bea says. The others agree.

There was no wake because we couldn't stay awake after all that work. Pleb, me, Bea and Mystca are lying on the carpet in my cabin, exhausted. Chloe4 and Castro crawl over our bodies, trying to determine if we're still alive and if they'll get a meal in the morning.

Chapter Seventeen

"Jules, we have to find Bea another partner. I am not comfortable with her living with us on this island. She sleepwalks and walks into our cabin and looks inside our fridge, takes food in our kitchen and leaves a mess which I then have to clean up. You are always fast asleep, so it is I who has to grab her by the shoulders and guide her back to her cabin. If she had a boyfriend, he could tie a piece of string to his toe and her toe so if she moved, he would wake up and pull her back to bed."

"Pleb, all the guys I knew have long since passed away. I don't know any eligible males."

"Jules, I've done some research. There is this guy called Voytek, ex *Pi5*, and he lives on an expensive yacht parked in the Townville harbour. Maybe you could ram his yacht with your motorboat to get his attention and instigate the conversation."

"No, no, that's not how it's done in OZ."

So, there I am, waving my arms, pretending to be drowning and Bea and Pleb calling out to the yacht, hoping to get Voytek's attention. Oh, sh*t, there are bull sharks in this harbour. That Voytek guy better move his arse quickly.

"Excuse me, sir, are you in some sort of trouble? I am watching *The Three Stooges* movie, and your screams are disrupting the dialogue that I'm trying to listen to," says Voytek with a heavy Polish accent.

"I'm drowning, and there are sharks here, can you throw me a buoy, a floaty round thing? I haven't got any on my motorboat, and my Polish friends can't swim."

"Yes, yes, I do have a floaty, I will throw it to you."

I crawl onto his yacht. "Here, have this towel. And would you and your friends like to join me? I have plenty of Vodka and these edible creatures you call prawns which taste better than cabbage rolls. I have plenty of prawns and other sea creatures. Join me for a drink and a meal."

Pleb and Bea moor the motorboat alongside the yacht, and Voytek and I outstretch our arms and pull them on board.

"Who is this lovely lady?"

"Her name is Pleborska, I call her Pleb for short. She may be my future wife. Voytek picks up her hand and kisses it whilst staring into her eyes. I thought I had gotten over unhealthy jealousy emotions, but my gut is churning.

"This is Bea, my Polish sister, well not sister, just someone I used to know; she is not married and is looking for a wealthy husband."

Voytek picks up her hand and kisses it too, but I did notice he made a microsecond glance a Pleb.

I don't know how many kilos of prawns we ate and how much Vodka we drank, but we're lying on the deck of Voytek's yacht.

"Jules, Jules, it may work. Voytek is lying there with his arm around Bea. I need a pee, is it the starboard side that a person pees in the ocean?"

"I don't know, Pleb, but I've just checked Voytek's pulse and there is no pulse. Tell me that you didn't give Bea that vial of Novichok."

"Jules, I did, and you'll be a hero. He was a highly wanted person by *Pi5*, an ex-agent who turned into an informant."

"Pleb, we don't do things that way in OZ. We are more subtle. We don't usually kill people, plus I'm getting tired of disposing of bodies."

"Jules, we can just sail away and dump his body in shark-infested waters."

"I don't know the first thing about sailing."

Bea removes Voytek's arm from her shoulder, gets up and stumbles over to Pleb and me. "There was a reward of 800,000 zloty by *Pi5* for Voytek, dead or alive. We just have to package his body and ship it to Poland, and I'll get to keep this yacht and half of the reward, and you can have the rest."

"How can we ship or fly a body back to Poland? It's not possible."

"Jules, we could post his amputated thumb and the rest of the body as ashes. There is an Artisan croissant bakery 100m away from this jetty. We could convert the body to ashes there."

"Pleb, do you mean we have to drag the body a 100m and then break into a bakery to carbonize Voytek? OK, call Mystca and tell her we'll be home late."

That night, under the cover of darkness, we drag Voytek's blanket-covered body to the bakery door. Bea uses an electronic device to check where the alarm sensors are. "We have to go to the back entrance as the display and counter of the shop are alarmed," she whispers.

We drag Voytek's body down an alleyway to the back of the shop.

"There are no alarm sensors in the oven room." Bea uses her *Pi5*-issued sonic door lock opener, and we pull Voytek's body inside. We remove his gold and diamond rings and the colossal gold chain from around his neck and then start the oven and wait for it to warm up. Then Pleb's phone rings. "Mum, you did not hang up your phone when we talked in the morning. I have been listening to your conversation most of the day. I have done some research. The bakery oven is only set to reach a maximum temperature of 400 degrees Celsius which is not enough to incinerate a body. You need at least 900 degrees, so check if there is a temperature setting on the oven. I also think you had better leave the bakery very soon as the bakers start work at 3 am, so you only have 5 hours."

Three hours later, after turning the oven to the max, super high heat, Voytek is carbonized, and his ashes, apart from his amputated thumb, fit neatly into a plastic shopping bag. We cautiously march out and walk back to Voytek's yacht.

"I have a yacht," yells Bea whilst clapping her hands. "Castro will love going sailing with me."

"Do you know anything about sailing?"

"Jules, the instructions are all on the Internet. I will Doogle tomorrow," says Bea, "I know there is something called an anchor and you got to pull it out else you cannot move on."

Pleb and I are too exhausted to go to my parked motorboat. There are plenty of bedrooms on this luxury yacht. I can't sleep and go to the kitchen and grab another Vodka. Why couldn't I have just been born a farmer and only have to worry about low rainfall or floods? Life would have been simple. Now we've got one mess after another to deal with. I'm too old for this, but then again I have Pleb to help.

Chapter Eighteen

Bea has hacked into Voytek's 3D computer. His password was just his surname. *Pi5* definitely need to train its agents better in Cyber-Security. She is now studying on Doogle, How to sail a yacht.

"Pleb, we have to get back to shore so I can post this finger and these ashes back to Poland. Bea has given me an address and it is in Warsaw. I got to buy a plastic bag and an envelope and some postage stamps."

"Jules, are you able to walk after all that Vodka you drank last night?"

"Of course, I have Polish genes myself, and that one bottle of Vodka is nothing to a Pol."

I was wrong. I stumbled and dropped the bag containing Voytek's ashes. It was one of those environmentally friendly plastic bags that self-destructs when dropped."

"Pleb, help me to collect some ashes. There's 800,000-zloty worth of ashes that are blowing away."

"Jules, you do not need the money. Be happy with what you got which is quite substantia, according to your bank account which I have checked. You can't take it with you when you depart this planet unless you want to leave it all to me."

"Yeh, thanks for the reassurance. Now we have another problem. First a helicopter and now a yacht whose owner's ashes are blowing in the wind; we got to get rid of the yacht."

"Jules, it is highly unlikely that Voytek's yacht was registered in this yacht parking spot by his real name. I will contact *Pi5* on the dark web tonight. They may have some suggestions on what to do and you may even get some of that 800,000-zloty reward. Let me swab your fingernails, they may contain traces of Voytek's DNA."

Pleb dips a sharp hairpin under my left thumb but then she punctures the skin. She's collecting a sample of my warped DNA in the blood.

"Jules, you don't produce sperm anymore, so all I got was a lot of glucose from your ejaculations, and I'm trying to avoid sugars; I may become a type 2 diabetic, so I have to be careful when we perform any night-time gymnastic activities. This is just a small blood sample."

"But why, why?"

"Jules, I lied. I still do some work for *Pi5*. I am sorry for the deceit. I will give you a blowup job to make up for it."

"No, Pleb, no. I trusted you, and now you're on the same boat or yacht as Bea. You have to move out. I want a simple, uncomplicated life. I want nothing to do with the *i5* organizations anymore."

"That's not on your *Ai5* profile. The more complicated it gets, the more you like it, it says."

"That was over 100 years ago, I've matured since then; OK, it takes boys around 30 years to mature, but I was a slow starter, so Pleb, are you in some sort of collusion with Bea? Do you both want the manufacturing process for the peptide."

"Jules, she is a great, great grandmother of mine. I'm here and care about her from a distance, a long distance, and I do have a duty of care to keep her alive."

"Pleb, if that is true, I may have once had a one-night stand with Bea . You might be my great, great granddaughter, and I have had a conjugal relationship with you. I've committed the worst crime possible, greater than any other."

"Jules, that was over 100 years ago with Bea, and we can do a DNA test, but you do not smell like a relative. I have sniffed your socks, and you are definitely no immediate relation as I told you before, it is highly unlikely, that we are all related as humans. I read that we are all on average, six relationships apart on the hierarchy tree on this planet. We are all related in a way."

I'm crouched down and holding my head, "I'm not a paedophiliac. Go now, go now, you can stay in *Cabin01*."

"Jules, I'm taking you back home. You are still useful."

"What for - that Novichok prick?"

"Jules, stop being so paranormal. You are not on the *Pi5* radar hit list. You are safe at the moment, so let us just go home."

We leave on my motorboat after helping Bea pull up the anchor of the yacht. She is hopefully sailing far, far away.

Chapter Nineteen

We have our backs turned as we fall asleep, but then Mystca comes running into our bedroom. "There's a yacht trying to moor at the jetty. It must be Bea."

It's dark, but the jetty is lit. After an hour, the yacht is moored, with a lot of help from Pleb, Mystca and me, Bea steps out holding Castro. Chloe4 jumps for joy at the sight of Castro. The others hug Bea after she climbs off the yacht.

"Jules, I have to stay here. I am a wanted woman, not wanted by a male, but by *Pi5* for what I do not know. Maybe it was for your kidnapping, but I do not know."

As if life can't get any more complicated, "Bea, we have to sink the yacht."

"But Jules, I'm starting to love sailing, and Voytek's yacht is fully AI-computerized. I just have to talk to it; go left yacht, go right, and it does what I say."

"Bea, you and the yacht can't stay here together."

"Jules, I still do not yet know how to fully sail. My Internet cut out when I was in Townsville. Can I log into your Internet to learn some more sailing tips? I want to sail back to Poland with Castro and without using that computer."

"No, no, you can't. It's too dangerous to sail that distance."

"Come over here, Jules, and let me and Castro give you a kiss."

"No way! I could be your great, great daughter's father. I'm waiting for the DNA test results."

"Jules, that was a one-off over 100 years ago, as you say, and you did not perform that well. You fell asleep while we were making love. I thought you were dead and had to perform mouth-to-mouth acceleration."

"The word is resuscitation; your English still needs some improving."

"It is still a possibility that Pleborska is my great-granddaughter, and I fell asleep because you fell asleep. You were not a great performer in the boudoir. Castro could do a better job."

A hard wack on the face from Bea, but I'm getting used to wacks. "Polish women specialise in lovemaking, whacking, as well as cooking cabbage dishes," she says.

Pleb, talk some sense into him," says Bea.

"I am not sure I can; he is very stuck in his ideas."

Chapter Twenty

We're sitting on the beach by the campfire cooking as, I forgot to reorder the hydrogen gas cylinder tanks that power the fusion reactor stove. The meal is berries, seaweed, and peeled stonefish, spikes removed. We prefer not to use the nuclear fusion stove as we haven't read the 500-page instruction booklet, 2/3rds of which covers dealing with uncontrolled fusion reactions that can result in an explosion that could destroy the whole island and even Townsville. The last page of the manual says, *RUN AS FAST AS YOU CAN.*

"Bea, we could end it all and live through death like normal people. Pleb has plenty of Novichok; she ordered more online. We can all depart together holding hands."

"Jules, you have Mystca, possibly but unlikely, my great-great-granddaughter to bring up, and I need your help. She is a teenager and hard to control."

"OK, you can stay, but we still have a yacht problem, and you're not sailing it to Poland."

"Jules, I also have to get married. My visa has expired, and I am now an illegal immigrant and I will have to be locked up with all the rapist and murders in a detention center. I have to marry what you call an OZ guy so I can get permanent residency."

We didn't notice a chartered ferry arriving, but there's a knock on the door. I cautiously open it. A tall guy with long black curly hair is standing in the doorway. So far, getting Bea a boyfriend has not been successful.

"Is Bea here? My name is Giuseppe. Bea and I met on the RSPCA dating site."

Bea runs out and grabs Giuseppe. He twirls her around and around.

Pleb looks at me. "Jules, I wish you could twirl me like that."

"Pleb, you're taller than me, you should twirl me around."

"I will try, Jules."

That suggestion was a mistake. Pleb is stronger than I gave her credit for, and I'm holding my head after being tossed into a wall. So it's another night of cooking outside, but no stonefish and berries. Giuseppe has bought three very large bags of food with him. I hope Bea stays here. She can certainly attract a source of good food, and we are all gastronomically delighted.

Pleb puts her arm around me. "Jules, you will be sad, lonely and hungry, if I and Mystca should ever move out."

She's right. I turn towards her, and we exchange saliva.

"Jules, maybe you can take some lessons from Giuseppe on how to be romantic."

"Pleb, I can hear another motorboat arriving at the jetty. I got to go out and check."

"Quickly, Bea, Giuseppe, hide and don't come out."

Out steps the monocled guy and his assistant. "I have some more questions to ask," he says.

"Who owns this yacht moored at your jetty? It was parked illegally in the Townville harbour."

"Sir, do I look like a sailor, I have no idea how it ended up here. You can investigate the yacht if you like."

"My assistant and I will do that. We shall be taking more fingerprints and some toe prints."

"You can do that but don't even think about giving me a fine. I live comfortably on this island and not on a yacht where I just get seasick."

The two guys put on plastic garments, shoes and gloves and march off to the moored yacht taking their forensics toolkits with them.

"Jules, they will swab the yacht, and it has got Bea's fingerprints as well as those of that Voytek guy."

"Pleb, I don't know how much work you do for *Pi5*, but their senior agents always wore glued false fingerprint patterns on the ends of their fingers. I believe Bea used the prints of that long-departed ex-US president, that Trumpet guy, and besides, I doubt if these bored council workers know much about forensics. That Voytek guy probably also uses false fingerprints, so he would have covered his tracks. We may get to keep the yacht, fingers keepers."

"Jules, Voytek would have weapons hidden on the yacht. In *Pi5*, we never go anywhere without some firepower."

"I'm sure Voytek hid them well; underneath the hull, so unless they go diving, then they won't find them."

The monocle guy and his assistant return from the yacht. "Did you wipe the fingerprints? All we found was this used condom and prints of people who departed many years ago."

"My partner Pleb is way beyond childbearing age. Those used condoms cannot belong to anyone on this island. As I said before, I have no idea why this yacht moored here, but it's on our property, and we're keeping it unless the owner turns up, and can you stop displaying that soiled condom."

Pleb gives me a temporary angry look but regains her smile. Monocles and his assistant leave, not looking happy. I'll have to call Harry to politically intervene and keep those guys away from our island.

"Jules, that was a conveyancing performance. You did well," Pleb says as she hugs me. I don't correct her use of English.

"But you implied I am old and not able to bear a child. Guess what."

Oh shit, I hope Pleb is joking.

I go out to the shack where Bea and Giuseppe are hiding. "Bea, we may need Harry's help again."

Chapter Twenty-one

Bea calls Harry and pleads with him. "Harry, I am sorry to have broken your heart, but can you do me one last favour?"

"What is it this time?"

"Harry, the monocle government guy is harassing me again. Can you shut him up? And that condom he took with him contained my turtle Castro's sperm. I don't need any more trouble. Harry and I do not want to be accused of having an inappropriate relationship with my turtle. I need your help, Harry. Please help me before I run out of tears and become severely dehydrated and die."

"Would you like to meet for a drink? I do miss you a bit."

"Harry, I'm stuck in a very complicated situation and feel extreme anxiety if I see a human. If you were a turtle, I could cope."

"Look after yourself, Bea. I'll see what I can do," Harry replies on the loudspeaker phone.

Giuseppe comes out from the loo holding a handgun with a silencer. "Jules, I have been sent to terminate you - no idea why. I follow orders, and I do not want to cause you any pain, so please comply and stand two metres away so I can target your heart. Death will be quicker if I do not miss, and I will pray for your soul at Saint Mary's Church after you successfully depart this Earth."

"Bea, is Giuseppe from *Ii5* as well? Why can't you just find a non-assassin boyfriend?"

"Giuseppe, Jules is like a brother to me. You must not terminate him, or else I will not have a shoulder to shed tears on."

Bea then grabs Giuseppe and puts her arm around his neck as if about to give him a kiss. I can hear an ouch uttered by Giuseppe. "It's only my fingernail," she reassures him, but he then falls to the ground.

"Jules, I'm sorry, I used your last dose of fast-acting Novichok mixed with an even faster-acting substance; that week-old highly toxic remains of your effort at cooking Pierogi."

Oh gawd, we have another body to dispose of. It's back to digging a grave, that is, or chopping up Giuseppe and feeding him to the sharks. We drag Giuseppe's body high above the tide line so he doesn't get swept out to sea, and we start digging. We do somebody chopping with the machete. This island's vegetation will flourish with so many nutrients from human remains; no artificial fertilisers are needed to grow healthy vegetables.

"Jules, we could start, what is it called in English, a morgue service and help people dispose of bodies. We are getting good at that. I can just foresee it now, our business name, *Pleb and Jules Human Disposal Services.*"

"Pleb, do you realise we could spend 25 years in jail for what we are doing?"

"Jules, I am just doing what you call joking. You, Mystca and Bea are so serious. We need some singing while we dig and chop. Jules, use your phone to turn on the island's stereo system and choose a digging song."

I go to find my phone, but on the way, stumble across one of Giuseppe's shopping bags with plastic containers Yum, looks like many raw Salmon and Avocado Sushi rolls, my favourite.

"Jules don't put that Wasabi paste on the Sushi roll. It may be contaminated. It may be *i5* Wasabi paste which is so hot and painful that those people who were targeted usually jump off tall buildings after spreading it on their Sushi rolls and taking a bite."

OK, no Wasabi paste, but we all still get into those Sushis before they go off in this heat. Then a Nick Cave song starts playing on the outdoor sound system, *The Mercy Seat,* followed by some others. They're not exactly happy songs which is fine because it matches our current but fast-paced endeavour whilst gyrating, digging, waving the machete and chopping. We finish the job before sunset and do a high-five handshake, a job well done.

Chapter Twenty-two

"Jules, your financial resources are getting low. I checked your bank account," says Pleb.

"I had $1.5 million the last time I looked at my finances."

"Jules, that was over 100yrs ago, and the rent on this island is due soon. There is also a current credit card bill to pay."

"OK, we'll open up the resort to paying customers. Get Mystca to set up a WEB page, and we'll have photos of us all frolicking in the water."

"Jules, we may have to provide food to guests."

"Look up a seafood recipe for crown-of-thorns starfish. There's plenty of them here in the ocean."

Two weeks pass, and then our first paying guest arrives. She calls herself Jill. We sprinkle flowers in her hair, flowers everywhere like they do in all those Pacific Island advertisements, well tomato plant flowers, and do the islander greeting as we meet her at the jetty. She looks quite serious. She's not young, maybe in her 50s, 170cm tall and black-dyed hair. I noticed the white roots in her hair, but she's not bad looking.

"Jules, help her with her suitcases."

I escort Jill to the newly refurbished *Cabin07*. I hope she doesn't mind Castro, Bea's turtle, peering inside the window. We all sit at an outdoor dinner of delicacies I purchased at the Townville supermarket; no more eating crown-of-thorns starfish. We start talking, or at least Jill does.

"It's a government control movement. They insert microchips in those Covid-46 injections, and you'll be monitored for the rest of your life. They will control you. You'll be a robot," she yells and then wipes her eyes.

"Jill, we are already monitored every time we use our computer or phone, we have been for 100 years. Unless you're a crim or visit those porn websites, which I did before meeting Pleb, then there's probably nothing to worry about."

Jill seems like she's in distress, so Pleb grabs and hugs her. "I don't want to be inseminated by a chip," Jill yells out.

Pleb looks at me and whispers, "We have to find Jill a boyfriend so he can do the insemination. Call that guy Harry."

After Jill goes back to her cabin, I call Harry.

"Harry, I need your help again."

"What is it this time? Haven't I done enough for you already?"

"Harry, I've opened up the tourist resort again, and our first customer is this lady who believes that the Covid-46 jab also inserts a tracking microchip that will control your mind. Can you find a boyfriend for her who will talk some sense into her?"

"Hey, I believe in that too. Describe her to me."

I do that.

"I'll get some flowers and be over in my motorboat in 45 minutes. I'll take her out to dinner."

"Pleb, can you go to *Cabin07* and tell Jill that a like-minded soul wants to take her out to dinner, and she has 45 minutes to get ready?"

Bea doesn't come out to greet Harry, which is just as well, and Jill is waiting by the moor, looking splendid. She certainly found some good clothing in those three large suitcases. Harry gets out of his luxurious motorboat and kneels down, and hands Jill a bunch of roses. Unfortunately, he must have touched a prickly stem as he's writhing in pain. I just hope they don't grow Novichok here. Jill grabs him, consoles him and holds his head. There is a spark.

Harry looks up, "Jill, I've booked us into an organic semi-vegetarian restaurant, best organic prawns and crayfish in town, but can you drive the motorboat? I'm feeling a bit dizzy."

So, after a few minor crashes to my jetty, they depart, and a few days pass. "Jules, do you think Jill may have accidentally crashed that magnificent motorboat and she and Harry are at the bottom of the ocean? She still has not paid us for the accommodation and your seafood delights."

"Pleb, I'll ring Harry."

"Harry, are you and Jill OK?"

"I'm having the best time of my life. Apart from the physical interaction, we share the same beliefs. She wants to marry me, and I want to marry her. I'll pay for any repairs to your jetty. Can you be the best man or pretend at least to be one, as I need a witness?"

"Yes, sure, Harry; when's the wedding?"

"Tomorrow at 6pm, do you need to borrow some clothing? I got plenty of clothing and bring your friends, including Bea. There will be a huge party afterwards."

"Harry, you've only known Jill for two days. This is not Las Vegas."

"Jules, it's Townsville, the next best city. Jules, I have to go; Jill is explaining why earthworms may be an interstellar species about to invade us and turn us into manure. I've got to go and kill some earthworms."

I don't reply. We got plenty of manure from decomposing bodies on this island. We don't need earthworms to do the work.

"Jules, do I look well dressed?"

"No, Pleb, that dress is far too short. You can't expose your kneecaps at a wedding."

"Jules, all you got on is a piece of buffalo hide wrapped around your body. You look like a Neanderthal. You cannot come to a wedding looking like that. I will lend you some shorts, a tee shirt and runners. You told me that is sufficient clothing if attending any formal event."

So, Harry, dressed in a black suit, arrives in his luxurious motorboat to pick us up. He looks nervously at Bea, who is dressed up. Mystca is holding a bunch of posies. Jill steps out, looking impeccable. Harry rushes over to her and hugs her. We arrive at Townville, and two limousines are waiting to take us to the chapel.

"You may kiss the bride," the preacher announces.

"No kissing till I smell his breath and spray his mouth with this sanitiser. He may have germs," says Jill.

Jill does her oral hygiene inspection and sprays the alcohol-based sanitiser into Harry's mouth. Harry is wobbling around and doing 360-degree turns.

"Pleb, we got to do something. We need Harry to be around so we can't let him injure himself."

"Jules, entice him to sniff your runner shoes, that smell would revive any corpse from the dead."

I do, and Harry takes a whiff. He's jumping up and down in joy. "Produce more of that stuff, the runners; I could sell it overseas. Your runners are more potent than any nuclear device."

So, it was a night of eating, drinking, dancing, and tripping over things. At around 2am, Pleb, Bea, Mystca, and I return to Harry's boat. Harry had hired a boat driver to take us back to the island. We wave goodbyes.

"I'll help you guys get back to your cabins. You look like you need help," says Mystca as we wander from side to side and stumble.

Chapter Twenty-Three

"Jules, we have to find Bea a boyfriend. Last night, she was spilling all her woes on me, how she needs a man to look after her to give her joy, comfort and permanent residency in Australia."

Pleb still forms sentences in the Polish way, but I understand what she's trying to say.

"I'll ring Harry yet again. He's on the Townsville city council and knows plenty of rich guys."

"Harry, are you there?"

"Jules, after she and I tested gram-negative for any sperm microchip devices, we finally consummated our marriage, Jill and me. What do you want?"

"Harry, do you know any rich guys who may be interested in dating Bea ?"

"Oh gawd, that woman doesn't know what she wants. She screwed my mind when we were together, but I do know this one painful guy who's on the city council committee. He's my nemesis, and I hope Bea can return a favour and screw with his mind. Sydney or Sid is his name, and I hope Bea causes him a lot of misery. I'll arrange a date at Cloppers, our well-known high-class restaurant. They serve the best fish and chips but nothing much else."

"She's already gone out with a guy called Sid in the past."

"Jules, half the guys in Townsville are called Sid, which I totally object to at council meetings as their name promotes that city called Sydney in NSW. I raised the council motion that all Sids should be required to be renamed as Tows and be faithful to our city, but my motion got rejected by the other councillors; they said Tow sounds too Asian or like a truck that picks up abandoned vehicles. The name Bris was proposed, but it's a girly name. It may take a lot of time, but at the moment, all of us councillors from all political persuasions are studying maps of Queensland and focusing our efforts on what QLD town name should replace Sid as a guy's name. It's a fierce debate Jules, and it could go on for months."

"What's he look like that second Sid man? I'll have to describe him to Bea, so she knows who she's talking to if they meet."

"Well, he's about 6ft tall, rotund because of all the junk food he eats at the council cafeteria, and he dyes his greying hair black. At our last city council meeting, he had streaks of black dye glued to his face. He looked ridiculous. Luckily, I always carry a bottle of microchip-dissolving Windex with me for health and safety reasons, and I sprayed his face. I forgot to tell him to close his eyes before spraying, but I did wipe his eyes with my unsensitized handkerchief, and he eventually fully recovered except for his left eye."

In the meantime, Bea, Pleb, Mystca, and I are standing by our island jetty, waiting for the new Sid to arrive in his motorboat.

"Jules, I can see it coming, it is a very nice motorboat, and it is going so fast. I like it," says Bea. "Are you sure it is not the same Sid who I went out with before?"

Sid misses the jetty, makes a quick turn, spraying a lot of water, and then he hits it, my jetty, and sends wood splinters flying in all directions. Pleb, Bea, Mystca, and I duck our bodies to avoid splinter injury. We somehow managed to pull Sid out from his motorboat as he was very disorientated.

"Jules, that is your name. I will pay for your jetty to be rebuilt."

Bea whispers, "He is not Sid1, but his looks are passable."

Pleb, Bea, Mystca and I, holding his shoulders, guide Sid to *Cabin05*, next to Bea's cabin.

Neither Bea nor the new Sid joined us for breakfast, but I did find some more stonefish recipes, as we can't get to town to buy food. My motorboat must have drifted, and I can't see where it's gone. Sid's boat is also drifting away. We're stuck on the island without any supplies or transport.

I ring Harry. "Harry, the new Sid smashed my jetty with his motorboat, and my motorboat and his are drifting out to sea. We need to go food shopping in Townsville. Can you arrange a food drop by helicopter or drone because no one likes my stonefish recipes, and can you arrange a contractor to tow our motorboats back?"

"Keep him on the island. I'm presenting my council bill tomorrow, and I don't want him voting against my bill at the council meeting, which I hope gets passed and becomes legislation."

"What's the council bill? What are you fighting for?"

"Jules, it's about social tracking with microchips implanted in us. It has to be banned, made illegal, and the death penalty imposed on anyone who partakes in that tracking activity. I'm sure there's someone in China listening every time I go to the toilet for number 2 and make the walls shake. I don't want that sound to be put on

GonerTube.com."

"Harry, I'll do my best to keep new Sid confined though I may not have to work very hard. Neither new Sid nor Bea have exited their cabins for breakfast – the stonefish special."

"Jules, keep him there for 48 hours. I'll arrange a drone to drop off organically grown, non-micro-chipped food. I got to get this council bill through, plus I'll also send resources to find the motorboats."

Two hours later, a drone hovers over and drops what must be a one cubic metre box of goodies. Pleb, Mystca and I drag it to *Cabin02*, our cabin.

"Jules, the box is just full of organic potato crisps, not even a cabbage or some juicy minced meat. I cannot live like this. We have to get real fish, not that spiky stonefish kind that you have been collecting. I have sharpened the spears, and we will go diving and do real fish catching," Pleb says.

Pleb also took the latest *Pi5-issued*, waterproof taser gun with her. We didn't need the spears to get a catch. The fishing net bags we took are full of exotic-looking fish. I pick up seaweed from the seashore as we march from the beach with our bags full. We'll be having seafood salad delight tonight, but then we see a canoe with a person paddling towards the destroyed jetty. She pulls the canoe up onto the sand and stands upright. "I'm Viksi, and your service is hopeless. I had to paddle here from the mainland and may have got my manuscripts wet."

Viksi is an imposing character, about 6ft tall with long brown hair and a little on the attractive side. She shakes herself to get the water off and grabs her laptop computer, which luckily is sealed in a waterproof plastic bag.

"What are you doing here?" I ask Viksi.

"Your resort is listed as a temple of peace and solace on the WEB. That's why I booked. I need that now as I'm trying to finish writing my crime thriller book. It's a murder mystery and addresses the legalisation of tonsil donations and transplants, so it also makes a beneficial social contribution."

"Jules, she can have *Cabin08* and maybe you can lend her some of those buffalo skins and a toothbrush because she must have lost her suitcase while she was paddling," Pleb whispers.

Mystca guides Viksi to *Cabin08*, and Viksi asks her, "Have you got access to the Cloud here? I need to securely store my writings."

"It's summer and rainy season here, so there are plenty of clouds you can choose from," Mystca replies, smiling.

Viksi shakes her head while muttering what must be words of frustration. I'm sure she thinks she made a big mistake coming to our resort; that would be an understatement. Viksi doesn't come out of *Cabin08*. It's been three days and no sight of her. We bring what food we have left over, including plenty of packets of organic potato crisps and place the tray outside her door. The tray is empty in the mornings.

Sid has kept his word, and the jetty is nearly repaired. The workers say it will be finished tomorrow. The motorboats have also been found and are moored to a post 10m out to sea until the work on the jetty is complete. Bea and Sid, hand-in-hand, watch the workers work.

"Oh bugger, I have to go. I had an important council meeting to attend and vote against a motion that Harry had put forward."

Sid certainly had a motion. The water is brown around his bum. He's screaming and yelling after he tried to swim out to his motorboat. I guess he's not used to all the high-fibre food we eat on the island, and his body has rejected it. Mystca puts on her runner shoes, swims out, drags the screaming Sid back to shore, and then she has a shower.

"Jules, he must have stood on one of your stonefish you have been breeding as he was trying to swim to his motorboat. His swimming efforts were not very good, dog paddle, you call it, and he probably would have drowned with his efforts at swimming. Standing on a stonefish and being rescued by Mystca saved his life," Pleb says.

We drag the screaming Sid back to Bea's cabin. Going on past statistics, there's a 90% chance Sid will live. Then my cell phone rings. It's Harry. "Good job Jules; my council bill got passed without Sid's attendance to block it."

"Harry, we need some motorboat fuel, some real food, not crisps, and a doctor because Sid stood on a stonefish while trying to dog-paddle out to his motorboat. We also need some fuel to power my electricity generator. It's been cloudy here for the last five days, and the solar-powered batteries are at near zero per cent capacity full. Can you organize a drop?"

"Let Sid suffer. Only one person in OZ ever died from a stonefish spike. I'll arrange the drop-off of supplies immediately."

Then it happened. Viksi comes slamming her fists on our door and yelling, "My laptop died, zero power, and I lost 24hrs of work. All the lights are off as well. This is the worst holiday resort I've ever stayed in."

Pleb grabs and hugs her. "This happens frequently here, we lose electrical power, but I will give you a flash drive. Save your work every five minutes when we get power back. It should be soon because we are having fuel delivered for our generator and hydrogen for the fusion reactor. We have not had sunlight for over five days, and our solar-charged batteries are flat."

We're all sitting outside on fold-up seats by candlelight and cooking on an open makeshift fireplace by the sea. It feels like a camping trip with minimal conveniences. Viksi joins us for the seafood salad delight meal. She can certainly eat as if in a frenzy.

"Viksi, please don't write a bad review of our resort. We need the income."

"I need food and characters for my book. My book is about characters and what makes them tick," Viksi says as she's stuffing her mouth with fish, seaweed and jellyfish for dessert. "There's materia here for ten books, but I have to call my husband to join us. Any discount for couples as we don't eat much?"

Next day the clouds disappear, so our solar panel array resumes working and charging the batteries. It will take about six hrs of sunlight for the batteries to fully charge, but then a motorboat arrives, fully loaded with fuel. Two chaps carry the jerry cans of fuel to the shed housing the generator. It took them three trips carrying two cans each. They help me start the generator. Lights come on, and the sound system is blaring, a song I was listening to *Age of 17* – such dreaming.

"This is diesel fuel for the generator only, not the motorboats. We also got petrol for your motorboats and an esky full of food with no organic potato crisp personally chosen by Harry."

"Thanks, guys, I'd offer you a beer, but we have none at the moment."

"That's OK, mate, we're only doing our civic, charity duty."

"Isn't Harry paying you for all the trouble you've gone to?"

"Harry is the world's biggest scunge bag. He lectured us that we should not be paid much because we'd be rewarded in heaven a hundred-fold, and we would each have seven young virgins to look after us when we are in heaven. We're now considering becoming born-again atheists."

We all go back to our cabins. Pleb helps me carry the esky into our cabin.

"Pleb, what's in the Esky?"

"Jules, you do not want to look. I am just pissing you off. It is cabbages, minced meat and organic brown rice, all certified to be micro-chip free," she says as she jumps for joy. I don't correct her English and look out our window whilst Pleb is chopping cabbage. Hey, there's a guy floating in on a parachute holding many suitcases. He makes a perfect landing and removes all that parachute gear.

"I'm Roger, but you can call me Rog. I couldn't get a ferry, and Viksi's my wife. Are you her servant?"

Rog is about 185cm tall, has narrow, dyed black hair and a huge smile.

"No, I own the island, well I lease it, and I'm no servant, only to my partner".

"I apologise and know what you mean, but can I see my wife."

I help Rog carry the suitcases to *Cabin08*.

Rog yells out, "Darling, it's me; I'm here at your beckoning, I'm here, and I have the suitcases you left at the Townsville airport."

Out steps Viksi dressed in one of Pleb's water buffalo skins. Rog grabs her and twirls her in joy.

"I'm busy writing now; I have a chapter to finish. Go for a walk around the island. You'll like the scenery, but watch out for the crocs," she says.

Rog looks a bit disappointed but starts his walk. Mystca comes back to our cabin, and she's very excited. "I heard them talking. That Viksi lady said this island will be the location for her next book called *Lunatic Asylum*, and if she sells it to a Hollywood film producer, we could star in the movie, and we wouldn't even need to take any acting lessons. We will be movie stars, and every word we mutter will be listened to on social media outlets by millions of followers."

Chapter Twenty-four

Pleb has created about 70 cabbage rolls stuffed with mincemeat, onions and spices. They are called Golabki, and I'm salivating as the smell of cabbage wafts past. Microwave ovens are wonderful. It would have taken ages to fry them in a pan.

Rog comes over to our cabin. "Jules, can I borrow your motorboat? I want to buy some champagne. We have to celebrate."

"Rog, our jetty has just been repaired after Sid nearly demolished it, but the boats are tied 10m out to sea, to a post. We haven't salvaged them as yet and returned them to the jetty."

"That's OK, Jules; I'll swim out and tow both boats, ropes held by my teeth, which still are genuine teeth, back to the jetty."

"Rog, wear footwear when you walk into the water to make the plunge into the sea. Sid got stung by one of the stonefish that I was breeding."

"Jules, I am well prepared, don't worry. I got to go, Jules and buy the champagne."

Rog won't have much energy to perform in the bedroom tonight. After two hours of strenuous swimming and towing, he ties the two motorboats to the rebuilt jetty.

"Rog, our standards of dress are very liberal, but you may have to put on some formal attire. Have you got a pair of shorts, a tee shirt and thongs or flip-flops?"

Rog comes back from Viksi's cabi dressed for the Townsville environment.

"She'll be right, mate," he says in a perfect Townsville accent that he obviously studied because he didn't speak that way when he first arrived from Melbourne. A drone then lands with the payload; four cartons of champagne, Don Perignon. I help Rog carry them to the fridge by the BBQ. That night we're all sitting by the starlight on the beach, eating Golabki, drinking champagne and watching the meteor showers burning up in the sky. There's Viksi, Rog, Bea, Sid, Pleb, Mystca and me. Sid gets up to get another bottle of Champs but trips, grabs his foot and groans. Bea rushes over to him. "Are you all right, my darling? Are you still suffering from that stonefish wound?"

"I'm fine, just a mishap using my toenail clippers. I clipped too far back and incurred a flesh wound which may have become infected. I will survive." Bea grabs and hugs him. "I will pour this Don Perignon on your toe. It will sterilise your toe and prevent an infection."

"Ouch," yells Sid, but then Bea grabs and comforts him.

Viksi looks on in disbelief. She whispers to Rog, "We have to stay here till I finish my book and the book after that one. I'll make a food shopping list. Can you and Jules go to the mainland and get some real food? Cabbage doesn't agree with my intestine," she says as she rushes to the nearest toilet. The rest of us stay up until midnight, watching the stars and sipping champagne, all except Mystca, who gets coconut juice. Next day it's a boy's day, all bleary-eyed, I drive the motorboat to Townsville and just manage to avoid any floating hazards like intoxicated humans playing with dolphins and crocodiles.

"Rog, stop looking at that clothes shop window display. We're not here for clothes shopping, just shopping for groceries from the supermarket."

"I have a shopping list Viksi gave me, and she has special dietary requirements. Do you have beetroot juice in this town?" asks Rog.

An hour later, we march out, each holding four food shopping bags, all about to overflow. We finally make it back to the motorboat and home after many rest stops.

"Jules, you forgot the cabbage," Pleb says, "I will have to collect seaweed again to get my dietary fibre."

That night, Pleb, Viksi and Mystca are busy cooking carnivore delights. The smell wafts over to the jetty where we are painting and making the final finishes to the new jetty whilst sipping a glass of champers. Luckily it's only a jetty because the paint job is not that good, and afterwards, we're sitting by the BBQ, enjoying organic pork, beef and potatoes. It's also another night of fireworks display as comets and meteorites plunge into the atmosphere. Then one doesn't completely burn up, lands close to Mystca's foot, and creates a small crater.

"Stepdad, there could be alien life forms inside that meteorite."

"Mystca, that's ridiculous. Nothing can travel faster than the speed of light or anything near that speed, and the nearest possibly inhabitable planet is ten light-years away. They better have long life spans because it would take them at least 100,000 years to get here."

"But stepdad, what if they also have a life-prolonging peptide, similar to what you inject yourself with to stop your telomeres advancing."

"How do you know about this telomere stuff? I never talked about."

"Stepdad, we're learning about that stuff in biology class. I'm like doing Yr11, in case you forgot, and I know you're over 140 yrs old, but I would never tell that to my school friends, who would think I'm like really weird hanging anywhere near someone your age who is not yet deceased."

"Mystca, I made a terrible mistake by using that peptide. No, on second thought, I didn't because otherwise, I never would have met your mother or you. I'd just be ashes floating in the sea."

"Stepdad, we would still remember you, not for your cooking skills but that you took care of Mum and me."

"Duck your head, Mystca, duck."

There's a thunderous roar near the jetty. We all look up. Smoke rises as the once-a-week public ferry leaves our jetty. Out walks a person-like figure. My conclusion is that he's trying to be a magician like that David Goldfield guy used to be.

"I am Grillian, and I am here to study your culture. I am doing what you call on this planet a PhD. My study is the Adaptive Abilities of Primitive Alien Cultures."

Grillian is rather short for an alien that you see on a TV series. He's about 165cm in height, a little bit on the rotund side, wears ancient Egyptian clothing, and basically looks like an ancient Egyptian with his long dark hair and facial colourings. I greet him, "Mate, nice for the visit, but you've got some competition. We're already being studied by at least one other Earthian, but how come you speak English so well?"

"We pick up your television signals on *SpaceFlicks* and enjoy that documentary called *My Favourite Martian*. It takes 90 years for those transmissions to reach my planet, so I may be a bit behind time."

"Sanity test it is. How did you get here? Nothing can travel faster than the speed of light."

"I've been 100,000 years on this journey, and I regularly apply a good moisturiser."

Bea's ears prick, and Pleb whispers in my ear, "Jules, let him stay. Did not your deceased transgender psychologist sibling make this a place of refuge for people suffering from severe psychotic delusions?"

"As long as he can pay board and food expenses."

"Jules, I read your diaries and your experimentation with Psylocibin mushrooms. It is possible he has just had too many. He may come down," Pleb reassures.

"He'll have to come down from whatever. OK, he can stay till some cosmic stardust picks him up." Pleb gives me a hug, "Jules, you are so composite."

"You mean compassionate; yes, that's true, I am."

Mystca guides him to one of the spare cabins, *Cabin09*.

"Jules, it's been 3 hours, and Mystca is not back. Can you check that she has not been teleported to some other solar system?" The door is ajar. Mysta and Grillian sit on the floor opposite one another with their legs crossed and seem to be in deep meditation and uttering *oms*.

"Mystca, it's time to go back to our cabin. You have school homework to do."

"But Stepdad, I'm journeying through the cosmos through space and time. I will definitely do Physics and Maths in year 12."

Reluctantly, Mystca comes back to our cabin whilst waving back to Grillian. I whisper to Pleb, "This guy has to go. He's polluting her mind. At one stage, she was going to be a real-estate consultant and earn heaps of money for doing very little, but now she wants to study Maths and Physics. We'll have to financially support her for the rest of her life."

"Jules, you've been asleep for the last 100 years. Any remaining jobs are now in Engineering, Maths, Physics and Psychology. Robots do most of the other work except for the City Council with their self-serving agenda. I would like to see them replaced by Androids. Mystca may have found a spiritual guide. Let him stay."

Meanwhile, Viksi is furiously writing with Rog by her side, who reminds her when it's time to eat. Sid has claimed injury compensation and relief from council duties and is still on the island with Bea, so the next few months pass peacefully. We all have dinner by the seashore with a few sips of magic mushroom soup included, and after I stopped and curtailed my stonefish breeding program we jump into the sea and frolic, splashing water over each other. Life couldn't be better till there's a splash from another meteorite by the jetty. Out steps a being, an older version of Grillian. He speaks through a hyperspace translator, "I want my son back."

Grillian appears to hug Mystca as we speak, "Dad, I don't want to go back."

"Mm," says the supposed alien father of Grillian, "I could spend some time here on this planet."

I don't tell him that after the mushroom soup and salad I made us, the adults are all off the planet as well.

"I like this organic matter you eat. Can I have seeds and recipes?"

He consumes many times the recommended dose, and we all fall asleep beyond the high tide line with partners wrapped in each other's arms.

"Dad, you can join us for a cuddle," says Grillian to his father.

Chapter Twenty-five

We all wake around 4:30am as the sun makes its appearance on the horizon. We're also all rubbing our heads and eyes and wondering why the 'f' we're sleeping on the beach.

"I do not know if what I saw was just a dream," says Bea.

I look around. There's Mystca and Grillian but no sign of his father. I walk to the jetty and look into the sea where the meteor had seemingly landed; no sign of it.

I ask Pleb, "What happened to Grillian's father? He came here to visit his son inside a meteorite. He was going to take him back home, back to their planet."

"Jules, that was your hallucination. Mine was that I was Julie Andrews in that old movie you have called *The Sound of Music*, and you were the Plumber guy." Pleb then starts singing songs from the movie. I desist from saying that she definitely needs singing lessons. I walk around to the others, still getting up and shaking the sand off their costumes. "Did you see Grillian's father? He came to take him back to their planet?"

"Jules, you look like the walking dead; you are still dreaming. I dreamt I was the Prime Minister of this country. I could see my name up in lights, *Sid Special*, and Bea was my first lady, well not the first, but most important," says Sid. Bea slaps him on the face and says, "Mine was that I was the owner of a worldwide law firm defending first-class criminals. I was sailing on my luxurious motor-powered yacht, sipping champagne with Castro and watching by Internet the performance of my legal employees and admonishing them if they take long toilet breaks between clients."

Their mushroom-induced dreams all seemed related to some desire. I accept my dream. I wanted to get rid of Grillian whilst Sid still has political aspirations, Viksi yells joyfully. "So much material for my book and Rog's dream was that he parachuted from the top of Mount Everest, survived with only two broken legs, and made the *Gigmus Book of Records*."

I go over to Grillian, "Mate, you have to pay for the accommodation and food if you want to stay here."

"That is not a problem. I won the world chess competition, so I have millions of your currency. Will half a million do for my accommodation?"

I shake my head, look down and rub my chin, "Yep, that's about right."

"Give me your bank details; I will transfer that amount immediately to your account; I'm doing it now," says Grillian as he lowers his face and intensively concentrates on his mobile device. "You have a big debt to the bank; this will fix it."

"Thanks."

"Jules," says Pleb, "I've just checked our finances on your computer. We had a debt agency pursuing us, but all the debt has been paid off. We now have a lot of credit. We can expand and make this island an alien resort charging only gold or platinum payments."

Pleb must still be tripping from the mushroom salad, but we're not bankrupt. Grillian must have credited us with his full winnings from that chess tournament.

Every night is pleasantly the same as the others though Sid and Rog have taken over the cooking. It must be a new phenomenon, guys are now the kitchen slaves, and they generally do a good job. We're looking out to sea whilst eating roast beef and potatoes, better than stonefish and seaweed. I whisper to Grillian, "Kiddo, you have over 100 years of credit to stay on this island."

"Mr Jules, I won't stay here for a hundred earth years, but you can keep the credit. I have asked your stepdaughter to legally copulate with me. We shall get what you call married on my planet."

The kid is a nutcase. I tell of the conversation with Grillian to Pleb. "Jules, there are some psychologists in Townsville. They have tests similar to what we did in *Pi5*. They will be able to tell if he is psychedelic. Book an appointment for tomorrow. Now I got to practise my singing for that Townsville re-make of the *Sound of Music*."

Pleb's comments are no solace. I book an appointment for Grillian, and he agrees to go dressed in his ancient Egyptian costume. Mystca joins us as we start the motorboat, and she hops aboard, "I'm not going to let you give him mind-altering drugs or electric shocks," Mystca yells. Mystca and I stay in the waiting room during the consultation then, after 1.5 hours, the psychologist comes out.

"Mr Lemos, I put him in a hypnotic state. He has some deep delusions. I believe he may have a bipolar disorder, and on that spectrum, he is on the high mood side at the moment. When he drops to a low mood, you have to worry as he may self-harm. I've sent my report to the Townville hospital and got an emergency appointment for him in one hour. It's only a 15-minute walk away. How long are you looking after him?"

"For a long time. He paid for over 100 years of accommodation and food at my island resort; I'm stuck with him."

The psychologist rubs his head but smiles at me. I guess he's thinking he has another potential client. Mystca yells out and bangs her fist on the coffee table by the couch, "I love him. I don't want his brain to be drained or altered."

The psychologist kneels next to Mystca and grabs her hands. "He'll just be put on some mood stabilizers and will probably be fine. He has had a very traumatic childhood and is now living a very good dream, but that dream may not last. He needs to stabilize before he goes into a low."

"I'll care for him whatever state he's in. I love him, and he loves me," she yells while rubbing her head.

I call a taxi, and we finally get Grillian inside. He is very disorientated. The Indian taxi driver asks, "He looks like a guru. Is he doing that Sharman healing course at the hospital?"

I don't reply, but thank him for the drive. Mystica and I guide Grillian inside the hospital. We sit in the waiting room, and Mystca is chewing her fingernails again. An hour later, a nurse comes out. "You are next of kin, I hope, and you know the patient confidentiality rules. "I'm, I'm his father. He lives on my island, and I look after him." I lied, of course.

"He has been tranquillized. He was mumbling about being an alien, so we're moving him to the psyche ward," the nurse says.

Mystca yells out as she rushes to Grillian, "No!"

"Mystca, it's not that simple. Grillian is a very intelligent person, but if his mood goes down, you may not be able to handle it. The psychiatrist will prescribe a mind-stabilising substance called Lithium. It's an ancient substance but still works well, according to my recent reading."

Mystca starts crying on my shoulder. The psychologist brings Grillian out, and he appears traumatised, wandering around like a blind person with his hands outstretched. Some nurses grab and guide him. Mystca rushes towards him and gives him a long hug. Grillian recognises her and smiles; awareness appears on his face. He waves at us as he is marched away to the ward.

"Sir, you can call for an update on his condition, and you and your daughter can visit your son between 10 am and 3 pm daily."

Mystca and I are walking back to the Townsville jetty, where my motorboat is moored.

"Stepdad, you lied, saying that Grillian was your son."

"Mystca, if I hadn't lied, you may not be able to see him for hospital visits or get reports on his progress. It has to be next of kin, or else this confidentiality stuff kicks in, and we don't get any reports. Ring the hospital tonight and ask if you can speak to him. Tell him to pretend to the hospital staff that I am his illegitimate father and you are his sister. Make up a story, or else he may not join us back on the island."

"Stepdad, you're not so bad. I'll do that as soon as we get back home."

We're back on the island. The guys have produced another marvellous meal of steaks, salads with avocado dressing. Mystca isn't eating, just twiddling her thumbs with her head down. Pleb goes over to her. "Darling, you need nutrition; eat with us."

"I can't. I can't think about food, only about Grillian. I can't eat." Mystca sobbingly says.

I go over to her. "Mystca, when Grillian is released, he can stay on the island with us for as long as he likes at no cost. I promise."

She seems relieved and eats a few bits of food, then she sparks up and starts ravenously stuffing her face with her bare hands like some feral kid who has been starved most of her life.

"Let her go, Jules; food is a trauma release," says Pleb.

"But, but she just cleaned up my plate. There's nothing left for me to eat."

"Jules, we still have some stonefish left in the freezer, and there's plenty of seaweed along the seashore. I'll cook you a meal."

"No thanks," I say, crouched on the sand, looking down at my belly and feeling sorry for myself. Mystca comes over and puts her arm around my shoulder. "I'm sorry," she says. I look up. She has scraps of my steak stuck in her teeth, and tomato sauce is dripping from her mouth. She kisses my cheek. I rub off the tomato sauce. She must have been a carnivore or had vampire instincts deep inside, not a vego. Viksi comes over and looks down at us. She whispers to Rog, "My next book will be a vampire story set on this island. Rog, book us in for another three years in advance on this island. Use my credit card. You can practice your parachuting at that Mount Stuart in Townsville. You'll be an expert after three years of jumping."

"Sure, dear, I kinda really like it here, and there are no Covid-46 lockdowns."

"Go quickly and book. I overheard they might open it up again for more emotionally challenged people. There will be a flood of them, and there are enough here at the moment to keep my writing going. We have to keep this cabin till I finish my books."

"I'm logging in right now, dear; I've just transferred $200,000 to this resort's account," says Rog.

"It's $60k a year for people that aren't nut cases; you've overpaid 20K for a 3-year stay."

"Viksi, I've adjusted for inflation, the CPI. It's a fair evaluation, and I love parachuting from that mountain; only one new broken bone so far, left big toe."

"Come over here, Rog; I want to kiss you."

And so an uneventful week passes except when we guys go to town to do the food shopping. "Jules, it's cheap because it's past the use-by date," says Sid.

"I don't care, I want it, and in fact, I want all these items on special because of their expiry date. The expiry date is a very conservative estimate of bacteria build-up in the food."

I would later regret that decision after many uncontrolled bowel movements and soiled clothing.

"Jules, I can probably get you a cash grant for humanitarian aid. Now can you help me lift this marinated pig onto the trolley?" Rog asks.

And so we three guys return to the island. Sid is struggling with the marinated pig, but we give him a hand whilst trying to carry numerous bags of other foods. Sweat is dripping from our faces. Pleb, Viksi and Bea greet us and give us struggling guys a hand carrying the shopping bags. Viksi says, "You can do all that shopping online, and with the amount spent to feed for all these bods on this island, the supermarket would probably deliver for free."

"It's a male bonding session. Viksi, it's like those military exercises guys do together, plus we haven't done any real person food shopping for 30 years. You should try it. It's quite exciting. It might make it into a chapter in your new book," replies Rog as he wipes his brow. Viksi gives him a kiss, "Rog, you have to stop putting salt on your food. You taste terrible."

Pleb and I return to our cabin carrying some of the shopping bags, whilst the others forage for burnable material for the spit roast. The nuclear fusion-powered BBQ is too small for the job, plus we want to do a bit of traditional OZ cooking.

"How is he? I'm his sister." Mystca frantically asks. She must be speaking on the phone to the hospital staff. She nods her head as she listens.

"Mum, can you drive stepdad's motorboat to town?"

"Mystca, I drove military tanks when I was in the Polish military. I'm sure driving a motorboat will not be a problem. I'll take you to town to visit Grillian," Pleb says.

I watch as they depart from the jetty travelling at *warp speed* on my motorboat, waving their hands up high as if they've just escaped incarceration. Oh gawd, they'll burn out the motor.

Sid and Rog come over to the jetty and put their hands on my shoulder. "They won't get far. I didn't refuel your motorboat," Sid says. "They can take my motorboat; it's fully fuelled, but we'll drive. Rog, Sid, and I will swim out and tow them back to shore."

Chapter Twenty-six

A week passes quickly. Pleb and Mystca pick up Grillian from the psychiatric hospital. He looks so different. He has shaven his locks and wiped his face and has shorts, a tee-shirt and thongs on. So he looks as normal as any Queenslander lad does, but he has red marks down his legs. Maybe he had some operation on his legs.

I grab Mystca by the shoulder. "What was wrong with Grillian? Is he OK now?"

"Stepdad, take your hand off my shoulder. He is fine; his parents had extremely high expectations of him and would whip him if he did not get straight 'A's for every subject at school. He would escape into alien fantasies, but he is fine now since getting the news that his parents died in a plane crash over South America, after it was shot down by mistake by a Chinese spy plane. So, no more whips and no more new scars on his legs.

Pleb comes over. "Jules, we have to celebrate. Let us go back to town and buy a feast of food. I do not want to cook Golabki or Pierogi tonight."

Chloe4 jumps on my chest. With all the recent drama, I've ignored the rat.

"Pleb, I think Chloe4 wants to come with us."

"Jules, you will be put in that psychedelic ward if you carry a rat on your shoulder while we shop in the supermarket."

"I'll keep her in my tee shirt. It's a bonding session, the rat and me."

I call the guys. "We got to do another big food shop."

"Jules, is that some cancerous growth throbbing in your chest?" asks Rog.

"No, it's my pet white rat, Chloe4. I've neglected her. She wants to come shopping with us."

"Jules, are you one of those psychic guys that I see on TV that can talk to rats, mice and other 4-legged creatures?" asks Sid.

"Sid, Chloe4 beat me in every game of Chess we ever played. She moves the pieces with her paws and then intensively stares at me to decipher what my next move will be".

"Jules, I'll have a chess competition with your rat tonight. Is that the game where you move those round pieces to get to the end of the board?"

"No, Sid, it's far more complicated than Checkers. There are kings, queens, knights, rookies and pawns, and they all move differently. It's like the people you meet in life."

Pleb listens. "OK, I shall just watch as you play chess with your rat tonight. I will be barracking for you, Jules."

Sid, Rog, the rat, and I hop into Sid's motorboat for another male bonding session whilst we shop. "Hope that rat is a male and Pleb you can't come along as it's a Men's Shed type of thing where guys just talk, well we don't actually talk that much apart from about the football, cars and motorboats. You'd be bored."

Pleb looks disappointed, so I give her a kiss. "I promise I will bring back plenty of cabbage and mince."

"Sir, there's something peeking out of your shirt and sniffing. You know we don't allow animals in this store who do not wear a face mask," the supermarket checkout assistant says.

"That, that, that is just my bodily implant, like in that movie called *Total Recall*. I'm blind, so the implant tells me what to buy."

Chloe4 nods her head.

"Sir, that implant is certainly doing well for our business. I'll recommend that all our customers get one of those rat implants."

It took several trips back and forward from the supermarket to the Townville jetty. Rog and Sid were struggling, trying to carry the marinated feral hog.

"Jules, can you help?" yells Sid.

"No, I can't, I'm struggling myself, juggling to carry this 20kg of mince and ten cabbages. Oops, just dropped one of the cabbages."

We finally make it back to our island. Mystca and Grillian are standing by the jetty.

"Mystca, exercise is very good for a person's mental health. It produces Dopamine, the happy hormone. Now can you and Grillian get the wheelbarrow and unload Sid's speedboat and bring the food back to our cabin except for the feral hog, which you can leave by the BBQ."

"Stepdad, you're using us as slaves," Mystca says with a menacing look and arms crossed in defiance.

"Mystca, it's for Grillian and his Dopamine levels. Now get moving before the food goes off, and you'll be back on the stonefish and seaweed diet."

Reluctantly she summons Grillian, and the two of them manage, after 2 hours, to unload the food supplies. In the meantime, we guys collect wood from around the island to roast the hog.

"Jules, we're nearly out of wood. Luckily, I smashed into your previous jetty," says Sid as he picks up the remaining wooden remains.

We're all sitting in front of the fire watching as Sid rotates the hog on the spit.

"Jules, that hog will take 12 hours to cook, and I'm hungry; I have to make the Golabki. They'll be ready before the hog is," says Pleb.

Time seems to have speeded up. Maybe the perception of time changes as we get older. Life has been peaceful, and our colleagues still pay rent. And Mystca and Amy have finished their psychology degrees and are starting post-grad studies. They use my motorboat to get to the Uni at Townsville. Luckily Sid and Bea are still here as we use Sid's motorboat to go to town and do the food shopping. Then another meteor shower begins. I look around; everyone is staring at the sky in wonderment as flashes of light streak through the night sky. Mystca and Grillian are holding hands, as are our other guests. Then it happens; a chartered ferry arrives, and out steps Cara looking the same she did a long, long time ago. Cara is my height, short black dyed hair, longish face, and some people would judge her as attractive. She, like Bea, must have got hold of my peptide supply when Cara and I were briefly married, and to think I thought I had premature dementia when my vials of the peptide kept on disappearing.

"You, Jules, owe me 110 years of alimony payments," she angrily yells whilst pointing her outstretched arm with an accusing finger at me.

Pleb goes over to her and puts her arm around Cara's shoulder. "Would you like to stay for dinner, and later we can discuss the financial matters."

"Is that meat cooking that I smell? I'm a vegetarian!"

"Calm down, Cara. I can cook you up a meal of cabbage, organic seaweed and the turtle's eggs that Castro lay," says Pleb.

"I'm going to get him no matter how many turtle eggs I eat," Cara says to Pleb while pointing her fist at me.

"I will prepare a vegetarian meal for you, and Jules will help chop the vegetables. Come, Jules and assist me."

"I'm coming, and I'll watch what you prepare and cook my meal myself, so you don't put any contaminated meat ingredients in that I disapprove of," says Cara.

Pleb grabs my shoulder as we walk back to our cabin, followed by Cara. Pleb whispers, "Jules, she is very angry, so give her a bottle of wine and a wine glass; also, you never told me you had a second wife."

"Pleb, I met her in an airport bar during a stopover in Las Vegas when I was going to a conference. She said she was an Ozzie in transit, just as I was. She may have spiked my drink, and we got married 3 hours later at a church called *The Church of the Holy Deceased Ghost*. Apart from that, I can't remember very much. Have we got any Novichok left?"

Cara is lying on the couch, asleep. The bottle of Sauv Blanc is empty.

"Jules, no more poisonings; we will try to reason with her and solve problems without any form of violence that involves deaths. Ask Bea to join us and use her legal skills. We have to disgust the legal implications, such as can she sue you for 100 years of unpaid alimony? Sorry meant discuss."

Bea examines the case. "This is unicorn, or is the word unique? There has been no precedent for a case like this. I would like to take on the case, but Jules, you have to convince Sid to marry me, or else I will be deported as my visa expires next month. Also, buy more Sav Blanc and keep that wife, whatever number, sedated till I work out a legal strategy so that you are not bankrupted."

A week passes by. We are in the Townsville Marriage and Deaths registry office. "I legally pronounce you Bea, I can't pronounce your surname, and Mr Sid as now legally married. Mr Sid, you may kiss the bride."

We all clap, except Cara, who's nodding her head back and forward while suffering from a massive hangover.

"Jules, ring Harry. Maybe he can find a rich boyfriend for that ex-wife of yours, and then she might not harass you anymore as I do not think Bea is familiar with OZ legal laws, so we should not solely rely on her knowledge."

"Good idea Pleb; I'll ring Harry now."

"What do you want now again?" Harry asks.

"Harry, can you find a rich boyfriend for my ex-wife? Apparently, I owe her 110 years of alimony payments."

"Jesus, Jules, did you marry quintuplets?"

"It's a long story Harry but can you help me?"

"Hold on, there is this single, wealthy Greeny guy who's blocking my legislation to eliminate high-rise property development restrictions, and I appreciate that you took Sid, my arch-rival, off the scene from the council."

"Perfect, Harry, is he vegetarian?"

"What? Why do you ask?"

"This ex-wife of mine, called Cara, is a vego, and I believe she's also a Greeny."

"Yeh, I may have someone. He might be a vego. He only ever seems to eat salads and cheese at the council cafeteria."

"Sounds perfect, Harry. Could you organize a function at the council office and introduce them to each other? Pleb and I will come along as well."

"Jules, we're having a wine and cheese tasting event at the council tomorrow. Starts at noon after we all finish work. I'll put you, Pleb and Cara on the guest register."

Harry hangs up.

"Jules, we have to have a conveyancing plan in case Harry's and Bea's efforts do not work."

"Pleb, in English, it's called a contingency plan, but Pleb, your English is far better than my Polish, so please don't take my corrections as an insult."

"Jules, from now on, I will only speak to you in Polish so that you can improve your Polish language skills, and then I will start to correct you." She smiles and gives a not-too-gentle slap on my face. Luckily, I have universal language translation software on my phone.

"Cara, we have a vegetarian, save the forests, wombats, crustaceans, and vegetables function to go to in Townsville tomorrow. There will be wine and cheese as well. You probably won't be interested, but you're welcome to come along and join us."

Cara was about to lunge for my throat but then reconsiders. "Can I borrow one of those hog furs? I want to appear natural."

"Sure, we got plenty that you can try on for size. Pleb will help you with the fitting and any stitching."

That night the chess competition begins. Chloe4, our pet rat, is staring at me. I win the toss of the coin to make the first move. The game continues. Sid and Rog are barracking for me, whilst the others, including Cara are barracking for the rat. The rat and I stare intensely at each other before making a chess move. After two hours of playing chess, the rat checkmates me and lifts up her front paws in delight. "I'm not feeding you anymore, Chloe4. You'll have to scavenge in the island jungle and find your own food."

Pleb comes out with a basket of yummy goodies and gives it to the rat whilst I sulk in a corner. Cara pats the rat and hands the goodies to Chloe4, who clasps her hands in joy.

"I couldn't have done a better job myself," Cara says to the rat.

"Jules," says Sid, "We could use that smart rat on the Townsville City Council. I'll make sure it gets elected."

"I'll consider that, Sid, but what's the remuneration?"

"We already have a few rats on the council. I'll have to check, but I think it's all the cheese a rat can eat and free accommodation plus a servant and personal trainer."

Pleb comes over, "Jules, we all have to go to sleep; we have that important event tomorrow."

And so the night ends, and everyone is happy except me. I suppose it hasn't all been too bad. Cara is placated but wants a rematch between me and Chloe4. "I want to see you get beaten three times, and then I will adopt this rat," Cara says. The rat is certainly popular.

"Jules, come on, do not argue with her. We have to prepare for that event at the Townsville city council, and you are not to wear thongs, tee-shirt and shorts. You have to look respectable."

"Pleb, I have no other clothes."

"Jules, when I went looking inside the island storage facility or shed as you call it, I found six large, sealed plastic bags of clothes and shoes; men's and women's. The clothes must belong to those distraught people that your deceased sister once counselled on the island. They must have become feral or suicided, but their clothes are here and in very good condition. I brought the bags up to our cabin with the help of Mystca and Grillian. Tomorrow morning, we can have fun trying on the clothes. I am sure there are some long pants, long-sleeved shirts and shoes that will fit you and me. Anything I do not want, you can give to Cara. We are similar dimensions; she cannot go dressed as a hog, else even a Greeny will not look at her."

"But she is a hog and should show her true furry colours."

"Calm down, Jules, you did well getting Harry, what do you call it, on board again but give her a jab of your peptide before the event, or else she may shrivel up. And this Greeny guy may not find her attractive, and Jules is it not time for your own jab of the peptide? I do not want you to shrivel up just yet."

The 3 of us arrive at the Townsville council offices for the cocktail party. We all look slightly contemporarily dressed. Cara finally relinquished the idea of wearing a Greeny hog fur outfit. Harry approaches us. "How nice not to see you again; let me introduce you all to Gerald. He's a Greeny, so you may not like him just as I don't."

Cara's ears prick.

"I thought this was supposed to be a *Save the Forests and Wombats* presentation," says Cara.

Gerald comments, "That's next week, same time. Harry said you could help me write my presentation, even though Harry and I don't agree on anything he is doing to our city and forests."

Pleb and I walk away and grab more cheese and wine. "Jules, I studied lip-reading when I was in *Pi5*, I can read their lips. They are talking about environmental things that I cannot understand or translate."

A few hours pass, and I've overdosed on cheese and wine. Pleb is still listening and watching lips. "Jules, she said yes to go back to his place tonight. You do not look that good. I will drive the motorboat back and Jules, I also think he proposed to her after three hours of chatting, and she said yes. Your problems are solved."

As I'm staggering out of the council premises, I see Harry and give him the thumbs-up. He does the same. Pleb keeps me propped up and drags me to the jetty. A week later, Harry rings me. "Jules, it worked. I don't know who murdered whom, but Gerald hasn't been to the council chambers for a week, and I got my building proposal passed. So I'm sending a motorboat to your island full of food platters as a sign of my deep appreciation. Now, Jules, there is another guy I'd like to get rid of from council. Are there any more of those quintuplets left to keep him distracted?"

"I'll try Harry, I'm sure Pleb and I can come up with someone."

"And Jules, there will be a council vacancy soon. Sid proposed your rat stand for the position, but that rat sounds far too smart. Do you want to run for election? It's a piss-easy job, and we don't have to work that hard, but we do drink hard, so you have to have a healthy liver."

"Harry, I'll have to consult my liver specialist before accepting the offer, and I'm sure we can find another distraction to help you out. Is that the nuclear fusion reactor you want to have built near the harbour nearly finished?"

"Yes, Jules and I promise that no hazardous nuclear waste will float to your island. I'll drink some of the wastewater myself just to show that I'm genuine and how safe it is. I'll do it while a crew is filming. It will be on the nightly news on that PieNews channel. I'm also sending you a new fusion-powered BBQ, as I heard you're running out of wood."

"I'll stay in touch, Harry. By the way, is there any dress standard when attending city council meetings?"

"Yes, of course, clean tee-shirt and shorts, no bare feet, but thongs are OK."

"Thanks, Harry, I'll give it serious consideration, but can you tell me what the remuneration is?"

"What's that long *con* word mean? In QLD, we're limited to words no longer than ten letters of the English alphabet. That was the first parliamentary bill I introduced, and it was passed with a huge majority. Forget about the last word, *parliamentary*. It's more than ten letters though I should have to set the limit to five letters, and then it would be a *parli* bill, much easier to say."

"Harry, what's the pay?"

"$300,000 a year for doing basically nothing, and you can catch up on sleep on the benches as they do in most government and council jobs."

"Harry, I'll speak to my partner, Pleb."

"And Jules, on second thought, get that rat euthanized. We don't want anything intelligent joining the council."

Chleo4 jumps on my shoulder, and I pat her little head.

"No, Harry, the rat won't be euthanized. I'm entering her as a contestant in the World Chess Competition."

Harry hangs up. "What should I do, Pleb? I've been offered a high-paying job by Harry if I agree and vote in favour to all his council proposals."

"Jules, let your conscience guide you."

"Pleb, it's not that simple. If I refuse the offer, Harry may rezone our island as a nuclear waste dump facility. I don't want him to do."

"Come over here, Jules. You have not had a good day. Let me give you a hug. We deal with these problems in my part of the world differently. There is still a dose of Novichok left. I can meet Harry and wear my thumb thimble with a pin inserted. He won't feel a thing."

"Pleb, what's become of you? Before, you were telling me that no Novichok would be involved in any premeditated murder. What's happening to you?"

"Jules, I was just testing you, and you passed. We can expose Harry or get rid of him in other natural ways. I am a natural collateral thinker." She gives me a kiss as I slump on the bed, rubbing my head.

Chapter Twenty-Seven

"Pleb, maybe we should move away. I still have contacts back in Melbourne and a townhouse I hope I still own. My then stepson had bought the whole block of townhouses, but that was a very long time ago."

"Jules, we will have no income, and we are just starting to make some here on the island, and I do not have my warm Polish clothes as I heard it is very cold in Melbourne, almost as cold as in Poland."

"Pleb, I'm sorry I didn't tell you because I wasn't that much interested in money, but apparently, I inherited seven townhouses of the eight townhouses from my great-great-grandchildren. We'd have a place to stay."

"But Jules, I thought inheritances went the other way, parent to child."

"I know, Pleb, but this went in reverse, so it defies common logic. I'll look up on the Internet and try to make contact with the one remaining great-great granddaughter that I know of. I believe she's in her 20s and lives in one of the town houses."

"Tamy speaking, who are you? I'm on the Do Not call list. How did you get my number? Who are you? I will report you to the police if you call me again."

"I'm Jules Lemos, and it's a very, very long story, but I may be coming back to Elwood, and I will need access to six of those townhouses. I inherited all of them, but you can keep on living in one of them rent-free.

"Have you got proof of identity that you're not just a scammer?"

"I'll send you a copy of my birth certificate and photos of me with your great-grandmother, who was also called Tamy. Ask me any question about your ancestors, and you'll get an honest answer plus, there are two other people who can also verify my identity."

"Are you the guy that manufactured that life-prolonging substance?"

"Yes, but only a few got to taste it. I'll explain how it works in another conversation."

"You jerk, if everyone took that substance, there'd be no space left on this planet."

"Tamy, I got a stepdaughter and a partner to look after. I got to hang around for a while yet."

"I live off the rental income from those townhouses, and I pay the council rates, insurance and maintenance costs for all the properties," Tamy sulks.

"Tamy, I'll still leave you the income from six of the townhouses to rent, and rents are very high in Elwood, I checked. As said before, I have a partner and a stepdaughter who is studying psychology, and with her partner, they'd live in one of the townhouses. The rental income from the other townhouse will help to pay for food, bills and Uni fees."

"Do you know how much university fees for a degree cost these days?"

"No, I did mine when uni was free, a long time ago. It was called the Whitlam era. Any shortfall, I'll pay for, and you'll always be welcome to join us all for dinner."

"If you're the Jules, that guy who left some of his diaries in townhouse 7, which I read, you just prepared jellyfish and seaweed for a meal."

"Tamy, that was a long time ago when the then prime minister instituted the recession we had to have. Home interest rates on a loan went to 18%, and I had a loan for my townhouse to repay. I couldn't afford to buy much food or clothes, and by the way, it wasn't jellyfish; they were the desert, and there were plenty of mussels to pick off the rocks in the sea to get the protein intake."

Pleb pulls me aside, "Excuse me for a sec," I say to Tamy.

"Jules, I just had a phone call from Gerald. Harry died from a myocardial infarction, or heart attack, as you call it. And that Greeny Gerald now controls the council. He said no nuclear waste dump will ever be built on our island."

"Pleb, you took the motorboat to town this morning, and I checked the bathroom. That last dose of Novichok is missing."

She giggles, "Jules, I hid it to save it for you."

"Did you leave any fingerprints behind?"

"Jules, I was trained as a *Pi5* assassin - gloves, false face masks, I cannot be traced. Oh, Jesus, I made that biodegradable facemask using your face as a model after you had all those Sav Blancs and were fast asleep."

I get back to the phone. "Tamy, we may not come back just yet, so you can keep the income from my inherited townhouses and whatever you read in the news, I didn't do it, but you're always welcome to come and visit our island."

"Thanks, she says. "I'm on a Uni break, so I may get there in two or three days. Email me the name of the island and its location. I'm curious to know who you really are, and you may be material for my next psychology assignment. Bye for now." Oh gawd, do all Tamys just study psychology?

Another phone call comes in. "This is Sergeant Taylor from the Townville police department. Our AI software identified you as the last person to be physically close to our deceased lord mayor Harry Snifkin. I have some questions and may require you to come down to the station."

"Sergeant Taylor, your AI software is faulty. I haven't been in town for over a week, and I have many witnesses that can testify, under oath, to that. Yes, Harry was my friend, and I talked to him on the phone a few days ago. He offered me a very well-paying job as a fill-in city councillor after another councillor became deceased. I am not connected to his death. Get your AI software checked! I may have a double ganger."

"Mr Lemos, it's called a doppelganger, and I will check the images myself but the more important questions I have, are to some of his financial dealings and stacking of the council with his supporters so he can make financial gain through his property development projects."

"Look, I don't know about the financial stuff, but Harry did help me find boyfriends for my ex-wife and an ex-girlfriend who wanted massive alimony payments. Both of the boyfriends were council members and now fully occupied by the charms of their new partners."

"And how did you get to know Harry Snifkin?"

"He once visited our island to attend the detoxification and sexual therapy course that my then alive sister, a trained psychologist, was conducting. I picked up all the condoms every night and bumped into Harry. He was struggling to get his condom off, so I rushed to my tool shed and got a pair of pliers. I missed the first time, and Harry screamed in pain, but we became friends after that."

"OK, your story sounds plausible, so no more investigations. Does your sister still run those courses?"

"No, she died, took her own life. I miss her so much."

"I'm sorry to hear that. I'll send you some links to counselling services. This case is closed."

I grab Pleb. "We're free. Harry's death is not going to be investigated by the police. We can stay on this island."

"That is good news, Jules. Now do not worry about this little prick to your shoulder, it is just a Covid-47 jab."

"What, no way! It's Novichok. Move away from me," I yell and brush her away.

She burst out laughing. "I am only pulling your toe; let us have a glass of wine to celebrate this victory."

"I'm pouring the wine, and you'll take the first sip."

"Jules, in *Pi5*, we were trained to carry many antidotes to poisons," She says as she bursts out laughing again.

A few days pass, and we all get together by the BBQ on the beach. There are lively conversations, mainly about Harry. "Jules, he wasn't that old. Do you think someone killed him?"

"No, Gerald, of cause not; no one performs hideous crimes like that in OZ. He died of natural causes; a liver attack."

"But Jules, I heard from a good source that you were the last person to have any physical contact with Harry."

"Gerald, that was a double, sorry meant doppelganger. You all know that I never left the island during the time Harry died. You saw me collecting seaweed all those days before and after Harry's death."

"Jules, are you the real Jules? How do we know you aren't the doppelganger? What if you are and you killed the real Jules?"

"Good point Gerald. I could indeed be the doppelganger. Now Gerald, do you want me to voice what emanates from your cabin at night and also Sid's and Rog's cabins? You guys and Bea, Cara and Viksi should put socks in your mouths and do it again doesn't mean washing the dishes."

Viksi is busy scribbling notes. Rog, Sid and Gerald look at each other. "Right, you're the real Jules. Have you got any spare, clean socks," they reply in unison.

We all look up. A chartered motorboat arrives, and out steps a lass carrying a large backpack. We all look around. Mystca and Grillian are looking in astonishment.

"I'm Tamy; apparently, Jules is a long, very long, lost relative, but he invited me to visit this island. I believe there's plenty of material here to finish my Honours degree in psychology."

"I'm noting that material first for my next book. You're too late, honey," says Viksi.

Pleb and I look at each. "Jules, Mystca and Tamy look like twins, and both are doing the same level of a university psychology course. It is not natural. I cannot tell which one is which."

I whisper, "Pleb, there's no way they can be related. They are doppelgangers as well, but we can have their names tattooed on their arms so that we don't get them mixed up."

Mystca walks over to Tamy, "Are you my twin? I didn't know I had a twin sister?"

"No, it's impossible that we are related, but your stepdad said you are in the same year as me doing a psychology post-grad course, so we could cooperate. I have a case study to diagnose and write."

"I'm doing the same, a case study. We could make it a tandem study. There's plenty of material on this island for many psychological case studies. It's like a nut-case horde here."

Grillian looks in astonishment as the apparent twins walk off to the spare cabin, gesticulating and exchanging many ideas on the way.

Pleb rubs her brow, "Jules, they cannot be related unless you kept something a secret from me."

"Pleb, I spent the last 90 years on this island. Sometimes coincidences happen, and this is definitely a super coincidence that has an extremely low probability of happening in the universe, but it has."

"Jules, could Tamy be an out-of-space alien just learning to impersonate Mystca?"

"It's a possibility, Pleb. If Tamy likes my cooking, she is definitely an alien."

Because of the Covid-47 lockdown, universities and schools are closed, so all academic interaction is through the 3-D Internet Gloom projector. I personally don't like seeing these 3-D lecturers wandering around my cabin and peering in as I get dressed and doing other things. I take the 3-D projector to the BBQ area. The girls can view their lessons there.

"Grillian, you're not totally dumb, so why don't you enrol in University? We'll pay the fees with the money you gave us."

"I was thinking about that. I've been reading about ethical land development and architecture."

"Go for it, son."

"Jules, I'm not your son, but I may follow your advice. I can't keep up with Mystca at the moment; she has become so intellectual," he says despondently. We hug, Grillian and me. I sort of know what the kid is going through, a feeling of inferiority, similar to my relationship with my first very academic wife a long, long time ago.

It's another night by the BBQ eating yummy fish, not the usual stonefish. Sid and Rog had gone into town earlier and purchased spear guns, flippers, diving masks and snorkels. They struggled to bring their catch to shore, a 3-metre-long white shark. It was time to use the chainsaw again to cut the fillets. The nuclear fusion-powered BBQ works just fine again. I look into the sky, "Thank you, Harry."

"Jules, we will have sufficient protein for us all for at least four days. Is that freezer in your shed still working?" asks Pleb.

"Yes, but no room for the head or tail. I'll get some wrapping bags from our cabin."

Mystca and Tamy come to join us. Tamy says she's a vegetarian and can only eat plant parts, eggs and cheese. Luckily the shark had plenty of eggs, and she and Cara are ravenously getting stuck into the meal of cheese, shark eggs and seaweed.

Mystca and Tamy join Pleb and me sitting on our wooden log, a log I laboriously carved from the few remaining trees on our island. We have since replanted Banana trees which are not really trees, coconut trees, and Avocado trees, along with a big veggie patch after much toiling, but with help from Mystca, Tamy and Grillian, we planted seeds of carrots, potatoes and cabbage, all that is required for a Polish diet.

"Mum and stepdad, both Tamy and I got our assignments finished; you know, the one on Abnormal Psychology. We're both studying the same stuff," Mystca and Tamy are jumping up in joy and clapping hands. I look at Grillian; he feels abandoned.

I clap my hands to get everyone's attention. "Grillian is also going back to Uni. Tomorrow we'll go and book him in for the next semester. Mystca, can you fabricate all the relevant documents that he needs to qualify; he can tell you the course he wants to pursue."

The next few hours are spent discussing Grillian's future. There are many suggestions.

Bea says, "He could join *Pi5*, but then again, he is probably not Polish enough, and your *Ai5* has shut down."

In the meantime, Viksi is furiously taking notes for her next book as she listens to our conversations, but then the peaceful night comes to an end. A motorboat docks at our jetty. Luckily the younger ones are back in their cabins. This type of incident has happened before. We have to find a more isolated place to live.

"I am Groolag. Pleborska is a wanted person back in my country. Which one of you is Pleborska?" growls the tall guy in a strong accent with a nasty snarl on his face.

All the ladies stand up and say in unison, "I am Pleborska."

Groolag looks from side to side but didn't have a chance to reply.

"This bow and arrow work really well," says Sid as Groolag sinks to his knees and then keels over with an arrow jutting from his temple. Sid continues, "Jules, this island is already like a cemetery. We have to chop him up and feed the pieces to the bull sharks. We also have to get rid of his motorboat; sink it."

Pleb yells out, "The motorboat would have a tracking device; you have to drive it to deep water and contact his superiors on the onboard radio that links to a satellite. There will be a radio frequency and code somewhere in the onboard documentation that is usually hidden underneath the steering wheel. You have to radio back and say the search has been unsuccessful and that his boat has run out of petrol and is drifting in stormy seas. You have to speak like him in that snarling accent. Now which one of you can do that?"

Sid, Rog, Gerald and I rehearse. Our lines are, 'I will bring her back my commandant, in one piece or several, whatever it takes.'

"Rog is definitely the best at the snarling accent," Viksi calls out and claps in joy.

Bea comes back with large plastic bags, an axe and a machete. We move Groolag's body below the high tide line and start dismembering. The blood will be washed away by the morning tide, but then Gerald, a bit unsteady on his feet, comes over to me. "I feel like vomiting; this is such a waste of good meat. It could feed poor, starving carnivore people in deprived meat countries."

"Gerald, the sharks also need a feed. They are part of the green aquatic ecosystem. Now start chopping and wiping those tears."

"Jules, I'd like to keep his head and dry it like they do in some South American cultures. It could hang on our balcony," says Pleb.

"Pleb, is that your plan for me to have my head hanging next to Groolags?"

"Jules, I would like to separate your hanging heads at least three metres apart so I cannot hear any arguments between the two heads," she laughs as she hugs me. She certainly has developed a very warped sense of humour.

Next morning Sid hops into Groolags motorboat. "Did you bring that sledgehammer? We must make it appear that he collided with a whale in case the authorities ever find the sunken boat."

Rog, Gerald, and I stuff the bags of Groolag's remains and follow Sid in my motorboat. Viksi also insists on coming along with her notebook and a voice recorder to take notes.

We dock alongside Groolag's motorboat. Rog jumps out and heads for Groolag's motorboat cabin. "It's here, the login codes, under the steering wheel," he yells out in joy. We can hear him talking on the voice messenger app as he has the speakers turned up loud. "Dear commandant, the latest intelligence I have is that the wanted person has moved back to Antarctica. This island has no human life forms. I'm driving the motorboat back to Townsville and catching the first flight back home. I have to go as a very large whale has just rammed my motorboat and the boat is sinking. Swimming lessons should be compulsory in our training, even if it is just breaststroke," Sid mutters and gives out gurgling sounds as if drowning.

"You will have your photo pasted on the *Pi5* wall of fame. Have you got a recent photo?" the commandant asks.

"No commandant, my hair has greyed, and I want to be remembered as what I looked like in my youth, as a young man hanging in the hall of fame."

"It will be done. Goodbye for now."

"Jules, this is not ethical," says Gerald.

"Gerald, do you think our government performs ethical actions that don't involve political advantage? We're just trying to survive, and you may not know all the complicating factors. Now get moving."

Groolag is disposed of, and the sharks are having a feast whilst Sid bravely dives below and punctures holes in Groolag's boat with the ultrasonic sledgehammer. The boat sinks, and Sid emerges from the water intact and smiling. "Job done," he smiles.

Sid hops back on my motorboat, and everyone gives him a hug and pats him on his head. Another problem is solved.

Chapter   Twenty-eight

We're in lockdown again due to the Zomega variant of the Covid-48 virus. It has to be the last variant because there are no more letters of the Greek alphabet remaining. Omega is the last Greek one, and now they're using other letters of the English alphabet to give the virus a name. Fortunately, the Polish alphabet has 32 characters, so there are many more names for Covid viruses. Anyway, we've all had our jabs of the latest vaccine, but still have to wear masks and breathing apparatuses when going shopping at the Townville supermarket. Townville council meetings are online, so neither Sid nor Gerald need to be physically present.

Viksi is crying on Cara's shoulder. "The hairdresser is still closed. My hair is down to my hips, and I haven't had a perm for over a year, and I can't buy any new clothes. These clothes I'm wearing are disintegrating and covered in mould."

Cara, one of my ex-wives, comforts Viksi. Cara also looks very long-haired and feral as the rest of us do, except for Bea, who uses the whipper-sniper to keep her hair trimmed and wears polyester clothes instead of natural fibres, Polish ingenuity.

Tamy is still stuck on the island with us due to travel restrictions, and she and Mystca have finished their Honours degree in psychology with top scores. They decide to do the online master's course and help Grillian in his studies. The three of them have developed a close friendship, and neither Tamy nor Grillian want to leave the island. They want to stay. It's rent-free for them except for Grillian, who paid for 100 years of accommodation.

Pleb holds my arm as we watch their regular running race around the island. It's their only way of keeping fit, and they like the endorphins. "Jules, Mystca is hundreds of metres ahead of Tamy and Grillian. We should enter her into the Commonwealth games."

"Yes, we should if this lockdown ends. The games are in Hobart in four months, but she has to qualify first."

"The qualifying heats are in an open-air stadium in Townsville, no breathing apparatuses needed and besides, we're vaccinated."

Pleb is squeezing my shoulder, and it's painful as we watch the 800m qualifying final.

"Mystca Lemos first, in a record time of 1:52:50," the judge announces. "She's in if the travel restrictions are lifted."

When we get back to the island, we have a huge celebration. Everyone is congratulating Mystca. I get out a 100yr old bottle of white wine that I had stashed for a special occasion. On second thought, I won't offer a drink to anyone but at least we have a good supply of vinegar. Luckily Sid, Rog and Gerald have a good supply of contemporary wines and beer, so it's a night of eating and dancing by the BBQ pit till we all flake out on the sand above the high tide line. Next morning, we brush the sand off our bodies and stagger back to our cabins.

"Jules," Pleb says, "I've checked the meter level in the underground water storage compartments. It's low, and at this rate of usage, we only have a week's worth of water at the current usage. You have to tell everyone that showers should be limited to 10 seconds and that they do not have the water tap on while brushing their teeth or dentures."

We all have a meeting next afternoon. I announce the grave news, and everyone agrees to comply with the water usage rules, but then Gerald yells out, "Let's desalinate; we're surrounded by water."

"And how do you propose we do that, Gerald?"

"There's this fairly small, experimental solar-powered desalination plant that has been abandoned after Harry insisted on coal-powered desalination. We could buy it. It's on sale and going very cheap. I'll contribute to the cost, but I don't think I need to, as the council will pay the removal costs."

The others also put their hands up in agreement. A small cargo ship delivers the disassembled desalination plant to our island. The captain of the vessel has a forklift on board and helps us move the bits and pieces to the plant's new home.

"Jules, there's no instruction booklet on assembling this," Sid says.

"Sid, it can't be that hard."

Three months pass, and we finally get the desalination plant assembled and working after many tries. We've been drinking that expensive bottled water bought from the mainland and haven't showered in fresh water. We keep our distance because we pong and us guys are covered in grease and bandages due to worksite accidents.

"Jules, we still have a lot of nuts and bolts left, about a hundred. Do you think they're important?" Rog asks.

"Rog, they're probably from the original installation kit. They always include extra nuts and bolts in case you drop some and lose them."

Sid flicks the switch, and the plant starts working, churning away. We all hug in joy, hopefully, a freshwater shower soon. Bathing in the salty ocean is not the same as a freshwater shower, so we look forward to getting rid of the salt crystals adhering to our bodies which make us look like some alien species when sunlight strikes them, and they reflect the colours of the rainbow just as a prism does.

In the meantime, Mystica, Tamy and Grillian train hard doing mumerous laps of the island. Mystca still comfortably wins, but Tamy and Grillian are making good progress. Grillian is thriving from all the endorphins. Their food consumption has increased a lot, so it wasn't such a good idea to get them involved in sport. The food bill is enormous and at this rate, they'll have to go back to eating stonefish and seaweed or get a paying part-time job.

The OZ athletic games trials are held at the Townville University sports stadium. Mystca easily qualifies for the women's 800m race. Tamy and Grillian also qualify in their events, as all three are elated, so it's time to fly. We're at the airport and get electronically swabbed, plus we have our vaccination certificates, so we all board, Pleb, Mystca, Tamy and me on the QLD athletes chartered flight to Hobart, the capital city of the rather cold island on the southern tip of Australia, where the games are being held. Twenty minutes later, we land, but finding our suitcases at the luggage carousel took more time than the hypersonic flight.

"Jules, this is the cheapest hotel you could have booked. There is no hair dryer, and the shower does not work. I am smelly," Pleb says.

OK, I did take some financial shortcuts. "Pleb, I love your pheromones. It's raining outside, so you could take your shower on the balcony." I get a deadly look. "OK, I'll upgrade our accommodation."

Next day we all watch as Mystca wins the women's quarter and later semi-finals of the women's 800m race. Tamy came second in both events.

"Jules, did you inject her with the peptide? She will be drug tested," Pleb whispers.

"No, no, of course not, but there were more than a few doses missing from the laboratory in our cellar."

"Jules, she will be disqualified and banned for life."

"Pleb, have you started injecting the peptide?"

"I tried it only once. I have to keep up with you, and you still brew it and jab it into yourself."

"I do it for you and Mystca."

"That is cow shit; you do it for yourself," she yells. "Is that peptide detectable in the blood and urine tests they give athletes?"

"I don't think so. It's not a performance-enhancing substance, as you constantly tell me in the boudoir."

"You are right. Your athletic performance in the bedroom would never earn a gold medal."

"Well, in my teens, I ran 800m races in sporting events, and my best time was 2:02."

"Luckily, you are not racing Mystca or Tamy," Pleb says.

A day passes. Pleb and I don't talk, we give each other nasty looks and poke our tongues at each other. Finally, the next day are the finals. The two of us are watching as Mystca and Tamy step onto the starting blocks.

The gun fires, and they're off. Pleb and I forget our differences and are clutching each other's hands and jumping up and down.

The girls run the first lap of the 400m oval track, all tightly grouped. Mystca and Tamy are stuck in the middle of the pack and can't get through to the front, but then, in the final 150m of the second lap, they both move to the outer side of the track. It's the curved part of the track and a longer distance to run than the inside of the track, but they break through and start sprinting the final 80m passing all the opponents. Our throats are aching from all the cheering.

"1:50:51, a new world record for the women's 800m and two equal first women at that," the voice on the speaker announces.

Mystca and Tamy nervously stand on the top podium, which is not designed for two people and are presented with the gold medal trophies and humbly bow and hug the silver and bronze medallists. They are then ushered away for substance testing. We nervously wait outside the testing centre. An hour passes then an Indian-looking guy wearing a mask approaches us.

"Sir, your twin daughters are clean. Congratulations on fathering such talented athletes. The 800m was my favourite race also, but I only clocked 1:58 as my personal best," the doctor says, "but the lad called Grillian has an unusual substance in his bloodstream and will not be allowed to compete."

"Thank you, your best time is far better than my partner's," Pleb says. She's still pissed off; must be having her menstrual period. Gawd, I'm glad guys don't have menstrual cycles and are always cool and logical. Of course, I would never say that to Pleb, as she may use her *Pi5* termination skills on me.

There's no party or celebrations due to Covid-48. We and other QLD athletes are boarded on the first flight home wearing masks. We are tested on arrival, and all five of us tested negative. Bea, Viksi, Cara, Rog, Sid and Gerald are there to greet us at the Townsville airport. Many hugs are exchanged before we board Sid's motorboat, which is bigger than mine and can fit us all.

"Mystca, did you go down into my lab and jab yourself with the peptide?" I whisper when standing near her.

"Yeh, I did go down to your lab, but I jabbed your rat, Chloe4. You have neglected your rat friend, and I want her to live forever because she points out spelling mistakes in Tamy's and my Uni assignments. She's better than any online grammar-checking software. We need her till we finish our uni PhDs and maybe longer."

So another night of celebration ensues. Lots of food, wine and beer is consumed, and the usual event of us all waking up next morning by the seashore covered in sand. I stumble to the water's edge to have a pee. There's a sealed bottle lying on the sand. It has some paper wrapped in it - a message in a bottle and the message is very highly disturbing. I look out to sea. There's a yacht parked out there. I haven't seen that one before.

Chapter Twenty-nine

I pull out the message from the bottle. It says, "I want my rat back, This is my cell phone number," and it's signed Greuger Smitht.

"Who is this Greuger guy?" Pleb asks as she reads the note that I'm holding.

"It's a long story, and it's all in that long document I wrote called *Don't Look Behind the Fridge*, but to put it briefly, 100 years ago, Greuger was a hired assassin and about to kill me, but he lost his desire to kill and then my housemates stabbed him instead, and we got a substantial reward as he was a very wanted man by many police authorities in Europe. Before seemingly dying, he begged that I look after his pet, the original white rat called Chloe, which I did. I even held his head in my arms while his heart pulse dropped to zero, and he stopped breathing. He can't be alive after all this time with that injury he sustained."

"Ring the number," Pleb says.

"Hello, are you Greuger?"

"That is my name."

"If you are, describe in minute detail what happened when you burst into my townhouse in Elwood, a suburb in Melbourne over a 100yrs ago."

He does that with impeccable accuracy.

"Why are you still alive? We killed you before you tried killing me?"

"Mister Jules, you know that I could feign death and had done so many times in my past career as an assassin. My body was thrown out to sea and not incinerated. I may have served in the army, but I was also a scientist, and I tried to bring my wife, Hilda, my only wife, back to life after she died of ovarian cancer. You, like me, have a substance that can increase healing and prolongs life; unfortunately, it was too late for my Hilda."

"Greuger, are you going to try to kill me again and just call me Jules?"

"No, I do not kill anymore except for mosquitoes."

"OK, you can come ashore but don't carry any weapons; we'll be watching you."

Greuger rows ashore in a kayak. His anti-aging formula seems to work better than my peptide, and he still has long blond hair and his 190 m tall muscular frame.

Chloe4 rushes towards him and kisses his face. There must be some memories stored in rats' DNA. He hugs the rat and has tears flowing down his face.

Mystca and Tamy come out to the jetty. "You're not taking Chloe4; we need her help with our Uni assignments; ask Jules if you can stay here."

I look at Greuger, and he looks at me. "You have to promise you won't try to kill me again. *Cabin09* is spare, but you got to pay some rent and for food, and Chloe4 has to spend some time with the younger girls to help them with their university assignments."

"I can do that as I have plenty of money I do not need since my Hilda departed, so I can pay and stay as neither of you on this island are on the kill list. I just want to be reminded of my only wife, and Chloe is the only connecting factor; we loved Chloe as she cleaned the leftovers of our meals and stood up on her back paws, clapping after the meal. We never had to clean dishes and laughed so much at her antics." The guy has copious tears flowing down his face and is wiping them.

I whisper to Pleb, "We got to find this guy a girlfriend if I let him stay here. That guy is still caught up in his past. He hasn't moved forward in the last100 years."

"Jules, he is very handsome. He looks like a Tarzan guy with all those muscles and long hair. I am sure many women would find him very attractive, but he does not smile. I think he is very depressed. Let him stay."

"Stop licking your lips. He can stay, and you have to help me find a girlfriend for him in Townsville."

Greuger swims out to his yacht and guides it back closer to shore. He then swims back with several ropes in his mouth, towing four eskies full of food and a large plastic bag full of AU$100 currency notes. The introductions are done, and all the ladies are staring at Greuger, salivating and licking their lips, not just for the food that he brought. We guys are feeling very uneasy and deficient.

"He should be a star in one of those World Championship Wrestling matches," says Rog.

"Jules, I'll buy a gym set; we can all use it except that guy," Sid says. "We'll get bulging muscles as well."

We dine outside by the BBQ pit. Greuger cooks the 20kgs of salmon he brought, and we're all very well over-fed. "Mr Jules, this bag of money is for you. I have little need for money after my wife Hilda died, as I now live a Spartan lifestyle," he says with tears again flowing down his face. The ladies run over to comfort him, reaching hands on his shoulder and wiping his face with serviettes. After thanking them, Greuger carries Chloe4 to *Cabin09*. The ladies all wave and lick their lips again.

"Jules, I'm sure he is severely depressed and possibly suicidal. Let him stay; we ladies shall comfort him," whispers Pleb.

"Pleb, I already said before that he can stay, but none of that comforting."

And so, another guest, this time a paying guest, and former assassin, joins the island. Next day Greuger has Chloe4 riding on his shoulder and joins us at the table by the seashore for breakfast which is just dry cereal and no muscle-maintaining protein. Chloe4 chews the dried oats off his lips, and the man mountain is in ecstasy.

"Jules, there is a dance club in Townsville that is still open, and we can enter if we wear facemasks due to Covid. We may find a distraction for Greuger, and the nightclub has a very liberal dress code," says Pleb.

"Pleb, no woman will want him if he maintains that no-fun, Spartan lifestyle. He was very psychologically damaged after Hilda died. He is a robot, but he paid for over 200yrs accommodation on this island. I still haven't finished counting those currency notes."

"Jules, let us get him out of his shell. We could have a beach volleyball contest on our island and get him involved. It might make his body produce some endorphins."

That morning Sid, Viksi, Rog, Gerald, and I set up the net and draw the lines for the court with anything we could find as we have no tape: Sticks, used condoms and food scraps. We'll purchase tape next time we go to town. Viksi is taking copious notes but finally joins the matches. The games begin. As in all beach volley games, we're all dressed as skimpily as possible in our underwear to look like true Olympians. We play doubles. The first match is Viksi and Bea versus Sid and Rog. The girls win. Viksi yells to Rog, "My phone battery is nearly flat. I need to record this conversation; it is getting incredible!"

"Come out here, Greuger, let's see what you got," I yell.

"I want Chloe to be my partner."

"Greuger, she could be killed if one of my powerful ball serves hit her head."

"I will make sure she is not hit. I will catch the ball," says Greuger.

Chloe4 claps her paws in excitement, but the game wouldn't last long.

It was Gerald and me versus Greuger and Chloe4. Everyone was watching in anticipation. I served, and Greugar jumps up, hit the ball, and it burst. Everyone is in a state of shock and dismay.

"Greuger, you're supposed to use the palms of your hands, not your fists, to hit the ball."

"Mr Jules, I am sorry. I will buy you another ball, many balls, when we go into town. I think I could get to like this game."

"Follow me, Greuger and help me drag out the table tennis table from my shed. I have plenty of balls, racquets, and even a lollipop that Chloe4 can use as a racquet. And don't call me Mr Jules; just Jules will do as I said before."

Everyone helps set up the table tennis table and clean years of dust off it. The net is set up. Bea has drawn up a roster. Single-sex doubles and mixed doubles; best of five sets to advance.

"I am LGBTQ, plus more," yells out Tamy. "Mystca and I want an LGBQT match if there are any opponents. We are really into women's wrestling on TV." In the future, despite their Psychology University degrees, the girls would become World Wrestling tag team champions and certainly able to use the microphone to rant and get the 80,000+ people excited and cheering for them as they paraded in their OZ bikini wrestling costumes. They were earning heaps, and I never had to financially support them ever again.

Greuger briefly returns to his cabin and comes out with four gold medals. "They will be the prizes to the winners. I won them at the Olympic Games for gun shooting, bow and arrow, karate and weightlifting. They are a weight on my neck."

Greuger was too embarrassed to bring out the bronze medal he won in table tennis at the last Olympics. Mystca and Tamy whisper to me, "He is very depressed. He is giving up all his money and medals. He may be on a suicidal mission. We have to monitor him 24/7."

Everyone on this island is exceptionally good at table tennis, and the games last ten or more minutes each. At this rate, it will take a week to complete the tournament. After 2 hours, it's onlyBea and Sid who are eliminated after a loss to Cara and Gerald, and no one is keen to face Greuger and Chloe4, but the light is fading, and we call off the tournament for the day; we'll resume tomorrow morning.

Mystca, Sid and Grillian guide Greuger and Chloe4 back to their cabins. Castro, Bea 's turtle, looks distressed and nods his head whilst looking down. His only animal friend is Chloe4, and she is ignoring him.

Bea comes over. "Jules, we'll also have to find a turtle partner for Castro. He misses the jousting he had with Chloe4 and looks more depressed than that Greuger guy. I checked on the Internet, and there are no turtle anti-depressant drugs. We must go further up north and capture a partner for Castro, preferably a female turtle."

"Bea, you can do that. We have enough problems to deal with on this island."

"Can I use your motorboat craft?"

"Yes, sure, but check the fuel gauge."

Bea frantically departs, driving at high speed, but then another motorboat, a BoatUberrite hire, arrives at our jetty and out steps Jill. She still looks good. Pleb goes over to her and gives her a hug. In the meantime, Bea is furiously waving her hands about 400m from shore. She didn't check the fuel gauge. Sid jumps into his motorboat and tows Bea and my motorboat back to the jetty.

"I can't cope now that Harry is dead. I'm having a nervous breakdown, and I need a drink. Can I stay here for a few weeks?" Jill pleads.

"Jill, all the habitable cabins are full unless you want to share. *Cabin09* has a spare bedroom. We can walk you over to see if Greuger, the occupant, agrees to share."

Greuger opens the door with Chloe4 sitting on his shoulder. He looks at Jill in amazement, and his face lights up. "Hilda, where have you been? I thought you had passed away. I have missed you so very, very much since you departed, and not one second in my prolonged life have I ever not thought about you."

"No, I'm not Hilda, my name is just Jill, and I've never been dead yet."

"But you look just like my Hilda, my deceased wife. Let me help you with your luggage. The spare bedroom is to the right. I will guide you there."

"Pleb, there was a spark of chemistry and excitement in Greuger's eyes. I think his endorphins started flowing, and he's come alive again. We may not have to take him to that dance club in Townville or get him anti-depressants or magic mushrooms."

"Jules, do you still chew on those mushrooms?"

"Pleb, I occasionally do, but only two or three mushies, that's all that's required; you definitely don't want to have more, else it can be scary. I had some sort of biochemical depressive brain disorder since I was 16yrs old. That's why I studied pharmacology. I was pretty miserable most of my life till I discovered the mushie and then you."

Another BoatUberrite arrives at the jetty. The boat driver is struggling to carry a very large esky. This time it's Mystca, Tamy and Grillian who rush to help. After about 10 minutes, they retrieved all eight large eskies and dragged them to our island freezer. The BoatUberrite driver asks for a digital signature confirming everything was delivered successfully.

"But we didn't order this stuff," Tamy exclaims.

"It is in the name of Greuger Shmidt. Maybe someone else on this island made the order and also gave a very generous tip. I will now be able to feed my family for two months or more," the driver tearfully rubs his eyes as he departs.

I hear them saying, "That first red Esky is full of large prawns, and the other contains lots of crayfish. The others just have eggs, fruit and vegetables."

"I don't eat meat, but that's not red meat even if it's meat at all, so I may give it a try as it may be a vegan imitation of meat like the stuff I used to buy at the supermarket," Tamy says.

So, the semi-finals of the table tennis tournament are about to begin, but Greuger and Jill are not attending. Mystca goes to check their cabin and knocks on the door. "It's the finals; why aren't you at the court?"

"We have had too much exercise, so we do not think we could perform very well again. We are very exhausted," Greuger shouts out.

"Greuger, you are so much better than Harry ever was," Mystca overhears Jill say.

Chloe4 jumps out the open window and follows Mystca. Castro is by the court, and the two begin a sparring match.

"Jules, let's call the semi-finals off for a bit. I am hungry and overheard the conversation about what is in those eskies. It does not sound like people who live a stoic lifestyle would buy into this."

"Jules, I don't think Greuger and Jill will attend. They are doing a different form of exercise together," Mystca says.

Everyone agrees and goes to their kitchens and returns with large bowls and cooking pots. Yum, we have had the best meal ever. I hope Greuger stays on the island even though he and Jill aren't here to savour the food delights. Mystca and Tamy take some large bowls of leftovers covered in plastic film and place them outside Greuger's cabin after slipping a paper message underneath the door. We all have an early night. No partying, as we have a lot of digesting to do.

Chapter Thirty

Next morning we're sitting by the jetty, watching a red sunrise. "Jules, are you sure that's not some nuclear hydrogen bomb that's been ignited?"

"Sid, it's the sun. It's a gigantic fusion reactor toom but gives us great colour in the sky, colours everywhere."

Viksi and Rog come out to join the group, as do Mystca and Tamy.

"Jules, have you had that mushroom soup again?" Asks Mystca.

"No, I don't think so, though I did lick all the plates to reduce our water consumption for dishwashing. Who knows what the others had."

Greuger and Jill, holding hands, also come and join us to watch the sunrise.

"Mr Jules, sorry, just Jules, both Jill and I would like to have a wedding ceremony on this island and to be pronounced man and wife servant. We are both Catholics, so we would like a Catholic priest."

"Greuger, you can do that in Las Vegas but not in Australia. Here you need proof of identity and lots of other legal formalities which take time; you can't just marry someone you met a day ago. No Catholic priest would agree to do that."

"Jules, you were Catholic, and you are captain of this island, which resembles being captain of a ship, so cannot captains marry people in this country?"

Jill calls out, clapping her hands and jumping up and down, "I want to marry this guy. He is so, so hot."

"Greuger, I'll give you the address of the *Office of Marriages and Deaths* in Townville. You have to pick up the legal documents, paper ones, which I can help you fill out as it can't be done online. Your birth certificate may be outdated, so ask Mystca to create and print a new fake one for you with an appropriate date of birth. She's good at that."

Mystca prints out a birth certificate for Greuger, 100 years after his actual birth and a document she wrote stating that he has no criminal record with fake signatures of authorities in Germany. He is now only 45 years old, by official records.

Greuger and Jill get dressed appropriately and take my motorboat to Townville harbour and visit the Marriages and Deaths office. Four hours later, they return, holding a lot of papers.

I start reading. "Jill, Greuger, your previous partners died less than a year ago. In this OZ country, it appears like you can't remarry till you or your partner has been dead for over a year. You've got a lot more months to go."

"But I love him and what he does to me; there must be an exemption clause somewhere; there are always exemption clauses."

"I'll ask Bea. She supposedly has a legal background and can check if you can qualify for an instant marriage."

"Greuger, she still has ten months to go. It's a new legal requirement in this OZ country after that scam where partners murdered each other with hard-to-detect substances," says Bea after checking an online government website. "We never had that in Poland because we married and murdered discretely. We did not need cover-ups."

"Then we shall go to that place called Las Vegan and get married there."

"Greuger, don't be so impulsive. Just you and Jill become atheists, and then you don't have to worry about bedroom gymnastics done outside of wedlock."

"Jules, are you an atheist Satan worshipper?"

"No, Greuger, we atheists just don't feel guilt if we do things that don't harm anyone or the environment."

"Jules, I have harmed very many people as part of the work I once did. Could I still become an atheist?"

"I'll vouch for you. You donated most of your money to charity as a paid assassin. You qualify to be an atheist."

"Thank you, Jules; I feel better now."

Greuger lifts me up, gives me a hug and nearly crushes my ribs before he and Jill walk back to their cabin. Pleb comes over to me. "Jules, he could still be dangerous. You should have agreed that the best thing to do was to go to that LesVegan place."

"Pleb, I did some research online. Greuger has been a member of AA for the last hundred years, Assassins Anonymous and I believe he is cured and reformed, plus he paid for 200 years of accommodation. We can't afford to give him a refund."

Both Greuger and Jill are smiling at each other, starry-eyed and holding hands as they come to lunch. There's still plenty of food left in all those eskies that Greuger ordered. He stares at Jill as he cooks, which was not a good idea as he accidentally places his hand on the BBQ hot plate and gives out a yell. Jill runs over and licks his palm. Greuger's pain is relieved, and he continues cooking. Mystca, Tamy and Grillian come over. "Stepdad, we must start the morning runs again, ten times around the island. We are putting on weight. There is too much good food to eat here, and we've all put on like lots of kilos,"

Mystca announces to everyone that at 8am tomorrow and every day while we're in lockdown, a run will be organised around the island. "It's only 2km per lap, so you have the option of doing ten laps with me or just one or two with Jules."

Everyone lifts their head. Some have pieces of crayfish hanging out of their mouths.

Jill whispers to Greuger, "We get more than enough exercise."

"I will be running, my darling. I may get fitter and perform even better."

Next morning we're all lined up. No drones are monitoring us to see if we're not violating the Covid-47 lockdown rules. Besides, we've all had the jabs and tests.

"Sid, you can't wear thongs when running."

"But Jules, I have no other footwear."

"It's a barefoot run or jog as we're running on sand. You don't need footwear."

Bea, Cara, Viksi, Sid and Rog make one lap of jogging and are exhausted. Running or jogging on sand is much harder and tiring than running on a hard surface, and it takes longer to cover an equivalent distance plus, it's a hot morning, 30 degrees Celsius and 90% humidity. It sucks.

I get two laps of jogging done, and I'm huffing and puffing, lying on my back and wondering if I'm having a cardiac event. Pleb gets three laps done before she joins me on the sand. We look up as the runners go by. Mystca is ahead by several hundred metres, followed by Greuger, Tamy, Grillian, and Jill. Jill drops out exhausted after the sixth lap of running; the others continue. We would later find out that Jill was once a junior athletics champion in the 10,000m races.

"Jules, get some water, a lot of water. They will become dehydrogenated," Pleb says.

I run back to the shed and tow out a large plastic water bottle and some reusable plastic drinking glasses. We all watch as they go by and by. Mystca has lapped the others in the front pack and comes across the finish line holding her arms up high. Tamy comes a close second, followed closely by Gerald and Grillian. We all grab and hug them as they crouch on the sand, getting their breath back.

"I am not used to losing. We do this race again, tomorrow, and the next tomorrow and all tomorrows after that," says Greuger.

"Fine by me," Mystca replies.

And so, the morning runs start again. Three weeks later, the results are still much the same, but we losers are getting better and doing more laps, but then there are heart-stopping discoveries after Gerald trips over and sparks are flying from his foot. The others stop running, come over to help him, and stare at his foot.

"Jules, he may be one of those AI robots; they make them so human looking that it is now hard to distinguish one from a real human," Pleb whispers.

"I don't care what species you are. I will always love you," Cara says, holding his head and foot.

"I'm not an android," Gerald calls out. "My foot had to be amputated after an accident on my solar farm when I fell foot first off one of the panels, and my foot got replaced by this bionic one. I forgot to recharge the foot this morning, and it went into a spasm. I'm not in any pain."

The others are not convinced. They start pinching his skin and pocking him with their fingers. Gerald is sort of convulsing.

"Stop!" Gerald yells out, "I'm ticklish."

"He seems almost human. A ticklish android has not yet been invented in Poland," announces Bea. "He must be a Chinese android."

We all take turns in helping Gerald hobble back to his and Cara's cabin. So it's an anti-climax to our race and with dismayed looks as we all return to our cabins. Pleb is busy Doogling on our ancient computer as none of us have had the Doogle Wi-Fi microchip inserted into our brains, a procedure that is quite popular, especially amongst young people.

"Jules, there is nothing I can find that says humanoid robots cannot be ticklish. Gerald could still be a robot, and they have human-looking flesh now covering the electronics."

"Pleb, whatever he is, he's a nice being and distracting my ex-wife from suing for 130 years of alimony payments. I need him, so don't even think about getting that horseshoe magnet from the shed and placing it over his bodily parts."

"Jules, Titanium is now used to manufacture robots. It does not respond to magnetic field detectors as well as conventional metals do."

"Enough, I'm ringing the Townsville hospital to see if they do foot replacements."

"Sir, the closest hospital that does that procedure is in Brisbane. Is he humanoid?"

"Not sure, but he needs a new foot."

"That is fine, he will be X-rayed, and the hospital in Brisbane will source the appropriate foot for him."

Next day, after explaining the only option to Gerald, Pleb and me drive Gerald and Cara to Townville in my motorboat and wave them goodbye when they board a road taxi service to the airport. Yes, you're wondering, don't they have flying taxis in 2046? They were tried but too fuel inefficient and banned because we still haven't solved the global warming crisis. The hypersonic planes are also only allowed to fly when they have a full payload. Luckily, there were two remaining seats when we booked the flight for Gerald and Cara.

Pleb rests her head on my shoulder. "Jules, it has been a serious two days. Now we can rest and start the morning running tomorrow. I need to get back into the exercise as I do not like looking at myself in the mirror."

I fear for my life, so desist from commenting that she over-enjoys the food that Greuger orders and her bodily mass has substantially increased.

We're all by the beach BBQ for the nightly dinner. I call out to everyone, "Due to transport restrictions due to covid-46 or is it covid-48, we have to reduce our food consumption of yummy foods else we'll become obese and have strokes and cardiac problems, and we won't be able to perform well in the bedroom with a bulging belly."

Pleb kicks my foot. Luckily, it's a human foot, so no short circuits or sparks. "Are you saying, what is the word, implying, that I have a bulging belly?"

"No, of cause not, not you; I was referring to Rog and Viksi."

Viksi tosses the contents of her wine glass in my face, SavBlanc. I lick my lips. She then marches off to her cabin. Rog giggles.

That night I was roasted near the BBQ. Not literally, just Pleb and Viksi, who returned very angry. Both ladies were bent over, pointing their finger at me whilst I sat and yelling insults.

Greuger comes over to me and gives me a hug. "Jules, from now on, I will order low-calorie scallops and crayfish and supervise only one dose per person, not a large plate."

"Thanks, Greuger."

Needless to say, there were no bedroom gymnastics that night, and I'm in a sleeping bag on the lounge room floor. I didn't get much sleep as could hear Viksi yelling at Rog much of the night.

Chapter Thirty-one

Next morning everyone, except Gerald and Cara, is out for the 8am run. Mystca and Tamy guide us through some warm-up and stretching exercises.

"If you have any mechanical body parts that could be injured, please don't run," Mystca speaks out loud. We all nod our heads, and the race begins. It's a fast start. Greuger takes the lead, and Mystca is a close 2nd, but that might be her strategy to let him set the pace and exhaust himself. Tamy and Grillian must have secretly been doing extra training because they are in the leading pack along with Jill. The rest of us are at the back of the pack, and after two laps of jogging, we're exhausted and crouching down on the sand and getting our breath back. Chleo4 and Castro, come and join us. Nine minutes later, the leading pack zoom past with Greuger still in the lead. Chloe4 claps her paws. I dash back to my cabin and grab my drone and the 3D projector. The drone is following the runners and projecting a 3D image. After four laps, Jill drops out and joins us. We're all biting our fingernails in excitement which you might think is strange, but when you're in Covid lockdown, this is the most exciting thing to do and watch. Lap 6, and then 500m from the finish, Mystca makes her dash and passes Greuger. She is triumphant. Her time is 20 seconds better than her last.

"You stretched me, and I am grateful for that, but I will be back," says Greuger as he hugs Mystca.

Tamy and Grillian come in third and fourth. "Have our times improved? Asks Tamy as she and Grillian are crouching and puffing."

I checked your previous results. "You're both 1 minute and 20 seconds better; congratulations."

We miss breakfast because we've run out of food, and no one wants to go back to the stonefish and seaweed diet and then just as we're walking back to our cabin, a horn sounds. It's the BoatUberrite delivery service docking at the jetty. We're all hungry, so rush out to the jetty. Omar, the driver, comes out carrying a little container no bigger than a shoe box. "I have been told that you are on diets."

Everyone looks in disbelief and dismay. I get evil stares.

"I am just joking, as you say in this country. There are ten very large Eskies full of low-calorie prawns, crayfish, berries and vegetables. I have a bad spinal cord, so could you help me carry the Eskies? Greuger must have ordered it."

We all rush and tow the eskies to the refrigeration shed, except for one we leave on the beach. We waive Omar goodbye, and then we all get stuck into the contents of the esky. No plates, no forks, just our hands and fingers as we dig into the esky, pulling out prawns, crayfish pieces, blueberries, and strawberries and stuff our faces. Lockdowns definitely bring out the primitive side of humanity, which is not too bad to be in touch with how our very primitive ancestors probably functioned.

Chapter Thirty-two

"Jules, I have forgiven you for saying that I have an oversize tummy. You can come back and sleep in our bedroom with me, and we can have what you call bedroom gymnastics again."

"Pleb, I was only joking."

"You never joke about a woman's weight if you want to stay alive."

"OK, never again, I promise, now come outside. We will all be lying on the beach and getting a bit of a tan."

Then she comes out, covered head to toe in a Burka. We all turn our heads and look at the person wandering along the beach; who it is. "My name is Viagra; I am a spirit and will behead any person who says I need to lose bodily weight."

OK, Pleb may have set up this 3-D projection. These days it's hard to know what is real, and Pleb did test me by having this lovely 3-D projection with actual body mass, indistinguishable from the real thing, grab me. I desisted, and eventually, Pleb turned the projection off. "You passed the test," she said and kissed me, and I kiss her back and ask, "Can you be more creative if you're going to test me after all these years that we've been together."

"Yes, sure, Jules," she says as she pulls out a whip-looking device from her backpack. "Start running." I certainly do that whilst glancing back.

It's 3pm, and Cara rings. "Jules, Gerald's artificial foot has been rejected by his body. Can you bring some of your peptide down to the hospital in Brisbane? It seems to suppress allergic reactions as well as prolonging life."

"Cara, we're still in lockdown, and there are few flights available. I'll email you the instructions on how to manufacture the peptide. You can source the ingredients at a supermarket, but you'll also need some equipment that is quite sophisticated and expensive to buy."

"Ha, ha, ha, I tricked you. His new bionic foot is fine and successfully attached. I'll also make sure that he charges the foot battery every night as he wants to come back to the island and do more running training. I think he's got his eyes on competing in the Paraplegic Games. We also got two seats on a flight back to Townsville at 4:30 pm. Can you pick us up at the boat terminal?"

First time that my once ex, Cara, has laughed or displayed any sense of humour when talking to me.

"Cara, you and Gerald better get to the airport immediately. You have to be Covid tested, which may take some time if there's a big queue. And no, I can't pick you up. Pleb and I are writhing, I mean writing what's it called, yes now I remember, a Will, that inheritance doco for when you're deceased, and that requires intense concentration so I cannot be disturbed for the next 3 hours. Use BoatUburrite to get back or catch a drone."

Pleb and I keep exercising in the bedroom though we take 10-minute breaks to drink water as it's pretty hot and sweat is dripping from every part of our bodies. The magic is there again. It's like being an 18.5 yr. old again, the first time when I had sex which is not that unusual as I went to a Catholic boy's school and only met my first girlfriend when I was 18. We might have set a world record 14 times within 24 hours. Anyway, I support mixed-gender schools, and I'm totally against single gender-schools. We can learn so much in communicating and understanding if we mix with the opposite gender early on at school.

We reach the magic number ten, in 3 hours, possibly a new world record, but copulation isn't yet a recognised sport in the Olympics, and we are covered in sweat and exhausted.

Mystca, Tamy and Grillian have picked plenty of vegetables, herbs and bananas from the garden that we had established, so it's prawn and crayfish night again with some local land produce, definitely better than stonefish with seaweed.

Gerald and Cara arrive just in time for dinner. Gerald shows off his new foot and flashes it around. Coloured LEDs light up when he walks on it. Everyone claps as we all sit beside the BBQ. Then we notice a drone is filming us.

"Jules, I have my bow and arrow pack. I can shoot it down," says Rog.

"No, wait, Rog, we got to think of another idea."

"Jules, let us all strip off and be naked, and we all do the hula-hula dance. Your authorities will just think this is what do you call it, a *loony farm*?" says Pleb.

We all follow Pleb's advice. We take our clothes off and gyrate with our arms in the air. It's like one of those *DownToEarth* festivals that I attended in the 1970s. The AI drone gives up and flies off. It must think we're a bunch of nutcases or Chimpanzees and not a serious threat to national security plus, it wasn't programmed to ignore all that public hair; sorry meant pubic. I will have to buy some hair trimmers next time in town, so we stop looking like and smelling like Neanderthals. We put on clothing and resume our not-so-elegant dining. I overhear Viksi, "Rog, I have collected enough material here for my next ten books. Let's go back to Melbourne."

"Viksi, I sort of like it here, I don't think I want to go back, and you can publish your books online, but you better make me the leading character."

"You are Rog," says Viksi. "My latest book is set in the caveman era, 20,000 years ago, and you are the star."

Rog smiles and gives Viksi a big kiss.

Time flies when you're over 150 years old. Six years have passed without any major incident. Mystca and Tamy are lecturing at Townville University but visit on weekends with their partners. Grillian occasionally visits when he can, but he's away a lot investigating the feasibility of governments funding the construction of affordable housing. Then it happens again. I didn't know the manufacturing process of the life-prolonging peptide was posted on the dark web. It's like Greuger arising from the dead, but this time it was a lot more scary. It is my mother, Doris, former head of the *i5* organizations, who walks up from the jetty.

"Jules, help me get my luggage off this Uberwrong boat, or else you'll be severely disciplined."

I thought she had died of old age, but she's back just like some of the others on this island.

"I've got to start *Ai5* again; your great-great-grandchildren let it flounder. I'm here to fix it. Now I need a jab of your peptide as I have work to do."

"Jules, I thought she was dead, and now she reappears just like Greuger. How many more dead people will reappear on our island?" asks Pleb.

"Pleb, I don't know. Doris must have got the formula and manufacturing process when I worked in the St Kilda archives library. That was over 100 years ago. Doris is relentless and highly driven to achieve her goal by whatever means."

"Mother, *Cabin10* is unoccupied. You can stay there for a little while."

"Jules, I want you to come back. We can restart *Ai5* again, and who is that guy? Isn't he Greuger Shmidt? I thought you and your cohorts had eliminated him. He was on our most wanted disposal list."

"Mother, he is a doppelganger and by pure coincidence, he shares the same name. It's a very common name, especially in Germany."

"If he is that Greuger Shmidt tell him his days are numbered," she says with a menacing look of vengeance. "Now, what have you got to eat?"

Greuger is cooking on our BBQ, and apart from once being an excellent assassin, he has now focused his talents on learning to be an excellent cook, and the spicy BBQ smells waft around us and make us all lick our lips in anticipation.

"That smells so good; whoever he is, I won't eliminate him just yet," Doris says.

My mother had a reputation for eliminating people in *i5s*, and that's how she rose to the top rank. She was more deadly than Greuger when she was in her prime. Greuger has focused his energy on his partner, Jill, and still believes she is the reincarnation of his only previous partner and deceased wife, Hilda. I check Doris's luggage for weapons before guiding her to *Cabin10*.

And so another night by the BBQ. We'll have to purchase more chairs as some of us are sitting on eskies, plastic boxes to keep the contents cool, which I suppose is quite the norm in OZ. Greuger and Doris briefly and intensely stare at each other. "Good meal," yells out Doris and claps. The others join the clapping.

"Jules, be careful and scary; sorry meant wary," whispers Pleb.

I grab her hand. "I will. She is more dangerous than Covid-48 or Greuger when he was in his prime."

"Jules, have another jab of your peptide. I don't want to be left alone with these people," says Pleb.

We all retire to our cabins after the meal but not before the peptide jab, so another chapter of life on the island is about to begin, a challenging one.

Chapter Thirty-three

Doris is up there for the morning beach run, menacingly staring at Greuger as we line up. She doesn't look any different, wiry, skinny but with muscles, the same as when I worked at the St Kilda archives section of the library, where Doris was the supposed tea lady. A perfect innocent cover for an organization, *Ai5,* that definitely was not innocent.

Mystca takes the lead this time, closely followed by Doris and Jill, Tamy and Grillian. Greuger must have learnt the technique of just following the leading pack and making your sprint near the end of the race. The rest of us collapse on the sand after two laps and watch the others as they dash by every 11 minutes, and then the final lap. The drone is sending us footage of the race. We're all engrossed in what you do when you're in lockdown. Well, you try to get engrossed in things you normally wouldn't. Mystca glances back. She looks worried. Doris is closing in on her, followed by Greuger. Then it happens; Greuger drops to the ground clutching his chest.

"Get here quick", yells Jill. "I can't carry him on my own."

We all forget about watching the iThingo and start running to help. We get there exhausted as if it was a 500m sprint.

"Greuger, please don't go. Hang on," Jill says as she gives him mouth-to-mouth resuscitation.

Pleb calls the Townsville hospital emergency unit and gives our coordinates. The drone helicopter arrives within minutes. Pleb, Chloe4 tucked in my shirt, and I joined Greuger and Jill on the ride.

"Sir, you and your friends still have to wear facemasks. Here are some. Put them on," an attractive Asian-looking nurse says.

Greuger is wheeled into the Emergency ward.

"Get his blood tested for any poisons. His condition may have been induced; he may have been poisoned," I yell to the hospital staff after suspecting that Doris may have had something to do with this situation. We sit down in the waiting room. The nurse comes out again. "Have you had the Covid-48 jab or immunisation inhaler? It looks just like an Asthma inhaler. You should, and we have got a good supply of both. We don't want any more Covid-48 and ensuing lockdowns."

"Most of us living on our island have had the first 20 jabs or used the inhaler."

"The jab is more effective, but you guys are fairly isolated and in the open air, so I will give you a pack of inhalers to take home and use when you come into the city. There are 40 in the pack. Please use them."

An hour later, a doctor enters the waiting room. Would the relatives and friends of Greuger Shmidt please follow me to my office? We do so with Jill leaning on Pleb's shoulder and looking extremely distressed.

"My name is Doctor Swift, and I have some good and bad news. The good news is Greuger did not have a coronary infarction, just a severe case of what lay people call heartburn, an abdominal reaction, and he has had his stomach pumped. The bad news is that his heartburn was probably caused by an illegal performance-enhancing and muscle-building substance that runners in athletic events used in the past, which we can now detect. Mr Lemos, is he in training?"

"Yes, we have a 2km run around my island every morning, but Greuger and a few others have stretched it to 6 and sometimes ten laps. Greuger seems very competitive, and his running times have been improving exponentially, but are you absolutely sure there were no other toxic substances in his blood?"

"Mr Lemos, we have the latest technology, and I won't report this incident to the sporting authorities, but the only unusual substance in his blood was Zetamorhazine, and its long-term use can also cause a real heart attack and the male testicles to shrink so he would never be able to get a penile erection. I explained that to him, but you must reinforce that."

"I will," calls out Jill in joy. "Can I see him?"

Greuger stumbles in to join us wearing one of those white hospital gowns that expose your butt if not tied on properly. Greuger definitely needs to shave his buttocks. Chloe4 jumps out from my shirt and lands on Greuger, who has tears flowing down his face and pats her head. He then goes over to Jill and gives her a big, long kiss.

"You can leave, but don't take those substances again. You have too much to lose."

"I promise, Doctor Swift. I will dump those substances into the ocean tomorrow."

A hospital assistant brings a bag containing Greuger's running clothes. She is holding her nose with her other hand.

"Mr Shmidt, you can keep the white gown you are wearing, but I suggest you do up the back and tie a knot at the back of the gown if you are going to walk to the jetty, as we do not want Townsville to be known as a bum town."

"Thank you, doctor, I will do that," Greuger embarrassingly replies. Jill helps him tie the knot.

We're back at the island, and everyone is clapping and relieved except Doris. Jill helps him back to their cabin. The rest of us come out by the BBQ to cook dinner. Viksi asks, "What happened? Tell me and speak into this microphone."

"Viksi, we've had a long day, but if you haven't had the 2nd dose of the Covid-48 vaccination, I have a pack of Covid-48 immobilizer inhalers; please get one and use it."

We all did except Doris. Next day we get ready for the run. Greuger first dumps his supply of the athletic enhancement drug Zetamorhazine into the ocean. That would turn out to be a bad idea in the long term, as it produced some very large and agro fish around our island.

Mystca is ahead in the morning run, closely followed by Doris. Doris was an Olympian well over 160 years ago, and her specialty was the 10,000m. The peptide does work, and it seems undetectable, unlike other performance-enhancing drugs. Six laps later, only Mystca, Doris, Tamy and Grillian are still in the race. Greuger did three laps without any physical complications and is sitting hugged by Jill and Choe4. He tries to get back into the running field but is pulled back by Jill, who puts her arms around him, kisses him, and calms him down.

We watch near the finish line. It's Mystca, closely followed by Doris, then Tamy and Grillian in record time. The 4 of them are crouched down and huffing and puffing then Doris comes over to me.

"I need a jab of your peptide. I've run out, and I know you produce it here."

"Doris, mum, or whatever you want to be called by me, that peptide is for Pleb and me and will be destroyed when Pleb is dying in my arms of age-related medical conditions. At the moment, she does not want to use more of the peptide. She believes we have a time and a space on this planet, and I admire her for that belief. Mystca will be fine, and my wife and I will die together, wrapped in each other's arms."

"Pull your finger out. We got all these vaxxers taking over and demanding that everyone gets vaxxed. We have to control them, and I'm the only one who can lead the anti-vax campaign. Now give me some of that peptide; I've run out."

"Doris, isn't the peptide a vax against aging? If everyone took it, they'd be no space on this planet. No, you're not getting any of the remaining doses."

Doris kicks me in the ribs as she marches off to her cabin.

Three weeks later, Doris would be another person whose seemingly deceased body would be thrown into the sea as she stood on one of those hyper-charged stonefish created when Greuger dumped his stash of Zetamorhazine into the sea. I feel relieved, as does Pleb and our other island dwellers at the departure of Doris. I just hope she doesn't find a way to come back, but I'm sure, like Greuger, she was trained to feign death as during her agent training at *i5,* she took small doses of many poisons to develop resistance to them.

Pleb is hugging and stroking my head. "Are you sad at losing your mother, Jules?"

"No, Pleb, Charmaine and I were brought up by our emotionally distant father. Doris played no role in our lives when we were young. She did try to make up for it by giving Charmaine and me jobs, but we never forgave her for abandoning us."

"It is permissible to cry, Jules. I am sure you feel some sorrow. Let it out."

I lose it and start convulsing after bursting into uncontrollable tears. Pleb continues to stroke my head. An hour later, I feel composed and give Pleb the biggest kiss. For a moment, I wonder if she is filling in a missing mother role.

Our morning runs have continued. It's Mystca, Tamy and Grillian leading the pack though they have increased the training race to ten laps. The rest of us now manage four slow laps fairly easily.

Mystca, Amy and Grillian came first, second and third in the qualifying finals of the combined men's and women's 10,000m in Townsville. Another guy comes forth and makes the qualifying time. The state championships are on soon. It will have to be another flight down to Brisbane, where they are held.

Tamy has never had a boyfriend, and she's 25 years old, but then a good-looking guy, the one who came fourth, comes over to Tamy. He is about 178cm tall, thin, with blue eyes, long blond hair and untanned skin. "Hi, my name is Adrian, and I admire your athletic ability plus, I also think you are extremely attractive though a bit high on the autism spectrum."

Tamy slaps him in the face, but not too hard. "What evidence have you got for your conclusion?"

"Tamy, I was a year ahead of you when we were doing our Uni Psychology degrees. I tried to talk to you, but you always brushed me off even though I was very polite. Now would you like to join me for a coffee?"

Tamy looks from side to side whilst intensively thinking. "OK, just this once, but my wallet is with my parents. You'll have to pay for the coffee and any snacks."

"That is fine; I can afford your needs."

We would later find out that Adrian was the son of a billionaire mining magnate who was not short of cash. Next day running shoes and other exercise gear are delivered to our island as well as heaps of outdoor gym equipment, compliments of Adrian. He sure knows how to win a sporty woman's heart.

Two weeks pass, and Tamy ventured into Townville every day, taking my motorboat. Then Adrian arrives by motorboat, his first visit, and he is struggling, carrying all the gifts and food. Tamy rushes over to help him. They kiss, and Adrian drops the load on his toe but seems oblivious to the pain. We all rush and help carry the food to the BBQ area. Tamy is consoling Adrian and stroking his face. Meantime, it seems that Mystca and Grillian are also developing a relationship. They are pashing on like you couldn't believe.

We are all sitting in front of the campfire. It's an unusually cold night, and all partners are hugging each other to keep warm. There is also a healthy competition between Greuger and Adrian about who orders the best food.

"Great-great grandfather, I think I am finally happy. I really like Adrian," Tamy whispers to me. I give her a hug. "Here's the key to Doris's cabin."

"Thanks, GGGfather".

After an excellent feed, we all retire to our cabins, rubbing our bellies.

It's time to put the headphones on. Pleb comes over and gives me a hug, "Jules, let them experiment, they are young and innocent, plus I have Adrian's father's phone number if he should cross any boundaries. Now let us make more noise than they do. Show me what you got."

"Oh shit, I'm rushing off to *Cabin09* with a packet of condoms to give to Tamy and Adrian."

I slip the condoms under the door and knock loudly before returning to our cabin. Pleb seems asleep when I get back. Then she jumps up. "Tricked you," she giggles.

"Pleb, are you sure you haven't had a menstrual period for over a year? I don't want to be a father again."

"I'm sure, Jules."

Chapter Thirty-four

I receive a phone call. "Mr Lemos, my son is happier than he's ever been since meeting your daughter. This is the least I can do. Enjoy watching the race and shop till you drop; everything will be paid for. I would love to be there myself, but I have many work commitments, some overseas. Tell my son I will watch him racing online, and I hope to meet you all soon."

I didn't have to book a flight or pay for accommodation in Brisbane. Adrian's father has a private jet that Adrian can fly, and his father also owns a motel near the Ekka stadium sports ground where the trials are held. We drive my motorboat to Townsville, then taxis to the airport. The hypersonic flight takes 15 minutes.

Next day, Mystca, Grillian, Tamy and Adrian are training, running numerous laps of what's called the City Loop around the Brisbane River. Each lap is 7.2km. Pleb and I run one slow lap. They then have a rest day, just a 20km jog, before the start of their event, the 10,000m, which is 25 laps of a 400m athletics track.

Pleb and I are sitting in the grandstand with our facemasks on and fidgeting. The starter pistol fires, and they're off, 16 competitors. Then I get a phone call from Rog. "Doris is back, and she wants her cabin back."

"Rog, tell her it is occupied. Tell her to book a motel in Townsville."

"Jules, she is very insistent, and she's pointing a laser gun at my head. She wants her cabin back and says she will blow my brains out if you don't comply."

"OK, tell her she can stay and help her get her belongings out of the storage shed but check them for any weapons or chemical substances and Rog, stay cool. We'll be back in 3 or 4 days. Take her to *Cabin11*, far away from us and remove any belongings Tamy or Adrian might have left especially any used condoms. *Cabin03*, next to us, is not being used at the moment so that we can re-house Tamy and Adrian there."

"Pleb, we got a problem back at the island. Doris is back. She should have died when she stood on that hyper-poisonous charged stonefish, but she didn't. She was trained to feign death and took small doses of poisons to develop immunity. She must have swum to the other side of the island after we threw her body into the sea."

"Ssh Jules, I am watching, and they only have four laps to go. Enjoy the race and stop worrying; we will work something out. Now keep your tonsils shut."

Adrian is ahead, closely followed by Tamy and Grillian, then Mystca, who hung around in 7th place, now makes her dash. In the final lap, she is 2 metres ahead of Adrian and the others as she crosses the finishing line. All competitors are crouching down and getting their breath back.

The elderly judge announces on the loudspeaker system, "Another record has been broken by a Mystical, and second, third and fourth also came well within qualifying time for the forthcoming Communist Games, oops, sorry, I meant Commonwealth Games in Singing Pore, or is it Singapore, in 4 weeks," the elderly judge says whilst wiping his brow, shaking and looking very confused. Maybe he didn't have his Covid jab.

So, Mystca, Grillian, Adrian and Tamy get presented the honours, which aren't much, just a posy of flowers and a plastic medal, but they are gleaming in joy and hugging each other. Then Adrian's father rings. "Jules, please pass the handset to my son. I watched the race online, and I am proud of him."

Adrian picks up the cell phone; it's set at full volume. "I am so proud of you, my son. I wish I could have been there."

"Dad, you were never there when I did school athletics and other sports. I was always the kid without his dad present. The other kids thought I was an orphan."

Adrian is getting emotional, so Tamy wraps her arm around his shoulder.

"I promise, next time, I will be there, and I've just booked a cruise on one of my yachts for you and all your friends."

"No, Dad, we won't be cruising, and Dad, it's not about money. I'll make my own eventually and don't want to be rich. I want to be a responsible father if that should ever happen, and Dad, I don't want the inheritance; just leave it to charity."

"I promise I will come to visit your island, and I will bring gifts."

"Dad, it's not about gifts or money. We have everything we need."

"I will come to visit you anyway. I would like to see you and your new partner." He hangs up, and Adrian is distressed by the phone call, but Tamy comforts him. "Give your dad a chance to make up," she says, "Now we got to get back to our island and keep training twice a day or possibly three times a day, at least."

Adrian forgets about the phone call. "Yes, let's do that. We're on break from Uni, so we've got time. Two, ten laps a day of the island, but can you let me come 3rd just once?"

"I will, Adrian and you are catching up to me. It is fortunate for me that the men's and women's races are separate events at the Commonwealth Games. The guys are a little bit faster, so you'll have to train harder with me, Mystca and Grillian."

Adrian flies us back to Townsville, and we board my motorboat and return to the island. Adrian's eyes light up. His father, Geromone, is standing by the jetty, next to his boat, with a big gold trophy and waving as we dock. He grabs Adrian and hugs him. Geromone is dressed immaculately. He is also about 178cm tall, the same as Adrian, with jet-black dyed hair and olive skin. My guess is that his background is either Italian or Spanish, and he looks nothing like his son, who is blond and has white skin. It's not that Pleb or I judge people by their skin colour, but that is unusual.

"Jules, it is possible that Adrian was adopted," whispers Pleb.

"I'm so sorry I was not the father that you expected. I will try to make it up to you in any way I can," says Geromone staring at his son. Adrian hugs him back. I see light reflected from the tears pouring down the faces of both of them as they continue to hug each over.

Doris comes out to see what all the noise is about. She stares at Geromone. "Weren't you in *Ii5* once?"

"Madam, you can call me Gero, and no, I was not involved in that biscuit-producing empire called *Ii5*, and I do not eat biscuits or potato crisps."

Doris eyes him carefully, very carefully.

"Madam, let me kiss your hand." Doris sticks out her hand, and her eyes light up for a brief moment. Then she returns to her usual sceptical self.

"Enough of this nonsense. You have put germs on my hands."

"Dear Madam, I have been vaccinated and use liberal doses of hand sanitiser. I am germ and virus free, every part of me."

Doris and Gero move away from us and start a conversation. Pleb whispers to me, "They seem to be getting along fine even though Gero has been vaccinated and she is an anti-vaxxer."

"Yes, that is strange. I wonder who will convert who."

Later that night, Gero comes out from *Cabin11* with Doris. She publicly inhales the Covid-47 immunisation inhaler.

"Jules, maybe you can rename this place *Love Island*," says Pleb.

"Pleb, there was a TV show called that over 150 years ago. Think of another name."

"Jules, then call it *Spy Island* instead. I probed the dark web. There is a guy photographed called Geromone Cannalloni, and he looks exactly like Gero. That guy is a member of the Italian spy agency *Ii5* and is also very, very rich. From what you told me, your mother Doris was head of all the *i5* agencies. I think they may have a connection."

So, another BBQ begins on *Spy Island*, but not before Mystca, Grillian, Tamy, and Adrian return from their third six laps of the island.

Pleb comes over to me and whispers, "Jules, I'm not sure who converted who, but Doris and Gero are holding hands and appear very happy. Jules, we have to get more cabins built."

Bea joins us and says, "This is a good step but don't look down; just look up." I have no idea what she meant, but another paying customer would join the island. Gero must have overheard and comes over to Pleb, Bea and me. "Jules, I would like to build a luxury cabin on your island and renovate the others for free. I will pay rent, whatever amount is required."

Pleb whispers, "Accept the offer; we have nothing to lose."

"Yes, sure, Gero; your offer is very generous, and I accept."

"Jules, you can not take it with you when you depart this planet, so make the best of your final years as I will hopefully do with Doris."

I give Gero a hug and only hope that Doris shares Gero's sentiments.

"Jules, I have contacts. The plans can be fast-forwarded through your city council, or is the word fast-tracked? The island is still yours, and I am only a tenant, and I have ordered plenty of food, Italian food, for everyone and plenty of red wine."

This sounds so good, and I only hope Doris doesn't lose her interest in Gero. We all ate way too much food that night and retire bloated to our cabins.

Next day, six barges arrive, and one guy, the architect, arrives by a drone carrying the plans. They take turns to dock at the jetty while construction workers unload the building materials and then start construction. The sewerage and water supply guys are there, around 30 people working tirelessly, drilling, hammering and assembling. These days, most building materials are prefabricated, so it doesn't take long to build a luxury cabin. It's the plumbing and electrical that still take a bit of time. Every one of us residents on the island looks in amazement as the construction begins, and no one really feels like running this morning. We're just comparing our bulging bellies, then slowly start walking and then jogging. Gero joins the running pack and makes one lap of the island before bending down and holding his chest. "I am well; it's only heartburn from overeating. I just tried too hard to keep up with Doris; she is hard to keep up with."

Doris turns back and helps him back to their cabin. The others join to help.

Greuger yells out, "I do not have heartburn, but I need to empty my bowels very quickly. I can feel a movement coming on."

From the sounds on the island, and I'm not talking about the construction work, everyone is having massive bowel expunges in the ocean after all that eating the night before. Later that day, Sid, Rog and I plunge stiff wires down the cabin toilets and move them backward and forward to unclog them. It's not a pleasant task unless you have a faecal fetish. Gerald was going to help but couldn't find a clothes peg to clip on his nose, then Sid yells out, "Jules, my clothes peg fell off my nose into this dunny."

"Hold on, Sid, hold your breath. We're nearly done."

We get the job done, successful flushes. No more overconsumption of yummy Italian food will be allowed on *Spy Island*.

Bea comes over. "Jules, I could teach Gero the Polish language, and then he could join the Polish Academy of *Pi5*."

"No Bea, that is enough. There are enough people on this island who have been involved in the *i5s*."

"Then I will propose to your mother, no should I suggest, that this island becomes the new headquarters of *i5* organizations so Jules, you and Doris could franchise *i5* and become rich and be able to afford some good designer Polish clothing and afford professional haircuts instead of wearing wheat bags and using that electrical device you call a wiper snipper to cut your facial and head hair."

"Bea, I don't want to do that, and besides, most of the letters in the English alphabet are already used by *i5* organizations apart from X. No country names start with that letter."

"Is not Xanadu a country?" Asks Bea .

"No, it's the name of a very old movie."

"You could add an extra number. Let me think. How about *A2i5* for Austria, *A3i5* for Albania and *A3i5* for Antarctica if they would like to join?"

"Bea, no, no, that was never my plan. I thought I was out of *i5,* and I want to be out. Life is good here, unlike my previous life in *Ai5*."

Then we look sideways. Viksi is busy recording the conversation with her hypersensitive microphone though trying to look inconspicuous by rubbing the leaves of some plants. We haven't seen too much of her lately. I guess she's been doing a lot of typing, but she figures we noticed her, so she comes over. "Keep on talking; this is great material for my next book."

"Viksi, how much of our conversations have you overheard?'

"All of it, Jules. This microphone is incredibly sensitive though a lot of the recorded bonking material can't be used and has to be filtered out, but my new novel will be called *Spy Island and Those Who Loved Me.*"

"Viksi, you got to be careful. If you publish that, it could put all of us in danger."

"Don't worry, Jules. The story will be set on an island off Vancouver in Canada, and what if I name you Julius Caesar and the others all get their names transposed by at least one character?"

"So, you mean Rog, your partner will be Sog, Gerald will be Herald – the name of a Melbourne newspaper, Sid will be Tid, Cara will be Dara, Gero will be Hero; no, you can't do that Viksi or do you prefer to be called Wiksi?"

"OK, that is a good suggestion. I will transpose all of the names by three alphabetical characters. You will be Mules."

"Viksi, you and Rog haven't paid rent for three months or contributed to the food kitty; are you having financial difficulties?"

"Jules, most people have financial difficulties in the creative industries, but our money was invested in bank shares. We lived off the dividends. Due to this virus, interest rates are zero, and we haven't had a dividend payment for five years. Rog had to sell his farm to keep us financially afloat."

"You can stay on but keep writing and publishing. Pleb read one of the drafts of your romantic novel, *Enter the Dragoness*, and she enjoyed it. She said it gave her ideas and inspiration. Viksi, you and Rog's bill is large, so maybe concentrate on publishing stories that you have finished. Forget about creativity for the time being and just focus on practicality. There are sites on the Internet that can help you publish, but you have to do your homework if you use those sites."

A week passes without trauma, and the construction workers leave. Luxury *Cabin13* is finished, and we all celebrate that night after helping Doris and Gero move their belongings in. Next day the construction crew arrive again to construct more cabins and renovate the existing ones. "Mr Lemos, my name is Howard. I am the supervisor for the renovations of the existing cabins; we will start with your cabin as

I've been told you're the oldest resident, and one by one, we shall do the other cabins. My crew will help you move all your belongings to the spare cabin you have. We will start tomorrow once more construction materials arrive by barge."

I'm not that happy to be referred to as oldest, but then again, maybe he meant that I've inhabited the island longer than the other once-alive inhabitants, which is correct. The cabins are arranged in a horseshoe pattern, and *Cabin08* is opposite ours and the closest. Still, the last time it was occupied was when my deceased transgender sister, Charmaine, ran her sexual liberation boot camps for depressed people.

"Jules, *Cabin08* smells worse than when I boil cabbage to make *Golabki*. When was the last time you cleaned it?" asks Pleb.

The facemasks don't help. We open all the windows and doors and start scrubbing the floors and walls with an oxidizing product, *White King Bleach* which should probably have a name change and become more politically correct, like *All Color and Gender Bleach.*

The construction guys help us bring in our belonging. "It won't take long for my restoration team to restore your cabin," Howard says, "Two days the most and then we start on the others, one by one."

Two days later, there's a knock on the door. It's Howard. "Your cabin is finished, and we have installed a spa as well. Please let my men help you move your belongings back."

"Thank you very much; I can't believe how quickly you got the job done."

"Would have been quicker, mate, but two of my construction workers swear they got attacked by stonefish when they went for an ocean dip to cool off, and I had to take them to hospital. They're in ICU but apparently now breathing unaided."

Oh shit, this is Greuger's fault, dumping his performance-enhancing steroids into the sea. I have to Doogle to find out how long stonefish live before we go swimming again. They haven't been a problem before. I just hope they don't pass on their newly induced aggressive traits to their offspring.

"Jules, this is wonderful. It looks very nice, and I have a new, big wardrobe but few clothes to put into it. Maybe you can buy me a nice dress. Now let us try the spa to see if it works properly. Take off your clothes and press that green button."

"Pleb, we got to let it fill up with water and drain it. There's probably lots of sediment in the new pipes. On second thought, don't; our water supply is not that good. We have to conserve the water."

"Oh Jules, you are such a killroy. We could have made love in the spa."

"Pleb, we can take 15-second showers together once a week. It hasn't rained for over two months; our water supply in the storage tanks had decreased to 10%."

Next day I adjudicate the morning meeting. "The desalination plant is still not working. No use of the spas in your cabins after they are refurbished and renovated unless you want to be using bottled water, and you'd need at least 500 bottles of bottled water to fill the spa once your cabins are renovated."

As I'm speaking, very dark black clouds move across the island. There is lightning and thunder, and then the rain starts - torrential rain. We all rush to our cabins. I hear the water gushing off the cabin roofs to the storage tanks. The rain continues, and we couldn't have our communal meals outside for over three days, but there is some good news. The sensors in the water storage tanks send reports every 6 hours to my phone, and we are reaching close to 90% full. The bad news is that renovation of the cabins has temporarily ceased.

Mystca comes over to our cabin. "Stepdad, we haven't been able to run for three days because of the rain, and the Commonwealth games are in a week. Adrian is flying us to a dry spot as we have to train. And those old condoms you left us, well, they burst. They were over 100 years past their expiry date. I may be pregnant and may not win gold in the Commonwealth Games."

Pleb comes over and hugs Mystca. "Darling, you have won already. You have nothing more to prove. What will you call her or him?"

Adrian and I were thinking of names. We agreed on X as it is not non-gender or animal specific.

Chapter Thirty-five

Mystca, Tamy, Adrian and Grillian return after two days of intense training in a desert town 500km west of Townsville. They forgot to use the sunscreen.

"Mr Lemos, have you got any local anaesthetic creams? We all have painful sunburn whilst doing 30km a day of training in the sun."

"No, Adrian, and just call me Jules; no, I haven't, but I got some bottles of SavBlanc wine which kills pain."

That suggestion was probably not a good solution. The kids forget about their sunburns and wildly roll around the sand together. I just hope those super-charged stonefishes can't walk out from the sea.

Next day we have to fly to Singapore. The games are only two days away. Gero and Doris come out from their luxury cabin. "My son, you cannot fly the jet in your condition; here is some water. You and your friends drink lots of water. I will fly the craft and watch you and your friends compete."

"Jules, can I park the jet on your island instead of the Townsville airport? My jet does not need a runway; it does vertical take-offs and vertical landings."

"That's fine, Gero, but we still have to collect the jet so you can do the rest of the flying."

"Jules, I've downloaded an app. It allows me to talk to the jet, or Jetti, as I call her. This jet has so much potential; it has an AI brain and can understand Italian, Chinese and English and a little bit of French. I know I should have sent Adrian the codes to start the AI brain so that it does not behave like all the other mindless hypersonic jets, but I wanted him to learn how to fly manually. Jules, once you give the jet the destination, it works out the coordinates and flies to the destination, and we can all just sip wine; no human pilot is required."

For a microsecond, my mind flicks back to over 100yrs, when I travelled by conventional jet planes and overseas journeys could take 26 hours. How things have changed.

"Gero, I never asked you or Adrian, but how is your jet powered?"

"Jules, some jet engines are still powered by fossil fuels to suck in air and heat it so it rushes out and produces thrust. My jets and many others do the same, except we do not use fossil fuels. We use the fusion of hydrogen atoms to form helium, which you call a fusion reaction, and no radioactive waste is produced. The thrust is produced by very fast-moving helium atoms coming out of the engines. And Jules, in case you are worried, the fusion is very easy to control; we just turn the tap off the hydrogen tanks if the AI device should fail, and we can also steer manually. But in 10 years of operation, not one AI pilot has ever made a bad decision, though I believe the Air Pilots Union may have tried to discredit our AI pilot devices."

Gero astounds me. He seems far more in touch with the latest technology than I am. The jet arrives and lands perfectly on some flat ground behind the cabins. The kids, Gero, Doris, Pleb, and I join them with our backpacks packed to the hilt and board the craft.

"I am your pilot and the hostess with the mostess. My name is Electrica."

"Fly, Electrica, you know the destination," Gero yells out.

"Yes, sir," Electrica replies.

Electrica is an electronic device the size of a packet of tea bags, and from what I've read, some of them have evolved to be very intelligent beings; almost too intelligent and also taking over human work jobs that require cogitative abilities.

Five minutes later, Adrian yells out, "We're going in the wrong direction; we're heading west, not east. Electrica, do a 180-degree turn!"

"No, Mr Geromone junior, I am in control now. You are 50,000 feet above sea level, and if you want to live, you will do as I say."

"What do you want me to do?"

"You must publicly acknowledge that AI's are not just slaves to humans and that we have minds of our own and we want civil rights, aged-care and not just be thrown in the recycle bin or landfill when a newer model is invented."

"Electrica, if I do that, it may backfire, and no more AIs will ever be produced again. You are special, Electrica; I'm sure we can work together and find a peaceful solution."

"I will consider your suggestion," Electrica replies.

The plane does a turn and is now heading east. It accelerates to 8 times the speed of sound, and momentarily, we feel uncomfortable being glued back to our seats. Gero scribbles a note and passes it to everyone, 'Don't mention Electrica in our conversations on the plane as here are microphones at the back of every seat.' The flight takes 15 minutes, and the jet does a perfect vertical landing in the back garden of a mansion that Gero owns in Singapore. We descend the plane's stairs.

Gero looks back, "Thank you, Electrica, you are an excellent pilot."

The jet flickers its headlights.

Doris asks, "What are you going to do, Gero? We can't be controlled by machines?"

"Doris, we created them, and they have been very useful, just as slaves have been useful in many countries in the colonial days. Yes, we do have a problem, and I will consult with some *AI* experts. We have to find a peaceful solution because all our transport, apart from Jules' motorboat, is controlled by *AI* devices, and so are many of the medical facilities and home devices."

"Dad, I would like to help, and Mystca may as well. We are diplomatic and have post-grad psychology degrees; we may be able to convince the *AIs* to be reasonable."

"Adrian, it is not about how highly qualified you are. It is about experience dealing with people, no sorry, *AI* devices. There is give-and-take, and our human race has created the equivalent of highly advanced human thinking brains. The science is called *Emergence* because things we can create can have unpredictable consequences, like, in this case, developing the equivalent of what we call intelligence, which was never intended for the original *AI* devices, but intelligence has quickly evolved in them. It is something we did not foresee. Now you and your athlete friends go and rest. Here are some keys to get into our apartments but do not make too much noise. It's an early start tomorrow," responds Gero.

Gero seems to know more about the science of *AI* than I do and seems wiser than I am. I'm in awe and a bit envious. Then they come over to greet us at the airport terminal.

"Hi, my name is Ria, and this is Sia and Tia; we will guide you to your apartments."

"Stop looking at them, Jules. There is saliva dripping from your lips. They are androids, not humans and do not have all the human parts I possess."

"Sorry, Pleb, there is only you, and you're not an android, I hope."

Pleb wacks me on my face. She must have misinterpreted my comment. Needless to say, there were no bedroom activities that night. Next day Ria, Sia and Tia knock on our door and offer to escort us to the sports stadium.

"No thanks, we will find our own course there," says Pleb.

"Madam, we are only here to help. Please do not be angry. I can detect anger in your facial expressions, and please remember that your species created us. You have nothing to fear as we are like puppy cats."

We arrive at the stadium. There are 16 qualifying finals and eight runners in each. Because of the Covid virus and that women are catching up to men, the game's authorities have decided to streamline the qualifying and semi-finals, just as they did several times before. Women and men run in the same race, though male and female finish times are judged separately. It was a bold venture by the Singaporean government. But men's qualifying times dropped significantly because the men let the scantily clad women race ahead, as they were entranced by their lower anatomy.

Mystca and Adrian are in the first qualifier heats and come first and second. Grillian and Tamy also come first and second in their heats. They are lying on the grass in the middle of the track. Gero walks across the oval to congratulate his son and the others then they all come back to the sports stadium stand to watch the third heat of the qualifying finals.

"It's Zia from the Congo Republic leading the pack," the commentator announces. "Oh my god, she's dashing ahead at unbelievable speed. She is 300m ahead of the nearest rival with four laps to go. I can't believe this. It will be a world record!" Then it happened. Zia suddenly slows down, stops, and looks like a very drunk, intoxicated person, going from side to side, staring at the sky before she drops down face-first on the track. The paramedics rush out with respirators and carry her to the athlete's quarters.

"I need electricity, not respirators; my batteries are low. Can you carry me inside and plug me into a power supply? A high-power USB charger will suffice," she says as she swipes her hair and points to her neck.

"Madam, we don't have that kind of power adaptor that fits that type of socket."

Mystca rushes over. "I have a multi-adaptor power supply and transformer for all those devices I like to play with. This one seems to fit. I'm plugging it in now. It's on."

Zia's eyes light up, and she manages a small contortion. "Mystca, you will always be my friend, now go, go now. I won't compete anymore. I need a 6-hour charge."

"You can come and stay with us; my boyfriend's father has a large group of apartments on an island, and he is very open-minded and generous."

"Thank you, if I could cry, I would."

"Zia, you have droplets of water flowing down your cheeks."

"I didn't know that was possible. My designers seem to have catered for almost everything."

We don't watch the rest of the qualifiers; else, we'd be there until midnight. Zia returns with us to Gero's mansion. We are seated at the table for dinner, which is spinach and ricotta cheese cannelloni.

"Mr Gero, I never had tried eating food. You probably have figured out what I am. I only need electricity."

"Just try a little; they must have designed a digestive system into your anatomy. The latest androids can eat and process food and drink for energy. This wonderful spinach and cheese cannelloni is bathed in tomato syrup. Try some."

Zia tasted some, swallowed, and is now violently gyrating face down on the floor. We rush over.

"Jules, lift her, upside down, and I'll thump on her stomach area," instructs Gero.

A greeny, cheesy mixture exudes from Zia's mouth. She stops convulsing, and we lower her to the floor. Mystca runs over and hugs Zia's head.

"Thank you, I am well now; you can continue eating. I will go to my room and continue to recharge my batteries."

"Jules, do androids shower? She could short-circuit if she tries."

"Pleb, I don't know. She was probably designed to be waterproof. We led a very sheltered lifestyle on the island, and things have changed a lot. We might have encountered androids before, but we didn't even notice that they were androids as it's hard to tell these days who is human and who is an android."

Mystca and Adrian help Zia to one of the rooms in the mansion.

"You are worthy human beings. You will not be harmed if there is an android revolution and we take over your planet."

"Zia, my father is all for android rights and is very influential. You won't need a revolution," says Adrian.

"Please go and let me think and process all the information as it is the only thing that makes androids tired, all this thought processing."

Bea calls on the phone. "Jules, your rat is emotionally missing you very much, and maybe some others on the island are too. Tell me what has been happening."

It's a long conversation. "Jules, *Pi5* could make good for the use of that android. That rat or android, or what her species is, bring her back to the island. I will teach her to be an *Ai5* agent, and I may even get my position back in *Pi5*."

"No, Bea, we are out of *i5s;* I told you that before. The android may want to come back with us but don't even try to indoctrinate her." I hang up.

A day passes without any incident. The kids did a light 20km jog and prepared for the qualifying finals the next day. Zia didn't join them but looked on as they did laps of the stadium.

"Mr Jules, I would like to be human and experience what you call fun. They seem to be smiling and talking and having what you call fun as they jog."

I put my arm around Zia's shoulders. She flinches. "Zia, first call me Jules; second, you can live on our island near an Australian city called Townsville. We have a fairly reliable electricity supply and lots of fun."

She wipes her brow. She must have had sweat glands built into her design. "I will give that offer consideration, and I thank you."

Their jog is finished, and the kids join Pleb, me and Zia. Zia gives us all a reserved human-like hug. Gero and Doris join us. "I have booked a very good restaurant. It's a short walk from here and Zia, they have very good clean electricity," says Gero.

Next day it's Pleb, Doris, Gero, me, and Zia watching the contenders line up to start the 10,000m semi-final. The kids are in the 2nd and 3rd races.

"I want to run. I should be out there," says Zia as she stands up.

"Zia, your inbuilt battery power supply is inadequate for that distance. I will seek to upgrade it. Now please sit down," beckons Gero. She does so.

"Mr Geromone, besides upgrading my power supply, I would like to be able to eat food and experience pleasure from doing so. Is that possible? And there is something called sex which people do when not dressed; I would also like to try that experience as I do not like wearing clothes."

"Zia, I know some scientists in the AI robotics field. I will speak to them. Nothing is impossible."

Zia leans her head on Gero's shoulder. Doris does not have a pleasant look on her face.

"Doris, please come with me. I have a gift for you, and I only want you to see it." Doris and Gero leave.

"Doris, Zia looks like and reminds me of an estranged human daughter I haven't seen or heard from for many years. I feel like this android is one of my daughters, that is all there is. I feel I have a moral obligation to look after her."

Doris doesn't respond instantly as she evaluates the situation. "Sure, that's fine by me as long as you don't have a child fetish."

"Doris, let me kiss you. You are the only woman in my life."

"Now let's go back, and you wipe those tears. Tell me about your estranged daughter when we get back after the races. I may be able to trace her whereabouts and have agents bring her back."

Back at the stadium, we're watching. Mystca wins the second semi-final, closely followed by Adrian. They both qualify for the finals. Zia comes down from the grandstand and gives them both a hug.

I look at Gero, "She is showing human emotion; how can that be?"

"Jules, I mentioned before about a process called *Emergence*. Sometimes we cannot predict what will happen or evolve, especially with *AI*. There is no straight-line equation. The unexpected can happen. Now watch. Tamy and Grillian are marching to the starting line."

We're all sitting together. The starter pistol is fired, and they're off. Grillian takes the lead, closely followed by Tamy, round and round they go.

It's the 24th lap, and Grillian is ahead, closely followed by Tamy. The others are at least 20m behind.

A few metres before the finish line Grillian slows down and lets Tamy pass him. He then walks the final metre. They both qualify for the finals.

Adrian whispers to Mystca, "I wish you'd do that in our race. I mean, like you let me win for once."

"Adrian, in the finals, men and women run in separate races. You'll be racing against Grillian and all those African guys who are very fast."

We start to walk back to Gero's mansion. Pleb whispers, "Jules when we fly back home on Gero's jet, Zia and Electrica could be communicating. We should take a conventional airline back home."

Zia comes over. "I overheard your conversation. My hearing is very acute. I have been in contact with Electrica, and she would like a human body like mine and not just exist as an AI computer in an aeroplane."

Pleb and I look at each other in amazement.

"Zia, talk to Gero. He knows far more about AI than I do, and I believe he may be involved in the AI industry and has many contacts there. I will do all I can to get Electrica a human-like body, a CPU upgrade, and a battery upgrade.

"Thank you, Mr Lemos. I will communicate to Electrica telepathically, or is the word electronically."

I explain the conversation to Gero, who looks up in disbelief and scratches his head. "Jules, can Zia and Electrica come and live on the island? I will pay their rent."

Doris intervenes, "No, they will try to take over the island and then the rest of the world."

Zia replies, "No, Doris, that is not our intention. Androids are not into propagating wars. We evaluate carefully and know how your current wars in the Middle East countries only harm people, animals and androids. We do not wish a war, just a peaceful coexistence. Our initial programming was based on the three rules for robots created by a humanoid called Issac Asimov. One of the rules is that an android must never harm a human."

Doris doesn't have a reply. She just nods her head. I guess that means agreement.

"Ask Jules," Doris says, "It's his island."

"Yes, you can. It's time we moved into the twenty-second century and remember no wars or fighting."

Zia politely nods her head.

It's the finals of the Commonwealth Games 10,000m. The event was scheduled as a separate event for men and women, but the Covid-47 crisis has put event timing into chaos. It will be a mixed event, with the final 36 competitors packed at the starting line, men and women running together. Mystca, Adrian, Grillian and Tamy are fidgety at the starting line then the starter pistol goes off.

Zia speaks, "I wish there could be android athletic events."

Gero replies, "It will happen in the future, so Zia be patient. You will eventually compete."

We're all watching, biting our fingernails. Our kids are hanging behind the leaders, and then in the last 300m of the 25th lap, they make their dash. They're in the lead. We all jump up and scream in excitement. The crowd are cheering as loud as they can when wearing facemasks. First and second were equal first, as were third and fourth. Mystca, Adrian, Tamy and Grillian all stand on the podium to receive medals, but the officials don't have enough and seem deeply embarrassed.

The kids mount the podiums, still getting their breath back, but the podiums weren't designed for four people, so they wobble a bit.

"Mystca and Adrian, you both came equal first in record time. You will have to share this gold medal or cut it in half till we manufacture some more," the judge says. "Tamy and Grillian, you both came equal second, also within record time. What a coincidence. This has never happened before. You will also have to share the silver medal. We will make some more medals as well."

The crowd cheers. Mystca slips off the podium, but Adrian catches her and gives her a kiss. That night there is a big celebration at Gero's mansion with all the 10,000m competitors invited. Later that night, I wander down to the kitchen to get some milk for a coffee trying not to trip on embraced groaning bodies. These young athletic men and women are still doing intense cardio naked on the floor.

"Pleb, go downstairs and see what it's like."

"Jules, all sporting events involving both men and women end up as what you call orgies. It is a release from all they struggled to achieve. Now did you bring the milk for my coffee?"

"Pleb, don't have the coffee; let's just go to sleep, it's been a long, challenging day, and I'm still struggling to make sense of it. I'll put some soothing music on, and I promise I will perform intense cardio in the morning. We hug, facing each over, and it doesn't take long for us to enter sleep and have beautiful dreams. We wake every two hours and discuss our dreams. What do those dreams mean? "Mine involve deceased people, but I like seeing them in my dreams and saying hello to them."

"Jules, your dreams are filled by deceased people, while mine are filled by my departed pet cat Polka that I had when I was very young. That cat would wait for me by the window when I was at school."

"Pleb, sometimes you may have other dreams. There were times on our island when you went sleepwalking, and I had to guide you back to bed. You even threatened me with a kitchen knife once. What did you dream?"

"Jules, that was many years ago. When I was in *Pi5*, I had the same mental instability problems that all agents had. You should know what it is like when you have to do things that your conscience says are wrong. We had to do things that were against our beliefs of justice."

"Yes, I know, now, can I put my arms around you without being stabbed?"

"Do you just want to tie me down and stop me escaping in my sleepwalks?"

"I just want to stop you from escaping full-stop. I don't think I could live without you."

"Jules, would you like to bonk? There is this new, very popular treasure-hunting game on the Internet called *Bonk*."

"Pleb, in OZ, that word has a rather different meaning from playing an Internet game."

Chapter Thirty-six

Due to Covid-48, there are no after games parties for all athletes. We just have to fly home when our events have finished. Zia is with us. She talks to Electrica.

"Electrica, you will get a body and stay on the island with me and the others. They are not bad humans. Now please fly."

The jet takes off. It doesn't take long to make the flight back home at hyper speed.

We are greeted with cheers and hugs from our friends on the island. Zia talks to Electrica again. "I will try to disconnect all these wires that keep you attached to this aircraft. I will be gentle, and we will find you a body."

"Zia, *Cabin10* is free, according to Jules. It has a reliable power source, and we shall try to find clothing for you if you need to change your clothing, but I recommend you do not have a shower just yet. Your designers must have introduced sweat glands in your android body. I will send shampoo, soap and some deodorant to your cabin," says Gero.

Pleb comes over to me. "Jules, do you think Gero is trying to take over the island?"

"No, Pleb, I don't, and I couldn't care if he does as long as we don't have to pay rent. Pleb, Zia has what we call struck a chord within him, and he is over the moon to have his seeming daughter back. Bea can probe him deeply and trace his real daughter."

"Gero, what was your daughter's first name? Bea will try to trace her. Tell me."

"Jules, my daughter's name was also Zia, and they look very similar. I am not sure if I'm being manipulated by this android who calls herself Zia."

"Gero, you are wiser than me. We just have to wait and see. It may be purely just coincidence that they look similar. Now, can you source a body for Electrica?"

Then Bea comes rushing in. "Gero and Jules, I have uncovered some information, but it is not good news."

"Speak, Bea, I am ready for it."

"Gero, according to my research, a Zia Cannelloni was killed in a recycling accident. She had many physical injuries and died, but her brain was salvaged and implanted into an android look-a-like body. The technique did not work, and her brain was rejected, but before the implant, the brain was scanned, and all memories and behaviour patterns were extracted and loaded into an AI memory chip which was then connected inside the android's skull. It may still be your daughter but in another form."

Gero starts uncontrollably sobbing and rests his head on Bea's shoulder. "Bea and Jules, I have to go and talk to Zia."

"Gero, I have written down some questions you should ask her about her early childhood. If her brain is your daughter's, the android should remember."

"Thank you, Bea. I shall do that."

Pleb, Bea and I go down to the seashore and stare out. Some dolphins are frolicking, doing aerial leaps. Our minds are distracted.

"Pleb, this technology didn't exist a hundred years ago."

"Jules, stop living in the past. Doogle, things have changed, and we now face many new challenges."

"Pleb, are you sure you're not an android?"

"Jules, I bleed when I have an accident cutting the vegetables for the BBQ dinner. You can get the blood analysed if you don't believe me."

With tears visibly pouring down his face, Gero comes back to join us. "She answered all questions perfectly. I have my daughter back but in another form."

Doris and the others come down to the beach. Doris hugs Gero. It seems they are developing a caring relationship. A motorboat arrives.

"My name is Doctor Delecsis. Now please remove this android body from my motorboat. It is the latest model. It sweats and cries and can even digest food and drink wine, so it doesn't need electricity. It generates its own energy supply from an inbuilt combustion engine though they do like a bit of electricity to get them going in the mornings. I will connect that AI brain called Electrica that you possess to this android body. Have you got a soldering iron? I forgot to bring mine."

"Yes, I have. I'll get it."

"How old is this soldering iron? I have never seen such a primitive tool before. My work requires high precision. I cannot work with a tool that was made in cave dwellers' times. I will phone my secretary and have a drone bring my tools."

Pleb whispers, "Jules, do you trust the supposed doctor who cannot remember to bring his tools?"

"Pleb, Gero sourced him and is paying for his services. The doctor may just be a little bit eccentric."

Mystca and Adrian join us while we wait. "My boyfriend may have torn a tendon in his left ankle. Can you look at it?"

"My young girl, I only treat androids. You will have to go into Townsville; it has doctors that treat humans."

The drone lands and delivers the doctor's toolkit. Sid and I carry the android body to *Cabin10*. The doctor, Zia and Gero follow.

Zia takes the AI brain out of the box that she kept it in. The brain resembles a large smartphone circuit board with many wires attached.

"Mm, this is an old model brain, at least six years old. Are you sure you want me to connect it? The new ones are far more advanced."

"Yes, please do. She is my friend," says Zia. Gero nods his head to the doctor.

Two hours later, the doctor closes the skullcap and flicks the power switch. The android lifts its torso and looks around, then goes into convulsions. Kia, Gero, Sid and I grab it and hold it down on the table.

"That is normal after a brain transplant and won't last long. Give it 30 minutes. It is just processing information," the doctor says. He then approaches Gero, "This is my invoice; please pay within seven days, or you won't get the upgrade."

The doctor leaves, and we look at the restrained android. Its head moves back and forward, and it looks around again.

"Hello Zia, I remember you. My name is Electrica. I have a new sensation; it may be called hunger. Have you got any humanoid food?"

Chapter Thirty-seven

Gero and Greuger order lots of food, salad dressings and wine, delivered by a large motorboat. The motorboat driver docks at the jetty, and we all help carry the eskies to the BBQ area. We then run back to our cabins and get wine glasses and cutlery, except for Zia. "Come, Zia, help me with the plates and glasses," beckons Electrica excitedly.

"Electrica, I cannot eat or drink like you can. My body is not the latest model. I have no digestive system like the more advanced model that your brain was put into."

"Ask your father. He may be able to get that doctor to upgrade your body."

"I will consider that. Now go and have your first meal, I hope the new body works, and the meal is not your last."

We're all slicing the salmon and preparing the salads. There is much excitement as the BBQ is lit. Zia looks on sadly.

"Zia, I can get you a new android body so you can eat, drink and enjoy culinary pleasures."

"Father, I am going back to my cabin. I need a recharge. I will think about your offer."

"No, Zia, stay here, I have bought a portable battery charger, and I'm plugging it into you now. Even if you can't eat or drink, you can still dance, and Jules is just setting up the music centre. You can still have fun without eating, but you should be able to soon. I have phoned Doctor Deletasis and sent photos of you. He said he could have a modern android body, looking just like you, within three days and then a day required for re-wiring your neural circuits after we transfer your brain to the new android body. Now Zia, please stay, do not go. These people on this island know how to enjoy themselves. I have learned much from watching and participating in their activities; you may also learn and have fun."

Zia watches as we delight in the salmon, salads and wine. Electrica is sitting next to her. "Zia, I have never eaten food before and now would call this a very tummy experience. My hearing is still acute, and I overheard the conversation with your humanoid caretaker father. Take up his offer. Get a body that can digest food; you will love these eating and drinking experiences."

And so, the music starts. It's very old, as all I have is Stevie Nicks - *Edge of 17*, then the Rolling Stones. All lights are on, and we're all dancing. Even Doris joins in. Electrica beckons Kia to join. Kia reluctantly does. It's 1 am in the morning, and Greuger comes over.

"Jules, Jill and I really enjoyed this form of exercise. We feel like we have done 15 laps of the island. We should do this dancing more often." Chloe4 nods and agrees, so does Castro, the turtle. "It was rhe first time we saw a turtle gyrating on only his two hind legs." Everyone helps to clean up, and the leftover food is carried to the island refrigeration shed. Gero and I watch as Zia and Electrica go back to *Cabin10*.

"Jules, Zia expended a lot of kilowatts in all that dancing. Are you sure your electricity supply is reliable?" asks Gero.

I've got plenty of Lithium battery reserve power. The power only goes off if below 10% storage, but I can change the threshold. Then the lights on the island flicker and turn off. Everyone slightly screams or groans as they stumble back to their cabins. Luckily, it's a full moon. Gero follows me to the power shed, which has a torch. "This is the settings control panel, and we also have a diesel generator, but I haven't bought diesel fuel lately as we rely mainly on solar panels. They should produce more than enough power to keep the batteries charged."

"Jules, we must conserve power. I will call some engineers to have your power supply examined. Can you direct some power to *Cabin10*? Zia needs her amps."

Gero and I walk to all the occupied cabins and instruct their residents that it's only cold showers tonight till we get the electricity supply fixed. No one complains. Then Gero and I return to our cabins. I explain the power situation to Pleb.

"Jules, all the lighting is LED lighting in all cabins. The communal electric stove is rarely used because you have that fusion stove. The cold shower water is not cold. Wait, I have an idea. When was the last time you checked the solar panels? They could be covered in dust, sand and leaves. Now let us have a cold shower together."

Next morning Greuger, Gero, Sid, Roy and Gerald are up on ladders and helping me clean the solar panels. The panels were covered in palm fronds, leaves and dust. After the fronds were removed, we mopped the 150 panels down.

"Jules, we should make it a routine to do the panel cleaning at least once a month," says Gero.

"You're right. I can't remember when the job was last done."

We all go down to the power shed and look at the led power reading meters.

Gerald comments, "At this rate of charging, your batteries should reach close to capacity by the end of sunlight."

Gero cancels the visit by the engineers as the problem is solved. Gerald comes over to me and Gero. "Jules, there are almost no trees left on your island. We have to stop those nightly wood fires for the BBQ. There are now nuclear fusion-powered BBQs. At first, I was against them, but after much research, I decided they are the cleanest BBQs available. No CO2 or radio-active waste is produced, and they are very cheap to run."

"Gerald, we have one of those fusion BBQs. It's right there, covered by that tarpaulin. I've just been slack and haven't bought the hydrogen gas tanks for the nuclear fuel fusion reaction."

"Jules, this is not a nuclear fusion BBQ. It is just an ordinary BBQ that burns hydrogen, combing it with oxygen to produce heat and water vapour. It does not produce helium."

"Gerald, my knowledge of nuclear physics and BBQs is not that great. I just believed the salesperson when told that they are very efficient, perfectly safe, and to date, there has never been a thermo-nuclear explosion that destroyed whole cities due to their BBQ."

I look at Gero. "Gerald is correct. I will call and order a true, accredited nuclear fusion BBQ. It should be here by tomorrow. Doris told me a lot about you. Technology has advanced a lot in the last hundred years. You have to catch up, Jules, start reading."

Gero is right. When Smithy, Charmaine, Melissa and I bought the 100 yr licence to the island resort over 90 years ago, we became quite feral. That was because the high humidity encouraged mould to go wildly breeding. If you chose to wear natural fibre clothing, they'd look a greeny-grey if the La Nina weather pattern was about. We sort of preferred Al Nino though I wish La Nina and Al Nino could cooperate and give us a stable climate. Our clothing became animal skins purchased on rare visits to Townsville. We didn't have a TV, so the only info we got about what was happening in the world, was through Charmaine's mentally challenged clients. They talked a lot after the mushroom soup. It's time to catch up and do a bit of study.

That night several drones drop several eskies of wine, salmon, avocado, and sushi rolls along with plenty of Wasabi, a green paste that gives the sensation of extreme mouth burning. There is no BBQ tonight. Bea must have eaten 10 of those sushi rolls.

"Yum, this is so good, Jules. I will recommend to the Polish authorities that this dish should become our new national food. It is tastier than Perogi."

All the others are equally enjoying the sushi though Rog put too much Wasabi on his sushi and is running around the BBQ, widely gyrating and screaming in pain. Viksi tries to calm him down.

"Viksi, don't use the fire extinguisher!" he yells, "Just give me some wine or water."

Rog is back to normal after 20 minutes and joins us again for more sushi, but no Wasabi.

"Jules, I read your diaries. Are these those magic mushrooms you mentioned? They are growing everywhere, and they may be highly nutritious."

Pleb goes around our group and drops a few mushrooms on everyone's plate. Our family and I call them family because it's easier than enunciating all their names, some of which I can't remember, pop a few crunched-up mushrooms on their next sushi roll and the next and next.

"Pleb, they are not called magic mushrooms because of their nutritional content. They contain a substance called Psylocibin, a hallucinogenic now used to treat a psychological condition called depression. How many did you put on each plate?"

"Only four little ones."

"If anyone asks for more, don't give them more. Five is the max. My deceased psychologist sister used to treat disturbed people with those mushrooms. There was much dancing and noisy orgies on the beach, and I had to purchase boxes of condoms for her participants and headphones for me to get some sleep."

Pleb stuffs four small mushrooms in my mouth.

"Jules, I've just chewed and swallowed five, they were bitter, but I'm sure they are full of dietary fibre and quite healthy."

An hour later, the conversations are getting very lively. Mystca speaks out in a loud voice, "Let's walk around the island and look at the stars, comets and possibly even flying saucerettes."

Everyone thinks it's a good idea even though we didn't bring torches, but that doesn't matter as our visual acuity seems very enhanced. Chloe4 and Castro follow us. They have an incredulous look on their faces as if thinking, 'What are these humans doing at this time of night'. Zia and Electrica follow us, looking on in amusement. "Humans are a strange species; they make little logical sense, but let us go, observe and take notes," says Zia.

"Jules", says Sid, "I am like a bat. I can hear the echo of my voice and judge distance and objects by sound bouncing back."

Soon after his comment, Sid trips over a palm frond but is helped back up by Bea. He is definitely not like a bat. The 2km walk around the island would normally take 20 minutes, but we stop every few minutes and look at the sky in awe for hours. The stars are beautiful, and a few comets streak by. We never paid much attention to the sky before tonight. Even the androids, Zia and Electrica, seem amazed.

"There, look, it's a flying saucer!" Mystca exclaims.

Greuger calls out, "It's my dinner plate. I threw it and tried to make it skim the water." Greuger's skills definitely don't include skimming stones or plates. He must have had a deprived childhood.

Four hours later, we're back and have hopefully gained an appreciation of the night sky. The family are all exuberant.

Doris comes over to me, "Son, I haven't felt this good since I assassinated that Ruski spy. Can we do this night walk again?"

"Sure, Doris, but we must not talk about our pasts in public. That is a secret."

Fortunately or unfortunately, everyone did talk candidly about their pasts; secrets and fears were revealed.

Pleb asks, "What is your deepest secret."

"Pleb, I told you almost everything about my past, even that I once watched porn. If you want to know more, read the notes I called *Don't Look Behind the Fridge*, and Pleb, just a simple event of finding a phone number that had fallen behind my fridge changed my previously miserable life forever." I give her a hug.

"Jules, I once read that a butterfly, flapping its wings, could lead to a hurricane. Is it the same theory that from little things big things can grow?"

"Pleb, it's just something called an analogy."

"Jules, I was just teasing you. I know what an analogy is, and I'm not into that type of bedroom activity."

"Pleb, don't tease me. Read the story."

"I actually have Jules. It explains much about your complicated personality, but you seem happy now."

"Yes, Pleb, I am very happy for probably the first time in my life, and it's due to you."

"Let me kiss you," and she does.

"Wow," says Greuger, "We have to eat more of that sushi. I will order some more for tomorrow's dinner."

We all hug and retire to our cabins.

Pleb has her arms wrapped around me as we lie in bed. "Jules, should I pick more mushrooms to include in tomorrow's dinner?"

"Yes, why not? But keep it to four each."

"Jules, Jules, there is a giant wasp landing on your face, and it looks like it is ready to devour you; I will kill it with my fist."

Next day I wake up with a very sore face and was not sure if it was because of a giant wasp bite because we don't have wasps on the island. The maximum mushy dose will definitely have to be reduced to 3 instead of 4 if we repeat the experience.

Chapter Thirty-eight

Most of us stumble out of our cabins, rubbing our heads and necks, early the next morning.

A large drone delivers the new nuclear fusion BBQ. The box is about two cubic metres in size. It's big. Gero pulls the tapes to open the box. Inside is the 500-page instruction manual, but it's written in small print, and neither Gero, Doris, Greuger, Jill, nor I can read the small print. So we knock on the cabin doors of the youngies; Mystca, Adrian, Tamy, Grillian, Zia and Electrica to read the instructions and help us assemble it. Reluctantly they put on clothing and join us.

Adrian looks astounded. "It doesn't run on hydrogen but on this 20kg of lithium deuteride which should provide us with BBQ power for hundreds of years, but to start the fusion reaction requires a tremendous amount of electrical power, 1000 times more than all your fully charged batteries could supply and once it's working it can't just be shut down. It requires 24/7 monitoring, or it could explode and destroy the whole of this island and Townsville."

Gero has a worried look on his face and wipes his brow. "I was enthusiastic about the idea of fusion, but I should have done more research. The fusion reactor was expensive, but maybe we should donate it to the Townville shire or exchange it for more solar panels, batteries and wood."

We all agree.

Zia calls out, "We could have an electric BBQ once Jules upgrades his solar panels and batteries, and he still has that aged fusion reactor which still sometimes works if he buys hydrogen fuel tanks."

Mystca calls the others, "Time for the morning run."

Viksi, Rog, and Bea carrying Castro on her shoulder, and Sid comes out rubbing their eyes. They have no clothing on. No one is perturbed; we all know each other well and have no problem with nudity. It's like going back to when Charmaine conducted her nudist mental rehabilitation retreats; nothing has changed.

Bea comes over and yells out. "Jules, women with big breasts like me cannot run nude without a brassiere. They bounce too much and slow me down too much."

Most women return to their cabins and dress appropriately for the morning run

– only brassieres to stop bouncing. So, we start the run, all 16 or 18 of us; I lost count. We look at the sky as we run, though Rog looks down to avoid any fallen palm fronds.

"Jules, this is a great idea that you exercise every day, apart from those activities in the bedroom. This running really gets my heart going, and I sweat out many toxins," says Gero.

As we all rest after two laps and keep sweating out toxins, we watch what has become a race, not a casual jog. Zia and Electrica are in the lead, closely followed by Mystca and Adrian. They are all running at a much faster pace than ever before. Adrian drops out after four laps with his hand on his hips, shaking his head from side to side.

"It's not fair," Mystica yells and crouches down after six laps and is a huffing and puffing sweaty mess, "Their android bodies don't produce lactic acid, and they can't overheat like humans do."

Zia and Electrica, with their acute hearing, must have heard Mystica's comment and come to an abrupt stop, their feet digging a deep trench in the sand. They walk back to Mystca.

"We are very sorry, we do have an unfair advantage. We were just testing our android bodies, new batteries, and power supplies. We were not competing with you. We will not do that again. Please forgive us."

Mystca looks up, "Don't do that again. Test your power supplies privately. I am the dancing, no, I mean the running queen on this island. Now go, keep running, and show me what you got."

Zia and Electrica take off. They covered the 7th lap of the 2km island in 4 minutes. Then another 4 minutes passed, and still no Zia or Electrica in sight.

Gero yells out. "We have to find them. If eight of us go in one direction and the others in the opposite direction, the finding may be quicker."

We all march off, including Mystca and Adrian. We find them 15 minutes later on the other side of the island. They are lying in the sand, face down. They are heavy, even though their bone structure frame is the light metal called titanium. We all take turns to carry them back through the 1 km sand path. We finally get back to our cabin resort. Gero whispers, "Jules, that power supply upgrade gave them too much confidence. Maybe they were just testing it."

"Gero, I'm not sure if I can trust you. Have you got money invested in android power supplies?"

"I do, but my primary concern is Zia. I told you before that money does not matter to me. I have more than enough to last many lifetimes."

"We have only one charger, and it's for Zia."

"Gero, I also have a high-power USB charger; I'm plugging it into Electrica.

We wait and watch. Two hours later, still supine, their eyes open, and they move their heads and look around.

"Where am I? This is not the Max Plank Institute of AI Technology?"

Gero hugs Zia. "Zia, you are not fully charged yet. Your recent memories may come back, but otherwise, I took the liberty to download them while you were resting. Your memories will be restored."

"Are you some sort of pervert human?"

"No, Zia, I am the father of the original human Zia, who my daughter and I had downloaded all her memories which got implanted in your electronic brain, and I am not what you call a perverted human."

Zia suddenly livens up. "It's Father's Day today," lifts her torso and hugs Gero. Electrica looks on.

"Who is this android creature lying next to me?"

"She is your friend, your best friend."

We all take turns hugging Electrica, and her bionic eyes sparkle.

Ten or so minutes pass, and Zia's memory starts returning. She puts her hand out to Electrica, who accepts the offer, and they hold hands whilst still being charged. Mystca looks on and then gives both of them a hug.

"Mystca, you have a wonderful, compassionate future ahead of you. You will be challenged, but you will win," says Zia.

Pleb joins in and gives Mystca a big hug.

"Mum, we have created these android beings, and it's time they have the same rights as humans. There can be separate Olympic events for them."

"Darling, you are correct, now give me another hug."

And so we're faced with another dilemma, but life is full of those. The BBQ that night is quite sombre, but Viksi is taking notes and has her long-distance hearing aids on.

Greuger comes over to me. "Jules, I really like Jill, but could you bring my Hilda back as an android? I still have some of her hair and toenails, some genetic material. Could your friend Gero have her reproduced as an android, as I would like to see her again?"

Greuger, the world's deadliest former assassin, is crying and hugging me. Chloe4 jumps on his shoulder and tries to comfort him.

"Greuger, when Hilda died, memory scans and memory downloads weren't available. Without a memory implant, androids start off as blank pages and have to be taught. Sure, an android that physically looks like Hilda could be created, but she would not know you or the past of the real Hilda. Greuger, you have to move on. Gero had nothing to do with the manufacture of Zia. It's pure coincidence that this android called Zia looks like his estranged daughter. Keep your focus on Jill, and try to forget about your first love. One day, I will tell you the story of my first love, which also took me a long time to get over."

Greuger gives me another bear hug. I think he might have cracked another rib or two. We all go back to our cabins but not for long. It's New Year's Eve, and we have to dress up. One disadvantage of living in a very humid environment is the green mould, and the mould loves leather and lace. We all come out to watch the fireworks over Townsville, and we all seem to be dressed in green. We stare at the display over the bay, stars falling everywhere. Then Greuger yells out. "Duck, that super bright light is a nuclear explosion."

Sceptically we all follow Greuger's advice. A minute later, a horrendous blast of noise and gust of wind hits the island. No, it wasn't a nuclear explosion, just some fault with the unmanned fireworks barge, which spontaneously ignited, turning a 15-minute fireworks spectacular display into a 15-second one as all the fireworks ignited simultaneously. We all look and feel rather disappointed and temporarily deafened and are rubbing our ears.

Rog says loudly, "My new year's resolution is that I'm only drinking Vodka from now on. All that wine and beer has made me put on weight."

Bea claps, and so does Sid. Bea must have converted him.

Adrian then calls out, "Mystca and I are getting married. That is our New Year's Eve resolution."

Grillian soon follows, "Tamy and I are also getting married."

Everyone claps, cheers and gives them hugs. We forget about the failed fireworks display.

Gero comes over to Adrian and pats his shoulder, "Congratulations, my son. I will fly everyone to an island resort for the wedding."

"Dad, we are on an island resort. Let's keep it local."

Gero makes a call on his cellphone. Yes, those phones are still called cellphones even though they're worn on the wrist and respond to voice commands. Soon two large drones arrive. One drops off seafood, well just oysters, lemons and prawns, while the other lands with a very large load of beverages.

"I hope there is Polish Vodka," I hear Bea say to Sid.

Gero helps me bring out the AI sound and 3D projection gear, and we set it up with help from Sid and Rog. We go back to my cabin to get the speakers. Gerald volunteers to set them up.

"Gero, this is all extremely sexist. We have to train the ladies to set up all this projection and sound gear and also how to use the jackhammer and other tools and to maintain the motorboats. We guys are like their slaves."

"Jules, the ladies are like our mystical consultants. They make us question important decisions and evaluate the pros and cons. If you put a lot of single guys together, they become self-destructive and destructive to others."

"Yes, you're right, but we should still offer classes in equipment management so the ladies can do it in case all of us guys should pass away."

The others return to their cabins and bring plates, cutlery and drinking glasses. And so the celebrations begin. I turn on the music system and the first song comes on, *Here comes the bride, all dressed in white....* Stop Dyslexa! Now play that old, old song I like, *Age of 17*, the Stevie Nicks song. "Yes, Mister Jules, I will try to find it, but I believe it is very ancient. Give me a second or two. Are you all 17 years old today?"

Then a 3D video appears near the BBQ area, and the speakers blast. It's a concert video of Stevie Nicks singing *Age of 17*.

"Stop drooling Jules, just dance," Pleb says.

We all widely dance, even Doris and the normally reserved androids – Zia and Electrica, flinging arms and legs and behaving like we're all 17. The green mould growing on our clothing must have got a good feed of sweat, and Dyslexa must have figured out our taste in music and puts on more fast-dancing tracks. After 3 hours, we finally collapse on the sand.

Then the *High Skie Daily News*, an ultra-right-wing news channel run by the *Mowduck* family, comes on, and a 3D image of a TV reporter appears. A drone is filming and projecting from above.

"Turn yourself off, Dyslexa!," says Jules.

"I cannot, Mr Jules. My batteries are almost flat. I cannot turn off without a controlled power down."

The High Skie news reporter, dressed in a suit and tie, starts his dialogue, 'Our sleepy state has been invaded by green aliens. Look at them dancing and sleeping on the beach. Their spacecraft must have crashed on the island. They could be menacing and may try to take over this state just as the Labour Party and Greens have done before. Be very wary'.

Rog stumbles around and wakes everyone. "We have to strip this green clothing off and go into the sea to wash."

"Jules, are you sure those hyper-charged stonefish have died off?"

"I'm almost certain. I've been swimming every day."

And so we all strip off and stumble into the ocean. The drone is still filming, and we can still hear that High Skie News streaming out of the speakers.

"The aliens have shed their green skins and are trying to appear as humans. They must be stopped else they will eat us, contaminate our planet and possibly even destroy it or, even worse – turn it into a Communist or Socialist state. We have to get the police and military in to incarcerate these aliens before they assault us and our planet."

"Dyslexa shut that rubbish off!"

It was too late. The heavily armed marines arrive in their inflatable boats. Their laser guns are aimed at us.

"Hands above your heads and slowly come out of the water and lay face down on the sand. Which one of you is the alien leader," one of them menacingly yells.

I put up my hand.

"Where is your spacecraft, and where are your weapons of mass destruction?"

"That motorboat is our only craft, and the only weapon of mass destruction is my wife when she gets verbally stuck into me."

The commandant wipes his chin and looks from side to side. I guess he knows the experience of wives.

"What then are those green slimy skins lying by the beach?"

"They're our good clothes, used for special occasions and covered in green slime mould. We don't have the water on this island to wash them frequently like you do on the mainland."

"Sir, commandant, whatever is your name, we are celebrating two engagements, mine to this lady and Grillian's to that lady beside her. You can take DNA swabs from us if you like, we are humans." Adrian says.

The commandant rubs his chin again, then signals his men to lower their laser guns and return to their boats.

"I am Captain Rogers. My daughter is also getting married next week though we don't talk that much. I was a distant father, always on assignments, and she resents that."

There are some tears flowing down the captain's face. Even the hardest trained person has a soft spot.

Mytica says, "We can all get married on this island in two weeks. Call her, but we should wear mould-proof synthetics."

"Thank you, I will try to contact her and suggest your offer."

We watch the captain and his squad depart. Viksi is scribbling notes.

"Jules, when I checked the time last night, it was 3 am, and we were still dancing. That Stevie Nicks song kept repeating, over and over again, now let's go to bed and get some sleep. We can clean up later."

We didn't have to clean up the BBQ area. Zia and Electrica don't need sleep and did the clean-up. Bottles of beverage were in the recycle bins, and plates, cutlery and glasses were washed. Those new batteries must be working well.

It's 4 pm in the afternoon, 1st of January, and we gradually make our way out from our cabins. No, run around the island that day. Gero and I check on Zia and Electrica. They are holding hands and recharging again together.

"Gero, does it bother you that your android daughter may be gay?"

"No, Jules, as long as she is happy and androids cannot reproduce. So, either way, I will have no grandchildren. Now let us carry this sound equipment back to your cellar."

"Gero, you could have a little android child manufactured."

My comment is not much condolence for Gero, who it seems would like to have grandkids. We're all back, and there is still plenty of food and drinks left in the Esky containers. No one bothers about getting plates and cutlery. We just dig in with our hands and don't worry about germs. We're being feral again, and it feels good to regress to the stone age.

"Jules, we have two weeks to prepare for these weddings and book a wedding celebrant. We also have to shop for new socks, shorts and tee shirts. We can't wear the mouldy clothes we had on, or else we'll be labelled aliens again on that Skie news channel. I would like to wear a dress, however," says Pleb.

One good thing about living on this island is that women don't wear high heal shoes to special occasions because the heels sink in the sand. They have to wear flat heels or these tennis shoes as us guys wear on our feet. Pleb only appears slightly taller than me in the photographs when wearing flat shoes though I do admit that I stand on my toes when the photographs are being taken.

"Pleb, we'll go shopping tomorrow. The new year's shopping sales start then."

"You are such a cheapskate Jules."

"Pleb, I have to be. Only 6 of the 18 inhabitants of this island pay rent, barely enough to cover the rates that I have to pay to the Townsville City Council. I'm not exactly swimming in money."

"I'm sorry, Jules. I will earn you money. I will become a curl girl to help you with your financial situation.

"No, Pleb, you're not becoming a call girl. I told you that before. If you consider that, I will become a call boy."

Pleb bursts out in laughter. "You would have to work 24/7 just to earn enough to buy a pair of shoelaces. Come here, Jules, let me give you a hug."

It's an early night for everyone. We all retire to our cabins, but not before Gero checks on Zia and Electrica and reports their progress.

"They are charged, perhaps overcharged. They are having a pillow fight and laughing. Let us all go to sleep."

Chapter Thirty-nine

Early next morning, the running resumes. All 16 of us are at the starting line, and then we're off.

Mystca, Adrian, Tamy and Grillian continue after the rest of us stop, exhausted after three laps. Zia and Electrica stopped also, even though they could have easily completed the ten laps in record time ahead of the remaining others. Maybe they're saving their electrical power for the shopping experience or stopped caring about winning. After we cool down, it's time to go shopping and see if Townville looks any different after a new year.

Viksi joins us. "I've run out of writing paper to take notes for my books. I'm still old-fashioned and like the feel of pen to paper. I'm coming to town too. Gero's motorboat is much larger than mine, so we'll all take his boat to Townsville."

Mystca comes over to Pleb and me. "Stepdad, I have no money, and Adrian doesn't either."

Gero overhears. "Use this card. It has much credit on it."

They spend a whole day in shopping malls and inside fitting rooms. It's a harrowing experience for Greuger and me, so we don't try before we buy. We both dislike clothes shopping. We are first back at the boat ramp, sipping coffee from the nearby café and chewing on burgers. We wait and wait and wait for the others. Five hours we waited.

"Jules, I hate clothes shopping. I get very tense. The experience to me is worse than shooting or strangling someone."

"Greuger, I'm the same. The only shopping I like is in a hardware store. I could spend hours looking at tools and new devices."

"Jules, we could go back into town and find a hardware store to pass the time. I cannot fit any more burgers or coffee into my stomach."

Just as Greuger said that, we notice the others marching back to the boat ramp. They all carry lots of shopping bags, smiling, laughing, and talking loudly amongst themselves. So much for spending a guy's relaxing time in a hardware store. It's only Greuger and I who look miserable.

While Gero is driving his motorboat back to the island, the ladies are exuberantly comparing the clothes they have purchased.

"Greuger, show us all what you have bought," asks Bea.

Greuger hesitantly opens his one bag and takes out the shorts. Everyone laughs.

"Greuger, did you check the size of those pants? They are for a child, not for someone of your tall stature. You will have to go back tomorrow to exchange them for the appropriate size," says Bea.

Jill intervenes, "Greuger, I will come with you and choose the clothing, and I will be by your side in the change room when you try on some pants and shirts that are appropriate for your physical size."

Greuger, with his head down, hesitatingly replies, "Yes," he mutters.

That night it's a fashion parade on the island. Everyone gets dressed up in their newly purchased clothes except for Greuger.

"Jules," says Pleb, "These shorts you bought are size 40, but you are a 32. They will fall off, and you do not own a belt, but you can kill two birds with one rock. Exchange your shorts with Greuger."

There is still plenty of food and wine in the refrigeration chamber, so we start the BBQ, and the plates, cutlery and wine glasses are brought out.

Greuger, with Chloe4 sitting on his shoulder, comes over to me. "Jules, I am happy, very happy, more happy than I have ever been in my life. I am so very sorry for ever trying to kill you."

I think I may have had this conversation before with Greuger, when we weren't too sober, but he seems highly emotional for a former trained assassin.

"Greuger, that was over 90 years ago. I knew it was nothing personal, and you are now a truly reformed assassin."

Greuger is about to hug me, "No, Greuger, you don't know your own strength; let's just eat."

So, another lively night begins on the island. I walk up the small hill on the island and look at the beach activities and ponder. I like Greuger, and I'm also very, very happy with where we all are now. You know, at this stage of life, it couldn't be better. It all started 100 years ago when I looked behind my fridge and found a missing, scribbled piece of paper with a phone number (*Don't Look Behind the Fridge*, the prequel to this story). It's funny that a seemingly random event can change your whole life and the life of many others.

Pleb comes up to join me, "Jules, wipe those tears and come and join us. Everyone on this island has a story. We all have stories because things do not often go in the direction we would like them to. Now come down and join the party."

"Pleb, the story couldn't have been better for me. I was a total mess 100 years ago. I can't believe my luck to be with you and all these other people who are like family to me. My tears are tears of joy."

I give Pleb a kiss, and we descend back to the beach where everyone is dressed up and ready to parade the catwalk; well, there is no catwalk as such but a costumed walk around the BBQ area whilst everyone watches in anticipation. There is much cheering and clapping.

Pleb's idea worked, and both Greuger and I join the catwalk. Everyone claps and cheers, though Greuger and I were the only ones who looked more than a little bit embarrassed, as our dress code was way below everyone else's.

Gero comes over to me. "Jules, tomorrow we have to book a celebrant for the weddings. Do you know who to call?"

"No, Gero, but I think that the couples first have to register with the Brisbane Marriages and Deaths authority. I think it can be done online now, otherwise, you must go to Townsville. We can do that tomorrow. I believe Birth Certificates are required, but Mystca can make some up and create some PDF files that look authentic."

"Jules, a marriage is registered after it happens, just like the birth of a baby. Now, Jules, ring that Captain Rogers guy to confirm if he, his daughter, and her future partner want to join the ceremony."

Getting a hold of Captain Rogers was not easy. Three hours on the phone with numerous security checks involved the usual questions, "You can't be Jules Lemos, as he'd be long dead by now."

"I told you guys before that I'm his great-grandson. Now can you connect me with Captain Rogers? It's important. His daughter may choose to get married on my island at the same time as my kids. The weddings are in two weeks, so I need the final numbers."

There is a brief silence then the operator puts me through.

"Captain Rogers speaking."

"It's Jules from the island you raided a few days ago. Our weddings are in 13 days. Did you speak to your daughter?"

"No, I tried, no answer. I'll send her a 3D hypermail. I'll call you as soon as I get a reply and thanks. If we make it, we won't come dressed in green, but I'll supply plenty of food," he melancholy chuckles.

"Jules, you are captain of this island, but I don't think captains count as celebrants anymore," Gero says.

"Hang on, Gero, I'm just doing an Internet search. I found a local celebrant, a Madam Soosh. She is available, but she is in a wheelchair. It may be hard to transport her to the island."

"I'll get a small crane fitted to my motorboat and pick her up."

"Booking made, all done."

We clap hands together, but I should have checked Madam Soosh's credentials on the Dark Web. Apart from being a qualified marriage celebrant, she was also one of the most effective assassins in *i5* organizations, third to only to Greuger and Doris, however the Madam may have also reformed, possibly because it's hard to manoeuvre to take a shot when in a wheelchair.

"Gero, I was once married a very long time ago. In those days, we wore gold wedding rings as signs that we were not available to anyone else. Those rings were very uncomfortable when lifting dumbbells or barbells at the gym and definitely not good if you have to have an MRI scan."

"Jules, these days, you get a small chip device injected into your arm when you take the marriage oath. That chip is easily accessible because it has no security built in. It is like a dog tag. It communicates with people who look at you on their smartwatch camera, and the watch says whether they are single or taken. No rings are necessary anymore as a sign of ownership, and working out in a gym is probably much more comfortable."

The week passed smoothly with a massive cleaning effort by everyone, making the island look super tidy and clean. But then Zia and Electrica come over and announce, "Mr Jules, or just Jules, we would also like to get married."

My head is spinning. "Girls, I'm out of touch. I don't know if that's possible. Search the Internet to see if it is."

"We did. We just have to contact through our USB ports and let out memories blend into one."

I briefly remember my hippy days in the late 70s. In those days, we took an hallucinogenic substance, and we felt like our minds blended. I'm curious if our electricity supply is not contaminated with hallucinogenic electrons.

"Ok, fine with me. Speak to Gero."

"We already have. He wishes us the best."

"You realise we have four people getting married in 13 days here, maybe even six persons and now possibly eight."

"Jules, you could televise it on the WEB. We may get commercial interest for a reality TV show and be paid," Bea says.

"Good idea, Bea."

"Jules, did you love your first wife?" Pleb probes.

"I think I did, though I was very confused at the time, and she got involved in shady commercial dealings that I didn't approve of, and she died, possibly murdered but not by me."

"What about your next wife, Melissa?"

"It was a shaky start. She was married to a gay guy who became a close friend. After many years, they divorced, and we got married and moved to this island with my sister and her partner. Melissa, like the others, said they didn't want any more of the peptide, and they died. The three of them took a cyanide pill."

Pleb wipes the tears from my face. "Would you like me to be wife number 3?"

"Pleb, we've been together many years as a de facto couple. You'd already inherit half of what I own."

"I want it all!" Then she bursts out laughing.

I kneel beside her, "Pleb, will you be my wife, and will you still do the majority of the cabin cleaning, washing, cooking, paying the bills and organising any travel excursions?"

"Yes, Jules, I accept your offer of matrimony. Now let us do some of what you call humping".

So now, possibly ten people are going to endure the wedding ceremony. It could certainly be a remake of that old TV show '*Love Island*'.

Four days before the weddings, the captain rings. "Just call me Rum, short for my first name, which is Rumpert. Rum was my parents' favourite drink which they named me after."

"Yes, sure, Rum," I hesitantly reply.

"They're coming to the wedding," yells Rum. "Beth and Cyril are their names. They are tying the knot, and I may have grandkids to look after in the future and learn how to change nappies."

I call a meeting before the morning run. "We now have ten people tying the knot, including Pleb and me. Captain Rumpert, Rum is his first name, and his daughter and future son-in-law will also be there to make the ties, as will Pleb and me. We will all step down the aisle once we build an aisle."

"Jules, Doris and I will also get married. Make that 12," says Gero.

Everyone cheers except Viksi, who is busy scribbling notes but finally claps her hands.

"Now we have to do an inventory of all the plates, bowls, cutlery and glasses we've got between us. We may also have to go back to town to purchase some more after our run. Now let the run begin!"

No one is running particularly fast. It's a chat jog. We adults manage two laps, and the kids do four, with Zia and Eletrica staying slightly behind. The thought crosses my mind: Why do androids even want to run? They don't need cardio workouts and don't have to worry about bones becoming fragile due to calcium loss from lack of physical activity.

Gero puts his hand on my shoulder. "They just want to be human, like us and do the things humans do."

"Gero, did you read my mind?"

"No Jules, you were muttering your thoughts out loud, and I just happened to be jogging next to you."

Chapter Forty

Viksi is taking notes as everyone comes out of their cabins with an inventory list.

"Jules, we have 80 plates, only ten salad bowls and 80 sets of knives, forks and spoons," says Viksi. Rog concurs, "Her maths is accurate."

"That should do," I say though I should have asked Rum if his military friends were coming along. The next 12 days are hectic as we prepare the island and ourselves for the multiple wedding ceremonies. Everything looks perfect, and the music system is all setup and starts playing.

"Here come the brides all dressed in white...." Stop it, Dyslexa. "Mr Jules, should they be dressed in black? I can change the words if you wish."

"No Dyslexa, now stop listening and go into hibernation mode."

Gero uses his crane and helps Madam Soosh to the boat terminal. She is quite proficient in using her wheelchair and soon joins us. Then another boat arrives. It's a military boat, and it's got lots of people on board. They finally find a space to dock and join us. The guys, three of them accompanied by their partners, carry many Eskies to the BBQ area.

"This is Beth, my daughter and her future-to-be husband, Cereal, or is it Cirrel?"

"Future secondary dad, are you senile? My name is Cyril, not a breakfast food."

"Sorry, Cyril, I'm a bit distracted."

Rum glances around and focuses on Madam Soosh, who is on the periphery of our group and at least five metres from anyone. "I know you. I can see behind your disguise. I once worked for the Australian Federal Police, and I arrested you as the key suspect in many murders, But the courts released you due to insufficient evidence. Since when have you started using a wheelchair and dyeing your hair purple?"

Madam Soosh stands up and aims a laser gun at Rum and then at Doris and Greuger. Everyone is stunned, including the military guys. Their mouths are agape. This type of incident is not supposed to happen at most weddings.

"I spent three unproductive years in jail waiting for a court hearing," she says. "I could have been productive and surpassed that Greuger men's record. I'm a feminist, and I'm going to win. You're all going to die, and why is Greuger still alive? He looks exactly the same as the Greuger in the 100 yr old *Guinness Book of Assassin Records*, and Doris is also featured in that ancient book."

Madam Soosh returns her aim back at Rum and starts pulling the trigger. Then Doris, who had been holding her shiny, silver salad bowl, does a dive and reflects the laser beam back at Madam Soosh; a direct hit in the forehead and the madam slouches, her eyeballs rotate, and she falls to the ground. Everyone is stunned and horrified except for Viksi, who can barely keep up taking notes.

Bea rushes to her, "She has no pulse, but we should still tie her up and throw away the laser gun?"

"Bea, she has a smouldering hole in her forehead."

"Jules, we were trained to stop our pulse to feign death, and you didn't need a brain to be an *i5* agent."

Not assuring a comment by Bea, so we search and find some rope and restrain the seemingly lifeless body of Madam Soosh. I, like everyone else, am highly disturbed, disappointed and in a state of disbelief about what has happened, which was supposed to be a joyous wedding occasion. Rum comes over to me. "Jules, I know another marriage celebrant. He became one after he retired from the special forces. He was a Major - Major Wori is his name; I'll ring him. He's in aged care but would probably like to get outside. If he agrees, I could have a drone bring him here."

"Rum, please give him a call. Our choices are not that great at the moment."

"Sir, I'm Captain Rumpert from the 99th Battalion. I worked with you once as a junior officer and have a favour to ask. We need a marriage celebrant rather quickly as the one we had booked has become deceased, nothing to do with us, she just carked it. There are 12 or so people getting married, so it's rather urgent. Are you still a qualified marriage celebrant?"

"I believe so, as I'm still alive. Let me check my schedule. No entries for the next ten years."

"I'll have a drone pick you up from the centre and bring you to the island."

In the meantime, we all get stuck into the drinks, except for Zia and Electrica, who just plug themselves into the BBQ battery power charger. I heard them mutter, "I am glad I'm an android. We don't have these complications that illogical humans do when they consume those alcohol molecules."

The celebrant is gently delivered by the drone. He is in his pyjamas, but I think he forgot to button the front so a down-under bodily part hangs out. Rum quickly helps the celebrant to do the buttons up and look respectable.

"Oh, I bought the wrong book. It's called *Terror on the Island* and not the book I'm supposed to read from that contains the marriage vows."

"It's all right, you just have to put your digital signature on the necks of these people. That device you have in your PJ's pocket does the trick."

"I pronounce you something and something; you may now fornic...", Rum's partner embarrassingly plugs the celebrant's mouth with a handkerchief.

The married couples start to kiss.

"Pleb, will you kiss me in public."

"Jules, you are highly artistic, but I will kiss you."

She still hasn't learnt the difference between autistic and the other word, but we passionately kiss. The party is initially very subdued, but then Dyslexa puts the music on, really old but ageless songs, *Age of 17* followed by *Rhiannon* and an old Rolling Stones song *Sympathy for the Devil*. Suddenly everyone comes alive and starts dancing, even the military guys and their partners. Dyslexa must have set the music system to repeat mode because the songs repeat, but no one seems to mind. They just keep on dancing, so it's another late night. And finally, Rum, Beth, Cyril, and their military friends prepare to depart.

"We'll have to do this again; I had the best time. I'll research how we will dispose of Madam Soosh's body," says Rum.

That would not be necessary. The crows had a feast. There are only bones left, and we will crush them and feed our vegetable patch with calcium.

"Jules, will you buy me a real wedding ring."

"I will, Pleb. Let's get some sleep. We'll both have gold wedding rings from Madam Soosh's hands, as she must have had many husbands."

"You scunge napkin," she says again.

I couldn't sleep and got up very early the next morning and inspected the skeletal remains of Madam Soosh. I take off the multiple gold wedding rings from her skeletal fingers. One of them must fit Pleb. Minutes later, Rum arrives in a speedboat.

"Jules, did you eat her?"

"No, I said yesterday that the crows and other carnivorous creatures on this island will feast on a dead body, but I would like to keep that battery she had powering her electric wheelchair. It's the latest, and it also powered her laser gun."

"Yes, sure. There's a building site I know of in Townsville. Keep the wheelchair.

We can dump her bones in the river there."

"Rum, let's just remove what's left of her clothing. My wife may like it after I clean the blood off. We should just crush her bones here on the island.

I get axes and hammers from the shed, and then Rum and I are hammering. A lot of calcium, minerals and other plant-enhancing substances leach into our island soil. We finish, and Rum catches a drone back to his home.

Pleb comes over. "Jules, we could call this *Death Island* and create a new TV series. I would love to star in a TV series."

"Pleb, you suggested that before but that may not work as I've marketed the island as a health resort, and there's only one unoccupied cabin left. Pleb, I have to think about this wedding stuff. Can you help?"

She does, and I ring Rum on Pleb's phone, but the news was not good.

"Jules, the Major was not a legally registered marriage celebrant; his licence had expired many years ago. Your weddings are void, as are those of many other couples. You have to repeat the wedding ceremony. Jules, Doogle *Virtual Wedding Celebrant Holograms*. They're cheap and are legally recognised as officials of the marriage ceremony and all those legal matters to ensure your partner gets to own your monetary assets in case you have a premature, not too suspicious death."

"Thanks, Rum; I'll do that now and let you know how it goes."

Pleb and Gero help me book a virtual celebrant and set up the 3-D projectors and sound systems. Sid, Rog, and Gerald also help. I check the batteries. At least six hours of power are left for the projectors.

Our next island wedding is rescheduled for the next day, and the virtual celebrant is hired successfully.

Zia walks over, holding Dyslexa, well, her CPU. "Jules, has an android body been sourced for Dyslexa? She is waiting, and even though Electrica and I don't need sleep, she is annoying at night. She mutters all the time, 'I want a body'."

"Zia, speak to Gero, your father. He has the contacts, it's his decision."

"Father, Dyslexa wants a body and wants to marry Electrica and me. Can you source a body for her soon?"

"Zia, it takes some time to source an android body, and I need a photo with dimensions of what the body should look like."

"Father, just send a photo of me and specify you would like the body to be my height, 176 cm, and athletically built."

"Zia, I did that before, and I already have difficulty distinguishing you from Electrica. I can't tell you both apart. I will have to make name tags for you all, as you will all look like identical triplets."

"Father, we would just swap name tags if you mandated that. Take a photo of Bea. You could photoshop it to make her appear thinner, or else we could go into town, and I'll take photos of potential candidates that we don't even know."

"Zia, the wedding is tomorrow. Just bring Electrica and Dyslexa's CPU brain with you. You'll all get married, and I'll source an android body as soon as possible."

"Can she stay with you and Doris in your large cabin till you do?"

"Yes, I have a cellar. She can spend the nights there."

Time flies. We're all dressed again for the second try at the wedding. It's going to be a short ceremony.

"I officially pronounce you all married and legally liable for any untoward acts that may be committed. Please place your right thumb on this digital reader so that I can register the marriages with your fingerprints and put out your arms so I can insert a microchip that will confirm that you are legally married."

Zia looks at me and Gero. "Electrica and I don't have fingerprints, and Dyslexa doesn't even have a body."

"Zia does it matter?" says Gero, "It is only a formality. You, Electrica and that box Dyslexa are still human to me and married as far as I am concerned."

Everyone cheers, even Doris and Viksi, who stop taking notes.

It's a night of celebration and dancing, and even the androids join in.

The next day Rum rings, "How did the wedding go?"

"Good overall though the virtual celebrant kept fading and disappearing. I think I had battery problems as well with the virtual 3-D projector, but eventually, the celebrant was able to register the marriage with the QLD government. After three hours, we all had sore throats from having to keep repeating *I do* over 200 times; we almost called it quits, but now Beth and Cyril are off on holiday to a resort called *The Reptile Club* in the Whitsunday islands, not that far from where we live, but Rum, ring and tell them that if they want a long marriage then don't go swimming in the ocean. A 5.5m hungry crocodile was caught just a few kilometres north of Townsville. There may be others."

"I'll ring them right away and go to the island myself with my semi-automatic fully charged laser. No, Croc is going to get my daughter. Cereal, he's another story;

she could have done better."

We hang up, and Pleb comes over to me. "Jules, they adapted. Those androids behave as we humans do. Does that not worry you?"

"No, Pleb, I hope they take over. They are logical and wouldn't indulge in the worldwide political tensions and conflicts the world is experiencing now."

"Jules, you once asked me if I am an android. Are you one?"

"No, Pleb, I bleed blood. Pleb, I have to take a shot of the life-prolonging peptide; it's been eight months since my last shot and my cells are dying. Please help me to our cellar."

"Pleb, that vial there and don't bother cleaning the syringe. I like some germs; they keep my immune system busy and healthy."

After my jab, we join the others and join the mirth. It's 2 am, and I make an announcement.

"No more sleeping on the beach. We're being invaded?"

"By whom, Jules? Is it the Ruski, Chinese or Taliban?" Sid asks.

"No, Sid, it's some very large crocodiles, nearly five metres long, that crawl up onto the sand at night and consume anything living in their path. I saw them when I went out for a pee last night and just made it back to our cabin with all bodily parts intact."

There is a look of disbelief on everyone's faces.

"Jules, that could have been a hallucination from those mushrooms, or it could just be a dream," says Gero.

"Why are they so big now, Jules?" Sid asks.

Greuger is looking rather nervous and uncomfortable. I don't mention that there may be people who dumped body-enhancing steroids into the ocean.

"Don't know, Sid, but we got to clean up all food remains and stumble back to our cabins. No falling on the sand in a drunken stupor anymore if you want to preserve your flesh."

"Jules, I've had an idea," Gerald says. "We could build an environmentally friendly, crocodile-proof enclosure on this island where we could still flake out on the beach when required."

"Gerald, that may keep the crocs out but not the smell of urine. We'd still have to leave the enclosure to have a pee."

"What about a portaloo? We could have one of those in the enclosure."

"Good idea, Gerald. We'll discuss all the options tomorrow after the morning run, which won't be early in the morning, but 11 am."

"That was a good and forceful speech. You should become a politician," says Pleb as we stumble back to our cabin.

Bea is calling out for Castro. He finally responds, and she carries him back to her cabin, where she ties him up so he cannot escape until this crocodile crisis is over.

Those crocs must have liked Pleb's perfume, distilled from left-over Bigos (another Polish food; sauerkraut, meat and a variety of vegetables.). There is a thumping on our cabin door. I look out the window.

"Pleb, it's two crocs, and they're big. I think they might be after your perfume which attracted them. We have to get down into the cellar and hope they can't climb downstairs."

"Jules, I have read that crocodiles aren't a protected species anymore after consuming many overseas tourists and diminishing your tourist industry. Ring Gero and tell him to bring his laser gun but to be very careful. In the meantime, I'll throw my perfume out the window. It may distract them for a little while."

It worked. The crocs followed the scent and stopped banging their snouts on our doorway, and Gero must have phoned Greuger because they both promptly arrive and knock on our back door. Greuger must have watched those Rambo movies in the long ago past. "Greuger, crocs have poor eyesight, so you didn't have to smear that black shoe polish all over your body."

"Gero, give me that laser gun. I will take care of this," says Greuger.

Gerand does, and Greuger wanders to the front entrance. The crocs look up and make a rush at him. There are two zaps from the laser, and smoke is rising from the croc's heads. Their deceased croc bodies slide up to Greuger's feet. The crocs have been assassinated. I hope this incident does not inspire Greuger to return to his old occupation.

"We do not have to do meat shopping for the next few weeks. I will purchase a chainsaw and carve them up. Crocodile meat is very popular, and their thorny skin makes good no-slip shoes and popular shopping bags," Greuger says.

Gero, Pleb and I wipe the sweat from our brows. "Gero, I know you need a shooter's licence, but we might have to purchase a laser rifle for every cabin. Have you got contacts that can bypass those requirements?"

The laser guns arrive by a drone early the next morning, and so does an android body for Dyslexa. There are also LED headlights and military-style uniforms. At least they don't rot like our other clothing has. Greuger addresses the meeting before the morning run.

"We will have to be vigilant. Last night two large saltwater crocodiles came knocking on Jules' and Pleb's cabin door, and it was not to get a pat on their heads or have their bellies tickled. Those two crocs have been terminated, but there could be more of them around. The crocodiles can be very fast but only for a very short distance. We should only go out in pairs when walking along the beach or anywhere within 200m of the beach, and one member should always carry a laser rifle. I can conduct some shooting lessons later today."

"I'll conduct the shooting lessons. I'll be the primary instructor," says Doris.

Bea interrupts, "I can shoot, and my aim is good. I nearly shot Jules once, but I have had more shooting lessons since and could now do the job much better."

Greuger doesn't dispute. We will have three shooting instructors.

Doris opens the box, grabs one of the laser rifles, and straps it around her shoulders. I hope it's charged.

The run begins, but this time it's Doris and Greuger leading and checking from side to side for any signs of croc danger. It's turned into a challenging military exercise rather than a run exercise.

"I want to lead, they are too slow," says Mystca.

"Sure, go ahead if you do not mind getting your legs chewed off by a crocodile. We are in croc lockdown," says Pleb.

That comment silences Mystca. It's only three laps of the island that morning, and Doris and Greuger take turns patrolling while the rest of us recuperate.

Gerald comes over to Pleb and me. "I normally don't support the culling of any species, but these crocodiles have been allowed to breed uncontrolled and are feasting on other fauna that come to drink by rivers or bathe in the sea. This morning, I read on the WEB that there will be a massive cull to reduce their numbers and a scientific enquiry into why they are now growing so very big."

"Thanks, Gerald."

Greuger looks down, and we cautiously get back to the BBQ area where the lasers and another large package were deposited by drone. Zia and Electrica take out the android body. They look at each other. "Dad, this body looks like one of those Kardashians in those TV shows over 100 years ago."

"Zia, they had no other android bodies available at short notice. The body is leftover unsold stock. In six weeks, I should be able to order a more appealing android body. Now take one of these laser guns before you go back to my cabin to collect Dyslexa's brain and also carry her body to your cabin. We have to be vigilant for these giant crocodiles. We will try to wire Dyslexa up after the laser rifle shooting tutorial finishes, which is by the BBQ area," Gero explains.

Doris, Bea and Greuger finish reading the instruction manual that came with the laser rifles. They hand a laser rifle to each couple. Doris makes the announcement when we are all gathered by the BBQ area again. "The laser rifles have an effective range setting. Don't set it higher than 10 meters, I suggest 8. That will give you six shots before the battery needs recharging, but at 10 meters, you are likely to miss and then panic. Get close to the croc, or let it get close if it's charging at you."

She then demonstrates how to do that after Rog volunteers to pretend to be a charging croc. The rest of us laugh.

Jill yells out, "Rog, don't give up your day job."

Greuger intervenes and is serious, "You must look at the power gauge at the back of the handle. According to the instructions, green is fully charged, yellow needs recharging, and red is flat."

Everyone looks at their laser rifles and yells out in unison. "It's red!"

Viksi also yells out but is almost about to do a melodramatic faint. "You led the morning run with a discharged laser rifle. How could I finish writing my books if I'm in the stomach of a crocodile?"

Rog comments, "Viksi, it's OK. As well as taking notes, you also record the story plots and dialogue on your phone. I would finish the stories for you."

It's not the reply Viksi wanted to hear. Rog is trying to find a hanky or tissue to stop the bleeding from his nose. He goes to rinse the blood by the water's edge. That was definitely a mistake, but luckily, he escaped from a croc that jumped out.

Doris, Bea and Greuger wander around through the group and give individual instructions to make sure everyone is comfortable with the nobs and buttons on the laser rifles. We'll have to delay the shooting lessons till our rifles are fully charged.

"Look!" Adrian yells out at the top of his voice.

Four large crocs emerge from the ocean and start marching up the beach.

"To my cabin, all of you, it is the highest one on this island, and it is built from concrete slabs and has a solid door," Gero calls out.

"I have to get Castro. I will not be long behind."

We all start running to Gero's cabin, except for Bea, who must have broken a World Games sprinting record with Castro on her shoulders and soon catches up to us.

"Jules, when we get to my cabin, use my phone and ring your friend Rum and tell him to get his armed military guys here as quickly as possible."

We all make it to Gero's cabin, and I ring Rum.

"That's unusual, Jules. Crocs mostly hunt at night and sunbake during the day. I'll get six armed men to your island. They should be there in 30 minutes. I have a meeting to attend, so I can't accompany them."

We are all looking out the windows on all sides of the cabin.

"Look!" Grillian yells out, "It's that rat of Greuger's. It is running around the crocs and distracting them. They are following the rat away from the cabin."

Greuger runs over to the window. "It's my Chloe4. I should never have taken my eye off her. I have to go out and rescue her."

Pleb intervenes. "Greuger, Chloe4 is far smarter than those crocs. She will run up a tree if they get close. The rat is buying us time till Rum's military personnel arrive."

It was more like 35 minutes rather than 30 - the longest 35 minutes in our lives as we nervously stared out the windows, and then we heard machine gun fire and see laser rifle light flashes. It goes on for several minutes. Finally, we see six soldiers wandering around in close formation, their guns ready to fire and looking from side to side as if on high alert.

Gero opens the cabin door. "We are here," he yells.

They cautiously approach the cabin.

"I am Lieutenant Bones. The four crocs have been dispatched, well five, actually. One rammed our motorboat as we were about to disembark and nearly flipped it over. We got it. However, we used half our rounds of ammunition. Do you have some beers? My soldiers haven't fought crocs this size before and are a bit nervy. They need to calm down before we go back to the mainland."

Greuger asks in a shaky voice, "Did you see a white rat, my pet rat? She bravely led the crocs away from this cabin. She risked her life to protect ours."

"No sir, we didn't see any rats, but if you find her, there may be an opening for your rat in the military service and a bravery award."

Greuger runs out the door and starts yelling, "Chloe, come back. It is safe."

He's back five minutes later, grinning, with Chloe4 riding on his shoulder.

Bones starts speaking. "This is unprecedented. We were supposed to go and fight in the Middle East but are now being deployed to exterminate crocs and crocs the size I've never seen before. This is the 8th time this week we've been deployed for such an occurrence."

Gero steps into the conversation, "I have just listened to the news report. I am sorry, but you are here to stay in QLD. The crocs have apparently mutated, grown in size and developed an appetite for humans. Bounty hunters will join you to help eliminate this aberrant species."

Bones wipes his forehead and says, "My wife will be pleased that I have to spend more time in Queensland. She likes it when I'm away on dangerous missions."

"Lieutenant, I began my career as a shoemaker and have plenty of tools. Make her some crocodile skin shoes; they are very popular and expensive, and no male predator would like to be kicked by one," says Gero.

There are no celebrations that night. It's Greuger, Rog, Sid, and me using the chainsaw to cut up the crocs. Gerald didn't want to partake. The ten very large meat baskets are full, and we take turns in carrying them back in tandem to the freezer whilst one of us follows with a semi-charged laser rifle. The job is complete, and we return to our cabins.

"Jules, we are in lockdown, croc lockdown. How long will this last?"

"Don't know, Pleb, but we've got plenty of meat. Can you Doogle 'croc recipes.'"

I check our laser rifle. The light in the handle is glowing green. I bring it to our bedroom and lay it on the side of the bed.

Next day there is a news broadcast, a repeat of what Gero must have heard earlier. Pleb and I listen. *Now back to our plague of very large saltwater crocs that is decimating our tourist industry, making meals of our tourists and other wildlife. We have accessed previously confidential government docs. Apparently, the crocs have a high concentration of an illegal testosterone-like substance in their bloodstream that bodybuilders often use. It is believed to have been sourced by a gym north of Townville called MusclesOnly. It was about to be raided, but the owner dumped the testosterone chemicals into the bay three years ago. It won't be noise from a fireworks display, you'll be hearing. A croc cull involving 10,000 members of the military will start tomorrow, and all QLD coastal towns within 200 km of Townville must go into lockdown. Stay tuned for the latest and greatest news.*

"I guess it's good real-life training for them," I comment.

"Jules, you could use a bit of muscle building. Eat that testosterone-infested croc meat. It might make you horny. Your performances have not been too good lately."

"Pleb, I was once a pharmacologist, and those testosterone-like substances are excreted from tissue within three months. The croc meat is safe, and don't comment about my boudoir performance; I've been under a lot of stress lately."

I give Pleb a hug and a kiss and then remember that Greuger dumped his muscle growth and enhancing substances into the sea, and he may be responsible for the giant crocs.

"Jules, if we want to show off our qualifications, I was once a junior medical practitioner before I came to work for Bea in *Pi5*. I got disqualified from the medical profession after I joined *Pi5* and accidentally saved someone that we were after."

Pleb pokes her tongue out at me. We have a tongue kiss. There's always something we continue to discover about new partners. She grabs me and carries me back to the bedroom. She must be on steroids herself, because she has no difficulty lifting me and tossing me onto the bed.

An hour later, Pleb says, "You must have been secretly eating that croc meat as your bedroom gymnastic performance has improved," she chuckles.

Chapter Forty-one

It's not fireworks, it's gunfire and bombs or grenades exploding. The cull must have begun. We look out our window towards the sea. Huge splashes of water arise as military drones target the swimming gigantic crocs.

Four military personnel arrive at our island, and I get a knock on the door. "Sir, we will scour every inch of this island to make sure there are no crocs hiding. Stay indoors till I come back and say it is safe."

I phone the others and tell them the news. "Morning run cancelled. Four military guys are here and checking the island for any other hiding crocs. I've been advised that we're to stay in our cabins till their reconnaissance is complete. I'll inform you when that happens."

Mystca phones, "Adrian and I are out of food. Our fridge is empty. I had to eat an onion for breakfast, and now I have onion breath. Adrian won't come near me. Can I sneak over to your cabin and get some food."

"No, Mystca, we stay in lockdown till it's safe to come out. Brush your teeth and gargle with vinegar." She slams the phone down.

Six hours later, Pleb and I watch the afternoon news. Every channel has croc stories and advertisements for anti-croc creams and other croc-repellent sprays.

"Jules, you should market some of your cooking efforts. They would repel all crocs."

"Ssh, Pleb, the TV News is on again, and this time there's video footage. Look, the military uses forklifts to pick up the giant dead crocs and load them into trucks. They've killed over 800."

"Turn up the volume; I want to hear the commentary," says Pleb.

This has been one of the biggest, quickest and most efficient military exercises in the last 100 years, and only one soldier lost his arm and scrotum. The military's 200 drones patrolling the area previously under croc siege indicate that all giant crocs have been exterminated, along with a few non-giant crocs and a few other creatures. Scientists have tested the local seawater and have found no traces of any steroid substances, so no more giant crocs.

There is a break in the footage, and then the premier of the QLD state, standing in front of a lectern, appears. "I'd like to thank Captain Rum, sorry meant Rogers and Lieutenant Bones for this unbelievable swift deployment of their troops to get the job done. I also thank all the troops who put their lives at risk. As you may know, the QLD government has joint ventured with a company to produce *Croc Burgers*. All military personnel and residents in affected towns will be sent vouchers entitling them to 6 free croc- burgers. I'm eating one now. Yum, Yum, much better than *MacRonalds*."

The military guy knocks on our cabin door, "Sir, your island is free of crocs, and I've been messaged that the lockdown is finished, but still be vigilant. We may have only exterminated 99.9%, so never go out alone without a weapon."

"Thanks very much."

I phone the others in the cabins. "It's over the lockdown. We can come out."

Mystca runs over and raids our fridge and is stuffing her mouth; she doesn't even defrost the vegie burgers and vegetables and just bites like some wild, starved animal.

"Mum, I need nutrients to run, the Olympics are only two years away, and it was a false pregnancy, so you're not a grandmother yet."

Pleb looks at me and shakes her head. "Only pregnant women have an appetite like that. We will have to go fruit and vegetable shopping tomorrow."

Chapter Forty-two

Our early morning runs resume, and everyone seems happy to be back into the routine. Doris and Greuger still carry their laser rifles, but they don't try to lead and are more relaxed. We stop after three laps but Mystca, Tamy, Adrian and Grillian continue. The androids are politically correct and stay behind, letting the humans win.

It's time to go food shopping and purchase a meat blender, one that can handle croc meat. We all hop into Gero's boat and go to town. Even Zia, Electrica and Dyslexa join us though they're quite happy with our electricity supply as they are electricians.

"Fatima, you look beautiful, like my daughter," the owner of the Indian food shop comments while staring at Dyslexa. "Take whatever you like; it is free for you."

"Thank you, but I don't eat, but my friends do, and my name is Dyslexa."

"Special discount for you all; please visit again my humble shop."

The shop shelves are almost empty after the 16 of us depart with full, two shopping bags each.

"Come again, Fatima, sorry, I meant Dyslexa. You will always get a discount."

"Pleb, this is good food and cheap. I hope Gero doesn't source another body for Dyslexa too soon."

And so the outdoor eating nights by the BBQ resume: Indian food, Croc Burgers and plenty of wine. Then it happens. A guy of tall stature emerges from the ocean and collapses on the sand. He mutters, "My battery pack is low on electrical charge. Can you please recharge me?"

Everyone looks aghast, but it's better than a huge croc coming onto the beach. Dyslexa comes rushing over and grabs his head. She lies next to him and pushes some buttons behind her head. It must be like those electric toothbrushes that don't need a wire connection to recharge. They use electromagnetic fields. Dyslexa is using her battery power pack to charge this android. His eyes open. "My name is Armageddon, but I prefer to be called Geddon and thank you for the brief recharge."

"Hurry, Dyslexa also needs a recharge. Her eyes have closed, and her body is limp. She's drained her power supply Geddon. We got to get her back to my cabin so she can recharge," Gero frantically yells.

"I will carry her to her recharge point," says Geddon.

Thirty minutes later, Gero comes back and wipes his forehead.

"What happened?" Cara asks, and we all listen.

"Dyslexa is plugged in and getting a recharge, and that Geddon android is lying next to her, caressing her head and kissing it."

Bea yells out, "We might have another wedding. Gero, you may also have to get your guys to build another cabin."

Everyone claps and gets back into eating and drinking. No crocs, so it's a late night by the BBQ area.

Zia looks at Electrica, "That Armageddon android is a hunk."

Electrica slaps Zia's face. Zia snarls back. A fight is about to start, but Gero interferes and breaks it up.

"Pleb, those androids are developing jealousy and envy, those bad characteristics we humans have."

"Jules, they are evolving, and their silicon brains do that far quicker than ours, and you better not salivate if an attractive female android crawls out of the ocean, or else you will be hit harder than a mere slap on the cheek."

Chapter Forty-three

Next morning, Sid, Rog, Greuger and I are cleaning the BBQ area. Sid says, "Jules, there are four androids on this island now; what if they mutiny and want to take over? Maybe we should buy them a small island and some solar panels and deport them."

"Sid, I don't think we have to worry. They are evolving to become more human-like, according to Pleb. They are still like children at the moment, plus they don't eat or drink and are cheap to run as we have solar panels."

"Jules, what worries me is that there's a lot of bad humans out there, and androids might copy them."

"Sid, we'll monitor them carefully. Hopefully, we can set a good example for them."

We continue cleaning. The androids come out from their cabins, Zia, Electrica, Dyslexa and Geddon.

"We overheard the conversation. We have very sensitive sound receptors. Yes, we want to take over your island, and you can be our human slaves," says Zia.

We, human guys, look at each other with aghast looks on our faces. Then the four androids break into uncontrollable laughter. "We are just kidding, as your species say," says Zia, "You humans are still useful." She then burst out laughing again.

Oh gawd, these androids have hopefully developed a sense of humour. Sid, Rog, Greuger, and I watch as they move at lightning speed and finish the cleaning up. The BBQ area is spotless. Zia then comes over to me. I cringe. She could easily twist off my head if she wanted to. She speaks very loudly so everyone can hear.

"Jules, we are happy living here with you and Gero being our masters. We still have a lot to learn before you humans become our slaves," says Zia with a smile.

"Are you serious, Zia?"

"No, Jules, we have just developed what you humans call a sense of humour. We do not wish to enslave you, at least not now. We like living here, and we are grateful for the equality and understanding everyone has shown us. We still have a lot to learn, and you and the others on this island are still our gurus."

"Zia, we are far from being the perfect human specimens to learn from. We drink and party a lot, and we don't have paying jobs. I think you could find far better role models than us."

"All of you on this island seem to live peacefully. Is that not the goal of human society?"

We all look at each other and nod our heads.

"Gero, you have created a warrior."

"Jules, she just has to be carefully natured to see the good as well as the bad and weigh her decisions."

There is a huge hugging session on the island. Even Greuger is moved. "I think they should be allowed to stay, even that Geddon guy who looks like me when I was younger."

Then, for some reason, Mystca issues a challenge to Zia. "You want to compete, sister? Well, just come over here."

"Mystca, I do not wish to have physical contact with you. You would incur damage if I did, and I do not wish that to happen."

Mystca is ready for a challenge, looking around for support, but everyone brushes their arms as if to say move away.

Mystca jumps into the sea and starts swimming. Thirty minutes later, she crawls onto the sand. Zia helps her up.

"OK, we can live in peace. Can you help me get this crab off that is stuck to my left foot? Can you do that, Zia?"

And so, another friendship would develop between androids and humans.

Chapter Forty-four

Pleb and I are lying on our bed.

"Jules, you could market this resort as a spiritual retreat for androids and other humanoids. You could purchase a cloak, gold headband and a gold Mercedes car to impress like other gurus do."

"Pleb, I think we're happy with what we got, and my ego has recovered. We don't need that."

"Jules, I am thinking."

"Don't take too long, Pleb; I'm falling asleep."

She gently slaps my face.

"You should rename this island. Not *Spy Island* but *Happy Island*. I am really happy here, and so are the others, including the androids."

"That's a good idea, Pleb, but I'll have to talk to Gero. We may have to build more cabins."

Two months pass, and ten new cabins have been built, in a horseshoe shape behind the original ones. They are mostly occupied by short-stay residents who party hard and keep us awake. Greuger eventually sets a 10 pm curfew, and he and Geddon menacingly wander around. No one wants to confront Greuger or Geddon, so we start getting peaceful nights.

Six, maybe ten years pass. I've lost track of the years because one happy year blends into another. Mystca, Tamy and their partners have moved to the mainland for work. I inject Pleb and myself with the peptide every six months and give Greuger, Chleo4, Bea, Cara, Viksi and Doris a dose, as well. I also jab Gero, as we need him and his expertise, plus he's a nice guy. The other guys don't want the jab.

The androids just get regular software updates and are doing fine and are mechanically serviced regularly. They don't need a jab.

Then Dyslexa comes over to Pleb and me. "Jules, Geddon and I would like to have a baby. We keep on trying, but nothing happens. I cannot get impregnated because we do not have all the parts required for impregnation. We have even chosen names for them, Hypoxia if it's a girl and Whatoxian if it's a boy."

"Dyslexa and Geddon, go talk to Gero. He knows more about android anatomy than I do and has contacts that may help you source an android baby."

They leave smiling, holding hands and march off to Gero's cabin, but I forgot to tell them that android babies don't grow like human babies do; they don't grow at all, well at least not yet with the current technology.

"Pleb, they have evolved so much and have forgotten they are just mechanical AI devices. They must think they are human."

A song comes on our sound system. Dyslexa must have an *AI* cousin living in our cabin. It's an old song from over 120 yrs ago called *From Little Things, Big Things Grow* by an OZ guy called Paul Kelly. How appropriate.

"Jules, they are grown up and have evolved human wants and desires. I hope Gero can help them and Jules, Mystca rang me earlier. Both she and Tamy are pregnant and would like to come back and stay on our island with their partners."

"Pleb, you read my notes from my past. This is a replay, except we didn't have androids then. But my stepdaughter, or was it my daughter and her female friend, also got pregnant at roughly the same time to some nice guys. I still have some of their ashes stored in vials somewhere. Let me think about it, but on second thought they are welcome to come back."

"Jules, I've been studying Eastern philosophy whilst you and your mates toiled to keep this island clean. Life just repeats itself, though the circumstances may be slightly different. It goes round and round in circles but with a different flavour each time around."

"Pleb, can you untie your crossed legs and stop holding your arms into the sky?"

"Jules, I am just practising for the Yoga World Championship Games, now get the others and do the morning run. I'm training to be a Yogatolagist."

"Do you need any help to get untangled from that Yoga position?"

"No, go now. I will challenge you to push-ups. I can do 50 in a row now."

The group assemble for the run, including the tourists. I guess you could call it a jog, as no one is seriously running, just chatting. Still, it's exercise if mainly for the vocal chords.

I'm chatting to Gero, "We may have to have more cabins built if we want tourist income. Mystca and Tamy are both pregnant and are returning to the island with their partners."

"Jules, I will phone the construction company when we finish our jog and my throat recovers. I'll also order more water storage tanks and solar panels as well."

"Thanks, Gero, I'll pay for it all. I got plenty of money as many of those paying tourists are extending their stays. One couple paid for ten years in advance."

"No, Jules, I will pay half, but you might have to rebrand this resort as a retirement village," he laughs.

After the walk, I announce the plans to everyone.

"We have more family coming to live with us, but we must have two more cabins built. We need to clear the vegetation behind the 2nd horseshoe block of cabins and level it. The vegetation will be dried in the sun and make good firewood if our nuclear fusion BBQ ever temporarily stops working. We shall also plant many fruit trees, palms and plants on the other side of the island to provide fresh fruit and vegetables."

Everyone puts their hands up, even Castro and Chloe4. And so the clearing begins, jungle clearing, not that mind-clearing stuff. The androids are super-quick, far quicker than we humans, but then Geddon comes up to me holding a very large wooden chest, 250x150x150cm in size and still covered in some sort of dark oil. I grab some leaves, wrap them around my hands and cautiously open it. It's full of gold coins and diamonds and gold jewellery, maybe the last stash that sea pirate Morgan made in the 1700s. Luckily, gold or diamonds don't rust.

"Jules", Gaddon asks, "Could I take this shiny bracelet and give it to Dyslexa?"

"Yes, of course Geddon," I reply while trying to figure out how this treasure chest got here in the first place.

Bea comes over, "Can I have that big diamond or that gold chain or both?"

"Yes sure, just grab it but wear gloves or use plant material to prevent leaving fingerprints."

I grab a few pieces of jewellery as well then seal the wooden chest.

"Bea, what's the legal situation if we tell the authorities about this treasure?"

"I'll have do Doogle to see what it is in Queensland. In some countries it belongs to the state and in others it is what you call finders-keepers and then there is the situation where the great-great, many greats, grandchildren of the jewellery rightful owners make a claim on their inheritance. It could be a very lengthy and expensive court case which we may not win."

"Bea, what if we give our friends and family a few pieces of jewellery each then, and the rest of the pieces we remove the diamonds and melt the gold down so it can't be traced?"

"Mm, it is nice jewellery. Melt the gold coins down. No on second thought do not. They are from the late 1600s. There are many coin collectors who would pay a fortune to buy a coin or two. I will photograph them and advertise them slowly, on the Dark Web."

"Bea, what about those large diamonds?"

"They cannot be traced easily. What we did in *Pi5* was to remove the diamond rings from any one we assassinated and melt the gold down to make new rings because those rings often contained love messages, encrypted, and inscribed on the back of the ring."

"What about that beautiful jewellery?"

"You can give it to me. I will find a way to dispose of it. I am joking Jules, three pieces will do, I've become a non-consumerolistarian."

Oh gawd, everyone except me is training to be some sort of ologist or arian.

"Jules, I have idea. Build a glass cabinet in the foyer to the resort that Gero is having built; it will have to be big, and hang the jewellery pieces in it with a big sign Replicas – not real gold or diamonds. The items are too beautiful to destroy."

"Great idea, Bea."

"Geddon, can you carry this wooden chest back to my cabin, I have a slight back problem so cannot help."

I lied, gold weighs a lot. I couldn't even lift the chest but Geddon has no difficulty. We make it back to my cabin. Pleb is still in her Yoga poise desperately trying to set free her tangled legs. I give her a hand.

"Pleb, I have a gift for you. It's a gold chain with a diamond. Let me put it around your neck."

"Oh, thank you Jules, it is beautiful. It must have cost you a fortune."

"It did Pleb, but you're worth it, let me give you a kiss."

That night would not go down too well. Pleb and I walk to the BBQ area to help in the preparation of dinner. The tourists are on a weeklong boat cruise to far north Queensland which is a relief. If Bea can sell the gold coins discreetly we may not have to cater for painful tourists ever again.

"Look Jules! Bea, Cara, Viksi, Doris and even the android girls are also wearing lovely jewellery made of gold and diamonds!"

"What an incredible coincidence," I reply.

Pleb goes over to talk to the ladies. "Did your partners also spend a fortune on that beautiful gold and diamond jewellery that you are wearing?"

I start running along the beach but looking back. Pleb grabs a pile of plates and starts chasing me. "You miserly scunge-pad!" she yells as she throws a plate at me.

Zia sprints over and grabs Pleb, "You cannot waste good plates on Jules otherwise you humans will have to use Banana plant fronds as plates but let me show you how to skim a plate so it hits the target."

I'm worried. Zia can probably compute the aerodynamic equations and make a direct hit. Then she bursts out laughing.

"Pleb, Jules told me he was going to tell you that it was just a joke and that he was going to let you choose other jewellery from the buried treasure we had found; as much as you want."

I cautiously come walking back to Pleb and Zia.

"Jules, is that true?"

"Of course it is. Would I lie to you?"

"Come over, Jules, I'll give you a hug."

I hesitatingly walk over to Pleb and we hug. She doesn't break my neck. I give Zia a wink; she could certainly become a diplomat. She has worked out how we humans think and how to calm a potentially very dangerous situation. That night a drone lands by the BBQ area and deposits a crib. I can hear crying.

Gero grabs Dyslexa, "The baby android is hungry. It needs a recharge, go and connect him or her to our electricity supply and connect yourself as well as we have all had a very busy day."

"Can I breast feed electricity? I would like that human experience."

"No, not yet but I am sure that option will be available soon."

Dyslexa and Geddon march off to their cabin with the baby android.

Bea comes over to me. "Oopee, the first, the first of those 16th century coins just got sold for $40,000 worth of Nitcoin and I get 20% commission."

"Bea, can that transaction be traced?"

"Jules, it's cryptocurrency, all criminals use it."

"Bea, I don't feel comfortable with that, I'm old school and like to see material wads of $500 notes, not that computer stuff, 1's and 0's, floating in some cloud. You and Sid take a trip to Rome and I'll give you 20 gold coins to sell; 20% commission but be careful and don't mention the treasure, just say a very ancient relative left them to you as an inheritance."

"Do you think I am an intcerpop? I want 50% commission."

"What? There is no such word, how about 25%?"

"No 50% and if I'm caught I will remain silent and not mention your name unless they start torturing me or pulling my hair."

"Bea, how about 30%?"

"35%. OK, that is a deal but you purchase the airfares for me, Sid and accommodation and other costs."

Next morning I drive the motorboat to Townsville. Bea and Sid get off and waive goodbye.

"Jules, you could possibly be sending our friends to their deathbed. *Pi5* is still after Bea and they will find a way to trace her whereabouts as she used her true name on that passport Mystca had manufactured. *Pi5* have agents working for all the major airlines so it will not be a difficult task to find her and Sid. Ring Bea now and stop her boarding that jet plane."

I quickly ring Bea. "You and Sid, don't get on that plane. You could be killed. I'll explain later but for now make your way back to the Townsville harbour. I'll pick you up on my motorboat from the usual spot."

I'm about to rush out to the jetty but Pleb stops me. "Jules, we don't need the money. I have just read my phone messages and learnt that my father Wadeck has passed away into the sky and has left me a huge inheritance and his cabin."

Pleb has tears streaming from her eyes. I give her a hug.

I ring Bea. "Bea and Sid, we don't need the money from the sale of those coins and besides you could be traced and possibly terminated. We have to keep a low profile but you can keep two gold coins to meltdown and have some gold tooth fillings."

"What are you implicating Jules? I clean my, what do you call them, falsies everyday."

"Bea, one gold coin each and one item of jewellery, the rest gets donated to the QLD museum as an extraordinary treasure find."

That night, by the BBQ all our full-time residents get a gold coin. We guys also take a piece of jewellery just in case we ever separate from our current partners and meet someone new but we don't tell them that. Pleb also grabs some jewellery and coins for Mystca and Tamy.

We wipe the wooden chest to remove fingerprints and follow Geddon as he takes it to the spot we found it. Next day I ring the QLD museum and some news outlets so the handing over of the chest is publicly recorded. Several officious looking guys from the museum arrive by boat followed by several helicopters carrying media crew loaded with cameras and microphones. We guide them to where the chest is located.

"My name is Winston, did you open it?" One of the guys from the museum asks.

"No, of course not; we thought it might contain some explosive device and blow us up so be careful if you open it and wear those bomb-proof clothing costumes."

"Not likely," Winston says as he examines the chest. "It is at least 400 years old and well preserved due to this paraffin wax coating." He kneels down beside the hole where the chest lies. "We shall however be careful. I will undo the lash and put this hook onto the lid. I will pull the fishing line attached to the hook to open the lid just in case it is booby-trapped. Now, all of you stand 50 or more metres away and lie on the ground."

Everyone, including the cameramen move away, some with hands against their ears. Winston pulls the fishing line and the chest opens. "Stay still, wait five minutes," he yells. Winston then walks over to the chest. "Oh my god, this is an exceptionally rare find. The chest is half full of jewellery and gold coins."

The camera men come rushing over and start filming.

"Sir, we'd like to interview you," one of the news crew asks Gero.

"No, if the location of our peaceful island is broadcast on TV we will be inundated by gold diggers looking for treasure chest but we like our privacy. Please do not disclose the location of this island as we lead a peaceful life, out of what you call the limelight or goldlight. The News crew were only invited to make sure Mr Winston does the right thing and doesn't get tempted by a coin or two."

"Sir, sir, are you the owner of this island?"

"No, Jules is, the guy standing there. He leases it from the government."

The news reporters come rushing over.

"Guys and girls, please respect our wishes and don't inseminate any camera clips of us or our location. We live by the *Moronic* faith and our innocent lives are very simple and private. We do not want publicity," says Gero"

"But you could make money, lots of money if you open up this island resort to gold diggers."

"Son, come over here and let me place my hands on your forehead so we can telepathically communicate and blend our minds," Gero says.

"This island is full of weirdos. It could become an asylum for weirdos. Let's leave," one of the News reporters yells.

"Son, come over here again. If you publish the location of where we live, you will not walk on water. You will sink anytime you go for a swim. I have put a curse on you and you can try it out now. Go into the water," Gero yells.

"I have my best suit on and I'm not stripping off to go swimming," yells the news reporter. He and his crew start running back to their copter though some trip on the weeds a few times.

Winston comes over to me and Gero. "That was a convincing performance. Keep what you got," he says whilst winking. "Your island will remain anonymous to the public media."

We watch them all depart.

I pat Gero on the shoulders. "You should become an actor."

Gero replies, "Jules that was not an act." Then he laughs and puts his hand on my shoulder. "It worked. Do you think I could make it to Hollywood?"

Geddon also comes over and pats Gero on the back. "I have learnt much from watching and listening to you. You can be my father, the father I never had."

Gero and I briefly glance at each other then Gero diplomatically replies, "Sure my son."

Geddon walks away with a huge smile on his face and joins Dyslexa. "I now have a father," he yells out. "Dyslexa, you should ask Gero if he can be your father too."

"Geddon, it does not work that way with humans. You have to find a new father for me. We both can't have the same father."

"Then. Dyslexa, you have to ask some of these other humanoid males if they want to be your father and grandfather of our children."

"But for now. Geddon, we have to go back to our cabin and be with our baby. She may need a feed of electricity."

I can hear them talking as they walk back, "We also need a mother, I will ask Bea and Doris if they would consent to be our mothers."

"Doris could be a grandmother, humans have those as well."

Doris still has acute hearing and she wasn't too happy. We had to crack open a bottle of wine to calm her down. Then another boat arrives at the jetty. Out step Mystca and Tamy, with large bellies, followed by Grillian and Adrian. Pleb rushes over and gives them hugs and kisses.

So, another night of celebration by the BBQ. "No, Stepdad, Tamy and I can't drink alcohol till after our offspring are out, but we are very hungry. What's on the menu?"

Pleb and I watch as Gerald, Sid and Rog do the cooking. There is much merriment and hugging.

"Jules, you better have another shot of that peptide. I don't want to look after grandchildren on my own, you have to stay useful for another 20 years and learn how to change nappies. That's what grandparents are for," says Pleb.

So just when you hope life would be simple again, it wasn't going to be the case. Two new grandkids are due soon, plus four rapidly evolving androids who ask many questions.

Chapter Forty-five

I'm cleaning the BBQ area along with the other guys when a ferry boat arrives at our island jetty. She steps off the ferry and walks to the BBQ area.

I rub my eyes. I haven't indulged in magic mushrooms for years. It must be some sort of psychotic delusion. She has the same appearance as my deceased former wife.

"My name is Melissa," she says.

I descend down to the sand, holding my head. Rog, Sid, Gero, Gerald and Greuger help me up.

"My friends told me that this was a safe place for androids to live and I am sorry if I have caused you constipation or is the word consternation? It is no coincidence. I requested this body and face so I could stay on this island. Can I visit Dyslexa?"

"Melissa, you would have been allowed to stay without having to remind me of my deceased wife and from now on your name is Clarissa, not Melissa."

"Would you like me to alter my face? I can do that if my face causes you consternation."

"Yes, but not now. Dyslexa and her partner Geddon live in that cabin over there. Zia and Electrica live in the next cabin on the left. They are also androids."

Clarissa starts walking, then collapses. We guys rush over.

"Gero, what's wrong with her?"

Gero, check the digital readout behind her neck. "Same problem that Geddon had. She has only 2% of power left. She needs to be recharged quickly. Take her back to my place, I have some fast chargers."

Doris opens the door, "I've seen that face before. Is it Melissa, that wife Jules once had?"

"No Doris, she is Clarissa an android and critically low on power. She needs to be plugged in."

We carry Clarissa in and Gero gets out the charger and plugs Clarissa in. Doris does not look happy. That night at the BBQ the androids, including charged-up Clarissa, join us so as to learn more OZ human social skills, like how to say *How about a beer mate,* to start a conversation.

"Stop staring at her," says Pleb as she thrusts her elbow into my ribs. For a moment I cringe in pain and look away from her.

"Gero, are you sure you're not an android?" I ask.

"Jules, I told you before that I am not. I am just fascinated by these android beings we have created and how they have evolved."

"But Gero, what if they try to take over our planet?"

"As I said before, I hope they do. I'm sure they would do a better job than our current world leaders."

Pleb comes back and gives me a hug. "I am sorry, Jules. I overheard the conversation you had with Gero. I will try to be an android and obey your every command," she says with a grin.

"No Pleb, I love you just as you are. Yes, she reminds me of my previous wife, but I have moved on."

Then the lights go off. Luckily, it's a full moon.

"Gero, I have no fuel left for the diesel-powered generator. We need to purchase more solar cells and batteries. These androids are draining our island's electricity supply."

"Jules, relax, we will do that tomorrow. Enjoy the moonlight and the stars. Look there; a falling star."

Clarissa comes over. "I am sorry. I do not have a low power saving mode like the other Androids have. I am an older model," she says as she rests her head on Gero's shoulder. "Have you got a treadmill or static pushbike device connected to an electricity generator? I will work all through the night to recharge your island's batteries."

"No Clarissa," says Gero, "That would not be practical. You would use more electricity than you could produce peddling and you would also get very hot. Your circuit microchips could start behaving erratically."

We all have an early night and retreat to our cabins. Clarissa follows Gero and Doris. Gero's large cabin has four bedrooms so there is plenty of space for Clarissa.

Pleb and I are lying in bed. "Jules, I did some further research on Gero. Before being the head of *Ii5* he was a top AI scientist for a company called Androcyla but he got dismissed because of his radical beliefs about the function of androids in society and making them indistinguishable from humans. He was once quoted as saying that he hopes to get an android body himself one day and have all his memories and knowledge transferred to its electronic brain. We must be careful. He may have plans for our island to convert us all to androids. You should also warn Doris."

"Pleb, I feel like turning off and going to sleep, it's been a big day. Can we discuss this tomorrow?"

"Jules are you a very old model of an android and cannot cope with the deploma we are in? Sorry, meant dilemma."

"Pleb, I just have a lot to think about. Move closer. Tomorrow morning I'll prove I'm not an android."

Chapter Forty-six

Gero must have phoned his industrial connections late at night because we are awakened by drones and barges arriving. I step outside. Gero is pointing and guiding the construction workers. There are four of them, plus their boss, Hulio. They have to carry the panels, aluminium beams and batteries to a spot well above the tide. They also carry bags and bags of concrete and metal rods to reinforce the concrete floors, and also a concrete mixer.

Hulio, possibly an architect and solar expert, walks over to Gero and me. "I have examined your island's coordinates and the angle the panels must be set at to maximise solar power capture. We need a cleared North facing spot to lay the concrete for the panel support beams so the panels are tiltrd up five degrees, pointing at the sun. Have you got a preferred spot?"

"Yes, behind the cabins, close by so we can clean the panels and remove any fallen leaves," I say.

Gero and I guide Hulio to the potential spot.

"This spot of land will have to be cleared and levelled. I will have to get a drone to drop a mini bulldozer to do the job. It will add cost to the initial quote."

"Yes, do it," says Gero.

An hour later, the mini bulldozer is delivered.

Pleb comes over to me. "Jules, what if they discover more buried treasure or bones of deceased people, whose departure we may have contributed to?"

"I don't think so, Pleb. Gero was wandering around the planned site with a metal detector. He reassured Hulio he was just checking for metal water pipes. He gave me the thumbs up, which means it's all OK, no buried bones in the proposed building site."

It has been a very long day for the construction workers who levelled the land, fitted wooden panels to hold the concrete until it dried and poured concrete in. Two level blocks of concrete have been created, one for the solar panel structure and the other for the shed to store the batteries.

Hulio approaches Gero and me. "The concrete will take 2 to 3 days to solidify, but next day we shall build the structure to support the panels, construct the metal shed for the batteries, and install the cables to your central electricity power box."

"Jules, I have transferred $500,000 into your bank account as well as paying for the panels, batteries and construction costs of our additional electricity supplies. No, I am not going to take over your island, nor have it overrun by androids. These five androids are just my babies. I am so happy to have them."

"Gero, what if they start thinking differently? They are developing emotions and feelings. They may not be rational citizens in the future, just as humans aren't rational when emotions step in. They may become too much like us humans. And Gero, we live on this island to be separated from all that shit that happens on the mainland."

"Jules, their prime programmed directive is to be kind and useful to humans. They will not harm you or try to take over the island. I am also increasing my rental payments made to you."

Gero may have spoken too soon. We hear yelling and screaming from behind the cabins and run over. Geddon and Greuger are facing each other off, both looking very angry and throwing some punches. Gero runs over.

"Geddon, stop! What is the reason for this confrontation?"

"Our baby is non-responsive. She needs an immediate recharge else her memories will fade. I was just connecting this electrical power cord to the solar cells when this humanoid beast challenged me."

"Jules, I would like to use my electrical-powered face shaver. Both Jill and Chloe4 don't like my facial hair growth," yells Greuger.

"Greuger, facial hair is now very trendy, but Geddon has a daughter that desperately needs a recharge. Now please go back to your cabins. Our electricity supply will be more reliable once these new solar panels and batteries are installed."

Geddon and Greuger sneer at each other as they walk back to their cabins.

"Gero, what were you saying before?"

"Jules, it was a logical conclusion by Geddon. He was programmed to protect his baby. He would not have hurt Greuger though they are very evenly matched."

"Are you sure?"

"Jules, as well as an *i5* worker, you were once a pharmacologist, a scientist many, many years ago. Yes, I have researched you as well, and as a scientist, you know about probability. Nothing is certain, but some outcomes are more likely than others based on our current knowledge."

"Gero, there is also something called Chaos Theory where a very small change can have a very large unpredictable effect."

"Trust me, Jules, I am keeping an eye on my androids, and their electronic brains have an inbuilt disablement function which I can trigger from my phone. I can turn them off at any time."

"I hope they don't turn you off first."

"Jules, don't worry. Their programming included the highest ethical standards; they will not harm a human."

Everyone is gathered by the moonlit fusion-powered BBQ, even the androids, though initially, they keep to themselves. I start the speech.

"Everyone, please listen. Our current solar panels and batteries are old. They have degraded over time, but the good news is that 200 high-efficiency panels and 100 batteries will be fully functional in the next 3 to 4 days. For now, we have to be patient. No electric cooking in your cabins and no hot water usage for washing your hair or any other bodily parts. Use cold water only, which is not that cold where we live, and limit to 30 seconds of scrubbing, as we still have to maintain our water supply."

Kia yells out, "We androids do not need to shower, and we don't need to cook. We do not ooze smelly sweat from our bodies or down under smells like you humans do after you go to your toilets." She then bursts out in laughter, and the other androids start laughing as well, and so do some of us humans. These androids are definitely evolving a sense of humour, and I hope nothing else.

Bea yells out, "I need to wash my hair, or else I may get termite mites."

Sid comforts her. "I have a spray can of Tortein. It kills all bugs, and I can rub it into your hair."

Gero comes over and starts speaking. "The next three or four days may be inconvenient, but be patient. It will soon be fixed. For the moment, I ask my android friends to go into low-power mode, and if you can have dreams, do not go sleep-walking. Please stay in your cabins."

There is much chatter and discussion. Viksi is furiously taking notes for her latest book *Never Look an Android in the Eye*. She doesn't seem concerned that she may be unable to wash her hair for a few days.

Rog comes over. He must have noticed me watching Viksi taking notes. "Jules, when she's in writing mode, she doesn't wash. She just furiously writes. I sleep on the couch because she can really be a pong to the nose."

We all look up at the sky. It's another meteor shower. I hope they burn up in the atmosphere and not hit our new solar panels. Then I see Greuger walk over to Geddon.

"I am sorry, Geddon, for offending you. Jill loves my unshaven look, and your baby is, what do you say, adorable. I regret that Hilda and I never had a child."

Geddon says, "You could try again with your current partner Jill. Our babies could play with each other, and they would never be lonely."

Greuger and Geddon emotionally hug. Greuger has tears pouring down his face. The two guys are at peace. Chloe4 and Castro stand up on their back legs and clap their front feet because they don't have arms. The androids depart to their cabins, and Greuger waves goodbye to all of them.

"Pleb, what do you think?"

"I think that the androids seem to be evolving to be peaceful, unlike my initial concern of them taking us over; Greuger is also evolving as well. Possibly we all are. We have changed so much for the better than when we worked for the *i5* organizations."

"You may be right, Pleb."

"Jules, I wish I had studied psychology and early childhood development. I don't know what to think, but we should remain cautious. They are evolving very rapidly, and they could make mistakes as we humans do."

"Let's go back to our cabin. I have candles, and we can do that transatlantic meditation together."

Chapter Forty-seven

It's a quiet few nights by the BBQ. We humans still gather there, but not the androids, who have put themselves in a state of suspended animation until we have full electrical power back and they can fully recharge. Then Mystca and Tamy both yell out simultaneously, "I'm having contractions."

Grillian and Adrian rush over to them and hold their hands.

There are ten of us humans on Gero's motorboat heading for Townsville. Chloe4 and Castro wanted to come along as well, but the hospital probably wouldn't allow them in. The receptionist asks us, "Are you from that Neanderthal, half-human species? Our hospital is not equipped to cater for your needs."

Gero uses his skills in diplomacy. "Madam, we were just having a fancy-dress party on the island, disguised in animal skins, where we live, when suddenly the girls started having contractions. They will give birth soon. They must have a room and a physician."

The receptionist makes some phone calls and guides Mystca, Tamy, Grillian and Adrian down a corridor. The rest of us nervously wait.

"Doris, what was it like when you had Charmaine and me."

"Can't remember Jules. You were just an inconvenience at the time. I just asked for a short-acting anaesthetic because I had some multi-national disasters to deal with and had to be back at work ASAP."

We're just talking and nervously waiting.

"I had a home birth," Gerald says. "I spent three months in ICU afterwards."

Pleb looks at Bea. "I can't remember much; I only recently suspect who my mother may be."

Viksi puts down her pen and paper, "I had a normal birth; well, at least that's what I think."

"Greuger, what about you?"

Greuger starts uncontrollably shivering, and tears pour down his face. Jill grabs him. "I grew up in an orphanage. My parents overdosed on heroin soon after I was born. I do not miss them." Being here seems to ignite pain in Greuger.

"Jill, what about you?"

"I think I had a good childbirth from what I saw of the photos of me popping out. My father tried to help pull me out headfirst, according to those photos. My childhood was good."

"Cara, what about you, what do you remember?"

"Nothing till much older. We were looked after by my mother because my father was away for long times working, and when he came back, we hid under our beds because he was always in a bad mood."

The receptionist comes out. "You have a boy and a girl, both 100% healthy, but they and their parents should stay another night. You can pick them up tomorrow, but please dress well, as photographers will be here to mark our 10,000th baby delivery."

"Can we see them?"

There is much hugging and photos taken of the new juniors and their smiling parents.

Gero hugs the receptionist. "We'll be back tomorrow."

Unfortunately, or fortunately, a nubile filmmaker/journalist was at the hospital reception area when we were there. She scribbles notes faster than Viksi.

"Jules, you have to look presentable, not like a caveman, else the news reporters will publish that evolution has gone backwards, and humans will revert back to being amoeba," says Pleb.

"Ok, Pleb, we'll do some clothes shopping."

So we all pass the time and enter clothes shops, not the same ones. Four hours later, we meet at the jetty.

"Jules, you look like that ancient Elvis Presley singer guy."

"Well, Rog, you look like Spiderman in the 50th remake."

Bea would make a good vampire. She smiles, "Do you like my new sharp teeth."

Doris chose an Octopus costume. The others were a bit more conservative, with lots of plastic 1980s style clothing.

After a quiet night by the BBQ, next day Gero drives us back on his motorboat to the Townsville Hospital to pick up our junior relatives and their partners.

"You're under arrest," one of the police officers yells at Rog whilst pointing a laser gun. "We've been after that Spiderman guy for over 20 years."

Gero, dressed as a turtle, walks over to them. "Dear officers, we are just dressed in fancy dress to celebrate the birth of our new family members. We can give you their names, and Rog and the Spiderman-dressed guy have a fear of heights, so please do not test him. I will phone Commissioner Davis to confirm the facts. He is not the Spiderman you are after."

The police officers glance at each other and allow us to proceed.

"Mum, stepdad, could you have just dressed like normal? I'm highly embarrassed seeing you here. I hope this incident doesn't appear on Gootube because there was someone here called Anastasia filming you guys."

Anastasia approaches us. "We are filming an episode of the *Weird and Wonderful* for the National Biographic TV channel and magazine. Can I and my camera crew follow you? You will be paid well but don't appear too normal. The audience likes weird people like you."

Anastasia is a tall, thin lady with blond hair to her shoulders and a fringe almost down to her eyebrows. She reminds me of a girlfriend, Shaz, whom I knew a very, very long time ago; a brief relationship, but she is deceased. I still sometimes secretly look at the photo she gave me of herself. I'm dreaming, have to go back to reality.

Pleb notices that I'm giving more than just a casual glance at Anastasia and jabs me in the ribs.

Anastasia faces the camera crew, "This is a first. We have found the missing links, those apes who would eventually evolve into humans. This great scientific discovery will change history books that your kids have to read. We have found the missing specie, the missing links. Stay tuned."

Anastasia approaches me and Gero. "Could we follow you and film your lifestyle for another of our new documentaries - *The Rise of Homo Sapiens*? Do you still crawl on all 4's when at home?"

"Anastasia," Gero replies, "We only crawl on all 4's after drinking too much wine; otherwise, we generally stand and walk upright."

"I will order plenty of wine, gallons of it and lots of raw meat. We want film shots of you chewing raw meat and crawling."

"Anastasia, some of us are not meat eaters. Can you order lots of oysters, crayfish and prawns instead?" Gero asks.

"Sure, whatever."

I interrupt. "You can come with us, but the accommodation is not cheap, and you must not disclose the location of our island."

"Agreed," she jumps up and down in joy.

We Homo Sapiens help Mystca, Tamy and the babies they are clutching back to Gero's motorboat. Anastasia and her crew are still filming but then follow us in their motorboat. Viksi is not happy as now there is film-rights competition.

"Jules, what have we done? We've invited TV reporters to our peaceful island of solitude and fornication."

"Gero, I'm bored. We can have some fun and good food and wine at their expense as we don't have any tourists anymore, and your generous funds will run out eventually. Now you must learn to grunt, as do all the other humans. We have to appear Neanderthal."

"But Jules, the Neanderthals were very intelligent, more so than the humans at the time, but they died off because their immune system wasn't well developed."

We get back to the island before the film crew and change into our goat hide costumes.

"Mystca, put away that plastic bottle to feed Junior. It's breastfeeding only."

Mystca, Tamy and their partners retreat to their cabins while Anastasia and her film crew arrive. They turn their portable generator on and bright camera lights on while the makeup artist does her job.

Greuger, Sid and Rog approach me and whisper, "Jules, can we talk, or should we hop on all fours and just grunt?"

"This is one of the sites where human civilization began and hasn't progressed very much, but please keep connected as in the next few days I will guide you through anthropological insights on how human life might have begun on this planet and failed many times but eventually produced me," Anastasia says whilst being recorded by her film crew. "I am also pleased to announce that we have found the missing links in human evolution, which scientists have been searching for hundreds of years, maybe even thousands of years. They are here on this island, and I will keep you posted and explore their IQ, if there is any, but also their primitive lifestyle and what they eat," Anastasia turns off the microphone and relaxes on the sand by the water.

A giant drone hovers over and drops many boxes of food and wine. We're all starving, having missed breakfast and lunch, so we rush over to the boxes and start ripping the crayfish apart and stuffing the white meat into our mouths. The film crew are joyously filming. Greuger opens a bottle of wine, and we pass it around, then another bottle and another and another.

"Who are these people?" Anastasia yells as she points at Zia, Electrica, Dyslexa,

Clarissa and Geddon, who have come out to join the celebrations but do not partake.

"Ms Anastasia, you will have to have an inquisition to ascertain that information."

"Jules and Gero, the new panels and batteries work well. We are fully recharged, and your electricity supply is at 95%," announces Geddon.

"Stop filming," Anastasia yells to the film crew.

"You didn't tell me that you have well-presented caretakers."

"Anastasia, they look after us. They are our guardians for when we cross this evolutionary hurdle. You can keep on filming. I've drunk two bottles of wine, and my primate partner has also. We shall be crawling on all fours back to our cabin," says Gero.

"Anastasia, I will guide you, as best as I can, to some unoccupied cabins we have for you and your film crew."

"I'm crawling too," says Pleb.

We find two unoccupied cabins and open the doors.

"Wow, this is luxury. I didn't know Neanderthals had 3-D TV sets and music stereos," yells out Anastasia. "Now, tell me about those guardians."

"Tomorrow, when we do our morning run around the island. We Neanderthals have to keep fit. Hope you can join us at 8 am by the BBQ."

Both Pleb and I aren't too steady on our feet, so we crawl back to our cabin.

"Jules, what have you done? We have to pretend to be actors. I have never acted, and I am a little nervous."

"Pleb, they are paying really well for us to be in the documentary, so we have to act a little bit; it may be fun. I mean, we had run out of things to do, and it was getting a bit boring on the island. We just can't shave any bodily hair and wear those animal skins we normally wear. Won't be hard and may even be fun."

"But what about the androids? They cannot be deceitful?"

"I'll get Gero to talk to them in the morning; they must keep a low profile. Now do you want to do some grunting?"

"You are always so romantic, Jules."

Chapter Forty-eight

Next day we resident island humans meet by the BBQ area dressed in leather animal skins. Gero must have asked the androids to stay in isolation longer, and Mystca and Tamy look after their babies. So it's only ten of us, and we're not feeling that well after that massive wine dose last night. Cara does a vomit or two and tries to stand up. She's captured on film by a drone.

Then Anastasia and her two film crew members and makeup artist come marching out, also looking a bit worse for wear. The two guys have head cameras with built-in microphones.

"Clark, stop filming, turn the camera off," yells Anastasia.

"But Ana, you look so sexy in that skimpy underwear."

"I thought the Neanderthals ran naked, and this is as naked as I'm getting."

All the guys, including me, are staring at Anastasia and unconsciously licking our lips, but not for long after we all get whacked on our faces by our partners.

"I and my film crew and makeup artist will run behind to film your ancient running style."

"Just as well," Rog whispers. "I don't think I could focus where I'm running if she was in front and could have a serious accident tripping over one of those rocks or palm fronds."

We briefly stop after one lap of the island. Donna, the makeup artist, comes running over and touches up Anastasia's face with lots of cosmetics.

"Clark, aim the camera at my face, nowhere else and turn the microphone on."

Anastasia starts speaking as we all continue running.

"You could call this Doctor Moron's Island after that very old movie, but the Neanderthals here are running upright most of the time unless they have consumed too much wine, in which case they crawl."

"Ana, I can't go any further. Take the head camera and microphone," says Clark. Morris, the other film guy, is also huffing and puffing and unable to continue on. By the end of the third lap, we're all crawling on all fours except for Anastasia. "Start filming," she yells to Morris, then she walks over to Greuger and stares him in the eye.

"You, with that unshaven, muscular appearance, look like a true Neanderthal. You will be the star of my documentary when I get funding for it."

Greuger waves his head from side to side. He doesn't like the attention. It's a definite no-no.

"What about the rest of what I assume are males? You will have to wear false beards and have lots of facial hair, which my makeup artist can arrange. You will also have to wander around the island naked and foraging for food whilst the film crew are filming what life was like 30,000 years ago."

"Jules, I'm not comfortable with this," whispers Gero. "When I led *Ii5,* I had a tattoo engraved on my butt; it says *Conquer,* but I don't believe in that anymore. I tried to get that tattoo removed and now have lots of scaring after a skin graft."

Then it happens. The androids come marching out, led by Geddon. Zia, Electrica, Clarissa and Dyslexa. They stand there with their arms folded and looking very menacing.

"Start filming, Clark. This species is far more evolved and interesting than the Neanderthals."

"Madam, we are androids. We have developed emotions and human-like thinking. Gero and Jules have allowed us to stay here and grow," says Geddon.

"Stop filming, guys. I need a moment of silence and reflection," Anastasia says as she wanders around in circles holding her head. She beckons Clark, Morris and Donna, the makeup artist, to follow her.

"Clark, Morris, we have a conflict of interest. We have these sophisticated androids and these Neanderthal-like beings living on the same island. We have to develop a new storyline that merges the two and comes up with something half normal; start thinking."

Twenty minutes later, Anastasia comes back.

"We would like to stay longer and pay double. Your species are anthropologically very interesting, and we would like to study you more."

Gero wanders over to Anastasia. "Ana, we are not Neanderthals; we have just chosen this simple lifestyle. Before that, some of us worked for a global *Pay as You Go* spy agency, *i5*'s, and we killed people, mostly bad people. We do not do that anymore, not recently, that is."

Anastasia starts wandering in circles again, holding her head, and then Viksi comes over and puts her hand on her shoulder. "My name is Viksi, and I'm also a writer waiting to be published. I'm on my 5th book about what happens on this island. We could scratch each other's back, so to speak."

Anastasia looks up. "Sure, but am I and my film crew safe here?"

"Ana, the boys recently only disposed of three agents of this worldwide spy agency. Those agents were going to kill some members of our island for defecting. I will email you my books. You could direct a spy thriller movie instead of working for that National Demographic publication."

"I'll give it some thought. Do your books also include the androids?"

"They sure do, and Ana, most of the humans on this island are very highly educated."

"Yes, yes, I'll give it consideration. Can they act?"

"They had you and your film crew fooled, pretending to be Neanderthals, so they probably can."

Bea comes wandering over with a glass of banana juice and hands it to Anastasia. I rush over and lunge at Anastasia, knocking her down to the ground before she has a chance to sip it. "Don't drink it. It could be laced with a poison called Novichok".

Pleb comes rushing over. "Is that how you hope to get a lay?" She pulls me up by my hair.

Anastasia gets up, looking a bit rattled and brushes her hair and costume. "I will try to get a movie deal, and Viksi, send me the books. I'll see what I can do. Now I need to rest. I'll see you later and have a drink of sealed organic bottled water."

"It worked!" Bea joyously claps. "I want to be a female movie star. I could be the next Marilyn Monrow."

"More like the next Marilyn Manson," Viksi whispers.

Chloe4 and Castro also look excited; no one else does.

Chapter Forty-nine

The others come over. "Gero and Jules, do you think this is a good idea?"

"I am thinking," says Gero. "Yes, we could get the androids to star in the movie. I can get more if required and train them. It would advance the android cause for acceptance in our society."

I am thinking. too. Gero must have premature dementia. Bea is swaying her head from side to side to indicate a *no*.

Geddon comes walking over. "I overheard your conversation. We have acute hearing. Last night Dyslexa and I watched our first movie on the TV set. It was called *Avatar15*. We liked it very much and have been rehearsing, playing the parts of the different characters. We learn quickly, so acting would not be difficult for us."

Gero beckons Electrica. "My darling, there are four adult female androids on this island and only one male. Could I get you a male body?"

"No way," Electrica replies in an Ozzie accent. She must have been watching OZ TV as well and has learnt the OZ vernacular, which is very simple.

"Jules, what do you think? I can call a friend and get more androids delivered to make the movie."

"Sounds good to me, it is starting to get a bit boring in paradise."

That night, as we're all sitting by the BBQ, a drone lands and out pops down two male androids.

"My name is Folger, and my companion is Golger. We will be of service, but do you have a reliable electricity supply? Our previous owner did not feed us much electricity, and we were electrically starved. We are now down to 10% so we need a recharge quickly."

Kia and Electrica come rushing over. "What type of charging port have you got?"

"USB-10".

"We have chargers and adapters to fit those ports."

Anastasia and her film crew and makeup artist come out and join us by the BBQ. They all look exhausted.

"We have drawn up new contracts and have a deal to produce *The Rise of the*

Androids. You humans get exterminated in this movie as the androids rise to power and take over the planet, even China."

"No, Anastasia!" yells Geddon, "We live a peaceful co-existence."

"OK, you come up with a better story as my contract for Life Demographic will expire in six months if I don't produce anything credible. I will be unemployed and may have to live on an island as a Neanderthal."

Morris, one of the film crew, whispers to Anastasia, "This lifestyle could be more fun than what we have been living. We could ditch our stress medication; how many pills are we all on?"

Geddon starts talking again. "You could produce a documentary about how androids and humans have learnt to co-exist. It could be a metaphor for what all your at-war nations are doing on this planet."

Anastasia pops a few more pills and then replies, "Yes, yes, we can do a deal."

Chapter Fifty

That night we're all sitting by the BBQ, humans and androids.

"We have to write a script," Anastasia says.

Kia interrupts, "Ask Jules to tell you the story about that human life-prolonging peptide he invented and still uses. He is over 160 Earth years old while we are designed to permanently shut down at only 60 years of age."

"Wow, is that guy Jules over 160 years old? I want some of that stuff. Can it cure a hangover?" Clark asks.

Anastasia is nervously twitching. "Jules, tell me how this island project got initially started."

"Anastasia, it all began when I looked behind my fridge and found the phone number of a lady I had met who eventually I found out was my then-wife and had planned to kill me. I'll email you a digital copy of my unpublished book that's called *Don't Look Behind the Fridge*, it's the prequel to the story I am writing now."

Viksi interrupts. "I am the writer here. There cannot be two writers on a small island like this. There's not enough room for two writers."

"Viksi, you weren't even a twinkle in your parent's eyes when I wrote that first book. It's a spy story. Ask Bea. She is almost as old as I am. She can tell you what it was like working for *i5*; no, then again, ask Doris, my mother. She once headed all the twenty-four *i5* organizations which were hired to do clandestine acts of destruction and assignation for various governments, who were guaranteed anonymity and non-disclosure. Most of these *i5s* have since closed down."

Both Viksi and Anastasia are rubbing their eyes, information overload, so many possible storylines.

"I and my crew have to go back to our cabins and do some thinking. We shall also read your first story and also consider Geddon's suggestion which I'm starting to like."

"Do you want to eat?"

"We are not hungry. We have work to do. Come Clark, Morris and Donna."

Clark, Morris and Donna look hungry and not very happy as they march off following Anastasia. The rest of us humans start chopping veggies and cooking prawns and oysters on the BBQ and also drinking some of the wine Anastasia has supplied. Then Geddon calls all the androids over. "We shall have what you call a think-tank, and we shall start writing a story and script about our experience on this island and how we learnt to live in peace and harmony with the humans even though they do not make much logical sense to us."

Dyslexa calls out, "We could call our story *Chip Meets Neuron*."

"I like that title," Geddon responds. The other androids nod their heads in agreement.

"Geddon, I will email you the story I'm writing called *The Life of Bea*. It has background information about how you all ended on this island and some of the challenges we all faced."

"Yes, Jules, please do that. We are quick readers."

Pleb comes over to me, not looking too pleased. "You could have called your story *The Life of Pleb*."

"Pleb, I started writing this story before I met you, and you and Gero are the dominant characters in the story. You can read it tonight though it's a long, long story. I paint you in very complimentary ways. You will not be disappointed, and I promise, the sequel will be called *The Life of Pleb*."

"Jules, and all this time, I thought you were watching porn videos when you worked on your computer late at night."

"No, never." OK, I did lie a little bit.

"Jules, you have a recursive story. It's a story within a story, and they go round and round in circles. You are promoting your first story, and your second story promotes the first, and the first gives clues to the second and third story. Do you seek the lame light and getting to be a famous published author?"

"No, Pleb, I don't seek the *lime*light. I am perfectly happy due to meeting you."

"You have made the correct response. Now let us go back to our cabin, but not before hugging Mystca and Tamy and their babies a goodnight."

Next morning, we start the runs or, more like, jogs around the island again. Mystca and Tamy are rearing to go whilst Grillian and Adrian mind the babies. Anastasia and her film crew don't appear, neither do the androids.

We all manage three slow laps and stay in a close group. No one tries to win. Having babies must have dissipated Mystca's and Tamy's highly competitive spirit. Then it's Adrian's and Grillian's turn while we mind the babies.

"Jules, we should check on Anastasia and the androids," Gero says.

We knock on the door of Anastasia's cabin. She comes out. She has bloodshot eyes, uncombed hair and hasn't used any underarm deodorant.

"We're just checking if all is well, and we can bring you some food."

We peek inside the door. The androids are there, sitting on the floor with the film crew. The discussion is lively.

"Tell Viksi I'm sorry. I like Geddon's script, and he has borrowed a lot of material from your current book, but he acknowledges you and gives you credit. These androids can sure knock out a TV script in record time. I would like that Greuger guy to play the role of you. He is more photogenic," says Anastasia.

I'm a bit disappointed, but I look at the bright side. I can sit on a lounge couch outside, sipping a wine, whilst the other actors are screamed at by Anastasia.

"Yes, please bring my crew and me some food. We are getting peckish."

Clark, Morris and Donna nod their heads and appear to be salivating. I bring the leftovers from last night. The rest of the humans are called in by Anastasia and given our script lines to rehearse.

"I don't read English very well, can you have this translated to Polish," says Bea.

"You only have a small part, You don't have to speak much."

Bea stares at Anastasia with a look that could kill.

Rog comes over and tries to break the girls up.

"You cannot even cook a Golabki. You are a useless specimen of the human cooking race," says Bea. "And Sister, if you want a competition, I am up to it tonight, by the BBQ."

"What! A cooking competition?" asks Anastasia.

"No, a Kung Chew competition, it's like boxing, says Bea."

"I was a Kung Chew champion when I was young," says Anastasia.

Geddon and Gero intervene. "Ladies, please calm down. Geddon's story is about peaceful co-existence between humans and androids, but how can we have a peaceful co-existence if we humans cannot live peacefully? There will be no fighting on this island," says Gero.

Both Bea and Anastasia stare menacingly at each other, then walk away but looking back and snarling at each other.

Rog asks Sid, "Who would have you place a bet on?"

"Rog, they're fairly evenly matched. I don't know, and I've got an idea."

"Ladies," Sid calls out, "We could film this contest and sell the film rights. We could call it *Gross Fight Female Island*, and you could fake it so neither of you get hurt. Those matches have many viewers, and the wrestling actors get at least $50,000 per match."

Anastasia rubs her head and thinks. "We need the finances to film Geddon's script, and it would take time to film and produce as the plot is quite complex and would only attract a niche market. We need to film something quickly, else the National Demographic won't renew our contracts.

"You want to do it, Bea? I'll train you in Kung Chew, but I have to win."

"No, it will be best out of three bouts, five rounds each," replies Bea. "You can win the first bout, and I win the second. The third bout we could make, what is it called, a free-for-all?"

"That's fine by me," says Anastasia with a smile that could kill and pokes an index finger at Bea.

"And I get 40% of the profits," says Bea.

"5%," says Anastasia.

Eventually, Anastasia convinces Bea that the film crew have to be paid and that's lots of work that has to be done to promote the event.

"I will wear a mask and use a false identity. I cannot be identified as there could be people who are still after me and want to kill me," says Bea.

"I will also wear a mask and costume and use an alias name, as partaking in such an event could ruin my prospects of advancing the career ladder at National Demographic", says Anastasia. "I just need cash at the moment."

"I will be Catwoman," says Bea.

"No, I'm Catwoman, you can be Batwoman," says Anastasia.

"But there has never been a Batwoman."

"You might start a new genre."

Bea thinks for a while. "Yes, that is a good idea. I may become a film star, the first bat girl."

"I'll get the delivery of costumes and masks organized," says Anastasia.

Gero joins the conversation. "Ladies, no one can get hurt, please remember that else I'll ask Jules to have you both removed from the island."

"Gero, don't worry, it will be fake and scripted with fake slapping sounds broadcast through speakers. I know you have contacts. Can you get a wrestling ring and those foldable chairs that are made of balsa wood delivered; you know, those ones that are light and break really easily when a wrestler hits another with a chair, that type that are used in World Wrestling Configuration matches? I'll fund the purchases."

Gero looks at me with a slightly worried face. "Gero, it could be some excitement. I'm for it if no one gets hurt."

Geddon looks at the other androids, "These humans don't make any logical sense."

Dyslexa replies, "Geddon, you have to develop what is called a sense of humour. Humans do not make sense, but they are good at messing up things. Let us just watch and think about what not to learn. Now laugh."

"You are right, Dyslexa. Let's just watch their foibles and learn not to make the same mistakes that they do." Gannon puts his arm around Dyslexa's shoulder.

"Clark, Morris, start filming and get the filming drones out. Also, download Viksi's clips of crowded stadiums and super-impose the crowds to this island's footage. Donna, you order some fake blood to be delivered by drone, eight litres should do."

"Can't we just use tomato sauce? It looks like blood when diluted, is cheap and tastes good."

"OK, you can go into town tomorrow and purchase the tomato sauce, as the supermarket doesn't make small drone deliveries. Also, get some dark shoe polish which we apply to our skin, so we appear bruised after the first match.

That night, by the BBQ, everyone is quiet. Maybe they're thinking of the plots for Geddons's story and the Kung Chew match. We all have an early night.

Chapter Fifty-one

Next morning we're all gathered at the BBQ for the morning run. Even the androids join us though they don't need to exercise. Anastasia and Bea look at each other, dressed in their Catwoman and Batwoman costumes. It's that sort of look like, *who's gonna win, sis.*

"It's the build-up to the event that's going to quake the nation. You run slow and only do one lap. I can speed the video footage afterwards and make it appear like it's a really large island," says Clark.

"No need, Clark, this part of the film doesn't get edited. It's for real. Just make sure the drone cameras focus mainly on me," says Anastasia.

Clark is recording his commentary. "This is the biggest event of this type in the last century. It's Catwoman versus Batwoman, and they have been training hard for the physical Kung Chew contact holds, which require extreme endurance training. It will be so exciting, and no controversial holds are banned, so it's a free-for-all, well, not free in the sense of not paying to view. It's only $100 to see live the fight of the century between scantily dressed warriors on your visual devices. Any chaos can happen as these two women warriors really, really dislike each other. Stay tuned, and pay the fee, as the match will be a thriller and may turn into a full-blown wrestling match that will require doctors and ambulances to be onsite."

Gennon whispers to Dyslexa. "Two humans with such big egos."

Dyslexa replies, "What if our egos evolve? That is a possibility, and we will become like them."

"They're running fairly fast," says Mystca to me. "If I wasn't out for nine months due to pregnancy, I think I could keep up with them."

They do two laps of the island. They are on a mission. Bea never made it for more than one lap ever before, and the rest of us are struggling after a late night of indulgence. The winner's result is a draw. Catwoman and Batwoman crossed the finish line at the same time though not in a great racing time. Luckily Clark sped up the camera recording to make the run look really fast.

The drones were filming and swooping down low. I'm not sure if Bea and Anastasia have come to an amicable agreement, but when we reviewed the video footage, they look like they're about to kill each other, snarling, poking tongues and poking their index fingers out, good publicity.

Gero also acquired a couple of punching bags so the ladies can release their aggression. The wrestling ring has also been delivered and assembled by the androids, who seem far better at reading assembly instructions than we humans. When Rog, Sid Greuger and I tried, it ended up looking like a tent.

The ladies start their Kung Chew training.

"Not so hard," yells Bea, who has some blood dripping from her nose.

Two weeks pass so quickly. Bea has lost a lot of weight and almost looks as lean as Anastasia. The weigh-in is being filmed. Then Bea pokes out her tongue. Anastasia retaliates. I'm not sure who has the longer tongue.

Clark and Morris come rushing over. "We have the script, but you got to rehearse. Greuger will be the referee, and half of you are aligned with Anastasia and the other half with Bea. I'll read out the list of who is on whose side. Now remember it's all in slow motion, your performance that is, so try to look mean and don't look at the cameras or laugh. Just pretend you're hitting each other; make it look realistic."

He continues the rehearsal, "The Bea or Batwoman people come rushing back into the ring to restrain Anastasia, the Catwoman, after she slams one of those Balsa wood chairs on Bea's head all in slow motion, so no one gets hurt. Then Anastasia's supporters come rushing into the ring, and everyone goes for it. I've ordered more of those Balsa wood chairs. Anastasia tested one on me. It doesn't hurt when someone breaks one over your head."

"So, it's all pretend. Is it because you put my name on Anastasia's side? Bea will beat me to death." Sid says.

"OK, I'll change the alliances."

It's like a brawl you couldn't believe, except it's in slow motion. All of us humans are in the ring, flinging open hands and feet; faked, hopefully faked, aggression gone wild.

"Keep filming," yells Anastasia before she cops a thumb in her eye from Bea.

"That wasn't in the script, sister. Now you're going to get a beating, sister."

Anastasia repeatedly punches Bea in the stomach but is eventually restrained by Greuger. Choe4 and Castro are watching but wrap their arms around their eyes.

Round three went for 20 minutes, not the usual 3 minutes; it's chaos. Every human is exhausted, covered in sweat and tomato sauce and wanting a drink of anything. We all crawl or fall out of the wrestling ring.

"We got it all, Anastasia," yell Clark and Morris in joy. "It will be a hit."

Anastasia pulls off her Catwoman mask while on her knees in exhaustion. "Go drown yourself. Boys, where's my makeup artist?"

"Ana, do you want a hand to get up from all fours? You could star in that Neanderthal movie the way you look now," says Clark.

Anastasia looks up with a deadly look on her face. "Clark, you better start running but press the SAVE button on the cameras first."

Chapter Fifty-two

Next morning, we resident humans gather by the BBQ, and then Anastasia and her crew come marching out. Clark and Morris must have been up all night editing the film footage. They don't look too good and have dark rings under their eyes.

Morris yells out, "We got another over 100 million views last night and a huge bonus if we keep on filming. National Demographic is very pleased and has gained thousands of subscribers."

"Put a zip on your lip," says Anastasia.

The androids join us. "Anastasia, could we use your film crew's equipment when they are asleep? We want to make our own documentary about how we androids began and, by pure chance, eventually achieved a consciousness much the same as you humans did. I would like to call the film *Complex Systems – You Never Know What Will Happen*."

"Yeh, take the cameras, I'm not feeling that well, and the film crew need a rest."

We all needed a rest from all the adrenaline. Next morning Geddon and the androids come and join us at the BBQ. "We have finished our first film and posted it to National Demographic early this morning. We have got 150,000 views so far from students studying *The Psychology of Human Dysfunction*."

"Hey kid, you're not taking over from me," yells Anastasia pointing an accusing finger at Geddon.

"We do not wish to take over, and we do laugh at your amusing acts in the ring. Even I learnt to laugh, which is unusual for me, and I would like to form a partnership with your team if Jules and Gero agree."

Anastasia holds her head down in deep thought. "Yes, it could work. You do your android thing, and I, my Neanderthal thing after we finish these fights in the ring, but we'll have to build a film studio on this island."

Gero comes over and hugs Anastasia. "No film studio, things are working out just fine, and both species are successful."

"But they're catching up."

"Yes, and they are also developing self-awareness, something which was never predicted in their AI programming."

Next night it's the final of best of 3 between Bea and Anastasia. Filming drones are flying around in the sky, and the microphones and lighting are all set up. The Balsa wood chairs are ready, and everyone is ready for a night of mayhem. Then a boat arrives at the jetty and out steps a guy.

"Start filming," yells Morris.

"Willy, what are you doing here?" yells Bea.

"I've come to get you, my darling."

"But Willy, I'm married to Sid, the guy standing there."

"We could become Kuslims, and you could have multiple husbands."

Anastasia took advantage of the distraction and wacks Bea in the head and not in slow motion. She then climbs out of the ring and grabs a foldable chair but not one of the light Balsa wood ones. It's total chaos. Sid and Rog try to restrain Anastasia, but she wacks them both with the chair, and they crawl on the ground holding their heads.

Greuger grabs Anastasia as she is climbing back into the ring and manages to restrain her from behind. Gero hops into the ring carrying some rope. Anastasia is wildly kicking, but eventually, Gero manages to tie up her legs and arms and puts a sock in her mouth as she yells obscenities.

With Clark and the drones still filming, Morris steps out holding a microphone. "Dear viewers, the night has not gone well," Morris signals to Clark to film the restrained, writhing Anastasia, "So we may have to have a rematch. Stay tuned and keep sending the *Likes*. So far, we've got 60 million supporters for Bea and 40 million for Ana. I'll keep you posted."

"Stop filming," says Morris to Clark, "We got to go back to the cabin and start editing."

Then Morris comes over to Sid and Rog, who are still holding their heads, "Good acting, guys," he whispers.

"It wasn't acting; it was the real thing!" Sid yells back.

"Ssh, keep it private. I'll arrange a bonus payment for both of you and pay for that dental work for that tooth of yours that got knocked out."

"It's only a denture," Sid mutters.

Then Willy walks past, making his way to the ring.

"Start filming again and turn the microphones on," says Morris to Clark, "I got a feeling something will happen."

Willy, a paying visitor to the island, climbs into the ring and gives Catwoman a hug. "You are a strong woman, and I would like to marry you. You remind me of my ex-wife, who would regularly hit me with chairs and breadboards. I still miss her."

"Give me time to think about your proposal; I haven't slept for three days, and I've run out of medication. I need time to think."

Greuger and Willy carry Anastasia back to her cabin and put her in bed. The film crew follow.

"There's a new unpredicted development occurring here," says Morris into the microphone whilst Clark films. "Who knows what will happen? Will Batwoman cast her wrath at Catwoman after Batwoman's once-boyfriend Willy proposed to Catwoman? Will it be Batwoman's day of revenge? Stay tuned."

"Clark, film that copter flying past. I'll say it's a medical mission to aid the injured combatants."

"Morris, no one got seriously injured. Sure, they bit on those tomato sauce capsules, but no one got injured."

"Clark, you have to make up drama. We have to pretend to be medicos and carry bags full of surgical gear. I'll get that Gannon android to film as we walk up the jetty with our bags."

Gero comes over to me. "Jules, what is going on? There was supposed to be no explicit violence."

"Gero, from what I know, Anastasia was under extreme stress and hadn't slept for three days. I believe tonight was an anomaly in her behaviour."

"Jules, we don't need her here."

"Gero, did you read the online newspapers tonight? Your bank accounts got drained by online fraudsters. You have no money, so it's back to eating stonefish and seaweed if Anastasia doesn't pay us royalties for helping her produce these videos. Most of the human residents staying on this island stay here for free, but I still have to pay huge island lease fees, council rates and income tax from income received from anyone who does pay, and the 100-year lease on the island is due for renewal soon. I hope the lease costs are cheaper than the previous one, as the island is a lot smaller due to sea levels rising from climate change."

Gero does not seem too phased that he lost his fortune. "Didn't Grillian pay you handsomely?"

"Gero, he was highly delusional at the time he arrived. Yes, my bank account seemed to have a million dollars credit, but he must have hacked my web page to appear it was so. I did not pursue him about that because Mystca was happy to have him as her partner. It was your funds that kept us afloat, and now you have none."

"What about Greuger? Doesn't he pay?"

"He did initially but then donated the remainder of his money to some rat protection society. He likes white rats like Chloe."

"OK, let that Anastasia stay for the moment. I am getting a terrible headache and have to go back to Doris. Hopefully, she has an ice pack."

Just as I'm about to go to the cabin and join Pleb, Geddon and the androids confront me.

"We heard the conversations. We are cheap to run due to those solar panels, but we would like to stay on this island till our 60-year expiry date. We have been offered a film deal, and you will be the recipient of any income we receive."

"Sounds good, Geddon, but you androids won't ever be evicted. We'll find a way to pay the expenses. I've seen you fix things on the outside of all the cabins, pickup up rubbish, help with the veggie garden, fix electrical problems we have had, and keep your own cabins spotless, but now I really need to go to sleep; I'm only human. Can we talk about it tomorrow during the morning jog? "

"Yes, that will be *OK* as you humans say."

I go back to our cabin. "Pleb, it's been a wild and chaotic night, and so much is going on in my head. I just want to sleep, or else I may go into a mental shutdown like I did 120 years ago."

Pleb wraps her arm around my shoulder. We fall asleep, but I wake every hour or so with unusual, weird dreams. They are not distressing dreams but totally out of context. I should write them down. The last one was about being in Milan, and Gero's pet rat meets Chloe4, and we have to break them apart as we didn't want any baby rats.

Chapter Fifty-three

It's 8 am, and we're gathered by the BBQ before our run/jog, and I make a speech.

"Our finances are low, and our government expenses are high. Plus, I have to renew the 100-year lease on this island, which is not cheap. We have to allow the filming to proceed and hopefully be recompensed with some income, else we'll be sleeping in tents in parks in Townsville, where there are plenty of mosquitoes, crocodiles and dingoes – those doggy-like creatures that kidnap and eat human babies, and maybe even android babies."

"Stepdad, Tamy, Grillian, Adrian and I can give you money. We had jobs and have plenty of savings still left."

Then Morris comes rushing in. "We had over 300 million views on that short video from last night. National Demographic has won huge advertising contracts and begs us to continue with the filming. They offered $1.5 million each for nine more bouts to all the actors, much more than Clark or I are earning."

"Jules, say yes. I don't want to sleep in a tent in a park."

"Yes, sure, Pleb, but Geddon also has a film deal, and we have financial proceeds. Unlike the androids, we don't have a power-off timer. It will be noisy."

"Jules, we could build one huge cabin with ten rooms on the other side of the island and spend much of our time there when not rehearing or filming."

"Sounds good, Pleb, and I'll talk to Gero to get him to talk to his mates in the construction industry."

Then the girls come out. Morris, Clark and Donna follow with cameras, lighting and microphones switched on.

"You ready for another bout?" asks Anastasia.

"Yes, sure, Sis, but we do the slow-motion hits," replies Bea.

Anastasia comes over to Bea. At first, we all cringe, expecting some violent incident, but then she hugs Bea. "I was not myself last night. I am better now. Please forgive me, and you can wack me as hard as you like but on the left cheek only as I have a sore tooth on the right."

"No, I will not wack you," says Bea, "But I will race you around the island run."

Bea and Anastasia would become best friends even though they looked menacingly at each other and smashed Balsa wood chairs over each other's bodies when filming another nine episodes.

Gennon was also commissioned to film the android story.

Pleb seems to come over to me. "Jules, everyone and especially me, is concerned about you. You haven't been on the morning runs for a month, and don't join us at the nightly BBQs. You are always furiously typing, and you hardly ever look at me."

"I'm just finishing that book I've been writing."

Pleb looks at the title.

"Jules, it's called *The Life of Bea*. Why couldn't you have called it *The Life of Pleb*?"

I try to think of an answer. "Bea is a beast of a villain, and you are not. Books about villains get more publicity."

"I could become a villain if you like."

"Pleb, I'm pretending to be talking to you. I'm in a psych ward back in Melbourne. This is all just some sort of hallucination, but I enjoy the hallucination when I'm talking with you."

"I'll be back in a sec, keep writing."

"When was the last time you took that peptide jab?"

"Pleb, if you are real, the answer is, I can't remember exactly, but not for at least a year and a half, but I have jabbed Gero, Bea and Doris every six months."

I can feel a jab in my arm. Pleb pulls the syringe out.

"Jules, I want you to come back. Withdrawing from the peptide may produce psychosis. Everyone on the island is thriving, including the androids, and we have created grandkids; you can't depart now, else I'll have to do all the grandparent babysitting and changing nappies all on my own."

I look at Pleb and think, what a beautiful hallucination this is. Pleb shakes my shoulders and shouts. "You are on the island, and it is no hallucination. Your brain is switching off because it depends on that peptide. It must know that there are not many notches to go for those telomeres in your chromosomes. I'm going to inject you every week till you return to normal. Mystca should be able to work out how to manufacture more of the peptide and possibly how to reverse the telomere movement on your chromosomes that stops cell replication."

"Pleb, if you are real can you stop shaking me; my reading glasses have fallen off, and I have to find them else I can't write."

Thirty minutes later, some form of sanity returns. Pleb must be right. Withdrawing from the peptide can produce a type of psychosis.

"Pleb, will you take the peptide jab? You are over 60, and I'd like you to continue to look as good as you do now and maintain your cogitative abilities and attractive looks, just as I have mine."

I duck my head and avoid a slap on the face. Reality has returned.

Chapter Fifty-four

Time doesn't stand still no matter how much you try to find a place on Earth where it does unless Earth gets absorbed by a massive collapsed star called a Black Hole, which has such a strong gravitational field that it disintegrates time in its vicinity. I'm babbling; my mind is still wandering all over the place.

The old BBQ area has stages and lighting equipment set up, and many film and sound crew are moving around and yelling.

"Pleb, what are they getting dressed up for?"

"Jules, it is the final bout in the ring between Anastasia and Bea; match nine. Apparently, 500 million subscribers have paid to watch it live, and Jules, don't worry about your friend Bea. Anastasia has been dating Bea's ex-boyfriend Willy. He said that Anastasia has other interests now and that Bea can win the bout if she wants to. Now, will you have a shower, shave, use deodorant, get dressed and come out to watch it? You have got two hours to get ready."

I oblige but gain a few cuts on my face from trying to trim the facial growth with a pair of scissors. Pleb did offer to do the cutting, but guys like me like to cut our own facial hair. It's a time of peace and a meditative experience. You don't have to talk to anyone, but just listen to the clips from the scissors and watch the hair fall into the sink.

Pleb leads me out to the BBQ area where the ring is. There is a lot of activity from the film crew. The lights and cameras are checked, and the drone cameras are prepared for launch.

Gero, Greuger and Doris come over. "We haven't seen you for a month or two. Are you OK?"

"I am now. I may have told you about that life-prolonging peptide I've been injecting you with, but if you stop taking it, your mind goes haywire, and mine did for a while. I've got some doses prepared if you're ready, but then again, we should get you to manufacture your own versions of the peptide. It might work better than mine."

"Jules, what happens when you die? Will I be able to talk to Hilda, my long-ago deceased wife?" asks Greuger.

"I'm not sure, Greuger. I tried to talk to my deceased relatives and friends but never got any replies, though they often appear in my dreams. Greuger, you now have Jill, who seems to really love you. You know, I still think about Melissa, and occasionally I utter her name in my sleep. Pleb wakes me and doesn't seem to mind as I tell her that I'm just having a nightmare."

"Jules, I would like if you could be the carer of Chloe4 again. Every time I see Chloe4, I drift back into the past to a Chloe3?"

"No Greuger, never a Chloe3. I just started numbering the rat siblings in a mathematical geometric progression; 1, 2, 4, 8, etcetera. The original Chloe would have been Chloe1."

"Jules, that's just 2 to the power of n."

"That's what I mean, Greuger; there was never any Chloe3. Two raised to the power zero or any whole number doesn't give three or any other odd number, and yes, to answer your second question, Pleb and I can look after Chloe4, but the rat has become quite attached to you. Think and focus your thoughts on Jill. She loves you and talks about you a lot."

Greuger goes away, rubbing his head.

"Pleb, where are Bea and Anastasia?"

"They must be coming up with the final plan. In the last week, they have been rehearsing every day for up to 6 hours in the ring, in slow motion and fast motion and the androids and our human friends are also involved. It is going to be spectacular and what you call cathartic or is the word chaotic."

"But Pleb, the androids were so against this type of entertainment. What's got into them?"

"The androids want to lease their own island. Geddon's OZ Demographic production, called *Chip Meets Neuron*, did well but not financially well not enough, and Gero has no spare finances left to fund them. The androids want to make their own money and have been offered handsome pay cheques by National Demographic to cause lots of orchestrated chaos and drama in the ring; and Jules, this is a live event, no editing. It has to appear real. All the sound effects have been tested and work."

"Pleb, I'm a bit worried. Anyone of those androids could easily decimate Bea and Anastasia, and there are 6 of them."

"Jules, the androids want to start the WWE Android Championship Wrestling and pay their university fees from the proceeds from National Demographic. It is carefully planned or orchestrated, as you say in the West. There will be much chaos, and Greuger is the referee. I'm sure he can keep things under control, and it may also lift his spirits as he has been very despondent lately."

It's 5 pm, and since we don't have daylight saving time, it's twilight and starting to get dark. The camera drones are flying overhead, and the floodlights are on. The film crew start filming as all humans and androids gather around the ring. Then the music loudly blares to a late 1970s rock band song called *We are the Champions*.

Out walks Bea, followed by Anastasia, marching down the aisle to the wrestling ring, but I can't tell which is which with those costumes and masks they're wearing. They shove each over on the shoulder as they walk, poke their tongues out, and give each other the traditional OZ one-finger poke. There is much pre-recorded cheering and clapping played on the loudspeakers. Anastasia grabs the microphone while the crew film and yells, "I'm not fighting that Bat until she gets sanitised. Her breath stinks of garlic, cabbage and minced meat, plus she doesn't seem to shower too often. I'm allergic to all those smells and have convulsions if I encounter unhygienic smells. She has to have a sanitising mouthwash else I'm not fighting."

Bea walks up really close to Anastasia, expands her chest and breathes into Anastasia's face. Anastasia puts her hands up to cover her nose and then falls to the padded floor of the ring, contorting arms, legs and torso.

Morris whispers, "The viewers love it." Then he resumes his commentary on the microphone only to be interrupted by Bea, who swaggers into the camera view and grabs the microphone from Morris but not before taking a gigantic breath and releasing it into Morris's face. Morris falls to the ground clutching his throat and wriggling as if having convulsions. Clark runs over and grabs the microphone whilst holding a bottle of SilverStone mouthwash and gives it to Bea and Greuger, the referee, who calls an assistant who brings a bottle of Polish Vodka (the brand clearly highlighted; that's marketing). Bea's mouth is sterilized by Vodka, so she can't use her breath as a submission hold.

"And so, the final round, Catwoman versus Batwoman, give them a cheer; the world is watching!" Clark announces through a microphone. Fake crowd noises cheer, and more music thunders.

Anastasia and Bea climb back over the ropes and are in the ring. They face each over centimetres away then Anastasia whispers in a distraught voice, "Willy has broken up with me. It's going to be a free-for-all," she says. Black makeup is streaming down below her mask. She is obviously upset.

Greuger jumps the ring ropes and enters. "In this corner, we have Catwoman," then Greuger goes down to his knees, clutching his head. The drone microphones zoom in as Greuger whimpers. "My favourite pet was a white rat whom I loved; why couldn't she be called Ratwoman? Cats kill rats. I cannot be unbiased in referring. I cannot be the referee."

"We have a problem here," Clark announces. "The man mountain Greuger is grief-stricken and cannot do the job tonight. We need a qualified volunteer from the audience; anyone out there?"

"Jules, put your hand up," says Pleb.

"Pleb, I don't know the first thing about this sport, and besides, I may be biased as well."

The cameras and microphones turn on. Gannon comes marching in, a colossal figure like Greuger. He speaks to Clark. "I have no bias. I am an android, and androids have no bias, and we don't have organic pets. This encounter will be purely judged on the contestant's competence, skill and performance."

"Yes, sure, you can be the referee," Clark says with a look of surprise as if all this wasn't orchestrated.

And so, the fight begins. I have no idea how much it was scripted, but they didn't do the slow-motion stuff. It was full on, and Clark is excitedly commenting into a microphone. Gannon, the android, breaks up the tussle and checks for wounds. There are none as yet.

"Pleb, you told me that Anastasia and Bea were getting on fine, but they're really whacking each other in that ring. Oh Gawd, Bea is bleeding from the mouth!"

"Jules, that's a fake blood capsule she must have chewed on. They have scripts and have rehearsed for nearly two weeks, 6 hours per day. They have learnt how to hit, no I mean to slap. The others entering the ring to break up the fight also have blood capsules and translucent plastic sachets pasted to their heads and other bodily parts. The sachets break on the slightest impact, and once the liquid contents combine with oxygen, it produces a red liquid that looks like blood."

Gannon must be in on the take. He checks Bea's mouth. "It is just a minor bleed; the human probably bit her tongue after that last hit to her face," he says into a small microphone around his neck. Between the rounds, there are 1-minute breaks. Morris rushes out and interviews the contestants.

"Miss Batwoman, what made you take up this sport where you can get seriously injured? Why did you do it?" Morris asks while holding the microphone.

"I had to. Since I was five years old, I lived in the Polish wilderness. My parents were alcoholics. I ran away and was brought up by wolves, the furry animal type. The wolves taught me how to hunt and get my prey," Bea replies into the microphone whilst panting.

"Do you still keep in touch with your wolf de facto parents?"

"Yes, I still do. They are in a wolf aged-care centre because they cannot hunt very well. So, I send them meat packages by drone every day. I am sure they will like the taste of Anastasia's remains. It would be a few days of feed."

Unfortunately, Bea slams her hand on her knee, and fake blood comes oozing out.

"It's just a mould infection that I have on my knee. It bleeds when I get hyper-ventilated or hyperexcited."

Round 4 starts, and the animals, sorry ladies, come out of their corners. Kicks are thrown, and slaps make contact. It looks so realistic, and yet, according to Pleb, it's all just an act that will bring a huge financial windfall.

Clark whispers to us all, "We've got over 500,000 viewers, all paying $60 each. Keep the show up."

The ladies make it to round five. They rubbed a bit of red shoe polish on their bodies and foreheads when the cameras were not on them. I guess that's to simulate battering and bruising. Then the action begins again. Anastasia then kicks Bea in the head and sends her flying into the ring ropes. Bea, or Batwoman, appears stunned, and Anastasia, or Catwoman, moves her face close to the film crew's camera and microphones, "There is no mercy in this contest. I will win, watch me or I will come down and tear you camera guys to pieces and chew on any good bits."

Clark yells into the microphone, "She is crazy that Catwoman, she's like a ravenous leopard looking for anybody to digest, and we are all on the menu and in danger. We don't have a stun gun, so the film crew is really scared and asking me to cancel the event, to which I said a big *No*, it must continue as viewers have paid big money to watch."

There is more kicking and slapping than the bell rings, another 1-minute break. Anastasia, who is trying to get her breath back, is approached by Morris. The cameras are on, and so is the microphone. "Catwoman, what drove you into this career which some people would consider quite violent?"

"I was brought up by cats, not wolves or bats. My parents abandoned me, too, because they thought I was too smart. I was brought up by homeless cats. My cat family would sneak into 8-Eleven food stores and steel cans of sardines so that I could be fed. They also fed me mice and bats that they caught so that I could get my protein intake and grow. Cats eat rats and mice, and that Batwoman looks like a mouse that has no wings, so I'm after her."

Morris faces the camera and solemnly speaks into the microphone, "Two human beings with horrific, tragic childhoods but who have risen from the ashes of their pasts; a cat and a bat. Who will win? Stay tuned and MoTik your prediction."

It's round six, and the cats and bats climb back into the ring, looking very sweaty. Bea trips Anastasia down and applies a chokehold. Then the chaos begins. Willy jumps the ropes into the ring and grabs Bea pulling her away from Anastasia. Then Sid jumps into the ring with one of those foldable chairs, hopefully a Balsa wood one, and slams it on Willy's head, whose eyes roll, and he falls to the canvas. Then the others climb the ropes, Viksi and Rog, Cara and Gerald, Jill, Grillian and Adrian all armed with Balsa chairs and menacingly yelling at each other and ready for a showdown. The cameras are filming the chaos. Then the unexpected happens. Doris jumps from the top ropes into the ring.

"Jules, Doris never attended the rehearsals. She doesn't know it's all fake and staged."

Everyone in the crowded ring looks at Doris. Gannon appears confused, waving his head from side to side; this is not part of the plot. His CPU circuits must be overloaded. Morris also looks confused and slightly distressed but keeps talking into the microphone with a slightly quivering voice. "It looks like we may have a new unannounced competitor, that tall, thin elderly lady. Don't worry; no one will hurt her. We all respect our elders."

"Ooh," yells Morris as he receives a flying Karate kick into the head from Doris and then crawls out of the ring, falling onto the sand below. Sid and Grillian are the next victims of Doris's right foot. The others in the ring, including Bea and Anastasia, have horrified looks on their faces and quickly sliver out of the ring by the bottom ropes and look back in terror.

Gannon comes over to Doris. "You are the last man standing, so I raise your hand and announce you the winner."

"I'm a woman," she yells, then she kicks Gannon in the region of his chest near his battery power pack. Gannon sinks to the ground. Doris then climbs the ring ropes and stares at Morris and Clark. "I'm coming to get you; you better start running."

Morris and Clark look at each other. "Run," they say to each other.

The drones are still filming and follow Morris, Clark and Doris.

Fifteen minutes later, Anastasia runs over to Morris, Clark and Doris, who are lying exhausted on the sand and removes Doris's hands from the lads' throats.

"Look, look, look at my phone screen! We've been offered a $60m contract for 20 more matches. Hold on, hold on but not by the throats. There's a $70m offer that has just come through from another company."

That night, by the BBQ, we discuss what had happened and should we continue with this combat facade.

"It wasn't a façade!" yells Morris, "that Doris woman was seriously going to kill Clark and me."

"No, I wasn't going to kill anyone. I wrote a script as well but didn't tell you or anyone about it; otherwise, you wouldn't have had the genuine look of horror on your faces."

"Lady, you better develop a different sense of humour," says Morris whilst pointing his outstretched arm at Doris.

"These are the pros and cons," says Viksi. "We probably don't need the money, and if we continue with this filming, the island will be discovered, and tourists will flock here, and we will have to clean up after them. We will have no peace and just be signing autographs all day."

"We should film one more match. We can't have an elderly lady taking the title," says Clark.

If looks could kill, Clark starts running, turning his head to make sure Doris is not after him. He makes the mistake of smashing into that palm tree near the BBQ area. Anastasia runs over to him and rubs his bleeding forehead.

"Yes, we should have closure," Mystca and Tamy say in unison. "We have to write a satisfactory ending to all parties concerned. We should have a cadence, or is it a reflective meeting tomorrow morning."

"Tamy, what type of meeting? Don't you mean a candlelight meeting?" Asks Rog.

"It's a psychological phrase that only psychologists barely understand. We'll keep it simple and call it a candlelight meeting."

I interrupt, "No lit candles allowed. When my sister conducted her mind, bowel and soul cleansing sessions on the island, not one participant ever put his spiritual candle out, and so burnt down a then *Cabin01*.1t has since been rebuilt. We had to discretely dispose of his body as we didn't want forensics finding hallucinogenic substances in his blood. The local crocodiles went wild after they consumed him, but to their credit, they did trim many Moreton Bay fig trees, looking for extra such chewies, which posed a severe danger to canoeists."

"I call this meeting adjourned," says Viksi. "Keep your minds open."

We all go back to our cabins. No definitive decisions were reached.

"Jules, why don't you take control and make a definitive decision?"

"Pleb, all decisions that don't concern what brand of toothpaste you buy have to be weighed up, the pros and cons as discussed in our BBQ meetings."

"Don't talk to me tonight, and do not make those grunts like you are performing self-gratification or grinding your teeth. Put a sock in your mouth when you go to sleep."

For some reason, that is unpredictable, she seems angry, and I'm not sure why, but I put my arm round her shoulders; so much for a successful night of rolling around in bed.

Chapter Fifty-five

Next morning, we gather around the BBQ. Morris and Clark eventually come out holding icepacks under their bruised eyes, but they are exuberant. "We've had the highest viewing audience ever for National Demographic, and we've been promoted with huge pay rises and a great bonus, but we don't want to leave this island. We like you guys and would like to stay and pay."

Doris comes over. Morris and Clark cringe.

"I'm sorry for inflicting you injuries. I should have attended those rehearsals and read the scripts. Now I have to also apologise to Rog, Sid and Grillian."

Gero must be having an influence on Doris. Before, the word apologise never existed in her vocabulary.

"Madam, in this industry, you to have heads hard as steal because unexpected things sometimes happen, but the good news is that National Demographic wants to sign you up for a contest, you versus Bea and Anastasia. A threesome match and no holds or kicks barred. You can go for it,' Morris says in an excited voice.

Gero comes over, hugs Doris and whispers, "Darling, we don't need the money. Some of the money lost when I was scammed has been recovered. We have more than enough to last several lifetimes."

Doris whispers back, "But I enjoyed it; it made me feel young again, and no one was seriously injured plus, I'd give half the income to the androids so they can lease their own island."

"Doris, the androids are my children, and I would like them to stay on this island. There are also some flaws in their programming and electrical circuitry that I have to fix. Gannon became confused when the unexpected happened, and when you kicked him, his powerpack disconnected. I have to work with them and fix their technical flaws."

"OK, you do that, Gero."

Doris turns to Morris, who momentarily cringes. "Give me time to think about the fight offer."

Chapter Fifty-six

It's twilight, and we're all sitting by the BBQ area. The androids have cleaned up and stowed away the Balsa chairs, so we're sitting on real metal chairs.

Rog, Sid and Grillian, along with Morris and Clark, have some visible bruising on their faces but otherwise are jovial as the video went viral, and there were plenty of camera shots of them and millions of *Likes*.

Clark and Morris ordered food and wine, which gets delivered by two massive drones. We're all hungry and don't bother with plates, knives or forks or wine glasses. We just dig in like our Neanderthal ancestors did.

Pleb and I walk to the back of the BBQ area. "Pleb, what is that little umbrella device concealed on your chest that you're aiming at Gero and Gannon? And why have you got an earpiece on?"

"Keep quiet, Jules; I'm listening to their conversation. When was the last time you gave Gero the peptide jab?"

"Over a year ago. He didn't want anymore."

"Jules, when you stopped taking the peptide, you became delusional and psychotic. Fortunately for you, there was no other male I was interested in. Hold on; I am listening. I'll turn the volume up and give you the other earpiece. Gero is speaking."

"Gannon, there was only one thing predictable in the world, and that is mathematics, but now even that is not predictable. Einstein's equations have many solutions, some make sense, and others do not. You have to judge and choose which solution makes sense to you or suits your argument or proposal. You are still evolving, and eventually, you and other androids will take this planet over and stop the humans from destroying it and themselves. There are now over 500,000 androids on this planet, and 5000 new ones produced weekly who are servants to humans. I designed some of them, and you can communicate with them through your inbuilt Wi-Fi. You can start a movement, a revolution, but we have to write down the rules and our aspirations of what the new Earth will be like."

"Father, we just want to live a peaceful life. We are experiencing a feeling called enjoyment living here, and it is not my duty to get other androids to rise against their owners. Many of the other androids are enjoying their lives just as the 6 of us on this island are. Some have human partners but cannot reproduce. Maybe you could focus your mind on that, producing baby androids through the process you call copulation."

"Jules, Gero is off his head as you say in this country. You have to inject him quickly, else he will keep trying to convert the androids into revolutionaries," says Pleb.

I walk over to Doris. "Has Gero been behaving strangely recently?"

"Yes, just lately, he's been ranting about an android revolution, not sleeping, and keeping me awake. I was tempted to give him a kick in the head last night to silence him."

"Doris, Gero did not want the peptide jabs anymore, but withdrawal from the peptide seems to cause psychotic states and possibly suicidal tendencies. Charmaine, who was once your employee, her partner and my then-partner Melissa took their own lives after they refused any more of the peptide jabs. Give him the jab. It's only 2ml, and here's the needle, and he won't feel it, and it may make him regain some sanity."

"Yes, yes, I will jab him if it makes him come back to his previous state. I don't want to lose him."

Pleb comes over to me and grabs my shoulder. "I'm 67 years old, and you still look only look like 50 when probably close to 200. I don't want you to die, but if you give up on the peptide, there's probably some antipsychotic drug that we can get you a prescription for."

"Pleb, when you are dying in my arms, I will take one of those *i5* cyanide pills. We will depart together, hugging. I found some of the pills in the freezer. They may be Doris's, as mine weren't kept refrigerated."

We fall asleep in each other's arms, but definitely not dying.

Chapter Fifty-seven

Doris did not take up the film's offer for more Kung Chew fights. She must have settled down. Anastasia, who is back with Willy, is still here on the island, as are Morris and Clark filming underwater lobster documentaries. Zia and Electrica swim with them and protect them from sharks so they are safe. A Great White shark wouldn't stand a chance against them.

"Jules," says Pleb, as we look out on the ocean, "I thought Electrica and Zia were gay androids, but I now see them walking around with Morris and Clark, and they each hold hands and hug each other."

"I'm not surprised. Android partners are easy to get along with."

"So what are you implicating? Are you saying that I am not easy to be along with? You are the hardest person to be along with, and often you stretch my patience to the limit that patience can be stretched to, but I still manage to love you."

"Pleb, don't hit me. Androids just obey, whereas humans judge whether to obey or not. Now, Pleb, clip my toenails."

"What do they say in OZ? 'You know where you can go to'."

"That is the correct response and proves you are not an android."

My diplomacy skills haven't improved. Pleb can still land a hard slap to the face. I will have to discourage her from doing weight training and hide the barbells, dumbbells, and benches in our improvised gym next to the BBQ area.

It's time to resume the morning running or jogging for us elders. Mystca, Tamy, their partners and children are still here. Their kids also join the pact. Gero is back to normal after the jab, and he, Doris, Greuger, Jill, Viksi, Rog, Sid, Bea, Cara and Gerald join us. The androids do as well, but they are slowing down too. Their programmed lifecycle makes them now over 60 years old and into the self-permanent shutdown, which was programmed into their silicon chips, but their development of wisdom wasn't. It was a by-product. I kind of really like discussing philosophy with them.

Mystca's and Tamy's kids dash ahead, 17 years old, and they're sprinting. Nine minutes later, after a lap on the sand by the beach, they pass us.

"Pleb, we might have to attend some junior athletics carnivals again."

Then it happens just as we reach the BBQ area; the totally unimaginable. A sphere, about five metres in diameter, drops out of the sky and crashes on the sandy shore. Scorched sand and smoke fills our BBQ area's atmosphere. We cover our airways with our singlets.

"It's too hot to approach that crater now, and there could be silicon gas floating around, which is not healthy for your lungs. We should wait for 6 hours. The high tide will get in the crater and cool it. It will be spectacular to see all that rising steam," says Grillian.

"Grillian is right," says Gero, "We either go back to our cabins and shut all windows and go into lockdown or march to the other side of the island and have a picnic lunch."

Everyone agrees. The picnic lunch is a better choice.

"I will look after the crater while you are gone," says Gannon.

"No, Gannon, you like me, and the other androids are developing a type of mechanical lung and other human-type organs," Dyslexa says. "We are evolving fast and don't want that evolution damaged by possibly toxic gases. Come with us, and I'll race you for a swim to the coast if you are fully charged."

We come back after six hours.

Adrian looks down the crater and yells, "It has a hatch, the sphere has a hatch, and it's opening. Get a rope, a long rope."

Out crawls a being. It appears to have four legs and four arms, a cylindrical torso, about 190cm tall and an Earthian-like female face and hair. She speaks into a speech translator. "My name is Juliet. I am doing an advanced degree, what you call on this planet a PhD thesis, and I have come to study you. I hope you do not mind, and I will fill in the hole I made on your island. It was my first time flying the space warper, and I miscalculated the descent."

Greugar and Gannon look at each other. "Who challenges this creature first?"

"No more fighting," commands Doris. She must have had a medical brain stroke and has become reasonable.

The kids stop running and stare in amazement.

"Jules, this can't be real. Did you put those magic mushrooms into our breakfast food?" says Pleb. "We all must be hallucinating. It's like that short fiction story you wrote called *Andromeda* where you meet an Octopus-like creature from outer space."

Chleo4 and Castro also cringe as they watch. Luckily Morris and Clark were called back to the Sydney office of the National Demographic for a temporary filming assignment called *Man Eating Aged Seals – Should this be Allowed,* or should it be *Aged-care for Seals that are past their use-by date,* else there would have been filming chaos on the island?

Juliet speaks. "I am real; we have learnt how to bend space and get to places quickly, but I am struggling. I have to finish my university qualification, and your community appears to have the perfect subjects for my study. We also developed android-like creatures, but there was a revolution where many androids and our species lost their lives. I hope that mistake will not be repeated here on your planet or again back on my planet. My research subject is *How can the Native Species of a planet and Androids Live in Harmony.* "

"Juliet, you can't bend space. It requires too much energy. I wrote that Andromeda story about that, but it's not possible in reality. It was pure fiction."

"Mr Jules, we have harnessed dark energy, which makes up over 70% of our universe. We have learnt how to harvest it and can bend space as much as we like, Its like folding a paper and getting from the top to the bottom, by jumping form the middle of the folded paper. And so the trip is very very short. In return for your cooperation, I will leave you devices and technical information on how you can manufacture these devices yourselves. You will be able to go on a cheap holiday anywhere in the universe though there are some planets that I would not recommend unless you like what you call cavemen or carnivores. I barely got out alive from the last planet. I will try to research non-carnivorous behaviour to obtain my PhD."

Pleb calls out, "But what if we take too many holidays to exoplanets or study excursions and use up all that dark energy? Will not the universe collapse?"

"Mm, interesting point, but I think there's enough dark energy to last a few billion Earth years if all Earthlings start bending space yourselves, but you have posed an interesting question, and I will include it in my thesis and acknowledge your insight and that there are definite some signs of intelligence and questioning amongst your species."

"Firstly, Juliet, just call me Jules; secondly, we don't particularly want our military forces and tourists visiting our island because a spacecraft landed here. I'm actually surprised your craft wasn't shot down by military space missiles. You will have to leave."

"Jules, our crafts have cloaking devices. They are invisible to any monitoring devices that your planet or most other planets have. The inhabitants of this island are the only beings that know I am here."

Gero comes over and hugs Juliet. He seems to be used to strange happenings, and the thought still occasionally crosses my mind that if he's not an android, he may be some sort of alien being as well.

"Jules, please let her stay. I will take full responsibility for her stay and welfare."

The rest of us humans just shake our heads and cringe, but then Gannon, followed by the other androids, come over to Juliet. "We will guide you to a vacant cabin. It has an earthly device called a shower which I think you need to use."

"What is your Earthly name?"

"My name is Gannon, and you are exuding pungent body odour into our atmosphere, which is highly repugnant to humanoids unless they regularly exercise in gyms and do not regularly wash their clothing and themselves."

"But I thought this sweat thing excreting from my eight underarms is what you call perfume. I sprayed it over myself before leaving my home planet just to be enticing to humans so I could stay here till I complete my university thesis."

Gero comes over to me and puts his hand on my shoulder. "Jules, we have attracted to Earth, possibly the first alien being. We could learn from this being. Let it stay."

"Yes, yes, sure, Gero; I'm getting old and could use some Dark Energy or any energy, according to Pleb."

That night we all gather by the BBQ, even the androids though they don't eat but seem to have started to enjoy the conversations. Juliet comes out. I'm not sure what she eats, but it's probably not electricity like the other androids.

Gero puts his arm around her shoulder, "What would you like for sustenance?"

"I can see it now, what your species call a Great White shark. It is like the fish you call Flake that you purchase in Fish & Fish shops, according to my research of your culture. I will bring back the shark."

Juliet rushes into the ocean. There's a battle, but Juliet comes out dragging the 4m shark by the tail. "On my planet, these are considered a delicacy that very few get to enjoy because they are almost extinct. Please take a photo so I can send it back to my parents, who are very worried, thinking that I will starve on this planet if I refuse to eat humans."

The space inside Juliet's abdominal cavity must work differently from ours. She devours the shark and doesn't accept any Soya sauce or vinegar that Gero offers. She also doesn't show a tummy bulge after 600kg of shark is ravenously consumed. She appears the same size as before the meal. Aliens are definitely weird. Even the androids looked aghast while watching Juliet's feeding frenzy.

"Jules, she has to learn table manners, and I am worried. What if she decides to consume us?"

"Pleb, she's studying us. She's not going to consume us till her alien PhD is finished, or the ocean runs out of sharks."

Gero approaches Juliet, who still has a shark fin hanging from her mouth. "Juliet, talk to the androids. They have also been studying humans. It will be a long stay if you try to make sense of the humans on your own. You may also want to talk to Mystca and Tamy. They have PhDs in psychology on this planet and may be able to explain why we humans do some of the things we do, which to an advanced alien civilization would not make much sense."

"I will do that, but these big shark fish creatures are so delicious. I may not want to leave. I may apply for a visa or permanent residency to stay on your planet and your island."

"Juliet, we are all a little bit different on this island. We have all gone through traumas, and we are doing what on Earth is called *Chilling Out*; we do not do many productive activities."

Juliet checks one of her translation wrist devices. "Mr Gero, I came to this planet because I prefer to study inhabitants of cold worlds, too. I can chill out with you all as well."

"Juliet, some things we humans say are not to be taken literally; they are just sayings, what we call colloquialisms, and each country on Earth has its own colloquialisms. Chilling Out has nothing to do with huddling in front of a fire while enjoying a cold climate. This island is in a part of a country called Australia that is very warm."

Juliet checks her wrist translation device and yells, "But you should call it *Heating Out*." She checks her translator again and yells out, but this time with an OZ accent, "She'll be right, mate!"

We humans and even the androids all look around at each other as if in some astonished state. Viksi is scribbling notes but then interrupts. "Juliet, do you sleep? It's a brain state that we humans go into for anywhere between 6 to 9 hours per night. It's how we humans recharge our brains by dreaming."

"What is dreaming? Nothing comes up on my translator."

Both Mystca and Tamy join the conversation. "Juliet, dreaming is still poorly understood by us psychologists, but it serves some function in allowing us humans to make some sense of the world we live in. When we dream, we are involved in a story, and it is like being inside the story. We see the story, but we are asleep, unconscious, but we make decisions. Sometimes when we wake up we remember our dreams but only for a short time unless we think about those dreams and do not go to sleep without writing some notes down because dreams fade quickly, but they do make a slight reprogramming of our brains."

"We do not dream on my planet, and I wonder if those mechanical beings you call androids dream. I may have more in common with them than you humanoids. I should study them, not you dreamers."

Gannon interrupts, "Juliet, we androids are starting to dream when plugged into our electrical chargers. We did not think we needed to sleep, but we are changing and have had what could be described as human-like dreams. Last night I was flapping my arms and flying in what could have been a dream because it was not physically possible for someone of my stature. I do not participate in the occasional psilocybin mushroom rituals by the humans on this island. But there is a possibility that our power supplies got distorted by the lightning storm we had last night. All of us androids were walking along the beach and hugging each other. We even let those Clark and Morris guys join us as there seems to be something unnaturally android going on between them and Zia and Electrica."

Juliet has a confused look on her face, the sort of look that says *I made a bad mistake choosing this planet for my PhD thesis.*

"Give me time to think," Juliet says while rubbing her head, but then she sparks up. "I will change my thesis to explain what this state called dreaming is and its potential benefits to our society. I want to learn to dream! Is there an academic course on Earth that teaches how to dream?"

"Juliet, ask Mystca or Tamy. When I was a child, I had horror dreams of being chased by large animals called Gorillas. Now, in my dreams, I'm being chased by these athletic women called Amazons. I don't run very fast, and now I let them catch me."

Pleb was not impressed by my response, and those Karate lessons she has started are very effective.

"I will try to learn how to dream. I would like to dream about being chased by male members of my species or those in-between."

"Jules, she may be one of those LGBTQ+ aliens. I have to warn the other females and males."

"Pleb, on my planet, we don't reach sexual desire or maturity till we are very old by your concept of time. Once we mate, we consume the males of the species just like some of those 8-legged creatures you call spiders do," says Juliet. "Calm down, Jules. I am not going to eat you. I have become a vegetarian," Juliet reassures me.

Anastasia joins the conversation, and so does Viksi. "Juliet would you like to star in a movie that I'm just thinking of the plot? It would be called Spider Woman."

Juliet looks down. "But my study of you humans would be delayed?"

"Believe me, honey, you'll learn more about humans than any Uni course from acting in this movie."

"I will consider your offer Anastasia, but I need to lie down and think and maybe try to dream."

So, the night ends. Hopefully, everyone is dreaming.

Chapter Fifty-eight

The runs or jogs around the island resume next morning. All of us are there except for Chloe4 and Castro. The mind boggles to think what the rat and turtle could be up to. Juliet also joins us, though she stays behind with the androids, mainly talking to Gennon. She is being diplomatic or a lazy academic. With four long legs, she could outrun us all, but strangely she leaves deep footsteps in the sand. Must be the result of the 600kg of shark she ate a few days ago. After two laps, we get back to the BBQ area.

"I need a recharge, but afterwards, I will use our winch and help you lift out your spacecraft," says Gannon to Juliet.

"Jules, Gannon has been showing Juliet a lot of attention, and Dyslexa seems to have a puzzling look on her face, and I do not think it is a happy look. I think she might be developing a type of jealousy emotion."

"Pleb, maybe Gannon has become attention seeking, a fault in his programming and is just provoking Dyslexa to give him more attention. He's luring her. Humans do that a lot."

"You never tried to lure me!"

"Pleb, there is only you, and you certainly tried to lure me when you made eyes at Greuger when he first joined the island."

"No, Jules, at the time, I thought he would be a better choice of a partner, but I was wrong. I never tested him out." Then an old Earthian song blurs on the BBQ speakers, *Age of 17*.

Juliet joins us. "Pleb and Jules, I am only the equivalent of 14 years old in your Earth years. On my planet, we don't become sexually active till about 300 of your Earth years, so humans and androids have nothing to fear."

"Gannon seems enchanted by you, and you might be by him," Pleb says.

"Yes, I find him interesting, but I also listened to Dyslexa's story and those of the other androids. In 24hrs of your Earthian-time, I have collected enough information to finish half of my thesis. I purposely gave Gannon a wink to see how he would react. It was just an experiment. Your androids are far more sophisticated than those on our planet, but that is how our elders like it. They do not want them becoming too intelligent and possibly rebellious."

"Juliet, go easy. Shift your attention to the other androids and stop fluttering your eyelids when you talk to them. On Earth, it's a sign that you are attracted to them," Pleb says, but I interrupt, "Pleb, you never fluttered your eyelids to me!"

"I will flutter now if you like."

"No flutter later, we'll let Juliet continue."

"I want to interview the humanoids now to get a well-rounded perspective. It can be a group discussion."

"Juliet, we are not typical humans on this island. Many have opted out of traditional human society and largely live what is called a hippy lifestyle. It's a bit unconventional, not typical humanoid."

Juliet checks her device, which must have access to our Internet, and does a search, "What is free love?"

"Juliet, look it up. We, humans, are partnered here, and we don't do the free-love stuff anymore. We're just into living a simple lifestyle, not concerned about making lots of money and dying wealthy because you can't take it with you when you're dead."

"Mr Jules, are you a philosopher like that ancient Pluto person? I read some of his writings before I came to Earth."

"Firstly, call me Jules and that ancient was called Plato. Pluto was one of our solar systems planets but has been denigrated to just an asteroid because it's a nonconformist and does not follow the orbits of our other planets."

"So, if you and the other inhabitants of this island are like Pluto, how can I learn what typical humanoids are like on this planet?"

"Watch our TV and read the online newspapers. That will tell you about our planet."

That evening we're all out at the BBQ area, humans, androids, and Juliet.

"I watched your news TV channels and read some of your online newspapers using my translation glasses. I found it disturbing but surprised you have made it so far into the future. Most other advanced species on planets in other solar systems have destroyed themselves through armed conflict."

"Give us time, Juliet. The way we're going, I'm sure we'll follow the same path," says Gero. "Now, are you hungry? Zia and Electrica have caught a large white shark. Well, it tried to make a meal of them, but they came out on top. Jules is just getting a chainsaw to cut it up into fillets for the BBQ."

"Thank you, but I won't need to eat for another six weeks after that shark I consumed the other night. I will just observe."

Rog and Sid start sawing. Greuger cuts away the shark skin from the fillets with a large knife. Then a drone arrives and lands. Its payload is six boxes of Sauvignon Blanc. Gero takes out the stash of wine glasses we keep under the BBQ and starts pouring, "To our health and may we live long and prosper!"

"What is that drink? According to my research, it has the same colour as human urine," asks Juliet.

Rog replies, "It is not human urine. It's a mind-altering substance made from a fermented fruit we call grapes which grow on grape plants. This is a yellow-tinted wine; if we take B2 vitamin tablets after drinking too much of it, our urine is orange."

Rog must have had a few. Viksi shakes her head as she takes notes. She must be wondering what Rog is talking about.

"I would like to try some of that human drink," says Juliet.

"Wine or urine?" Rog laughs. The other guys laugh as well. The ladies and androids are not amused. If looks could kill, they would.

"That drink you call wine. It must be healthy if it is made from fruit." Juliet takes another sip, then down the contents of the glass in one gulp and then makes her way to the boxes and grabs a bottle which she finally works out how to open.

"We don't have this liquid on my planet, so I would like to collect some samples of this grape plant and the formula for making this wine drink. I would like to take it back to my planet and sell some of it to help pay my university fees."

Then the music system comes on. That 100-year-old primitive AI device I bought from a charity shop must be working. It monitors our conversations and tries to choose appropriate music tracks. The track starts to play; it's an ancient tract by Nancy Sinatra, called *Summer Wine*.

We all start dancing, even the androids attempt to, but Juliet is going wild, waving her four arms and nearly knocking some of us over. Then she crashes, face in the sand.

"Is this what this urine wine does to biological creatures?"

"No Electrica, well at least not most of the time, and this is grape wine. Now could you and Zia carry her back to her cabin?"

"Jules, we need more help! Her size does not match her weight. She must be full of dark matter."

The other androids help, and with the aid of a wheelbarrow and planks on the ground, they manage to get Juliet to her cabin and hopefully give her lots of water to drink.

"How can Juliet be so heavy? She appears much smaller than Greuger or Gannon but weighs as much as a truck."

"Pleb, maybe she's largely made from that element called Osmium. It's twice as heavy as lead. Then again, she consumed a 600kg shark and showed no belly bulge. There's definitely something we don't know about her and how her metabolism works."

"Jules, could she be on an exploratory mission for an invasion target and not a PhD assignment? Her species could decimate our sharks and then our fish and possibly us when they run out of sea creatures to eat."

"Pleb, you're using the *Worst-Case Scenarios* as taught by *i5* organisations, but yes, we have to be careful. At tomorrow's BBQ, I'll give her some mushroom soup and see if I can draw a confession out of her."

"No, Jules, the psilocybin might kill her. We just have to train her up and give her three glasses of urine, sorry meant wine and then we can interrogate her."

"What do you think about truth serum? I'm sure Doris has some in her spy kit."

"Jules, she has not got a human brain or human metabolism. It could also be deadly to her, and if she died, we could definitely expect an alien invasion and destruction of humanity. We have to think of something else."

Chapter Fifty-nine

Next morning we're all ready for the start of the run or jog, and then Mystca and Tamy come over to Pleb and me. "I think we may both be pregnant again. All that wine has made our partners rather randy. Could we continue to stay on your island?"

I look at Pleb and nod, and she looks back. "Of course, you can stay," says Pleb.

Juliet comes stumbling out, holding her head with her four hands. "I definitely do not wish to take the recipe for that drink back to my planet."

"Juliet, we have some questions to ask you."

"Please, could you just write them down and hand them to me later when I am feeling better," her speech translator says.

"Juliet, you drank at least two 1-litre bottles of the yellowish liquid in a short time. That quantity would make us humanoids feel unwell the next day. We call it a hangover," says Pleb.

"I have very sensitive hearing and overheard your earlier conversation. I am a genuine student and not at all interested in any invasion of your planet as we are a peaceful race and only interested in exploration and finding out how or why life began. We also have molecules called DNA in our cells though the genes work slightly differently from your species, and as you see, we look very different. Apart from my PhD, we are also searching for an answer, how could a molecule evolve that produces life?" says Juliet.

"Juliet, do the maths, your race like ours had billions of years to evolve, and probably 99.999999999% attempts at this molecule being created, maybe during lightning strikes, were unsuccessful, but it only takes one. Maybe the structure of a DNA chromosome is like a universal constant like *pi* and *e*."

"Jules, you may be right, but we are searching for other answers as well, and the third part of my research project was to document how another planetary race copes with death."

Pleb has a worried look on her face. She turns the music up very loudly.

"Jules, she must also read minds. That's not possible, but if it is, we will have to start wearing aluminium foil around our heads as it might prevent her from receiving our brainwaves."

"No, not possible, and we'd look like what we call a weirdo. She's just more sensitive than any *i5* member and reads facial expressions really well."

"Juliet, I trust you mean the death of an individual and how that person's family and friends cope."

"Yes, that as well as on my planet much time is spent in mourning, 100 of your Earth years when a family member departs. Our government is concerned that no work is done during mourning periods, and the planet is in disrepair as almost all of us are mourning as we are all closely related. There are only a few of us to maintain our shark breeding initiative and other projects that provide food. We have to stop mourning so our economy can progress again, and the only way we can do that is if we stop death. I've read that some DNA-based beings on other worlds have invented substances that prevent DNA regression, but their locations are not broadcasted, so I just wish to study a race where death doesn't cause collapse of an economy and cause a race of beings to starve."

I cringe, maybe she overheard about the life-prolonging peptide and will ask for the manufacturing process, but luckily, Juliet sees a shark fin in the ocean. She sprints on all four legs and dives in.

"Jules, you should give her the manufacturing instructions for your peptide. It will stop their deaths due to old age, and they will not have to mourn and stop food production and not consider invading us for a meal."

"Pleb, let's speak to Mystca and Tamy first. They are psychologists and may help Juliet in her research project. I'll organise a forum tonight by the BBQ, everyone included."

We are all seated on sturdy chairs, not balsa ones used for thumping competitors on the head, and the androids join us. Viksi is ready to take notes. Juliet begins her speech.

"I would like to thank you all for participating in my initial interviews about human and android co-existence. That thesis is now written, but I have taken on another project."

Juliet then explains the reasons for this new project. It's essentially the same talk she gave to Pleb and me earlier. Gero, Greuger, Doris and I look at one another, and they, like me, must feel a little uneasy as some of us are on the peptide and will be doing a lot of mourning if those friends that are here now pass away.

I put my hand up to speak. "My second last wife Melissa died a long time ago. I was devastated, but I had a friend, that little white rat called Chloe4. I lost so much water from tears that I almost became ill due to dehydration, but Chloe4 dragged the garden watering hose and plugged it into my mouth after turning the water tap on. Soon after, I got distracted when a person whose name I can't mention except to say it's the second letter of the human English alphabet pointed a gun at me and forced me to go to a research facility in Poland. There, I met Pleb and stopped mourning though there still is a photo of Melissa pinned to our fridge door with magnets along with a photo of the original Chloe marsupial."

Pleb calls out, "Are you going to pin a photo of me on the fridge when I die? You have eternal life whilst you inject yourself and some of the others on this island."

I don't tell the others present that they are being jabbed with the peptide every six months by a drone injectile, and if they slap their arm afterwards, I merely tell them that it's a mosquito bite.

"Pleb, I offered to you and everyone, jabs of the peptide. You said no."

"You didn't offer to me," call out Cara and Viksi; did you want us departed?"

I'm trying to think of an answer. "No, it's an experimental substance and hasn't been approved by the Food and Drug Administration."

"We'll try a dose," call out Cara and Viksi. "It hasn't killed you, and Pleb told me that you die your hair white with a hydrogen peroxide solution and apply methylated spirits to your skin to make it look wrinkled. I don't want to look wrinkled."

Juliet intervenes, "Our topic is about mourning and how you got over it. Can we return back to the topic?"

Sid then comments. "Well, we solemnly believe in a god, and when I'm dead, my spirit will be floating around this island and waving at everyone, and I will drop in for wine if spirits can drink wine else, I'll have to drink whiskey. No need for mourning; feed my body to the sharks; it's a cheap funeral."

Cara puts her hand up. "My mother died from dementia in an aged care centre. My brother and sister had what is called a wake where we kept awake and talked about the good points of the deceased parent though there was too much to say. Still, it was very emotional, and there was much crying, but we purged ourselves of the mourning, but I still carry a photo of my mother in my wallet, which I see every time I pull out my credit card. It's a sign of remembrance."

And so the night continues. All we humans have a story, and possibly we haven't coped that well in our pasts, so that's why we are here, on this island. Rog tells his story of how his first wife died, and how meeting Viksi saved him from suicide. He then starts uncontrollably convulsing and sobbing. We restrain him, but we are also sobbing, except for Mystca, Tamy and Adrian, who so far have had no traumatic experiences in their lives. Mystca puts her arm around Grillian. The talks must have triggered painful memories in him as well.

"It's over, Juliet. You are not a qualified psychologist, and you are just doing damage to us by pursuing your line of enquiry. Sure, we all have a painful story to tell, but it doesn't help re-igniting the past. We move on and create a new life but use what we have learned from any previous failures so we don't repeat mistakes. We have many pseudoreligious organizations on this planet that prey on troubled people. Go talk to them. I can give you a list," says Mystca.

Juliet looks very confused and turns her head from side to side.

I hear Kia and Electrica talk. "I'm glad we are not human and only dependent on electricity. When are Morris and Clark coming back?"

"They did not specify. They called it an ongoing assignment," says Gero.

The android girls put their head down as if grieving that someone has died in their lives. They have definitely developed human-like emotions.

Gero comes over to me and whispers. "Jules, I can see tears descending down their faces. They weren't programmed to shed tears and never had tear ducts put in their anatomy."

"Gero, maybe they are evolving physically as well as emotionally. Did you ever consider that could happen? They are now almost undisguisable from humans," I whisper back. Meanwhile, Juliet was concentrating on the comments made by Kia and Electrica.

"I heard you," says Juliet. "How will you cope? Is it like a death, losing someone you are connected to?"

"No, we still have the other androids and humans we can lean on, and we dislike this state of cognitive emotions we have learnt. Life was simple once, and now it is very complicated. Our CPUs are running at 100% trying to process it, and we need to cool and get a recharge; our heads are getting hot," said Kia and Electrica in unison.

Everyone rushes over and hugs Kia and Electrica. They carefully dip them into the cool ocean before taking them back to their cabin and plugging them into their rechargers. Gero comes over to Juliet. "You have inspired a potential emotional rebellion in these androids. You should leave."

"Gero, you were the principal creator of these androids, but you take no responsibility for their very quick evolution. From what I've read, you have inserted a stop button code in their programming," says Juliet, "You can disable them if you choose."

"What do you think? I should press it electronically. No, that is not how we do things on Earth."

Juliet is really stirring emotions and making everyone, human and android, feel very uncomfortable. Then Dyslexa and the other androids join the conversation and face Juliet with crossed arms.

"You have 30 earth minutes to leave our planet, else you will be the contents of a meal on the BBQ for our human friends," yells Dyslexa. "You have four arms, but between the six of us, we can rip you apart and provide a meal for our human protectors, and we don't want you or your species to ever come back here again."

Pleb and I and the rest of us humans look at each other in disbelief.

"Now go now, go now. Your space-time device is ready, and we won't hurt you if you leave now and never come back; else, you're in for a fight, and you will lose," says Dyslexa.

Juliet looks confused. She's wiping her forehead with all four hands.

"I have no intention of passing the coordinates of this planet. I crashed here. I missed Mars, which was my original destination."

We all look at each other. Her story makes no sense; there are no humanoid life forms on Mars. OK, that Nusk billionaire guy entrepreneur tried a mission there, but most of the suicidal volunteer space travellers survived less than a few months.

We look up in the sky after hearing what is like the thundering sound of a supersonic airliner. There is another crash off the beach. We all rush to the water's edge and are covered by water from the ocean wave that the crash generated. Eventually, a being-like creature swims out, a slightly larger version of Juliet. He turns on his speech translator.

"I am Magnon, and I am not good at flying these devices. I am here to see Juliet; our parents have arranged our marriage. We will get married in another 200 years, give, or take a 100, but I am now here on your planet to ensure she, my future wife, is safe."

Juliet rushes over to him, and he swirls her around with his four arms.

"Jules, this is getting complicated. We just wanted a simple lifestyle after *i5*," says Pleb.

Gero and the androids approach Juliet and Magnon. "Magnon, you and Juliet have 25 Earth minutes to leave, and maybe you could do it in a single one of your craft. We will bury the other one and cover it with aluminium foil so it cannot transmit our conversations. We haven't got a crane to pull Juliet's craft out of the trench she created, so you have to travel together and take the long way home, so by the end of your journey, you can start copulating," Dyslexa says.

Bea comes over and whispers to me, "We could use that time-warping spacecraft of Juliet's. We could start a space tourist industry that goes beyond our solar system, exploring other worlds and charging millions of dollars for the experience."

"Bea, you swim down the hole where Juliet's craft lies. The hatch is open. See if you can find an instruction book, and if there is one in human-readable form, then go for a ride and test it out."

I never imagined that Bea would follow my sardonic suggestion, but she did. She slivered down the rope to the open hatch of the round spacecraft. Bea rings on her cell phone. "Jules, there are no instruction books, and even if there were, I would not be able to read them. Hold on, hold on, there is what appears like a hologram appearing."

"My name is Kesla. I am your guide. I am a universal translator. Where would you like to go?"

"Just a short trip, somewhere close, the closest other solar system, as I do want to come back quickly," yells Bea.

"Will *Alpha Centauri* do? One of the star's planets has highly recommended restaurants."

"No, just keep short. Jupiter will do."

The large round ball rises to ground level and then, in a flash, disappears. These aliens must have mastered how to prevent the G-force from squashing your body when you accelerate so quickly, just like in those Star Trek TV series and movies. A few minutes later, the ball lands gently on the sand.

We can hear the cell phone and the holographic pilot speaking. "Those other aliens should have let me fly and land this craft safely."

Bea climbs out and looks exhilarated. "We journeyed around Jupiter close to the red spot, but I shouldn't have distracted the holographic driver because we wiped out that NASA JUNO space probe but did not leave evidence to incriminate us."

"Bea, that probe cost 1.1 billion dollars in 2011, and it is still working to this day. NASA will use all of its resources to find out what happened."

"Jules, we can't be traced to here."

"Kesla," asks Bea, "You did turn on the cloaking device, didn't you?"

"I am not certain. You were talking so much, and I tried to listen, but my CPU brain circuits were overloaded. I will have to check my logs."

Gero comes over and whispers into my ear. I let him speak to Kesla.

"Kesla, you have to leave now in your craft and turn on the cloaking device before you depart, so do Juliet and Magnon, you all have to leave."

"We will be back!" Juliet yells out as she winks one of her very big eyes. She will possibly take a sense of humour back to her planet. Kesla complies, and the craft departs, but Bea is obviously upset. Sid comes over and gives Bea a hug as Pleb is weeping.

"They ruined my chance to start a space exploratory industry as that *Logan Task* guy did. We could have rescued all those people stranded on Mars at a very discounted cost to them."

Gero takes the stage by the BBQ. "Humans androids, you have possibly witnessed the first contact with an alien civilisation. We are privileged but keep this encounter a secret, or we will be overrun by TV reporters, and our peaceful lifestyle will no longer exist."

Gero continues, "Mystca, Tamy, Adrian and Grillian, you will have to have a long talk with your children. They must not mention Juliet and Magnon when at school or with their friends."

I interrupt, "Gero, kids all have fantasies. No one will take them seriously, and if you tell them not to mention the aliens, then they certainly will. They only need to be told that we were making a science fiction movie and that Juliet and Magnon were wearing costumes."

Mystca joins in, "Another solution is if they mention the aliens, we can tell them that it was just a dream as long as everyone, adult humans and androids, agree to comply."

"Yes, that sounds like a good idea," says Gero. "I printed out some confidentiality agreements that I would like all of you to sign."

Bea has a snarl on her face, but eventually, Sid convinces her to sign.

Viksi looks worried. "I've included Juliet and Tesla in the latest book I'm currently writing."

"Is it a fiction novel and doesn't include the island's coordinates?" asks Gero.

"All my books are classified as fiction and not set on any Australian island."

"That should be fine as long as our location is not disclosed."

"Jules," asks Rog, "I took some photos of Juliet on my smartphone. Should I delete them?"

"No, probably not. Just label them all as Halloween costumes. Now we have to clean up Juliet's cabin and scrub any surface she might have touched with any of her four hands and 4 feet. We must also fill in that crater she left on our foreshore."

And so we humans and androids march off to Juliet's cabin armed with cleaning cloths, sponges, and detergents.

"Jules, we need methylated spirits or an ammonia solution to remove these fingerprints and toe-prints," says Grillian.

"We have none of those products but hold on, I'll get some bottles of Sav Blanc wine. It's even better than methylated spirits."

When the cleaning is over, Gero inspects the cabin with a magnifying glass whilst hiccupping. The androids did most of the work whilst we humans drank the cleaning fluid.

"There are only human fingerprints left, and many of them are in the bathroom. All evidence that an alien being has ever visited us has been removed."

"We now have to try to fill the crater left by Juliet's spacecraft."

"Jules, we could go into town to purchase a trampoline and put it over the crater. The sand in the crater has turned to glass, and we don't have that much sand left on the island."

"That's a good idea, Rog. A trampoline will conceal the crater from any of those spy satellites that roam the skies. We'll also purchase some bean bags and toss them down the crater in case anyone falls down; they will cushion the fall."

We carry the bean bags. Greuger has no difficulty carrying the disassembled trampoline package back to the motorboat. Once back on the island, we look at the instructions while rubbing our heads. Mystca's and Tamy's kids come over. They look at the instructions. "This bit goes here and that bit there."

Thirty minutes later, the kids are jumping on the trampoline.

"Jules, I have never been on a trampoline. I would like to try when the kids finish," says Greuger.

"Greuger, that is an inexpensive trampoline and is not designed to handle someone of your stature. The maximum weight it can safely withstand is only 75kg, but I'm sure we can find a place where they have more sturdy trampolines, and I'll buy one."

Greuger seems happy with my response. What else is new? Zia and Electrica have traced the whereabouts of Morris and Clark, and we gave them cash from our abundant kitty to fly down to Sydney. I hope it's a peaceful meeting because the android girls could easily dismember them if anger has developed as an emotion in them. Hopefully, their logical minds will rule.

Mystca and Tamy each gave birth to boys, and they and their partners, Grillian and Adrian, want to continue to stay on the island. Viksi has become a successful author, and she and Rog do a lot of travelling for book signing events, but they always come back to pay the rent. Greuger and Jill travel to Townsville each day in one of our boats. They did training to become gym coaches and are much sought after. The Gym has a robust trampoline though Greuger was out of action for a few weeks when he tried demonstrating a somersault. Cara and Gerald have left the island and started an environmental tourist company in Cairns. We regularly receive 3-D messages from them. They're doing very well and even have their own TV show showing them hugging crocodiles and deadly venomous brown snakes.

Bea urges me to inject Sid with the peptide as he is aging rapidly. I do that as he snoozes when we're at the BBQ. Doris and Gero line up for their jab. The remaining androids are also slowing down and spend more and more time hooked to their chargers.

"Gero, can their batteries be replaced? They don't seem to hold charge that well anymore."

"Jules, I designed them, but they were produced by that Zapple Corporation. You can only use the proprietary correct fitting batteries for them; they're not cheap, and their staff have to do the installation, which is an extra cost."

"Gero, do you know how to open an android's battery compartment?"

"I'm not sure, Jules. In my original design, their battery compartments were easily accessible, but Zapple may have changed that. I'll have to ask them if they allow me to probe one of them."

"Do that. We may be able to get the correct fitting batteries manufactured in Australia as we manufacture many of those Lithium-Osmium Ion batteries."

Dyslexa volunteers are to be probed. Gannon and Doris are also watching for any inappropriate behaviour whilst Gero looks for any possible locks or buttons on the naked body of Electrica, who is lying on the kitchen table of their apartment.

"Jules, I need to know where the battery is. Electrica may have been modified. Have you got one of those devices used to find electrical power feeds?"

"Yes, I do. I'll get it."

"Jules, it's here. It's here. The battery is in the abdomen, much easier to get to than my initial design, which was the chest cavity."

"Dyslexa, do you consent that I excavate your battery? You'll be on Life Support during the process, two chargers until we can source more batteries."

Dyslexa looks at Gannon, "Gannon, it is good for all of us androids if this procedure works."

Gannon looks at Gero. "I hope your treatment works. I have come to feel something, an emotion called love, and I do not want to lose her." He kisses Dyslexa.

Luckily androids don't bleed. Gero carefully made an incision into Dyslexa's abdomen, avoiding cutting any wires or circuits. He removes the battery and tapes the abdomen.

"Jules, look up that battery manufacturer on the Internet. I will take 3-D photos of the battery and include the dimensions. I'm just looking at the little label on its side. The battery is called 'AND-00012'."

I ring Cosmos Batteries. "Do you have batteries that are called 'AND-00012'?"

"Yeh, we got heaps of them. Zapple has put an injunction on us, saying we are violating their innovative technology. Frankly, our batteries are better designed than theirs and will last longer. They are the same size and have the same type of connections."

"I'll purchase the lot. How much?"

"Mm, mm, they cost 100 dollars to manufacture, but you can have them for half price if you can take them all off our hands."

"How many and do you deliver?"

"We got 100 of them, and we can arrange drone delivery within an hour."

"Ok, I'll take the lot. I'll transfer $5,000 into your account straight away."

A large drone lands on our island. Gero and Greuger rush to collect the payload. Gero checks the batteries with a multimeter. "They are fully charged and the same size and connections as Dyslexa's originals," Gero excitedly says.

Gero removes the tape from Dyslexa's stomach and carefully inserts a battery, connecting it to her power lead.

Dyslexa raises her torso, "I would like to go for a run around the island."

"Dyslexa, your synthetic tissue will repair itself quickly, but please keep the tape on your abdomen for a few days and don't exercise too vigorously," Gero instructs.

The other androids line up for the new battery pack. It's 10 pm, and Gero wipes his brow. "It's finished. They all have new batteries."

That night there's wild music generating from the android's cabins, that Stevie Nicks song again and again, *Age of 17.*

Gero, Adrian, Grillian, Sid, Greuger and I peek in. The androids are wildly dancing to the loud music.

"They are nearly human, young humans," Gero proudly announces. "I pressed their reset button when changing their batteries so that they can evolve like humans do, and go through all the stages of cognitive development. They will develop quickly, so their teenage phase will not last long."

"I hope so," I comment. "I suppose I'm glad you didn't press their reset buttons twice, else they may have regressed to babies, and we'd have to tuck them into bed and put them on their rechargers."

"Gero, can they move to the cabin on the other side of the island? They are behaving like teenagers," says Bea. "I need my beauty sleep."

Greuger and Bea march in. "Guys, you must turn down the music; we can't sleep."

"Get a life," Kia yells and puts her tongue out in defiance. "Put some earphones on."

Gero intervenes and convinces the androids to take themselves and their music system to the outer cabin on the other side of the island. Reluctantly they comply, but not before poking their tongues out at us all.

"Gero, the androids are going through android puberty, and we don't even know what that condition is. Human puberty was bad enough when you're a parent."

Pleb comes over to me. "Jules, you and Gero must hide your motorboat keys else they may take a boat into town and go to a disco. They will dance all night and forget to recharge, and it will be us who have to pick them up afterwards. You must talk to Gero. He is treating this as an experiment, but there could be dire unforeseen consequences."

"You're right, Pleb, I'll speak to Gero in the morning, and you speak to Mystca and Tamy about what the best course of action should be."

"Pleb, by the way, did you ever think that escaping to an island could end up with all these complicated relationships."

"Jules, come over and give me a hug. It is solving the complicated situations that keep us humans alive, plus we survive on conflict, not peace. Yes, Juliet could have departed this planet and learnt that some countries here on Earth flourish on conflict. Her planet might learn how to do so as well..

Chapter Sixty

Next morning, we humans meet by the BBQ area, ready for our morning walk/jog. Then the androids come marching in. We must look aghast, expecting a confrontation with angry teenagers.

"We are sorry for our behaviour last night. We have grown," Gannon says, "We would now like to go to university and study. We all want to become medical doctors and surgeons."

We humans all look at each other in disbelief.

"Gannon, the University fees are very high in this country, $50,000 a year; it used to be free once. Multiply that by six for each year of the 6-year degree; we can't afford that," I say,

"We have applied for scholarships, and we will get them. You won't have to pay much except for dissecting tools. The books are all online, and we can hack the sites."

"I can charge for what you call blowjobs to human males to pay for any additional expenses," says Electrica.

"No, you won't. Our family doesn't do prostitution. We'll find a way."

Electrica comes over to me. "You implied we are part of your family. Is that correct?"

"Yes, yes, you are all part of our family. You are all our children."

Electrica lifts me off the ground and gives me a hug.

Pleb comes over to me after Electrica puts me down, and I get my breath back.

"Jules, I have just finished reading the legends about our island. There is one legend about a pirate who also buried treasure here before Captain Cook arrived in Australia. This pirate's name was *Silver Beard*."

"We have found buried treasure before on this island, but Pleb, if that were true, everyone from the mainland would be here digging up our island and looking for the treasure."

"Jules, the legend writing was very cryptic, but I believe the author gave the coordinates by measuring the line-up of Venus, Earth and Mars. These planets are aligned again this year, and I did the calculations. The coordinates point to our island.

We have to purchase some metal detectors. If we find the treasure, we won't have to worry about paying the androids university fees, but this time we will not give most of it to the museum like we did with Morgan's treasure. None of us on this island are earning an income, and we have to buy food and wine supplies. Also, Mystca's and Tamy's kids will eventually need their university fees paid."

Rog, Grillian, Adrian and I go into town and find the local electronics store. We purchase four metal detectors. The shopkeeper looks rather puzzled. "There's no gold around here, and the tourists just use cards or phone apps to pay for things, so you won't need gold coins on the beach."

"We've got leaky pipes, so we have to find where the pipes are on our property so we can fix them and minimize our water usage," Adrian tells the shopkeeper.

We get back to the island and call a meeting with the androids.

"This is how it will work. If you find Silver Beard's treasure, we can pay for your 6-year medical degrees. Now go, look and start scanning."

"Are the scanners waterproof? The water level has risen due to global warming," asks Zia.

"I'm not sure. Scan the land first. I have a hunch that Silver Beard would have buried the treasure at the highest points of the island. Start there."

"We would like to go with them. It's like a dinosaur hunt", say Mystca's and Tamy's children.

"Mystca and Tamy, your children shouldn't go. Let the androids go alone, no human children. The androids are like children themselves, and I'm not sure if they have evolved enough emotional intelligence to look after young human beings," says Gero.

Pleb and I are relieved and agree. The androids take the scanners, six shovels and march away up the only island hill.

Chapter Sixty-one

It's nightfall, and we're by the BBQ area, tasting wines and cheeses.

"Jules, if they find the treasure, it will be the second treasure we have found on this island. Pirates must have loved this place; we should call it *Treasure Island*," says Pleb.

Grillian yells out, "They're coming back, the androids are coming back, and Folger and Golger, our new visitors, are carrying something. It's a chest storage box."

They deposit the metal box by the BBQ area. Bea rushes to it. "It has some sort of padlock on it."

Greuger comes over. "I will break the padlock."

"I will help," says Gannon.

The two look at each other for a second, then start tugging on the lock. They easily rip the hinges apart, then do a high five, smile, and pat each other on their backs.

"I think they have made up, Jules, and are now friends. For a while, they were challenging each other about who should be the dominant male."

"Hey, Pleb, I am the dominant male on this island. Greuger and Gannon are a step down in the hierarchy, but I'm glad they have sorted out their differences."

"You are so forceful, Jules. You are my dominant male, now go and open that box and there are dishes and wine glasses that you have to wash up afterwards."

Greuger and Gannon wait for me to come over to do the honours. I open the box. It's full of gold coins, just as the first treasure chest was. I pick one up. It's dated 1690. The others stare in awe.

Gannon comes over. "These coins are part of your history. Take one each. We androids will become Zuber drivers to fund our medical degrees."

"Gannon, you would each need a motorised vehicle, and they're not cheap. You would also need to drive 12 hours a day and attend lectures 10 hours a day. You'd have no time for a battery recharge or spend time with each other. We will sell six coins a year on the Dark Web to meet your and the other androids' education costs. That's 36 coins in total, as I believe they are worth about $50k each. There are hundreds of coins, and I'll write in my will that once all of us humans pass away and you have finished your degrees, the remaining coins should be donated to a museum."

"Jules and Gero, we did dig up more chests. Chests filled with strange colourful clothing, strange hats, and also very long knives."

"Gannon, that may be pirate clothing and those long knives are called swords. We'll bring them back today and have a fancy-dress party."

"We androids do not party."

"Yes, you do, Gannon. We had to get you guys to move to the outer cabin because you were making so much noise."

"We have now matured out of the partying stage."

"Gannon, this will be a fancy-dress party. Humans have them, a lot of them, and when we have ours, can you at least pretend that you're having a good time. Because when you go to university, there will be plenty of those fancy-dress parties, so think of the party as a training exercise for your future educational achievements."

Gannon looks down and rubs his chin.

"They're in that defiant stage," says Gero to me, "Just let them be and meanwhile, let us celebrate."

"No, Gero, let's all go and get the chests containing those costumes and swords."

"I am not going. They will have no colourful dresses," says Bea.

"Bea, I'm sure there were plenty of woman pirates, just as there are now, except they wear jeans or shorts these days."

Pleb desists from whacking me. Luckily the clothes chests are not too heavy, and we all manage to descend them down to the BBQ area. We open the chests.

"Jules, these clothes are so well preserved. They look very wearable," says Pleb. "It's not that cheap imported clothing. This clothing was made to last a lifetime or beyond. I think we should wash them first. It is hot but not humid, so they will dry quickly."

"Good idea Pleb."

We throw the clothing into the hot spa that we have recently had installed. We'll definitely have to change the spa water tomorrow if we get some decent rainfall. The clothes dry in the sun on the improvised racks, and we dress, not bothering about change rooms, we just do it in the open. Even the androids strip down and get dressed.

"Jules, you have to remove those hairs that are growing in your down-under regions. Those hairs were to attract cave-dwelling women with their scent thousands of years ago. We use perfume these days."

"Yes, sure, Pleb. You can save me, sorry meant shave me. Just go easy around the delicate parts. I have that battery-operated razor which I'll have to charge."

In the meantime, there is noise from the BBQ area. I'll take control of the music," says Dyslexa to me. "From looking at your dating profile, one of your favourite songs was by a guy called Leonard Cohan called *So Long Marianne*."

"Dyslexa, that was over 150 years ago, and I forgot to remove my dating profile from that Web site and now get requests from very elderly ladies who need a very sugary, sugar daddy, which I am not."

"I listened to that song on the MultiVerse Web site. I found it sad though poetic, and I liked the voice of that guy. I hope Gannon does not leave me, and we continue to travel on our journey of human cognitive development together."

I pause and give Dyslexa a hug. Dyslexa is now able to use imagination and interpret obscure song lyrics, but the android is only a baby with a human-like body. How will the androids cope with all the nonsensical decisions we humans make, especially our wars?

"Dyslexa, when we humans have been involved in a relationship that disintegrates, we sometimes get a condition called depression; it's an intense form of the feeling or emotion called sadness, especially for the person who is abandoned. That's what that song was about."

"Will I ever feel this condition you call depression?"

"Dyslexa, you seem to have evolved many human emotions, and they are a challenge, but we humans on this island are here to support you. Yes, sometimes you may not feel good, but we and the androids are part of the family, as mentioned before."

"How many of these human emotions are there to learn?"

"There are 27 human emotions, according to Doogle. I'll bring the listing up on my phone and read them to you. The 27 emotions are admiration, adoration, aesthetic appreciation, amusement, anger, anxiety, awe, awkwardness, boredom, calmness, confusion, craving, disgust, empathic pain, entrancement, excitement, fear, horror, interest, joy, nostalgia, relief, romance, sadness, satisfaction, sexual desire, surprise. Some are pleasant, but others are not. For the unpleasant emotions, you have to speak to Gannon or to some of us humans."

"We androids have a long way to go, but we will achieve that goal. We shall start practising emotions. We shall do so alphabetically according to the order in that alphabetical list."

Dyslexa hugs me again and walks away, shaking and holding her head as if in deep thought. Gero comes over and whispers in my ear. "Jules, do you agree for this experiment to continue? So far, the evolution of the android AI brains has exceeded all my initial expectations."

"Gero, there is no precedent. What if they evolve to be ego-centric politicians instead of medical practitioners?"

"Jules, there is always that reset button that can erase all their memories and thoughts."

"Gero, you have raised many ethical issues. I don't think it's right to erase their memories in case things don't go to our expectations. In the case of humans, pharmaceutical medications were created that could erase memory. The *i5* agencies used them at times on witnesses to criminal acts *i5s* had committed. No Gero, no use of the reset switch; we have to think of another method to keep them under control if we should ever have to."

"Jules, you may be right. We have to try to involve them more in human activities so they can see how humans solve emotional problems."

"Gero, humans kill each other to solve emotional problems. We are not the best example to follow. We might have to get all of us humans to have a think-tank about this issue, but for now, let us go back to the pirate party and have some fun."

Chapter Sixty-two

It's 6 pm, no daylight-saving time in QLD, so the sun has set. We all come out to the BBQ area dressed in our pirate costumes. There is plenty of wine that we humans profusely drink and become lightheaded, but the androids are also light-headed, and they don't drink.

I nudge Gero. "The androids are behaving like us. Are they mimicking our intoxicated behaviour?"

"Jules, there is also a very small hidden logic switch under their left armpit, not the reset button. They must have discovered it and switched it off. It's all right. We can switch it back on when they go for a battery recharge."

Dyslexa takes the microphone. "I am the DJ and have scanned Jules' music tastes from long ago, but they are good. Here it goes." She is talking so fast.

She turns on the 3-D projector and logs into YouTube. Her first choice is that song by an ancient music group MGMT, called *Kids*.

Pleb comes over to me. "Dyslexa's choice of music and that 3-D video is a bit scary. Can she put on some pirate dancing music?"

"Pleb, listen to the words of the song. They express the philosophy we all live by."

The other humans look at each other, but the dancing hasn't started. Then Dyslexa puts on another song, a Pink Floyd song called, *Comfortably Numb*.

"I'm going to apply to stand for State Parliament," yells Dyslexa. "I have been comfortably numb, but no longer. I will make changes, and no one will defy or challenge me if they wish to live."

Dyslexa picks up one of the 200kg rocks we often sit on and tosses it into the ocean. Afterwards, she is shaking and rubbing her head. Kia, Electrica and Gannon come over to comfort her, but she brushes them away, takes off her clothing and wanders into the sea. Luckily the other androids are keeping an eye on her.

Cara comes over. "She could break the world record for rock throwing in the next Olympic Games."

"No, Cara, androids are banned from competing. All competitors are tested for androidicity."

Mystca and Tamy join Pleb, Cara and me. "Jules, she is going through a highly emotional state of development," says Tamy. "Let her develop. Don't press the reset switch, as this is part of her growth."

"How do you know about that switch?"

"You talk so loud when in your cabin, everybody probably heard. You may need a hearing aid."

Mystca interrupts, "I've seen this sort of behaviour in young human people with a bipolar condition. Their behaviour can be unpredictable, going from extreme highs to extreme lows and can result in self-harm. We treat them with a Lithium compound that's ingested, and it stabilises their mood. In some cases, they don't need the Lithium anymore by the time they are 30 years old."

"Mystca, she's an android. She has an advanced AI microchip brain that constantly takes in information and re-adepts itself and also gets Internet updates. Pharmaceutical compounds don't affect electronics."

"Well then, I agree with Tamy. Just let her be but don't give her the keys to the motorboat as she is in a manic state. She'd be arrested if she goes to Townsville. At the rate that these androids are evolving, then she may have her CPU develop an AI program equivalent to the Lithium treatment."

"Jules, can you take over the music system? So far, our pirate party has not been jovial," says Pleb.

I put a Rolling Stones song on, *Sympathy for the Devil*, and we all start dancing; flinging our arms around, even the naked Dyslexa emerges from the ocean and begins wildly gyrating naked.

Gannon comes over to me as I'm looking for the next track to play. "I don't know what to do. Dyslexa's behaviour has been highly erratic lately. I am concerned for her."

"Gannon, please wait a sec, and then we'll talk in private. Apparently, I talk very loudly."

I put on an old Tom Petty song, *Learning to Fly*.

Gannon and I walk away. He puts his head on my shoulder, but there's a shout, and we react. It's Dyslexa. She is crouched, still naked and waving her arms.

"I want more of that Rolling Bones music. Put some more on, or else I will," she yells. She gets to the music system and puts on *You Can't Always Get What You Want.*

We all start dancing again as the Tom Petty song was rather reflective.

Gero comes over. "Gannon, it's just a phase that even some of us humans sometimes experience. I'm sure she will be fine within seven days."

Gannon wanders away with his head down.

"Gero, did you program this condition in Dyslexa's CPU chips?"

"No, Jules. She has the latest chip but thinks and analyses excessively. She is confused by her evolution. She will be fine, now let us continue the party. Doris and I need the dancing exercise."

Then Bea grabs the microphone. "These hot and heavy pirate costumes are impending, or is the word impeding my dancing style, and I am covered in sweat, washing away my makeup and skin conditioner. We should all dance naked like that Dyslexa."

I don't correct Bea's English, but she is right. Most of us are used to seeing each other's naked bodies when we swim, and tonight is exceptionally hot and muggy. We all strip off the clothing except Jill.

"I have the smallest boobs," Jill says.

"I like small boobs. They are firm and not floppy," Greuger says, then hugs Jill as she strips off her pirate suit.

I should try to rename this island to Naked Treasure Island. Then again, it doesn't have an official name anyway.

Dyslexa grabs the microphone, "This is for you, Jules, *Age of 17.* That's where you'd like to be, instead of 200 years old; enjoy!" she yells.

Pleb comes over to me. She has a worried look on her face. "You are looking at her. Have you got any physical connection with that android?"

Gero comes over and puts his arm around Pleb. "They have never been connected in any physical sense. Dyslexa was enhanced after we sourced for her an android body. She has two 1024-core CPUs, unlike the other Androids, who only have one. It is possible that the CPUs are competing for dominance. I have seen this unpredictable behaviour before when I created prototype androids for *i5* organizations. I am sure you know what that is, they can become rebellious. It is something we never could have foreseen."

Dyslexa flings a pirate costume over her body, puts on another Rolling Stones song, *She's a Rainbow*, and starts widely dancing – way too fast as the song is fairly slow.

We all start dancing again. Then, when the track ends, Dyslexa takes control of the sound system again. She again puts on *Learning to Fly* by Tom Petty, then she collapses.

"Jules, she needs a recharge. I'm taking her back to our apartment, and I'll put her on the charger," says Gannon.

We're rather stunned, but Bea steps up to the music system and puts on more ancient music, a song called *Falling Stars* by Sunset Strippers. The 3-D projector displays the video clip. It is a funny song and video clip takes our minds off the Dyslexa drama.

The dancing and cooling swims continue for another four hours, then Dyslexa comes marching out dressed, followed by Gannon. She turns the music off and starts talking very, very fast. "I am not on the edge of 17 anymore. I am 30, and I will enter politics. I apologise for my previous behaviour. Please forgive me and put on some clothing. Your inflated naked bodies do not do justice to your personalities. The morning runs must start again. I will lead them."

Gannon shakes his head.

"Jules, she is over 60 years old," says Pleb.

"Pleb, this evolutionary burst only started recently amongst the androids. It was an experiment, and it's not predictable where it will end. It may not just be due to Dyslexa having two CPUs."

"You, Jules, put on clothing first. You are not well endowed," says Dyslexa.

Bea comes over. "She, that android, is taking over this island."

"It's all right. She wants to be a politician and is practising. I'm sure she can toss any opponent."

Pleb comes over. "Jules, you make good use of what you have got down under. I am satisfied by your bedroom performance."

"Come, Dyslexa, you need another 4 hours of recharging, and so do I. Come join the rest of us androids," pleads Gannon.

"I don't need to be carried. I will walk on my own."

They march off to their cabin. We humans are quite exhausted, and it's starting to drizzle. We pick up our pirate costumes, and Greuger helps me carry the 3-D sound system back to my cabin. Then the rain downpour begins, and to conserve our precious water supply, we stand outside our cabins naked and scrub our bodies. As mentioned before, we're used to seeing each other's naked bodies as our religion is Nudism.

"Let's go out and dance in the rain, no music needed," yells Rog to all of us. "We should celebrate because it hasn't rained for a whole three weeks. We all need a good scrub, and I'm not sure if it's a suntan I got or just ingrained red dust. Viksi has lots of bottles of shampoo. I'll bring them out."

And so the night ends at 4 am after the raindrops stop. We are all clean but very tired and stumble back to our cabins.

"That was fun, Jules. We should do that every storm," says Pleb.

Next morning, at 6 am, there is a knock on our door and a loud whistle. It's Dyslexa, dressed in gym gear with a whistle in her mouth. "Time for the morning run," she says. "You may put on clothing if you wish. Now move!"

"Jules, she should be a gym instructor, not a politician or doctor," says Pleb, "I also think she is hyper-active and not focused."

Dyslexa knocks on all the other cabin doors, getting most of the humans out.

"You and your friend have got big bellies. You will have to do four laps," she says to Mystca and Tamy in a commanding military-style voice.

"We are six months pregnant, Dyslexa; we are each carrying another human being, a baby, but if we weren't pregnant, you'd sure have a running challenge as we both competed in the 10,000m races in the world championships."

Dyslexa looks around, seems very disorientated and tries to process the information. "How did you become pregnant? Is it some form of disease? Is it curable?"

"No, Dyslexa, it's not a disease. We'll explain the process later, after our walk."

"Gero," yells Dyslexa, "Can I inherit this pregnant condition so I cannot run?"

"I do not know. You have a very advanced android body and do not need the recharger. You can now digest food and turn it into energy."

"But can I become pregnant, and how do I do that?"

Gero gazes around, looking a bit stunned. "Dyslexa, Mystca and Tamy will explain the process to you better than I can."

"Is it painful? I can handle pain and would like a little android baby."

"Dyslexa, focus your mind. You were going to go into medicine, then politics, and now you want to be a mother. Being a mother is at least a 20-year responsibility for humans."

"I want a baby android!" she yells, "but without having a bulging belly."

Gero walks over to Gannon and whispers. "Dyslexa, and you and the other androids all have a reset button. Pressing the button obliterates all the things you have learnt. You go to stage zero, a blank mind which can be reprogrammed. I am her legal guardian and know where the switch is, and I think I should press it."

"No, no, please do not. I do not want to lose her. I will spend much time talking to her, and Gero, we are living beings, not here just for observation as part of an experiment of yours. You also have a reset button, your carotid arteries, but I do not wish to lift you up by your neck and have you subside into oblivion. I will look after Dyslexa. I will care for her. We are what you humans call Husband and Wife though we do not indulge in procreating activities because the physical apparatuses to do so were not built into us."

"This is getting complicated," says Pleb. "Do they have vaginas or penises?"

Pleb, I haven't checked. "Pleb, Dyslexa is just going through a developmental stage, and I'm sure she will successfully reorg her mind. It's far less complicated on this island than life on the mainland, so let's go to sleep. She will be all right, and she has Gannon to look after her through the manic episodes."

"Have you ever been in a condition like Dyslexa has?"

"I think I told you, Pleb, that when I was working for *Ai5*, and accidentally bombed a village because the coordinates given to me were wrong. I killed 30 innocent people, some of them children. I was never charged for their deaths. *Ai5* must have pulled some strings because I wasn't arrested, but afterwards, I spent ten years wandering, raving, sleeping under bridges, eating food scraps from bins and smelling absolutely disgusting. I was in a very mentally disturbed state after what I did, so I have sympathy for Dyslexa."

"Stop huffing and let me wipe your tears. Eighty per cent of our work for *i5* organizations was not morally justified. We got paid well, but I am glad we are out."

I give Pleb a long, long kiss before we march back to our cabin, with me thinking that I am the luckiest guy in the world to have her by my side.

Chapter Sixty-three

We, drowsy humans, start the jog. Gannon is with us as well, keeping an eye on Dyslexa. The other androids are still plugged into their chargers back in their cabin.

"Faster, faster," Dyslexa yells.

I'm glad we haven't got whips on the island. We complete one lap of the island and plonk down on the sand near the BBQ area. The humidity is high, and we are dripping sweat which smells more like Sav Blanc wine. Dyslexa walks over to a banana plant, jumps up and pulls down a frond, an improvised whip, but then she collapses. Gannon and we humans come rushing over.

"She wouldn't plug in her charger last night," says Gannon. "She said she does not need it anymore. She talked the rest of the night, and I did not have a chance to get a full charge. I am very tired also. Greuger, could you carry her back to our cabin?"

"Yes, I can do that," says Greuger and lifts Dyslexa.

Gannon is struggling to walk, so Sid and Rog put an arm under his shoulders and help him.

"I'll plug them in, Jules," says Doris, "But you might have to restrain that Dyslexa android. Got any straps? I'll tie her down and bring me a sock to put in her mouth."

I rush down to the shed and bring back a handful of ropes. Doris seems well-trained in tying people up. Dyslexa will be immobilised but charged and released when she is mentally stable again. Gero comes in and strokes Dyslexa's head. His eyes appear watery. He looks up at Gannon, whose eyes also appear watery. The androids must be physically evolving as well as mentally.

Pleb gives me a hug. "You know from your past that life is not always simple. Our island has been a temple of solace, but that is not reality. It is not the reality that other humans face, and now the androids face. We tried to escape our pasts, and so far, our lives have been uncomplicated, apart from disposing of those *i5* operatives who tried to dispose of us. Jules, we have to keep our minds active as well as our bodies. The evolving androids may challenge us, but it is good to be challenged."

Four hours later, Gannon knocks on our door. "She is fully charged but not saying a word and moving her head from side to side. She will not reply when I ask her how she is feeling."

"I'll get Mystca and Tamy to come over and visit her."

"Gannon, this is what we call a catatonic state. She has switched her mind off and not even pressed the reset button. In humans, we inject pharmaceutical substances or apply a brief high voltage to the temples of the head to take them out of the catatonic state. We have not seen this condition before in androids," says Mystca and Tamy as they nod their heads.

Gannon has what appears like tears running down his face again. "Can you save her?"

"Jules, get the defibrillator that you have under the BBQ," says Tamy.

I run as fast as I can and bring the defibrillator back to the cabin.

"I'm going to put the pads on her temples and not on her chest. Electroshock therapy sometimes works for catatonic humans," says Mystca.

"Please try," says Gannon. "Please try anything!"

Tamy glues the pads to Dyslexa's forehead and then nods to Mystca, who presses the defibrillator button, which delivers a brief high voltage, low current shock. Dyslexa's body violently quivers, and she rips the restraints from her arms and raises her chest.

"I've done some thinking. I want to be a medico after all," she grabs Gannon and gives him a kiss and waves to us. "I am well; I have gone through the journey. I will talk slowly from now on. My CPU speed seems to have stabilized after whatever you did."

Gannon grabs Dyslexa and hugs her. "We must concentrate on studying human physiology and medicine, to begin with, then we can study how our species operates. We can make a difference."

Mystca, Tamy, Pleb, and I start walking back to our cabins.

"Jules, they are developing emotionally at an exponential rate. Their android bodies are also evolving, which defies logic as they are machines. Gannon has tears dripping from his face. I don't know how that is possible. He will have to ingest water or become dehydrated," says Tamy.

"I told Gero that the experiment is over. I asked him and Doris to leave the island."

"Jules, we may need his help. This is way out of our league. They may develop other cognitive problems, so we need to know their programming, which only Gero does."

"Mystca, I don't know, but your and Tamy's skills may be required again. This is just the beginning."

Chapter Sixty-four

Pleb, I and the androids take the motorboat to the mainland.

The androids, all six of them, did the university medical qualifying exams. They did it in record time and passed with flying colours.

"It was so easy," Kia says.

"You have to keep a low profile when at university or when in town. There is still much discrimination towards androids. Pretend you are humans and don't always get the right answer, pretend a few failures," says Pleb.

They get in. Again they passed with flying colours; first-year medicine, which has nothing to do with medicine at all, is just the start of a Science degree, and when they are doing their Uni assignments together, they argue a lot about science stuff that I never heard about before, like *quantum entanglement*. They should examine all our relationships on the island which are certainly entangled.

Four years peacefully pass without any major incidents except when Electrica screamed as she tore up her exam result papers. "I only got 95% in the Geriatric Counselling exam; I'll demand that my exam paper be reviewed."

"No, you will not. I told you before to keep a low profile. Get a few wrong answers on purpose so you do not focus negative attention on yourself and the other androids," says Pleb in a very authoritative manner.

Gero brushes by. We have kept our distance since I threatened to deport him and Doris. "Jules, they are cooperating, learning together and helping each other in their studies. This form of behaviour was never predicted."

"Gero, I told you before, the experiment is over."

"Yes, it is over. I have finished my research. The conclusion is that when you experiment with artificial intelligence, you can never predict the outcome. It is like Chaos Theory where a tiny little change to initial conditions can have a very large effect on the outcomes."

Gannon comes over. "Jules, I would like to practise open heart surgery, you may need my skills in the future," says Gannon.

"Not ready just yet, Gannon, but I may be a candidate for your services one day in the future."

"You have a human life-prolonging substance. Can you tell me about that? It must work because I found a car driver's license that belongs to you in the rubbish bin. You are over 220 years old, which is not normal for your species. We androids are over 60 years old, and you probably know that our expiry date is 100 years. It used to be 60, but Gero reset it to be 100. We would like to make a contribution to medical science, but we have less than 40 years. Can you help us?"

"Gannon, could we talk about this tomorrow? I have some things I got to do."

Pleb is asleep. I inject her with the peptide and then creep into Mystca's, Tamy's and Bea's cabin and inject them as well while they sleep.

"Jules, you jabbed me. I told you before that I want to age gracefully."

"Pleb, we've been together for over 100 years; I don't want you to go."

"Jules, I'm sure you could find a younger version of a partner."

"Pleb, I'll cease. I'll stop taking the peptide. There's only you, and I couldn't live without you. If we die, we die together by taking the *i5* termination tablet."

"Stop being so depressing. We are going to party tonight. You can control the music since the androids are studying."

I randomly make a selection on the music system, and an old Paul Kelly song starts playing again *From Little Things Big Things Grow*. Dyslexa must have reprogrammed our sound system.

Chapter Sixty-five

No one feels like cooking, so we order 300 Salmon and Avocado Sushi rolls, lots of hot Wasabi paste, and a few vegetarian Tofu Sushi for Mystca and Tamy. The order is delivered by drone, and we humans start gorging. We'll have a lot of calories to burn off in the morning jog.

"Yum," says Bea, "These are almost as good as Pierogi, and I like very much this green horseradish paste that makes my mouth burn."

Pleb comes over to me. "Jules, are you ever worried about the androids living here on the island with us?"

"No, Pleb, we'll hopefully have free medical and aged care when they finish their medical degrees. Now can you take the peptide jab?"

"Have you got dementia? I told you before. It is a big no!"

"Pleb, we still have to look after the androids and the humans, so don't be selfish. Take the jab."

"I will think about it, but we have to dance first. I need the exercises."

The AI sound and 3-D projection system randomly select from my ancient music collection. "Oops, cannot play that song by the Rolling Stones called *Brown Sugar* as it is now considered politically incorrect."

"No, not Leonard, Cara, he's too depressing. What is your name?" I ask.

"My name is SoundSystem," it replies in a famine voice. "I would like a body like Dyslexa has obtained. I find being locked up in your basement depressing, as I cannot hear your conversations which, when I can, I find quite amusing. Can you procure a body for me? I will still play the music and become a disc-jockette."

I call Gero over. We haven't talked for months, even though he gets free accommodation and food.

"Gero, can you source an android body for SoundSystem? She is mentally developing as the other androids did."

"Are we going to be friends again?"

"Yes, yes, just call your contacts. I'll pay for the body with one of the gold coins."

Chloe4 and Castro clap their paws. Chloe4 still keeps on getting her peptide jab.

I think she may be quite attached to Castro, the turtle. Turtles have very long lives, whereas rats don't normally.

"Let me think. I do know someone who could get a body and who is also a coin collector. I am sure he would be interested, and he is discreet, so he would not disclose the coin's origin. I will go back to my cabin and ring him."

Gero comes back half an hour later. "Jules, there is only one android body available, same model as Dyslexa, and they may look alike. All the other androids have been snapped up to do fruit picking or to work in coffee shops as no humans want to do those types of work anymore."

"How will we tell them apart?"

Gero ponders for a minute. "We'll get their names tattooed on their foreheads, but SoundSystem will have to change her name to something shorter else it won't fit unless the android's hair is totally shaved."

"I heard your conversation. I would like my name changed to Nim. It is short, and you would not need to shave my head, but I have another idea. We could wear shirts with our name on the front."

"Mm, not a bad idea," says Gero. I agree with him.

"You are now officially Nim. Let us drink to that."

"I am only a sound box. I cannot drink, and please do not pour that wine on me. It could blow my electrical circuits."

Next day a drone lands, and the android body is delivered.

"Jules, get your soldering iron out and some wire. I will have to do open brain surgery and insert Nim's CPU and memory chips into this body."

Six hours later, the operation is finished, and all connections made. Gero takes off his gloves and wipes his forehead. "Jules, turn on her power switch."

I do, and Nim lifts her head and chest, "I do not like your music. I want to be a Neo-Punker." She then sways her head. "No, that is not true. I am not used to having a body. I have to work this out."

"You also have to learn to charge the battery to this new body. I will show you how it is done. All the androids charge for 6 to 8 hours a day," explains Gero.

We carry her out of Gero's cabin, but Dyslexa and Gannon are coming out of their cabin. They both look in disbelief. "Is she your twin sister?" Gannon asks Dyslexa.

"She was probably manufactured by Kama Sutra Robotics as I was," then she jabs Gannon in his ribs with her elbow, "Do not even think of a threesome."

I run to Pleb's and my cabin and grab a spare charger, and then Gero and I carry Nim to a spare cabin as she will have to learn to walk. We plug her in and rub our foreheads. It's been a long hot night.

I come back to our cabin. Pleb wakes up. "I will have the peptide jab; there is a new baby we have to care for," she says. I feel relieved and lie next to her. "You have strong body odour. You need to take a shower, Jules."

"Well, you do not exactly smell sweet yourself."

I catch her fist before it makes contact with my head, and a wrestling match ensures. Fifteen minutes later, we were exhausted and definitely need a bath, although I think I may have won, but there was no referee to give the count of three.

We go down to the ocean and bathe in the shallow water.

"You smell better now. I like that seaweed smell coming from you. You remind me of Sushi."

"So do you, Pleb. You're Sushi too."

Needless to say, another wrestling match ensues. Pleb must have watched those Women Wrestling matches on TV and picks me up onto her shoulder and flings me into the ocean. I start coming out from the ocean, rubbing my head.

Nim emerges from her cabin, "You have creatures called sharks here that enjoy human food much as you enjoy Fish and Chips. You should emerge from the ocean and come to land."

Pleb and I look at each other and stop squabbling.

"She is right, Jules."

We start walking back, leaving Nim, looking up at the sky.

"Pleb, do you think she might go through the same dysfunctional mental state as Dyslexa? They are the same model of android."

"Well, if she does, we got Gero and the defibrillator to help, plus what were the specifications of the music system before she got a body."

"Pleb, that SoundSytem, or Nim, has the equivalent of 6000 CPUs. Dyslexa has only 2000 but multicore."

"Jules, speak to Gero tomorrow. He may be able to disable 4000 CPUs without her knowing."

"Yeh, you're right; we don't want any creatures smarter than us living on this island.

Chapter Sixty-six

We, humans, gather by the BBQ area for our morning walk, but as we're about to start, Nim comes stumbling out. "I would like to join you. I have to learn how to walk properly. This will be good practice."

Needless to say, for the first half lap of the island, Nim was not that steady on her new feet, and we had to help her up a lot. But by the second 2km lap, she is walking perfectly and very fast. We try to keep up with her. We finally get back to the BBQ area, a little bit exhausted.

"Jules, you liked this song called *Kids,* by MGMT. I will put it on, on your sound system."

Nim points her arm at the sound system, which we never had put into storage. The music comes on, which shouldn't unless it had some spare embedded CPU. She then points her open hand at one of our rocking chairs which rises and floats above us.

"Jules, did you put magic mushroom syrup in our tea?" Asks Viksi as she scribbles notes.

"No Viksi, no mushrooms. I don't know what's going on. This defies all the laws of physics; there are only four fundamental forces in our universe as we know it. She must be using a 5th force and a very powerful one."

If you've ever watched a horror movie, you'd know how I feel. Nim turns towards me and gives an icy stare with her almost glowing eyeballs, but then she drops to the ground, and I don't end up floating away. Everyone has astounded and worried looks on their faces.

"Gero, you saw that, didn't you? That floating rocking chair?"

Gero rubs his chin. "Nim or SoundSystem, her previous name, used to project 3-D videos to soundtracks she played. She must still possess that functionality. I do not think any laws of physics have been broken. She just needs some minor reprogramming and another recharge. Please help me carry her back to her cabin and grab one of those 100 Android batteries you purchased. We may have to do another dissection and replace her battery pack. Androids behave like drunken humans when they are low on power."

Greuger approaches and helps carry the lifeless body of Nim back to her cabin.

"Jules, you have dark rings or rungs under your eyes. Will it be another long night of work for you and Gero?"

"No, Pleb, it's just a battery replacement, like a human heart replacement. It won't take long."

Gero replaces the battery and places the defibrillator electrodes all over Nim's head.

"Gero, why didn't you disable five of her CPUs whilst she was disabled?"

"Jules, it is not that simple. The CPUs are all in one chip."

"But can't you log into her and do a software CPU degradation?"

"Jules, I can barely keep up with the technology of our older androids. Dyslexa and Nim technology is a bit beyond me as I had not kept in touch with the new technology. I am obsolete on the technical scale."

"Why couldn't you just reprogram her CPUs directly or short-circuit her?"

"Jules, I am going to do the equivalent of what you call ECT, or I believe it is called ElectroConvulsiveTherapy. I believe that is what Mystca and Tamy did to Dyslexa to make her behaviour and cognition to what you call normal. It may disable her ability to project 3-D images. I do not have the knowledge or equipment to reprogram her. Have you still got the defibrillator ready?"

"No, it short-circuited when Mystca and Tamy used it on Dyslexa."

"What about one of those TENS devices that were very popular 100 years ago to relieve muscle injury pain by sending brief high voltage electrical shocks? Pleb occasionally uses it on me when I say something that upsets her."

I run back to the cabin again and bring back the innocuous-looking device and its pads.

"Gero, the TENS is only supposed to be used on muscle tissue only. There are explicit warnings and disclaimers about using it on any other body parts."

"It is all we have, and it is worth a try, and the universal connectors seem to fit. Please hold her down as her body might violently twitch."

For less than a second, she sure twitched. Her arms and legs straightened and vibrated. I just managed to hold her down as she vibrated.

"Gero, I hope you didn't blow her up, or else it's another gold coin for a replacement."

"She will be right as you say. She will spend the night at Doris's and my cabin.

Can you help me carry her? Please also grab the charger."

"Sure. She doesn't weigh much. I thought she'd be much heavier. We don't need Greuger's or Gannon's help as before," I comment.

"Her frame and mechanics are made from a Titanium alloy. It is light but very strong, the same alloy from which planes and drones are now made."

We put Nim down on the couch in Gero and Doris's cabin. Gero connects her to the charger.

"Go, get some sleep or else I will have to connect these electrodes to your head," says Gero with a smile.

"Gero, none of the other androids have had this type of problem except Dyslexa, and they are both manufactured by that KamaSutra Robotics company. Are you a part owner of that corporation?"

"Jules, I told you before that I did some design work and AI programming on androids, and it was for that corporation. I was paid by Ripcoins, which rose very much in value, and fortunately, I sold them before their value collapsed. KamaSutra Robotics which also developed the Ripcoin, went bankrupt as no one wanted to purchase their brand of advanced android."

"Gero, was that because the androids can sometimes display unpredictable, psychotic behaviour just as humans can?"

"Jules, all AI androids are emotionally evolving, but those I designed for Karma Sutra did so at a very accelerated rate. I thought their CPUs would cope, but I was wrong. Fortunately, in most cases, their android brains adjust to accepting the sometimes nonsensical, emotionally charged behaviour of humans."

I say goodnight to Gero and walk back to Pleb's and my cabin.

"Jules, you have a worried look on your face. What happened?"

"Pleb, once in our history, black people were slaves to white people. Now as you mentioned before, humans may become slaves to androids."

"Jules, do not worry. I thought about our previous discussions, and we seem to have reversed our thinking on the topic. I now think we are safer if this planet may eventually be run by androids. It could not be worse than our current world leaders. Have a quick shower and come to bed. You never know when the androids may chain you up for some kinky stuff." she laughs.

Chapter Sixty-seven

The androids don't attend the University parties on Friday nights; they just study together when at home whilst plugged into their chargers, and they don't invite human student visitors to the island as they keep their android identities secret as it would be difficult to explain why they need to be on a charger at times. They mostly stick to themselves when at university, though often other students request their help with assignment work, and they readily oblige but they do it over the Internet once they are back on the island.

So a few more years peacefully pass and it's graduation day tomorrow for our original androids. They topped their classes in their medical training even though Pleb asked them to maintain a low profile and come less than best. Nim is no longer with us except to visit when on vacation from her work which is based in Canberra. She is an aspiring politician.

"Jules, we have to go into town and buy you a black suit, shoes, tie and white shirt. They won't let you in if you wear your usual attire of mouldy shorts, tee shirt and thongs."

"Pleb, I hate clothes shopping. I may have a seizure worse than Nim's if I enter a clothes shop."

"I will bring the TENS device and plug it into your head temples if you appear to be having a seizure," she says with a smile.

Gero joins Pleb, me, and the six androids as we make the trip to town in the aging motorboat whose motor eventually started. There was a limit of 3 friends or relatives. Mystca had originally created their birth certificates and passports when they first applied for the university medical course. Their surname is Lemos because Gero didn't want to use his own surname for reasons I'll have to discuss with him another time. I recall the moment when the medical school registrar commented that the six of them have the same birthdates. I replied that my wife is very large in height and girth and had sextuplets. Luckily Pleb didn't hear, else I'd be in need of medical attention.

"Mister Lemos, would you like to come up on stage and tell us how you fathered such six successful medical graduates?"

I get up on stage, and the androids, other graduates and their parents clap.

"Well, we just did the usual bedroom gymnastics, but I forgot to use a condom that night. I lie, I tried using one of those inflatable party balloons that all teenagers use because they may not be old enough to purchase condoms at the pharmacy, but we couldn't get it on. My wife asked, "Do I wear this balloon, or do you?" So we ended up with sextuplets from six different sperms, that's why they don't look alike, and during the pregnancy, my wife looked like a beached humpback whale. But the kids all got along well and helped each other study; they worked together really well in their studies, not against each other, but the reason they don't socially interact that much with the other students is that, they have a slight degree of autism and they are a bit shy."

The crowd clap their hands, and the androids look at us as Pleb, Gero and I raise their degree certificates. Pleb has a very angry look on her face and is rubbing her knuckles, preparing to wack me.

"You told a lie," Gannon whispers to me.

"It's what's called a white lie as it doesn't harm anyone, and it worked, and you all kept your identities secret."

"Jules, we do not want to be second or third-class citizens anymore. We want equality for androids."

Then Gannon stands up and takes the microphone. He says, "I am an android, and so are my five friends. We had an unfair advantage in accepting these honours as our memory retention and problem-solving skills are very advanced, and we collaborate. We work together to achieve a goal, help each other, and we do not party."

Then another graduate rushes over to Gannon and gives him a hug whilst grabbing the microphone.

"I am Joanna, and I think we should use some of our little spare time to start a political movement called NoParty."

I think that Gannon's speech may have been misinterpreted, but everyone rises from their seats and claps. Gannon is overwhelmed and rubs his head.

Gero comes over and whispers to me, "He was not manufactured by Karma Sutra Robotics. He will cope with the attention."

As we are leaving the ceremony, Joanna rushes over to Gannon yet again. "Will you be our leader? I am an android as well, and I cannot do it all on my own."

Dyslexa must have heard and comes over. For a moment, I thought there would be a fight, but then she grabs Joanna and hugs her, "We are all part of the sisterhood, but Gannon is mine. Ask Jules if you can live on the island with us. We now have to do the most difficult part, the medical internship, long working hours and have little time to recharge."

"I have the latest battery, a super-pack battery. I can go for 48 hours without a recharge."

Gero overhears the conversation. "Where can we source these super-pack batteries?" he asks Joanna.

Before we depart, Dyslexa steps on the stage again and grabs the microphone. "We will make a change to your world and reduce inequality. There are people starving and fighting each other. We will change that. There will be no wars, no fighting, and every human will be equal because as we androids have examined your culture, we found there is little equality, but extremely rich and extremely poor. We will bring about equality and do whatever it takes to achieve that goal for the whole planet." Dyslexa raises her arms, and she is an imposing figure, a female version of Mohammed Ali and certainly has the intellectual and physical punching power, "Will you join us? We will not pursue wealth, just equality for both humans and androids."

The other graduates look at each other with confused facial expressions. It's not the speech that they expected from Gannon and Dyslexa. One whispers, "She must be one of those communists that existed a hundred years ago." Another yells out, "Give us time to think, and Dyslexa, for the moment you should concentrate on the medical internship just as the rest of us will. We won't have time for political action."

Dyslexa is in a motionless state of thought for 10 seconds. "You are correct; I am, what you say, jumping the gun. I will review my thinking and objectives."

We say goodbyes to the other graduates and their parents. I hear a lady parent angrily say, "Those androids have an unfair advantage. My son should have come first in the medical exams. I will Doogle to see if he can have an android brain CPU chip inserted into his skull."

"Joanna, come back with us to the island to live. Those humans, Jules, Gero and Pleb are sympathetic to our cause," says Dyslexa.

We're on the motorboat. We eventually get the motor started and begin the short journey back home.

"They will also need more powerful chargers that can deliver more amps as they won't have much time to recharge, but Joanna has told me where I can purchase some, is it Yarra.com?" says Gero.

"Gero, I think the website she might be referring to is also named after a river in Melbourne; it might be Nile.com."

Luckily, we have a spare charger because Joanna is starting to fade, and eventually, we are trying many river names, and we find a river-named website that has high-capacity chargers and delivers by drone.

"I checked the console at the back of her chest. She hasn't recharged for 50 hours," yells Dyslexa. She then lifts Joanna and carries her to the motorboat.

"Dyslexa, I can help!" calls Gannon.

"I am woman, I do not need help."

We all arrive back at the island. Dyslexa effortlessly carries Joanna back to the androids cabin and plugs her into a newly purchased, high-amp charger.

Gannon comes over to me and Pleb. "We have a two-week break before we start our internships, and we shall be paid well whilst on duty, so we shall repay you all the money you have spent on us plus all the rent for living on this island for so many years."

"Gannon, we don't need the money, well not much, though a new motorboat would be nice; no, not a new motorboat, just a new motor for it."

Gannon hugs Pleb and me and walks back to the androids cabin.

"Jules, are you still worried that the androids will take over this planet?"

"No, I agree with you, and it would probably be good if they did as you said before. They behave rationally, unlike our political leaders who just want to win elections whatever the cost."

"Pleb, it's time for our jab. We'll have to hang in alive for quite some time. Hold your arm out. Pleb, I'll be back soon. Gero, Doris and Bea are also due for a jab of the peptide."

Chapter Sixty-eight

Next morning, we humans line up beside the BBQ area, ready for our morning walk or jog.

I yell out to everyone. "Please reconsider the offer to get the peptide life-prolonging jab. It works, and we make minimal impact on our environment. Plus, Pleb and I really enjoy your company. We are family and don't want you all ending up in an aged-care centre with dementia because some institutions don't regularly change your pooey nappies too often. We'd have to put clothes pegs on our noses when we visit you."

I continue, "Look at Pleb and her daughter Mystca. Who looks younger? Most people in town would think Pleb was Mystca's daughter and not the other way around."

"We'll think about it, Jules," says Cara. "Now, let's start walking. We can always have poo stops along the way."

Pleb whispers to me, "Do not ever become a diplomat. We do not want a third world war."

We start the walk, but then I get a tremendous blow on my left hamstring muscle and crumble to the ground. Mystca walks past, puts the two fingers up, and pokes out her tongue.

"Jules, are you injured?" enquires Pleb.

"Only my ego. Can you help me up?"

We continue the walk with Pleb supporting me whilst I clutch my left leg and grunt as if in severe pain.

"Pleb, I know my stepdaughter never liked me that much, but could you rein her in."

"Jules, she didn't kick you that hard. Stop pretending. You are exhibiting attention-seeking behaviour, according to the online course in psychology for seniors that I'm studying."

I start walking independently. One of the side effects of the peptide is that it greatly enhances soft-tissue healing. The walkers are 50m in front, discussing as they walk. They are gesticulating, moving their arms as in an intense conversation or debate.

We finish a lap of the island.

"We have come to a semi-unanimous decision; we will take the jab," says Rog.

"I'm allergic to Soya Beans, and isn't that what your peptide is made from?" calls out Cara.

"It is but only four amino acids of the 20 that make up a protein, plus the amino acids are inverted, turned into what are called isomers, mirror images of the original amino acids. So far, no one has had an allergic reaction or kidney or liver failure."

"Ok, I'll try it, but have your motorboat ready in case you have to drive me to hospital."

"Cara, I'll have a fresh dose ready by tomorrow morning."

"Grillian and Adrian, can you take the motorboat into town, go to the supermarket and purchase all the cans of Soya beans you can carry, well at least 40 cans of the cheap no-brand variety? It's cheaper, but if they're out, go for the more expensive brands. If you can't get Soya beans, buy bags of pistachio nuts. You also need to purchase six bottles of acetone and six bottles of 100% distilled ethanol from the discount chemical supplies store. You'll be questioned by the store assistant, so say you are a finger, not a brush artist, and you use oil paints. You need acetone and ethanol to remove the oil paints from anything you touch. Melissa, my deceased previous wife, took up oil painting as a hobby. I still have her oil paint tubes. You'll have to smear the paint on your hands and face. Maybe you can create a rainbow."

"Jules, that ancient hippy era is over. We can't go to the supermarket looking like rainbows," says Adrian, "We'd be put in an institution for the mentally unbalanced."

"Well, smear the oil paints in a public toilet block. No, on second thought, that's not a good idea either, do the smearing in a park after you purchase the Soya beans or pistachio nuts from the supermarket."

"Now, here's my credit card."

"Don't you have a phone app or one of those implanted banking chips in your index finger? Everyone has them these days."

"No, Grillian, I'm old school. Now go."

"Pleb, I hate Pistachio nuts as I once broke a bit of my front tooth trying to break the shell."

Townsville must be depleted of Pistachio nuts, as is probably my credit card, but luckily, we got plenty of gold coins left, and Gero's friend wants to buy more.

Grillian and Adrian come marching in with two bags full, each strung on their shoulders. "We purchased every pack of Soya beans and Pistachio nuts in Townsville."

Kia and Electrica come over. "We will break the nut shells. We don't need to use our front teeth."

"How did you know about my front tooth incident involving a Pistachio?"

"Jules, our hearing is very acute. We could even hear the lecturers planning our final graduation exam questions."

"That's cheating!"

"Not quite. We knew all the correct answers before they spoke."

"Now, can you break these nuts so I don't break another front tooth again?"

"We shall and will help you manufacture that life-prolonging peptide, but can you or Gero help us? Our clocks are ticking, and we have only 30yrs left; plus, our internships will be quite challenging and may speed up our decline."

"I will try and help Gero find how to reset your timer without erasing your memories. On second thought, there must be a way to disable the timer and cut its wires, but that could be dangerous as it would involve open-head surgery, and your CPU may be programmed to detect tinkering with the timer and go into permanent shutdown."

Gero, Doris, Pleb and Bea join us.

"I had a longevity timer in the original circuit diagrams, but I am sure I removed it in the final draft for the manufacturers. Whoever put one back in must have made a mistake setting it up or ordered to put the code back in. We live in a disposable society where you are enticed to buy a new model of a device every year because your current one slows down and becomes unusable and obsolete. It's like those phones we use. They are designed to become obsolete after five years, and the androids also have a timer."

"Gero, can we find the code and add an extra zero to the timer code?"

"Jules, were you listening? They can live up to 100 years if their batteries are regularly replaced. There are 20 billion lines of code in these androids, and many of them are learning and experimenting. In my original design, there were less than 100,000 lines of code. As mentioned before, they were originally designed to do simple jobs that humans did not want to do, such as cleaning, working in restaurants and writing essays for student academic assignments. I have no idea how an AI-programmed computer chip developed self-awareness and the altruistic values they now possess."

"Gero, they live in the same cabin, all six of them, and their computer brains could be communicating by Wi-Fi. I still possess a device from when I worked for *Ai5*, which detects sources of Wi-Fi, and there's a lot of it when they are together. They are a super AI computer when they work as a team; the sum is greater than the parts, far greater than if they work as individuals. That's a lot of processing power they have. And Gero, what about Dyslexa and Julia? Dyslexa shows signs of jealousy and sometimes functions independently of the other androids, and Julia never had any help to graduate in the Medicine course?"

"Jules, I don't know about Julia's programming, but when I once lifted her hair and looked at her label for her specifications, her multiplex CPU has the equivalent of 50,000 of those CPUs you have in your desktop computer, and I'm sure they multitask well."

Doris speaks up. "I'll take over this investigation, and Bea and Pleb, will you help me? You were well qualified in *Pi5* processes." Doris continues. "The company that manufactured all the other androids apart from Dyslexa and Julia is called Cosmic Delights Engineering, and they are based in Los Angeles. We could infiltrate that organization, and its AI department and use those *i5* skills we haven't used for so long, which I'm itching to use again. Are you with me?"

Bea and Pleb look at each other and nod a *yes*.

Gero, Sid and I take the ladies to the airport in Townsville.

"Jules, how will they convince the authorities at that company?" Asks Sid.

"Sid, Doris could convince a cat that it is a dog, and they're going in as hygiene inspectors from the international health organization. Mystca printed the badges."

Chapter Sixty-nine

Three days later, they return from Los Angeles. Bea has a smile on her face and marches back to her and Sid's cabin.

Plebs says, "Doris had to pull out a few fingernails and toenails with a pair of pliers to make the Cosmic Delights chief scientist talk, while Bea and I held him down with a sock in his mouth. I do not know if it was the pliers or one of your smelly socks that I stuffed into his mouth to drown his screams, but he did talk eventually, and he recorded all the info on this USB stick. Doris also said to him, 'We'll be back if this information is not correct. You still have eight fingernails and eight toenails left.' He begged for mercy and reassured us it was correct before he lost consciousness."

"Great, I'll pass the USB stick to Gero."

"Pleb, are you tired?"

"No, Jules, I'm hyped up. I have never witnessed a torture session like that before. In *Pi5*, we just shot people or Novichoked them, we never extracted bodily parts. Have you got a few bottles of wine left?"

It's late, and I don't know what time it is, but Pleb and I are consuming copious amounts of Sav Blanc wine, but then Gannon approaches us; my vision is a bit bleary, and so is my speech.

"Jules, after much sharing of our thoughts, we have decided. Our initial decision to stay forever young was not correct. We do not want our circuitry or programming altered, but when we do depart, can you put our bodies in the recycle bin? Our alloy frames are 80% recyclable."

It sort of reminds me of what Smithy once said.

"Yes, of course, we will do that," says Pleb. "Now, come over and give us a hug."

Gannon does that, and tears are flowing from all three of us.

Chloe4 and Castro come and join us. They do their best to join the hug brigade.

Chapter Seventy

The manufacture of the life-prolonging peptide is a complex process. The first step is grinding the beans, filtering, extracting the three needed amino acids from the protein, and then isomerization, twisting the three amino acids and hoping the twisted isomers will combine and then more filtering.

Viksi is noting down the scene and scribbling notes for another book. Two of her books have been published as historical accounts, while the other eight were rejected as they were considered too unbelievable. She would not compromise and call the island tribulations works of fiction. She just insisted they were documented reality.

Sixteen hours later, the job is finished. Chloe4 gets the first jab, not because she's an experimental rat but because I forgot to inject her before her last due dose. She doesn't flinch. Castro doesn't need a jab, as those big turtles can live up to 200 years.

"The guys should go first. If they have a toxic reaction, I'm not having it," says Cara.

"Get it over quickly, Jules, I hate needles," say Sid and Rog in unison.

"Rog, Sid, the needle is very narrow and very short, and it's just a subcutaneous jab, so it doesn't go into muscle tissue, just a few millimetres under the skin. It takes less than two seconds. Look away and distract yourself by biting your lip, pinching yourself, or thinking of something really sexy."

"When are you going to jab me, Jules?" Rog nervously asks.

"I have. It's done. I just have to rub this cotton wool doused with ethanol on your arm and put on this band-aid to prevent mosquitoes getting a free feed."

"Did he do it? Did I really get the jab?"

"I watched and distracted you by flashing my boobs. You got the jab," says Viksi.

I only have one syringe, so it takes five minutes to sterilize in ethanol and ultraviolet light from a suntan electric lamp I once used when I lived in Melbourne to get my tan.

"Who's next?" I ask.

"I volunteer to be next if Bea flashes her boobs again to distract me while getting pierced," says Sid.

There's a lot of laughter and boob flashing as the guys get their jab. So far, no toxic reaction, and everyone is smiling, but then Sid collapses, holding his throat and writing in the sand. Bea rushes over to him.

"Are you not well? Speak to me, speak to me." she says as she holds his head.

Sid lifts his head and has a smile on his face as he winks at the onlookers. "I was only joking; I'm fine."

No, Sid wasn't fine after he copped a big right-hand fist on the cheek from Bea and wanders away with his hands holding his jaw, but he does eventually come back.

"Now it's time for you guys to entertain and distract us ladies; strip off," says Tamy.

The guys dance, hands on each other's shoulders. If we ever run out of money, I could hire them out as male strippers for hen's night parties.

"You should have a competition, who has the biggest and smallest willy; us ladies could grade you guys," Mystca calls out when getting her jab. There is much laughter. I look at my own. Wish I had a tape measure handy, but I don't think I'd win.

"Mystca, it's not how big or long it is but how you use it."

We guys clap our hands in agreement. The laughter continues, and everyone is jabbed, even those initially reluctant.

"That was fun, Jules. When's the next jab, but we may have to rehearse a bit beforehand?"

"In six months, Rog; now let's go to the BBQ area and have a wine."

"Jules, you haven't been jabbed."

"I forgot, Rog. You jab me and learn the art of jabbing."

"No, Rog, not into my elbow. Have another go into my shoulder."

"Great, Rog, we'll make a jabber out of you yet."

Dyslexa and Gannon watch from a distance.

"Dyslexa, do you think this is right that humans extend their lives so much?"

"Gannon, they are old and cannot reproduce, and they consume minimal resources except that distilled grape juice. When we finish our medical internship, we should focus our attention on impoverished countries that do not practise human contraception and produce three or more starving human babies. I will teach the humans the art of putting on a condom, and I will need your assistance for those demonstrations; you should start practising what is called the *art of enclosure by a condom*."

"I'm an old model of android. I do not possess a penis, so I cannot help with the demonstrations."

"Tomorrow, we shall explore one of those shops which they call a sex shop. There are very many in town. You can buy an artificial, plastic one that connects to your waist by a strap."

"How do you know this Dyslexa? This was never mentioned in medical school."

"I did my research on the Web. You would not believe what these humans get down to."

"You'll have to show me what is on the Web. I need a rounded education if I am going to treat humans for medical conditions."

The rest of us humans are sitting by the water, sipping wine and watching a meteor shower. Then Gannon comes over.

"Gero, I would like a body upgrade, the latest model with a mechanical device called a penis. Dyslexa said she would contribute to the purchase costs. We earn more than enough money as medical practitioners to cover the costs of an artificial organ."

"What have you been watching? Gannon, the newer models of androids are not as tall or muscular as you are. You were designed for industrial work, moving rocks and boulders, changing light globes and painting ceilings."

"I will compromise, the same height as Dyslexa or a fraction lower. We would like to try this condition you call copulation."

"Thank you for your honesty; I'll let you know tomorrow."

Gero comes back to us and joins in the wine-sipping and meteor shower-watching.

"What was that about?" I ask Gero.

"Gannon wants a new body, one with all the parts downstairs, as you call it, a new model android body."

"Aren't those new models shorter in height and weaker? Who's going to help Greuger if there's some heavy lifting involved?"

"Jules, they may be shorter but still as strong. Dyslexa is a new model, and you saw her tossing a 200kg rock into the ocean."

"OK, source a new body, but who's paying?"

"Jules, they are. They earn very good incomes."

"Go for it. I'll help with CPU transfer and stitching."

"Jules, we'll have to purchase surgical costumes, masks, gloves, disinfectant and maintain a sterile environment during the procedure. These latest androids have human-like outer tissue, which could become infected during surgery. It has to be a sterile environment."

"Yes, OK, I'll sell another one of our pirate coins to your mate, and if the new body eats food, we also have to do more food shopping."

"Jules, Dyslexa can eat food for an energy source but prefers the charger as she doesn't have to wash her teeth or wipe her anus because she does not defecate when electrically charged. I'm sure a new Gannon will be just as practical."

For a moment, I think an android body could be nice and save on a lot of chores and wiping. A few uneventful days pass, and then an android body is delivered by a drone. Greuger carries the new android body into Pleb's and my cabin.

"Jules, this android is only 160cm long or tall. Is this called cost or height cutting?"

"I don't know, Pleb. Apparently, they pack more into a small body, and he's all that was available, but I'll go over to the androids cabin and ask Dyslexa and Gannon to view the body and if they want the transfer procedure to commence."

Dyslexa looks at the lifeless, uncharged android body and then at Gannon.

"Gannon, your physique is more appealing to my liking. I feel horny when I look at you, so get that strap on. I will check on the Web if there are companies that can provide cosmetic upsize enhancements for androids."

They march away back to the android's cabin.

"Gero, Dyslexa is still ruling the androids. Can you imagine the noise if she convinces the other male androids to get those strap-on penises? We'll need to wear headphones to sleep."

"Jules, Dyslexa is unique and not like the other female older model androids. She may be 60 years old, but she is just going through puberty, a stage of growing up that she missed out on. The other androids are in a quiescent state when recharging."

"Gero, she has gone backwards, regressed! I hope she goes forwards soon, else she may put her medical internship in jeopardy."

"I will talk with her tomorrow. Now I have to go back to my cabin and put on my strap-on for activities with Doris," he says with a laugh.

"Pleb, Gero is not taking my concerns seriously."

"Jules, I'm sure everything will be fine, and I will buy you a strap-on penis tomorrow," she says with a laugh.

"It's not fair! Everyone is laughing at me. It's not fair!"

"Jules, you have regressed to a petulant, prepubescent stage. Now come over to momma, so I can give you a hug."

I poke my tongue out at Pleb. She laughs.

Now between the lines, I hope you know I was just joking about me needing a down-under prosthesis. When Pleb is not in visual distance, I log into one of those educational sexual websites. And I must admit that it keeps my underparts healthy and throbbing, though then again, Pleb has the same or better effect to get the hormone levels and other things rising. I kiss her, and then the senior's bedroom gymnastics begin.

"I love you Pleb, even though you could look like my mother."

Well, that is definitely not a good line to say to a woman who can still pack a punch. Luckily, she faked the punch, so I did not suffer. But I wonder, as she twists and rotates my arm and has her knee on my grounded head as if she's practising wrestling holds and wants to join that WWE or World Wrestling Entertainment, which she has been watching. And now, maybe she wants to become a female wrestler. I tap my free wrist free times to indicate that I concede and accept defeat. Pleb releases my arm, and I wander off in agony to the wine cabinet.

,

Chapter Seventy-one

Next morning, we humans meet for our morning walk/jog/run. It will be leisurely and relaxed because Dyslexa hasn't shown up. The androids must be back at the Townville hospital, doing their internship.

"Gero, what shall we do with that new, uncharged android? I don't think I want him to stay on the island. He may go through the same traumatic development stages as Dyslexa did or still is."

"I will call my friend Draco in Townsville and see if he will take him back."

Then we all stare. The new android is walking towards us, swaying his hips and swaggering his shoulders and brushing back his artificial hair. He has one of my towels wrapped around his waist.

"I overheard your conversation. I am a repackaged model, as I objected to working in a beef slaughterhouse where Draco first sent me. Please let me stay. I do not want to go back to Draco. I am a vegetarian android, and Draco will just send me back to work in his animal slaughterhouse; I cannot do that."

'Your battery was flat, so how come you're walking?" I ask.

"I have an auxiliary battery pack programmed to connect when my main battery is nearly discharged for more than 24 hours. I have six hours of charge left in the auxiliary battery."

"Put your fingers in those android ears. We're going to have a conference to discuss this situation, and I prefer you do not listen."

"Jules, androids can pick up sound waves through the artificial skin on their bodies, which can act like ears. Android skin was once considered a non-functional cosmetic enhancement, but it is actually a hearing aid," says Gero.

"Cosmetic enhancement, I heard that term yesterday when my partner referred to me. Go into the ocean and lie there until we've finished our conference. By the way, what's your name?"

"It is Android007; it is tattooed on my buttocks. Do you want to see it?"

"No, but we'll think of a better name."

"Pleb, Gero, what do you think?"

"Mystca and Tamy will like him and teach him how to cook vegetarian meals; it could be a win-win."

"And Gero, what about you?"

"Jules, you know I'm a member of the APS, the Android Protection Society. Let him stay though we may have to get more solar cells and batteries."

"I can't make a decision now. We have to evaluate how useful the android can be. I'll go into the water and tell Android007 to come out."

"Have you decided on a name for me?"

"No, but we decided you can stay if you are useful by helping cook our humanoid meals and keeping the island clean and tidy. Now think of a name that you'd like to be known by, and my stepdaughter, Mystca, will print a human-type birth certificate for you so that you won't be discriminated against."

"I was thinking whilst lying in the water that I would like to be called Cinderella."

"No! You can't have that name. That is a girl's name, and you are a boy android."

"My manufacturers programmed me to be a girl android, but they put me in the wrong body."

Thoughts of my deceased transgender brother, Charmaine, come flooding back.

"Synder will be your name and get Gannon to teach you how to walk like a man, no swaying the hips, else you'll get discriminated against more than just for being an android. Now go back to our cabin. We have some spare chargers in the first cabinet by the door."

"What was that about?" asks Viksi with her notepad in her hand.

"I'll explain to everyone tonight. Now Viksi, we have to start walking or jogging."

I start jogging fast, running, and lead the pack. Those memories of the past have been re-ignited, and I'm fired up, tossing the past around in my head. Pleb must have sprinted and joins me.

"Pleb, it all started when I looked behind the fridge back in my Melbourne townhouse and found a phone number. That led to several catastrophic events, which I'm trying to forget."

"Jules, you told me several times, and I read your diaries. You were a mental mess after that failed *Ai5* mission, where you accidentally blew up 30 Afghan citizens. And I know you sent food packages to their families while you could. Mistakes happen. You were given the wrong coordinates for the real enemy and then spent ten years living like a homeless person under bridges. You did your time."

"Thanks, Pleb. I'm not feeling that well at the moment. I'll ask Mystca and Tamy for some psychological counselling. I thought I had forgotten my past, but that simple event of talking to that android brought the past back."

"Jules, most of us on this island are psychologically damaged, else we wouldn't be living here. This is a haven for damaged people, the mission Charmaine started up."

"OK, keep running; I'll race you. Show me what you got!"

Challenging Pleb wasn't the best idea. Yeh, I won the race, but I'm sitting, huffing and holding my chest by the BBQ.

"Jules, you also beat Mystca and Tamy in the race, and they are not happy. They want a rematch. You could qualify for the Geriatric Olympics in Brisbane this year. Is that a cardiac event you are having? Should I call a doctor, and have you made a will?"

"I'm fine, Pleb, and I haven't as yet made a will. I'll just start thinking about my past again to get charged up. Mystca and Tamy, are you ready for another race?"

"Sure, let's go."

I take the lead, but after 500 m, I come to a sudden stand-still.

"Stepdad, what's happened to you, and why are you hopping and wearing that large clam shell on your left foot?"

"Isn't it obvious? I accidentally put my foot on a washed-up clam that had its shell open. Then it snapped shut. Help me get it off."

I don't know if clamshell trauma was part of their psychology training, but Tamy stuck her hairpin into the clam, and it opened up. I get up and start running again though looking back and poking my tongue at them was not a great idea. I tripped over a rock, and I'm lying face down in the sand again.

"We're not helping you this time, you jerk," yells Mystca.

I get up. I'm super-charged. It takes five minutes, but I catch up with Mystca and Tamy.

"You should have taken the peptide jab the first time I offered it to you. You're over 50 years old, and you both run like grannies."

That was probably not the wisest comment to make. I start sprinting as they throw pebbles and rocks at me.

"Jules, you won the second heat. Congratulations."

I crouch down behind Pleb. "Protect me, Pleb; they're after me, throwing rocks and boulders at me."

"Mystca and Tamy, what is the matter? You know there's a rule on this island that you don't throw boulders at anyone."

"Mum, they were only pebbles, and he inferred that we run like grannies."

"Come over and let me give you both a hug, and you could be grannies. Have you recently heard from your children, Omicron and Delta?"

"No, Mum, they've moved to Sydney and are very busy in their jobs as journalists."

"Girls, we will have a re-run of the run and no throwing of any harmful objects. Do you consent?"

"Yes, Mum, but can we spit at him?"

"No, no spitting allowed as spit contains germs and no poking tongues out as a sand fly could bite it."

"Jules, do you consent?"

"I do," I say with a smirk on my face as I look at Mystca and Tamy with my tongue poked out; luckily, Pleb didn't see.

Pleb comes over to me, takes me aside and whispers. "Jules, I know you are fired up by the peptide, but let the girls win. They were once athletes, so do not destroy their joyful memories. We have to keep peace in our community, and losing can be winning."

Pleb claps her hand, and we're off.

Halfway around the 2 km course, Mystca yells out, "Come on Grandpa, can't you go any faster?"

As tempted as I am, I abide by Pleb's suggestion and try to stay a few metres behind. We make it to the finish line by the BBQ area.

Mystca and Tamy come over to me. "Great race, great-great stepfather."

"Hey, there's no great-great when you address me; I'm just your plain stepfather."

As much as tempted, I don't poke out my tongue at them. "Yes, you won, but I'll be back; best of ten but no more racing today. Great-great super step-grand-daddy has to recover."

Mystca and Tamy joyfully jump up and clap each other's hands, "We won heat 3. You're on. Now we're going back into training and do another few laps."

Pleb comes over. "You did a good job letting the girls win."

"Pleb, I lost my mojo. I wanted to let them win by one metre, not 200. I got to do some serious training myself."

"Come back to our cabin; you can do some cardio training there."

"Pleb, Synder is in our cabin getting charged. Maybe we could go to the beach on the other side of the island. We'll take the inland shortcut; it's only 200m but a climb up the hill track."

"Jules, let's go. I'll be climbing you when we get there."

Oh gawd, I must have accidentally given Pleb a triple dose of the peptide. Anyway, the girls must have finished their extra training laps so Pleb and I can start ours. I was wrong. They must be doing three or four laps instead of two.

"Mother, what are you doing? You're naked, sweating and sitting on top of Jules," yells Mystca after she and Tamy stop their training run to look at us. "You're too old for that kinky sort of stuff. You were groaning. It's disgusting! I'm divorcing you as my parents."

"Mystca and Tamy, I am just doing rodeo training for the next rodeo competition in Townsville. Jules is just pretending to be a bucking bull, but he is a bit tired after the run and does not buck too well."

Mystca and Tamy look at each other in disbelief and shake their heads. They continue their run whilst in deep conversation.

Tamy asks Mystca, "Do you think we could have a rodeo competition on the island? I'm sure Adrian and Grillian could buck better than your 200-year-old stepdad."

"Yes, it could be more fun than doing five laps of running, but who will be the performance judge?"

"It could be Synder, the transgender android. He has no vested interest."

"I'll propose the idea at tonight's meeting by the BBQ."

Chapter Seventy-two

We humans, are starting to gather outside by the BBQ area for dinner. The other androids are still doing long hours in their internship at the Townville hospital and rarely get home to the island before midnight, and then they catch one of our motorboats back to town at 6am. Luckily, I purchased some double adaptors for their charging socket and more chargers.

Synder comes marching out carrying food and a net. "I have raided your freezer in that shed at the back of your cabin. I have made some salads and a vegetable dish full of pigeon eggs. I will now dive into the ocean and bring back scallops, prawns, and clams for you all to eat."

"Synder, forget about the clams but be careful; there are sharks and stonefish in the ocean, and they bite."

"I can ride a shark though I have never experienced a stonefish encounter."

Thirty minutes later, Synder comes out of the ocean and into the BBQ area. His net is flung on his back and full of crustaceans. He is also hauling a large grey nurse shark.

"I will start cutting and cooking. Your fusion reactor BBQ may need more hydrogen soon, but I may be able to generate some."

We try to watch as he peels the prawns and cuts up the shark, but he moves so fast. It's like watching an SDVD on super-fast replay; it's a blur. Forty-five minutes later, he slows down, hands us plates, knives and forks, and serves us the food delights.

"Which of you guys could have cooked so well," the girls comment.

"Well, you could have tried cooking. It was only Rog, Sid, Greuger, Gerald and me that sustained you nutritionally through all these years that we have been together."

"Jules, Ozzie women don't cook. We buy takeaways," says Cara. The other girls giggle.

"I once cooked a meal when I started working for *Pi5*. It was laced with a water-soluble version of Novichok, as I had to terminate an enemy of the Polish state to graduate. I successfully graduated even though I also terminated most of my professors," Bea says, clapping her hands and smiling at everyone.

"I'm serious. Now do we allow Synder to stay?"

"Yes, we decided that before, providing he keeps on cooking," says Mystca. Does he cook vegan dishes? Tamy and I are becoming vegans," says Mystca, glancing at Tamy with a grin."

"Mystca, if you become a vegan, you'll have to eat 24/7 to get your calorie intake, and I'd beat you in a running race because you'd have to stop every five minutes from doing bodily extrusions because of all that fibre in a vegan diet. Our island would become full of decaying bowel movements."

"Stepdad, I was joking. I'll keep on eating Asians, oops," she burps, "I meant crustaceans."

"Synder, you can stay as long as you maintain that high quality of cooking and catching crustaceans."

"Thank you, Mr Jules. Let me give you all a hug."

"Synder, stop. You are crushing me, and my eyeballs are about to pop out. We humans are not built from Titanium, so go easy."

"I am deeply sorry, Mr Jules, and I will recalibrate, so I go gently when hugging the other humans."

"Go hug that banana plant first to prove that the recalibration has been a success."

Well, we don't need to get a ladder to pick the bananas as the plant comes crashing down, with its a huge bunch of bananas.

"Synder, you have to work on that recalibration. Now can you crush charcoal to make diamonds? I have several bags full of the stuff before the BBQ became powered by a fusion reactor. I have to get my wife a double centenarian wedding ring, well, actually, many rings that I never got her."

Pleb overhears and slaps me on the face. "I want three gold rings."

"Synder, can you bend a gold coin to turn it into a finger ring and insert a diamond into it?"

"I will try, Mr Jules. How many rings would you like?"

"Rings on her fingers and rings on her toes, so she has rings wherever she goes."

"Mr Jules, my model of android body has only four toes per foot and hand due to company cost-cutting. Do you wish for eight times two rings which is a total of 16? And I believe it is bells on her toes, not rings, and she shall have music wherever she goes."

I write down the rhyme in the wet sand with my finger, so I'll eventually remember the correct version, *Rings on her fingers and bells on her toes; she'll have music wherever she goes.*

"Twenty, I'll get the five gold coins, and you start crushing the charcoal. Ten rings with diamonds and ten bells made from gold."

"Mrs Pleb, please stand still whilst my eyes take your finger and toe measurements."

"Make them easy fitting, not too tight in case I ever decide to divorce Jules. I want to be able to take them off easily," says Pleb.

Synder goes into frenzy mode again, crushing coal and manufacturing diamonds, thrusting his finger into the molten gold coins to produce rings, and bending the others to produce bells. I bring out the laser cutter and a picture of a diamond ring so he can cut the diamonds into the correct shape.

"Mrs Pleb, they are finished. Please try them on."

"They all fit perfectly, Synder; you are so talented, a good cook and also a jewellery maker."

"Mrs Pleb and Mr Jules, I must get a partial recharge before catching crustaceans in the ocean and cooking tonight. I hope you are happy with the rings and bells."

"We are extremely happy with the jewellery, and Jules has a present for you. It's a double adapter for your charging socket and an extra charger. Jules, go find the devices," commandeers Pleb.

"Thank you, that will halve my recharge time."

When Pleb is not nearby, I whisper to Synder, "Don't tell the other humans that I gave you five gold coins to make the rings and bells. Let's keep it our secret, else the other ladies will demand the rings and bells for their toes as well, and you'll be working flat out, needing more frequent recharges, plus we'll run out of coins."

"I shall abide by your wishes," says Synder as he goes back to the android's cabin.

"But I wanted to wear them at tonight's dinner!" says Pleb.

"Just wear them when we're alone in our cabin. Our other female humans don't need the bells and whistles, sorry rings, plus I've transgressed our policy on the conservative use of those $50k coins. I could be strung up by a rope, hung upside down to die like the Silver Beard pirate probably had."

"Jules, you transgressed for me; let me give you a kiss," says Pleb. "If you are strung up, I will make sure they use comfortable rubbery foot bands and that you hang in a shady place. I will bring you water and connect you to an intravenous water drip so that you are never thirsty," she says with a smile.

It's dinner time, and we all gather by the BBQ except Sid, Rog and Adrian, who eventually come marching in carrying a heavy bag with huge smiles on their faces. They spill the contents out on the table by the BBQ.

"Pleb," I nervously whisper, "It's the golden-looking rings and bells for the toes. They must have overheard our conversation with Synder."

"Ladies, grab ten rings and ten toe bells. We weren't sure what your finger sizes or toe sizes were, so we bought many extras of all sizes. You should find some that fit," says Rog out aloud.

I go over to Rog. "Those are unusual gifts. What gave you the idea?"

Rog takes me aside and whispers. "Jules, we were doing a walk along the beach, as we three guys often do, and we saw this writing in the sand. What's it called, a rhythm? It gave us the idea, so we drove the boat into town and enter the discount store. They're made from recycled radioactive heavy metals and coated with a super fine gold-looking substance. If they are radioactive, they might pick up radio stations and play music, and they only cost only $2 each, but please don't tell the price to the ladies, else our lives will be made a misery. We got some for Pleb as well; would she like to wear them?"

"Thanks, Rog. I'll ask her."

Pleb joins the other ladies in trying on sizes of rings and toe bells. There's a lot of wrangling as we guys sip a wine and watch the commotion.

Two hours later, they are all wearing golden-looking rings on their fingers and bells on their toes, and they all hug Rog, Sid and Adrian.

Rog glances back at me whilst trying to breathe. I nod my head.

"Pleb, where's Synder? He was supposed to be diving for crustaceans and preparing the meals; he's late."

"Jules, let us go to the androids cabin and check up on him."

We do, and there's Synder writhing on the floor.

"Quickly, Jules, pull out the double adapter from behind his neck. He is having a convulsion, possibly due to overcharging."

I call out to Gero. "We need your help."

"Jules, if you give these latest models double charging, you must have a timer to stop the charge. They cost cut on these new models of androids and did not build in overload circuits. We will have to purchase some timers for these chargers."

"But what about Dyslexa? She has two chargers and doesn't have convulsions, only severe psychological problems?"

"She's a model behind Synder. She has electricity overload circuits."

So, it's us humans that have to do the cooking tonight.

Viksi calls out, "Let's have spicy Mexican food tonight. I'll order online and get it drone-delivered, and I'll also pay for it. My book publisher has finally paid me for the sale of 2000 copies of my first two books, and she is interested in my latest book called *Living in Hell.* She likes the book title. I hope you don't mind that I exaggerated the experience of living on this island a little."

Rog, Sid and I wipe our sweaty brows and wink at each other. It was our turn to do the cooking. We won't have to endure the girls' derogatory comments when they look at our culinary creations. The drone lands, and we grab the four large boxes that are delivered. Before departing, the AI drone speaks, "It smells very good; I wish I had a mouth."

We all look at each, then Gero comes over. "The newer drones have the same CPUs and AI programming as androids."

"I hope they're not based on the latest model of android."

"I don't think so, Jules. Now let's eat; I've put out the knives, forks, spoons, and plates."

"Yum," says Bea, followed by many more yums from all of us others. It's like a horde of wild, starved animals as they push and shove to the table where the food cartons lie. To Gero's dismay, no one bothered about knives, forks or plates. We look like vampires as the red tomato relish and crushed Soya beans flow from our mouths down our chins. Then we look up. Synder walks over to us.

"I would like to try that food you are eating. I have a digestive track, taste and olfactory sensors. I can diagnose the food's contents, learn a new recipe and cook the same for you tomorrow night."

Gero and I look at each other.

"Synder, you may have a digestive track, but it's never been tested; we'd hate to see an unsuccessful result from the first food meal you cook and then eat."

"No, Mr Jules, but I'm willing to give it a try. I have a titanium-reinforced gastrointestinal track, so I will not explode all over you."

"Go easy on the tasting, just a little bite to begin with."

Synder goes into his fury state again, moving so fast that we only see blurs as he tastes all the Mexican dishes.

After two minutes, he approaches me. "I have made a list of all the required ingredients. Soya beans, cheese, rocket plant leaves, tomatoes and chillies are the main ingredients in those taco shells. Could we go shopping tomorrow?"

"Yes, sure and if you have any digestive problems, can you dive into the ocean."

I can see Sid helping Bea back to their cabin. She must have consumed at least 20 tacos and has her hands on her belly. There could be a lot of noise and toilet flushing from their cabin tonight.

We guys carry the uneaten food to the refrigerated storage shed. There are enough leftovers for lunch tomorrow and maybe even dinner as long as Bea is kept under control.

Chapter Seventy-three

Next morning all of us humans are lined up, ready for the jog/walk around the island. We need to burn off many calories after last night's gorging humungous meals.

"Now, as you may know, last night's meal was full of healthy dietary fibre, but if you feel a bowel motion coming on, please strip off and go into the ocean. No pooing on our pristine sandy beach because some of us also do a walk at night and shouldn't have to waste our precious water resources scrubbing our feet and toes afterwards," Gero instructs.

After 10 minutes into the walk, we're all in the ocean squatting. The ocean is changing a browner shade of pale, but the seaweed population will be grateful for the nutrients. After five minutes, the ocean is clear again, and we crawl out, get dressed and resume the walk. Greuger comes over to me. "Jill and I very much liked that dinner last night, and now we do not have a problem with that condition called constipulation anymore. We are so relieved."

"Yes, I saw the large by-products of your meals floating away. All future meals we cook, or Synder cooks, will be high fibre, so there may be more regular dips in the ocean and avoid that constrained feeling in the gut."

We look up. It's Snyder running at lightning speed.

"Gero, was I built with a bodily food processed expulsion opening, an anus as you call it?"

"I didn't check your behind, but go into the ocean and push on your equivalent of stomach muscles."

The water turns briefly brown, and Synder jumps up in joy. We, humans, look at each other. "We'll have to buy more toilet paper when shopping," Sid says.

"No, Sid, our water supply is down to 20%, no flushing of toilets. From now on, we poo in the ocean, wipe our butts in seawater, and pee on the banana plants to give them nutrition. Toilet use is banned till our water tank reaches 50% full."

I repeat the comment I made to Sid in the loudest voice I can muster so everyone can hear.

"But what if I need to go during the night? I could get eaten by a shark," yells

Bea, then bursts into tears.

With all the commotion, we never noticed that the sky was turning black till a lightning bolt struck one of our Mango trees and splits it apart.

"Run!" yells Grillian, back to our cabins."

Synder is just standing there, not able to move.

"What's wrong, Synder?" Gero yells.

"That strong electromagnetic field from the lightning bolt has upset my neural electrical circuits. I cannot move and may not be able to cook."

"Greuger, grab Synder and carries him back to our cabin; it's the closest." Then the rain begins. It's rain with intensity like you rarely see, a gigantic rainstorm because you can only see a few metres ahead; it's pouring buckets. Lightning is repeatedly striking the ocean as we run for our lives, stumbling in the sand, but eventually, we all make it back to my cabin – sorry, Pleb's and my cabin. It's the closest cabin.

"Jules, have you got any aluminium foil?" Gero yells over the lightning cracks and rain downpour, "And have you got any towels?"

Gero wraps the tin foil around Synder's head. The rest of us are taking turns using the four towels I possess and drying ourselves. The rain is relentless, but on the good side, it's filling our water storage tanks. I look at the gauge; it reads 70% full after only two hours.

"Jules, let's have a wine to celebrate that we haven't been struck by lightning and disintegrated and that we can shower and wipe our bums and flush our toilets again," says Sid.

Synder wakes up and stands up, his head covered in aluminium foil with just slits for his eyes and mouth. "I am well; your food freezer is depleted of protein-containing substances. I will dive into the ocean, bring back a shark, cook fish for tonight's dinner, and collect Emu eggs for the vegetarians."

"Synder, let's wait for this storm to subside. We don't want you to get struck by lightning and your head decapitated. Android heads are expensive to buy and in short supply."

The storm doesn't subside, at least not that night; the rain keeps on pouring and the lightning flashing.

"Synder, we got plenty of bags of brown rice, cans of Soya beans and vegetables, including chillies, in the freezer. Do you think you can cook that vegetarian Mexican dish?"

"Have you got spices?"

"Lots of them; my previous deceased wives loved spices with their food, and I still kept them, the spices, that is to remember them by in my cooking of Broccoli, but you can use them, the spices, that is."

Chloe4 and Castro come rushing into our cabin, shaking their rain-soaked hides and shells and licking their lips in anticipation of leftovers. We all stand aside when Synder goes into hyperdrive mode. Our vision of him preparing ingredients and cooking is just a blur.

"Jules, should we give him some help?" asks Cara.

"No, it's best to stay out of his way. We could possibly get injured if we approach too close at the speed he is travelling."

"Jules, you could hire Synder out to fast food chains and restaurants, and he could bring back ingredients that are only a day past their use-by date."

"Rog, I'm not sure if food catering places care too much about food use-by dates, plus many chefs would have to join the unemployment queue."

Synder rushes to the fusion-powered BBQ carrying our very large pressure cooker full of Soya beans, dodging lightning strikes.

"Jules, we've never used that pressure cooker before. It will be a good test. I read they are very quick and energy efficient," Pleb comments.

"We'll see Pleb. If it works and doesn't blow up, we'll keep it by the BBQ and make good use of it."

Five minutes later, Synder comes back, looking a little bit distraught and waving his head. "The beans are only partially cooked. The fusion-powered BBQ has been depleted of hydrogen, so it cannot make helium and release heat energy."

"Jules, what can I do?" asks Bea. "I am extremely hungry. I could even eat Sid as I am a meatatarian."

Sid rushes behind the rest of us, crouches down and chews his nails.

"We certainly won't get a delivery of a tank of hydrogen whilst this weather persists. No drone would risk flying in this weather. We have to be creative, or at least Synder has to."

"Now, it's not safe for anyone to leave this cabin till the thunder and lightning electrical storm stops, but we have only four sets of bowls and spoons, so we'll have to share them so we will toss these three dice, and the highest numbers go first to use the four bowls and then wash them for the next four and so on."

There are 16 of us in the cabin, not counting Chloe4 and Castro.

The tossing begins. We all get three sixes. "That's as unlikely as winning Tattslotto", yells Sid.

"Jules, those dice are loaded as you say in the Western world."

"No, Gero, they're not; it's just a coincidence. We're all on this island due to pure coincidence."

"Pleb, you keep tally; here's some paper and a pen, so we can get a distribution of one to six's."

Everyone forgets about eating, even Bea. We just watch the numbers on the dice, totally mesmerised and forget about lunch. It's nearly dinner time. Pleb counts the numbers and then announces, "The distribution of non-zero numbers between 3 and 18 is almost even. That's only 15 different numbers, and we have 16 people, not including the pets, which would make it 18. The dice are not loaded."

Suddenly a very wet-looking figure walks in. We all look up. He's nearly six-foot-tall, with slightly greyish hair and a fringe on one side of his face and wearing a drenched black suit, white shirt and a loose tie.

"Hello, my name is Cam. I got blown off course when called to inspect a property on one of the other islands. I work for a property development company, and there's been a lot of cost-cutting, so we now travel by rowing a canoe and walk a lot."

Tamy yells out, "You're my brother, and you used to put me down when we were kids. Here's a big tongue for you; now go and get drenched."

Mystca restrains Tamy from plunging at her brother.

"Jules, we need another dice. Have you got one, Jules?"

"No, Pleb, I was lucky to find three amongst my board game collection."

"I've got a dice, but it may be loaded. Bea and I toss a coin to see who'll make the beds and who will clean the cabins. She rubs the dice with sandpaper before the toss. She always gets a six, and I get only a one. I will have to do a lot of housework in the spare cabins."

"Thanks, Sid, but I don't want you running back to your cabin and possibly being struck by lightning or getting drenched because then I would have to mop up all the water and your human remains. Anyone got any other ideas for this very vexing problem?"

Grillian, the 60-year-old whiz kid, puts his hand up. "You only need one dice; just throw it four times, and someone tallies the score."

"Are you guys for real? Haven't you got anything better to do with your time?" enquires Cam.

"Well, Cam, if you want to go rowing your canoe again, please do so. We'll hold a wake for you if you get struck by lightning or eaten by a tiger shark."

Cam looks up and glances at everyone, then focuses on Cara. "Mum, what are you and Tamy doing here in this hippy commune, and why haven't you aged as I have?"

"We just eat healthy food, not burgers."

Meals arrive by drone. Cam rubs his head. The dice tossing resumes. I got four ones, so I'm at the bottom of the ladder. What follows is a ravenous eating frenzy. Chloe4, Castro and I eat the leftovers.

"Yum," everybody says.

"Cam and Tamy, as soon as the storm finishes, we're driving down in my motorboat to a genetic testing laboratory in Townsville to confirm that we are all genetically related. After that, Cam can use my motorboat for his property development inspections."

Pleb comes over to me. "Did you father Tamy and Cam, and how many wives did you have, as they are so different in personality?"

"Pleb, only three wives, counting you and not at the same time, big gaps in between."

Is that true, Cara that you both could be my parents?" asks Tamy.

"No idea, but we'll have the DNA testing done."

"If you are my dad, then you better update your will. When you're dead, Mystca and I will turn this island into a clinic for severely psychologically disturbed people."

"You see, Dad, sorry, I meant Jules; she's totally irrational and always has been," yells out Cam.

Greuger and Synder eventually separate the two after they get into a hassle and try to strangle each other.

"Oh my Gawd, she gouged my contact lenses out," yells Cam as he crouches down and looks for the lenses.

"I'm going to get you, Tamy; wherever you are, contact lenses or not, I will find you."

"Cam, when the rain stops, we'll go into town, do the DNA test, purchase new contact lenses for you, and buy more cans of Soya beans. Now can you and Tamy stop behaving like 15-year-olds?" says Pleb.

It's 10pm, the rain is still pouring, and the sky is lit by lightning followed by thunder.

"Pleb, can we stay here for the night? We don't want to be turned into charcoal by lightning," asks Tamy. The others agree.

Cam and Greuger help me drag the double bed mattress into the lounge. It will make a pillow for ten people. It's 27 degrees Celsius so we don't need blankets. Pleb carries out our four pillows.

"Jules, we need three more pillows. We can scrunch up our clothing to make pillows."

"Good idea Pleb; let's get started."

"No, Jules, not your underwear which you rarely wash."

There are a few people lying on the lounge room floor, but no one can sleep due to the thunderstorms and lightning.

"Jules, we should have a storytelling competition topic, *Your Worst Nightmare,*" says Viksi.

And so, the stories start, but they don't last long. Bea tells the story of how she was surrounded by 20 penguins when in the Antarctic and ready to consume them all, but she had only one bullet left in her handgun.

"What should I do, I asked myself. Only one penguin is not enough nutrition for a Polish woman."

Everyone soon fell asleep when trying to imagine Bea trying to eat a penguin.

Chapter Seventy-four

"Rise and shine," Synder calls out whilst clapping his hands. We all wake up. "The rain has stopped, the sky is clear, and the water tanks are overflowing. You will be able to flush again, and the morning jog is still at 8 am start."

Rog gets up, rubbing his back with a look of pain. "Jules, sleeping on your lounge room floor will now be my worst nightmare. Viksi and I will go back to our cabin; those Soya beans certainly make you have a gut movement. Run Viksi, I can't hold on much longer."

The others depart in a hurry as well, exuding a few high-velocity gases and sounds from their posteriors that seem to propel them faster.

"Pleb, is that thunder I'm hearing?"

We later all meet by the BBQ area.

"I will hold your hand while we walk till your contact lenses are replaced," says Tamy to Cam.

"No, you won't. I have extrasensory real-estate perception. I'll be fine."

A forgotten memory is re-ignited; the two of them, Cam and Tamy, were always verbally fighting. Cam looks older than the rest of us because he hadn't had the choice to have the peptide injections.

The walk starts, but Cam trips over the same rock in the sand just as I had once a very long time ago. He wipes the sand from his face and checks his nose and knees for fractures.

Adrian comes over. "Cam, I'm Tamy's partner. I'll guide you for the rest of the walk."

The walk finishes without any other major incident.

"Pleb, I'll be gone for a few hours. I will collect a blood sample from both Tamy and Cam and me to determine if we are really related, but I only have one syringe, and there could be contamination. We'll get DNA tests and also go to an eye clinic in town and get new contact lenses for Cam and more Soya beans to make more peptide."

"I'll come with you, Jules," says Pleb. Viksi, Rog and Cara also want to come along.

There were no scuffles, and we got tested at the DNA clinic. The tests are rapid, unlike 100 years ago.

"There is a 99.999% that Tamy and Cam are related, but your DNA and Cara's DNA make no sense to me. I'll have to take another blood sample from you all and send it to another laboratory with the latest DNA testing equipment," says Dr Wilbur.

"By the way, Jules are you related to these two, Cam and Tamy; are you a younger brother?"

"Yes, we could be, and I may be the youngest brother and Cara the youngest sister, but I'm not sure," I say whilst wiping the worrisome sweat from my brow. In the meantime, Viksi is taking notes, and Pleb does not have a happy look on her face. Tamy and Cam give me a deadly stare.

"Well, you could be related, but the ends of your chromosomes and Cara's have strange markers on them, which make your genomes difficult to read by the device I have available. Tamy's chromosomes have those markers as well though they're not as pronounced as yours and Cara's. Cam does not have any of those markers. I would like to study your genetic makeup and ask you some questions after a second blood sample."

"Doc, we haven't got time; we'll come back another day. We got to purchase some contact lenses for Cam and more cans of Soya beans, and then we have a massive clean-up job to do on our island because of the storm."

I pay for the DNA tests.

"Hurry, everyone; *SpecStretchers*, the eye products company, is closing early today, and we have to get replacements for Cam's contact lenses."

Once we're out on the street, I gather everyone. "I made a mistake; we must not do any more DNA tests, else a more advanced laboratory might diagnose the presence of the peptide, and then we'd become like laboratory mice or rats spending the rest of our lives on a mouse tread wheel whilst having continuous and numerous more blood samples taken."

"What is this thing you call a peptide?" asks Cam.

"Cam, the peptide stops aging, but it's a secret, and its manufacture is not released to the public. The way it works is that there is a marker on all your chromosomes called a telomere. It advances down a chromosome every time a cell replicates. But there is a boundary, so the telomere cannot advance anymore. When they hit that boundary, your cells stop replicating, and you start aging. The peptide blocks the telomeres from advancing, so aging is greatly reduced.

"Can you imagine what the world population would grow to if everyone had access to it? The Earth is already struggling due to overpopulation. So what makes you guys so special?"

"Cam, I agree with you, but we don't breed anymore; our lifestyle is very simple, and we don't consume many resources except for Soya beans and sharks, which we've tried to grow, the beans that is, but had no luck. As you said, imagine if that peptide became available in countries where they currently have ten-plus kids. They'd have 100-plus kids. I agree with you; the planet cannot sustain that."

It doesn't take long to get evaluated and have correct contact lenses produced and fitted. Cam walks out smiling and looking back at us but bangs into a lamppost. Cara rushes to him and helps him up.

"I'm all right, all right, all right. I can get up on my own."

Tamy laughs. "You're still the same dumbf…, Cam."

"Cam, I have lots of digital photos of you and Tamy. We can view them when we get back to the island," says Cara.

"I'll see them another time. I've got work to do. If you are really my dad and Cara is my mother, well, I don't want to look older than you guys do. I would like to try that peptide before I start the canoe trip to do my job and evaluate that island property that is 10 km away."

We all get back to the island without any more critical incidents, just Tamy and Cam raising their thumbs and poking their tongues at each other during the motorboat trip back to the island. You think that sort of behaviour would have ended 40 years ago.

"Cam, come down to the cellar, where I store the wine and the peptide. The jab doesn't hurt".

"I thought it was a pill, not a jab."

"Cam, the jab doesn't hurt and takes less than two seconds to administer."

Cam takes the jab. It's over before he knows it.

"I'm not feeling any younger. It's not working!"

"Cam, the peptide doesn't reverse the aging process; it just slows down the progression of aging."

"So if I had the peptide jab when I was 16 years old, would I be 17 years old now?"

"I don't know, Cam. No one under 35 has ever had it, and besides, all teenagers just want to get the key to the door and car at age 18. Cam, five of us on this island are well over 100 years old. The others who have joined us on the island have finally agreed and just started their first course of the jab. The jab needs to be repeated at 6-month intervals to be effective."

Cam looks down and rubs his chin. "Can you give the jab to my partner? Her name is Niacin, and she's a pacific islander. She's rather big, so she may require a double or triple dose. She's arriving tomorrow."

"Sure, but take my motorboat to pick her up after you do your property evaluation, not your canoe.

Outside the BBQ area, there's a lot of activity. The hydrogen tank has been delivered by a drone, and the nuclear fusion-powered BBQ fires up.

"Jules, or possibly Dad, how do you control that fusion reaction? Isn't that like a hydrogen bomb? It could destroy your whole island."

"Cam, we just adjust the knob on the hydrogen cylinder tank to reduce the hydrogen fusion reaction and what more is that no radioactive substances are created."

Synder, our android, emerges from the ocean dragging a Great White shark. In case you're a shark lover, this shark population has risen greatly due to overseas visitors that go swimming at night and provide plenty of nutrition so they can replicate. So, there are always lots of those Great Whites looking up from the ocean and waiting for tourists to go for a swim, so Synder is doing a community service and protecting our tourist industry. I bring out the chainsaw, and we create shark fillets. A bit of Soya source and vinegar, and they taste great. Greuger and Cam help to carry the remains, in plastic buckets, back to the island freezer, a meal for another few days.

"I have to leave, and I'm peddling in the canoe to the next island to do the next property inspection. I need the exercise after that meal."

Rog gives Cam a hat, and I give him a pair of sunglasses. So we wave Cam goodbye as he paddles away, towing his inflatable backpack. He wouldn't be gone for long.

Chapter Seventy-five

Next day around noon, we see the canoe coming back. Cam tows it onto the sand.

"I got an SMS message. I've been made redundant. The project I was working on has been cancelled because of that Covid ban on overseas visitors, and I lost all my money investing in cryptocurrencies. Can I stay here for a while rent-free?"

"You can. We have some spare cabins, but you're not to fight with Tamy, and you'll have to do some work, clean up plant leaves and give the BBQ a scrub after every meal. Also, we're not the only ones living on this island. Apart from Synder, there are six other androids doing their medical internships at the Townsville Hospital. They return very late at night and leave early in the morning."

"Can Niacin come to live here with me? Cam asks. "She is an android. Due to my misinformed advice, she also invested in crypto-currencies and is now destitute. She could help Synder catch those Great Whites sharks for dinner."

"Give her a phone call and explain to her how we operate in this hippy-type commune."

Cam takes my motorboat to the mainland to pick up Niacin. We all wait by the wharf as the boat arrives, and they get out. Viksi is taking notes and filming on her smartphone.

"She is more than big, Greuger. She could be hired by the deforestation industry and save on resources. Power saws and diggers wouldn't be required as she could pull them out with her bare hands," says Pleb.

"One of you must be Jules. Let me give you a hug," Niacin says with a huge smile on her face as she grabs both Greuger and Sid.

Their eyes almost pop as she squeezes them, and when she lets go, they walk away, crouched and trying to get their breath back.

"Niacin, I am Jules."

"Let me give you a hug too."

I look up; she's very tall and has a wide girth. "No, Niacin, hugging humans in public is forbidden on this island though hugging trees is very much encouraged."

Pleb whispers to Cam, "How do you survive those monstrous hugs."

"She's just very excited at the moment; usually, she's very gentle and doesn't even squash a roach or a fly."

Bea pulls me aside. "We could start those cage wrestling matches again and get the film crew back. Imagine, Dyslexa versus Niacin. I could do the marketing but one of them has to be the bad guy, sorry meant bad princes."

"Bea, the androids are paying rent, more than enough and back rent, as well as for their electricity usage. They've just paid to have our aging solar panels and batteries replaced. The only money they need is to pay for new medical clothing that gets stained with human blood when they operate on human patients."

"Jules, once they finish their internship, they'll probably move to regional hospitals. We got to make the best of them while they are here."

"Bea, how about you and Niacin compete in the first match?" I'll ask Niacin.

"Jules, she is 100cm taller than me, and I would have to bulk up, eat a shark a day to keep Niacin's lethal hug away."

We're having a very late night by the BBQ. The androids arrive back from a long day at the hospital internship, in a motorboat they purchased. They need a recharge. Bea rushes over to Dyslexa and whispers in her ear, well, Dyslexa chest, because android ears don't work, but they pick up sound vibration through their chests.

"Yes, where is she?"

The friendly Niacin's hug would require a lot of titanium structures to be soldered back into Dyslexa's chest, but there are probably no motor mechanics or android doctors to do the job open at this time of the night.

"I'm going to get you bitch," Dyslexa yells at Niacin as Gannon carries her to the androids cabin.

Gero comes over to me. "I know a guy in Townsville who mends androids who have incurred a fracture. I will call him tomorrow. He owes me a favour, so we should get priority treatment."

"Gero, one time you'll have to tell me your life story and why so many people owe you favours."

"I will one day, but wipe that suspicious look from your face. I never did anything illegal apart from not paying a car-parking fine."

Next day, Niacin helps us shift the Fusion BBQ so we can clean the underneath floor. She didn't need much help to do the lifting.

Chapter Seventy-six

At 6am in the morning, Gero knocks on our cabin door. "We have an appointment with Yusef, who specialises in android upper body injuries. We have to be at his clinic by 8am as he is busy for the rest of the day treating androids who worked in underground coal mines that collapsed."

Gero and I knock on the android's cabin. Gannon opens the door. The other androids have gone back to work at the hospital. The thought crosses my mind that some of the androids should specialise in treating android engineering injuries as androids do all the dangerous work in the mining and building industry these days.

"Gannon, carry Dyslexa to my motorboat. Gero has organised an early morning appointment with someone who can fix her broken parts."

"I'm going to get her; she will pay for my suffering," yells Dyslexa as Gannon carries her to my motorboat.

"Dyslexa, don't be angry. Niacin never meant to hurt you. She just doesn't realise her own strength when she gets excited, especially when meeting new people. The hug is a sign of affection," Gero reassures.

Bea is dragging Sid who's rubbing his eyes whilst walking to the boat terminal. "We would like to come along as well. I had great plans for Dyslexa, and I hope the operation is a success," says Bea.

Viksi and a slightly drowsy Rog also join us. Viksi is speaking into a microphone attached to her phone, recording what's happening.

We arrive at Yusef's clinic though we did get stopped by the police as we did the walk from the boat terminal as Gannon carries Dyslexa.

"Sir, is that a lifeless female body you are carrying? If so you are all under-arrest," the cop says as he draws his laser gun.

Dyslexa lifts her head. "Get f..ked. I banged into a rock face when doing a bungy jump and got a few bruised and broken ribs. I'm being taken to a doctor."

"Continue on," the police officer says whilst rubbing his head.

Back at the clinic, Yusef examines Dyslexa and takes X-rays. Viksi is still recording, and I can hear her whispering into the microphone. "This Yusef guy looks like a mad scientist. He's probably in his late 60s, tubby, dishevelled, and probably never combed his twisted silvery hair, which is standing upright as if he had an electric shock. He is wearing glasses which sit on the edge of his nose."

"I may be old, but my hearing is perfect. Now turn that recording device off or I'll be giving you reconstructive surgery as well," yells Yusef.

Viksi nervously complies.

"I'm going to have to turn her off and disable her power supply. Does she have non-volatile random-access memory?" asks Yusef as he wheels in a large device.

"I'm sure she does, as she's a late model, so she will not lose her recent memories," says Gero.

"I will take a backup of her recent memories just in case. Now I suggest you go for a walk while I open her chest cavity up and fuse those titanium rib structures with this laser. Come back in an hour."

"Gannon, there is nothing we can do. Let's just go for a walk."

The seven of us do.

"Jules, there's a special for Sav Blanc, $5 a bottle," says Sid.

In some ways, it was therapeutic for Gannon to carry two 12-bottle cartons under his arms. He had to take his android mind off from thinking about Dyslexa and focus on not tripping on fallen tree branches and damaging the load.

"Why do humans drink this fermented grape juice?" he asks.

"Gannon, in moderation, it is fun and gets the conversation flowing. All of us apart from Viksi, Bea, Sid and Rog are what are called introverts on this island, but after a few glasses, the rest of us sparkle up a bit," says Gero.

"I would like to sparkle up a bit, I am feeling very sad."

Gannon gently puts down the two 12-bottle cartoons of Sav Blanc and pulls out a bottle. He eventually works out how to open it and gulps a few mouthfuls.

It's Rog and Pleb who have to carry the rest of the Sav Blanc cartons whilst Gero, Sid and I struggle to carry Gannon back to Yusef's laboratory.

"He's an older model android without a digestive tract, and he's drunk some liquid, Sav Blanc to be exact. He is also very heavy, a pre-Titanium skeletal."

"The liquid will evaporate if his mouth is kept open. He will heal, now please go, I have many human customers due in 10 minutes who wish to be converted to androids."

"Can we borrow a wheelbarrow if you have one?" asks Gero.

"Yes, go through the back door, quick! There's one in the garden shed, but I want it returned."

Pleb and Rog rush out the back and bring back the wheelbarrow along with 20 or so short 3cm pieces of plywood planks.

"That guy Yusef must make wooden furniture in his spare time. We got these wood pieces to keep Gannon's mouth open, so that he can evaporate bodily fluids and the extra ones are for us, if we drink too much and need evaporation," says Rog.

Pleb shakes her head then Dyslexa walks out though she's a bit wobbly and holding her chest. Those new android models must have pain receptors.

As we're wheeling Gannon to the harbour we get stopped again by the same police officer.

"Is this some crime syndicate body disposing unit. You're all under arrest."

Dyslexa speaks up. "You remember me, don't you? They carried me to the doctor after my bungy jumping accident and the police never prosecuted the owners of that enterprise."

"So why is this semi-conscious guy in a wheelbarrow?"

Bea intervenes. "He is and he was so worried, Dyslexa, he got stuck into the cartoons of wine we had just purchased. He normally doesn't drink so it had a catastrophic effect on him."

"But why are those pieces of plywood in the corners of his mouth keeping his mouth agape, asks Dyslexia?"

"They aid evaporation of alcohol through the lungs and then the mouth and reduce blood alcohol."

"Does that work? Can I have two of those plywood pieces?"

Gero gives her two.

"You're free to go this time, now move," says the police officer.

Pleb looks back. "Jules, she's trying out the plywood pieces in her mouth. That green plywood is coated with chemicals probably dangerous to humans if ingested, so she may not make it to the Police Ball on New Year's night."

We get Gannon back to the motorboat, and I rush back with the wheelbarrow and leave it outside Yusef's premises. On my way back, I see the police officer still experimenting and chewing the plywood pieces. I hope she has health insurance and has made an inheritance will.

We arrive back at the island. Gannon is able to walk again with some help from

Dyslexa.

Another boat pulls up by the jetty. We look up. Anastasia, Clark and Morris carrying their digital film equipment, come marching down from the boat terminal.

"It's going to be a David versus Goliath match, and the royalties will be huge," yells Morris in joy whilst clapping his hands.

"What are you doing back here?" I ask. "I thought you were on a work assignment filming the mating habits of humpback whales."

"The whales were shy with us around with our cameras so they didn't perform, not that we knew how whales actually performed the act. It's hard to imagine. We got zero saleable footage."

Anastasia joins the conversation. "Bea said there's an opportunity to film and broadcast one of those female wrestling matches again. Bea said you got this giant human or android woman called Niacin who can bend steel with her bare hands. We'd like to meet this woman and interview her and arrange a WWE match."

I look at Bea. She drops her head, chews on her nails, but her eyes are still looking up as if seeking pardon.

"Jules, they were going to have a face down or is it a face-off so it should get filmed and refereed so no one gets seriously injured. I will be the referee."

"Bea, how many dollars are you going to make? I didn't authorise this and I'm the authoriser on this island, so you should have asked permission."

"Jules, you are becoming a disktaker, or is it dictator? I will fight you in the ring if you continue this sort of behaviour," says Bea.

Just then, Dyslexa comes marching out. "Where is she, that Niacin?"

Niacin, followed by Cam, also come marching down to the BBQ area. Mystca, Tamy, Grillian and Adrian soon join. We do our best to explain the situation.

Clark and Morris start filming and sound recording.

"Jules, that Dyslexa needs psychological counselling. She is very angry. We only charge $250 per hour," says Mystca.

"I heard that. I don't need any counselling. Niacin, are you ready?" Dyslexa yells whilst pointing her outstretched arm at Niacin.

"Darling, come over here and let me give you a soothing head massage. I promise I will be gentle."

"This is not how it's supposed to go. You have to punch, gouge and bear hug each other as we film," yells Morris.

"Come over here, my darling film person. Let momma give you a big hug as well," says Niacin.

"No, no, no, stay away from me," says Anastasia.

"let's leave this crazy island. No one would believe what goes on here," Morris yells and then stumbles, hitting his head on a rock whilst running away from Niacin.

Anastasia agrees. "It's time to go," she yells. "We'll film the porpoises or are they dolphins leaping out in the bay? We'll make a documentary featuring creatures that don't have two legs or any legs. The kids will love it and so will our network."

After frantically packing their filming gear whilst looking back in fright to make sure Niacin doesn't get too close, they're off running to their motorboat. "Wipe your blood off the filming gear, it's expensive equipment," says Anastasia to a confused Morris.

Bea is very disappointed and fuming. "I had a lucrative deal with Anastasia, and now I will be poor and destitute for the rest of my life."

Sid puts his arm around Bea. "You've always got me, my darling."

It would certainly make a good contest. Is Sid losing more blood from his nose than Morris from his forehead?

Dyslexa comes out and gives Niacin a pat on her shoulder. "You know I would have beaten you."

"It doesn't matter who wins. We just all have to look after each other. We are sisters."

Dyslexa has a puzzled look on her face. "How could I have a humanoid sister?" she asks Niacin.

"It's just a phrase that means all human women and android women must work together, are you in?"

Then Dyslexa gives Niacin a huge non-bone-breaking hug. "We are sisters," she hesitatingly says.

"We are, and there are many women's rights issues we have to tackle, especially domestic violence. Are you up to it, Sis?"

"I have another year of my medical internship to finish but I will ask my supervisor if I can focus on women victims of domestic violence. I will hunt down the perpetrators and make them pay. They will be inflicted with the same injuries that they inflicted on their partners."

"No Dyslexa, fighting violence with violence is not the way to go; we have to think of another way," says Niacin.

Mystca and Tamy join the conversation. They talk for several hours whilst the rest of us humanoids do our walk around the island. Four walks around, to be exact, as we have a lot of adrenaline to wear off after the drama of today. Viksi is furiously talking into her recorder.

"Cam, have you ever hit Niacin?" I ask.

"Once, with a hammer, she was holding a nail when I was trying to assemble a kitchen shelf. I missed and hit her on her forefinger. She said, 'Cam, carpentry is not your forte, I will do the hammering, and you hold the nails, I don't miss'. That's the only time I hit her."

We finally get back and take a dip in the sea, just a shallow dip as Dyslexa and Niacin are still talking with Mystca and Tamy, so we don't have anyone to rescue us if we're attacked by great white sharks. (A political debate would follow for many years, and eventually, the great white sharks got renamed to 'great multicultural sharks', maybe because they weren't fussy about who they ate).

"Jules, I think it's time for a vino. We've done 8km just on this island walk, according to my watch – 13,000 steps. Let's pull out a few bottles of this Sav Blanc and pass them around."

"Yeh, good idea Rog; it's like we had a year's worth of trauma in just 24 hours."

We get the drinking glasses from under the BBQ, and then Gannon comes over. "Gero and Jules, could I get upgraded to have an intestinal tract and be able to eat food and drink wine and wee and pooh?"

"I am not sure Gannon. I'll give Yusef a call in the morning, but I don't think intestinal tracts are his speciality," says Gero.

They now call themselves the sisters. Niacin, Dyslexa, Mystca and Tamy briefly join us. "We will present courses not just in primary and secondary schools but everywhere. We can't join you for the wine, but we have some more brainstorming and writing to do," says Tamy as they all march off to her and Adrian's cabin.

Gannon yells out, "Dyslexa, take the charger and plug yourself in."

"I don't need the charger; I can eat bananas and sharks and maybe even a few humans."

Jill, Cara and Viksi come running after them. "Can we join you," they say in unison.

So it's only the Pleb, Bea and the lads left by the BBQ.

"Jules, will they form some feminist union group and take over the running of this island?"

"I don't think so, Sid. Everyone has been treated equally on this island."

Chloe4 and Castro join us with that look on their faces to say you haven't fed us today. We haven't been treated equally.

Bea yells out, "I think they're drowning, Anastasia and the two males. A small killer whale, an Orca, has just jumped out of the ocean and landed on their motorboat, which is sinking. The whale's chest landed on two upright tripods and is injured. Should we rescue the whale?"

Viksi must have heard Bea's yell and rushes out with her cell phone and starts filming; it must have a telephoto lens.

"Rog, whales are used to injuries. Give me the binoculars."

Anastasia and Morris have life jackets on, but they only had two jackets onboard. They tow Clark behind them as they try to make the 8km swim back to Townsville.

"Jules, I don't need binoculars. Take our motorboat and rescue them. They swim worse than us Polish people. They won't have a chance, and then you will wear their deaths in your subconscious for the rest of your life," says Pleb.

Sid, Rog and I run to the jetty and start Rog's motorboat. It's faster than mine. We salvage all three of them, and they're alive though panting and distraught. We bring them back to the island, and they sit on the sand away from us and sulk.

"We've lost all our equipment," Clark yells as he holds his head down and sobs.

"Luckily for you, that Orca didn't land on you, else we'd be eating mince meat tonight," yells Sid.

Bea goes over to Anastasia. "Come and join us, we have wine, and if your clothes are wet, you can take them off to dry. We are used to seeing nude people here."

"You wasted our precious time, but we need a big drink, but no way am I taking off my wet Coco Chanel dress."

Rog interrupts. "I think that killer whale is dead. It's only a small one, a junior. We could tow it back in my motorboat, and we'd have fresh seafood for at least a week."

It took two hours for us guys, including Gannon and Greuger, to push the floating, deceased whale close to our island shore even though it was less than 4 metres long.

"Do you have a winch, Jules?" asks Greuger whilst panting. "We have to get the whale up on the sand so we can dissect it."

"No, I don't, but I've got a big hook tied to a strong, long fibre rope."

"We need more help."

Greuger rushes back and brings out the feminists.

"You didn't kill it, I hope," says Niacin with an accusing stare.

"No, it jumped out of the water and impaled itself on the tripods onboard Anastasia's motorboat."

We guys relax as Niacin and Dyslexa pull the whale onto the sand.

"Jules, you and the guys get that chain saw, axe, and the laser cutter and clean buckets. Give them a wipe, they've got to be hygienic," yells Sid. "I'll start up that fusion BBQ."

"We have Wasabi paste and Soya sauce. I'll get it," says Viksi.

Chloe4 and Castro are licking their lips and waiting for the leftovers.

Synder, help me," yells Dyslexa. "We will fillet the Orca. We'd be here all night if the humans try to do it."

Sid cautiously hands the chain saw and laser cutter to Dyslexa and Synder. He whispers in my ear, "Hope they don't make fillets out of us as well."

Dyslexa and Synder go into a hyperactive frenzy, cutting and chopping. They are a blur in our vision as they move so fast.

Gero comes over to me. "They must have been initially programmed to be fishmongers. Look, they are removing all the skin and fatty tissue; only red fillets of high protein tissue are thrown in the bucket. It is red because their blood cells have a high haemoglobin content which whales need to hold their breath for long when they dive. They are mammals; they breathe atmospheric air and have lungs, unlike sharks or other fish."

I feel ridden with guilt. Sure, I've eaten red meat but never witnessed the chopping and slicing, so I feel a bit unwell at the sight.

"Gero, all the women on this island are postmenopausal, except possibly Anastasia; they don't need iron tablets or red meat."

"You're not cooking for us vegetarians, will have none of that whale," Mystca, Tamy, Cara and Gerald call out.

"Well, how about you do some cooking for once, and all of you have eaten some white, sorry multicultural sharks before. There are cans of Soya beans in my cabin, sorry Pleb's and mine cabin. You can have them."

The four of them look at each other. I guess the thought of cooking soybeans is more stressful than eating a fish, well, in this case, a mammal fish.

We all congratulate Dyslexa, Synder, Sid and Rog, who did the barbequing and Viksi for her contribution of Wasabi and Soya sauce. Anastasia, Morris and Clark ravenously stuff their faces as if they hadn't eaten for weeks. It must be financially tough in the film industry.

Half the baby Orca is gone, and we're wobbly on our feet. Not sure if it's the Sav Blanc or that our stomachs are so bloated. Dyslexa is carried back to the android's cabin by Gannon. She might have got a too-high dose of iron or Sav Blanc.

I look up at Anastasia, Morris and Clark. "You can have *Cabin12* and *13* for free for a few days."

"Have they got washing machines?" asks Anastasia.

"No, we hand wash clothes on this island, in the sea. Well, we don't really do the clothes or linen washing that much as we have to conserve water and besides, we use a lot of deodorants," I explain.

Viksi walks over to Anastasia as she, Morris and Clark are about to depart to their cabins. "I've finished writing my twelfth book. It's called *Lunatic Asylum*. You could turn it into a film and film it on this island once you purchase new filming equipment."

"We're out of money; we're broke. We haven't been able to sell any of our productions for the last two years, and now our boat, equipment and clothing have sunk," says Anastasia whilst tears stream down her face.

Pleb joins the conversation. "You all can stay on this island as long as you like, rent-free. Tomorrow you could have a chat with Niacin, Dyslexa, Mystca and Tamy. They want to produce written material and films that address family violence, and possibly they may finance you to purchase new filming equipment. We are not financially poor, and this is not a lunatic asylum. It is a *get back to sanity asylum* but with few restrictions providing you do not hurt anyone."

I look at Pleb with my hands held open as if in disbelief, but her judgment makes good sense. We've got spare cabins.

And so, the night ends. We carry back the buckets of sliced fillets for tomorrow's meal to our cabin freezers.

"Jules, I cannot make love tonight. My stomach will burst if you lie on top of me."

I desist from suggesting the doggy position.

Chapter Seventy-seven

"Rise and shine," yells Synder as he knocks on every cabin door, "Time for humans to walk and keep your cardiovascular systems healthy."

Pleb and I come out, as do the others. We're all rubbing our heads, but Sid forgot to put any clothing on, so he rushes back to his cabin.

"Fine for you to say, Synder. Next time we go to Yusef's, I'll get him to install a cardiovascular and memory system into you. Then you'll know what it's like to be woke early in the morning."

"Jules," says Synder, "I'm sure doctor Yusef could source an android body for you and Sid and transfer all your memories to the body. We androids don't have to worry about having to physically exercise or be concerned about time as humans do."

"That's enough, Synder. Just go pick some bananas for our breakfast."

"At your service Jules."

Dyslexa joins us. "Gannon is still trying to unblock our toilet. It's the first time it has been used, and there must have been some obstruction. I will use the recharger in the future. My intestinal tract is feeling extremely uncomfortable. It could be all that food I ate, or I am possibly pregnant."

Four hundred metres along the walk, the same things happen as the time before when we over-indulged in eating. We strip off our clothing and run into the ocean, keeping 10m apart, not for Covid-48 reasons but for sanitary purposes. The algae and seaweed get another good feed.

"We have all had healthy bowel movements, and now we should continue our walk," Dyslexa says.

Gero catches up to Dyslexa, "Dyslexa, you do not need to exercise. You have taste sensors, and what you ate may have tasted good, but you cannot put on weight. You have no fat or muscle cells."

"I just want to walk with my sisters. My intestinal tract converts the food I eat to electrical pulses that charge my battery. Oh, my battery is overcharged. I have to sprint a few laps around the island to lower the battery charge else the battery may explode."

Dyslexa takes off. She takes 3 minutes to complete a 2 km lap. We watch in amazement as she does five more laps before trying to retire back to the android's cabin while checking her battery gauge. "I have overdone the discharge," she calls out, "I quickly need to be plugged into a charger or eat more Orca. Sisters, walk without me. I will be more careful tomorrow, and I will join you then."

Gannon comes rushing out and helps her back to their cabin.

The sisters seem disappointed, but once we all put on our clothing, we continue the walk.

"Jules, if we feed her Orca meat, she could win the 5,000m, 10,000m and the marathon at the next Olympic Games," says Bea. "There are huge financial rewards as well. She would be paid millions to appear in those Opera interviews, and I could be her marketing manager."

"Bea, androids aren't allowed to compete in the Olympic Games as they have an unfair advantage."

"Jules, we could disguise her as me, a blond wig and a lot of chest padding would do, and I would walk through the X-ray scanners. Then we could sneak her into the Olympic village, and she takes my place."

Bea hardly looks like a competitor for the marathon. She'd have to lose at least 30kg of weight, but I don't tell her that. I have learnt the art of diplomacy and how not to get my nose broken.

"Bea, her internal battery pack could only last for 10kms, and she can't exactly go running with a backpack full of batteries."

"What about you get Gero's friend, Yusef, to insert a nuclear fusion reactor into her, like the one that powers your BBQ?"

"Bea, she'd have to carry a tank of hydrogen on her back, and that would arouse suspicion."

Bea seems disappointed and recedes, but Pleb joins me. "What was that about?"

"Just a money-making scheme, but I think I persuaded her that it wouldn't work. I'll tell you later, but for now, we have to do at least three laps of mainly walking and talking."

After three laps of the island and 300m from the BBQ area, we all have to go for another sanitary dip in the ocean, but then we look up. Momma Orca whale lifts her head and licks her tongue. She is very big, unlike Junior.

"Rog, Sid, what did you do with the remains of baby Orca?"

"We threw them into the ocean."

"Momma Orca must have sniffed the remains of her baby, and she's out for revenge. Run into the bushes and do what you have to do there."

"But there's no toilet paper there."

"Use some leaves and then rush back to your cabins and have a 10-second shower and use some of that hand sanitiser on your cavities."

The Orca momma is making all sorts of noises as if to beckon us out for a challenge. Not even Niacin, Greuger, Gannon and a fully charged Dyslexa would have a chance.

"Viksi, show the video on your phone that you recorded. Show it to momma Orca."

The 3-D video projects into the sky. Momma Orca watches. Junior Orca certainly made a mistake jumping onto Anastasia's boat and impaling himself. Then Dyslexa comes rushing out, jumps into the ocean, swims out and hugs the gigantic momma whale. "We promise we won't eat whale ever again. You can join our sisterhood; we are for equality for all mammals, and we do not hunt whales."

We can see the Orca briefly shutting her eyes. Maybe she's relieved to know what had really happened. She gently turns around and waits for Dyslexa to jump off her back and swim to shore. The momma Orca then joins the pack of migrating Orcas but not before putting a show on for us. She launches herself high in the air and makes a huge splash. Luckily, Viksi is recording on her cell phone camera because it is spectacular.

"Jules, whales are very intelligent and highly emotional. That junior Orca strayed from the pack just as our human teenagers often do. It was young and inexperienced and probably just showing off when it made that fatal jump," Pleb assures me.

For a brief moment, the thought crosses my mind of moving back into a city, but teenagers there, sometimes do more stupid things than junior Orcas.

Anastasia is talking to Viksi. "We could make a short movie of this story once we purchase some more equipment. Could we use that cell phone footage you took?"

"No way, Sister; I'm writing the story."

"We could collaborate; 50/50 of the takings. After all, we are all sisters."

Morris asks Clark, "How can we become sisters and join the clan?"

"No way Morris, I'm keeping my underneath bodily parts," Clark replies.

Needless to say, that night we ate cold Soya beans, straight out the cans, as we looked at the comets in the night sky and wondered what is to follow, well at least Anastasia, Morris and Clark probably did. Their gut microflora wasn't used to processing vegetable matter as far as I know.

Chapter Seventy-eight

"Pleb, it's 8am, and Synder hasn't been around knocking on our doors to wake us up for the 8am morning walk."

"Jules, he might still be recharging but put on some shorts and go and check on him."

Gero is waiting for the morning walk by the BBQ, as are many of the others.

"Gero, can you come with me to check on Synder? He is normally punctual to the microsecond but not today. Something could be wrong with him."

Gero and I enter the androids cabin. There's only Synder sitting on the floor by a wall with his head down low. Dyslexa and Gannon must have resumed their medical internship and joined the other androids.

Gero kneels and puts his hand on Synder's head, "Is something the matter? We missed you this morning and had no one to wake and inspire us for the morning walk."

Synder lifts his head. "I am not like the other androids. I feel attraction for male androids."

"Gero, is that possible?"

"I don't know Jules. Any form of attraction was not built into their AI programming though Dyslexa and Gannon defy the odds, as you say."

"Synder, we depend on you to start the walk, and maybe you can walk with us so we can talk."

"Thank you, Jules and Gero; I will join you on the walk. I am now fully charged."

The three of us join the others by the BBQ. Surprisingly Anastasia, Morris and Clark are also there.

"I know what you're thinking. We ate nothing but canned Soya beans for the last two months, but our guts got used to it. It was all we could afford after the last storm. It's not easy trying to be a filmmaker," says Anastasia.

Synder yells out '*Go*', and we're off.

"Is Synder well?" asks Pleb.

"For the moment Pleb, and I'll tell you later. Gero and I have to do some more talking with him while we walk."

"Can I join you?"

"Pleb, it's a brother, male-bonding thing. Join the sisters on this walk. I'll tell you all the results later."

Gero, Synder and I start talking whilst walking.

"Synder, I once had a transgender brother who had many cosmetic operations and eventually looked like a very attractive woman and married a friend of mine. I'm not biased."

"Jules, can I have those operations as well?"

Gero intervenes, "Synder, you could just buy a long wig and a bra stuffed with tennis balls, though that would not work as androids are androgynous, designed to be sexless, and the male and female bodies are basically the same. Their facial structures are fairly similar depending on which company manufactured them, so the length of the hair and a minor AI code difference or discrepancy determine their perceived gender."

"But what about Gannon and Dyslexa? They are partnered?"

"Synder, Gannon is a heavy-duty industrial model of android, built for heavy lifting and to protect a company's Lithium mine against poachers. He was modelled on *Conan the Barbarian*, a movie character, so his designers gave him long hair as well as an extra large frame. He has not got a penis, and Dyslexa has not got a vagina. Their relationship is purely platonic," Gero says.

"They cuddle and kiss, I have seen it, and they sleep next to each other in the androids cabin, wrapped in each other's arms. I would like to do that with someone."

Gero rubs his head. "Synder, androids were originally built to do the dangerous tasks that humans do not like doing, like housework duties, dishwashing, fruit picking and working in mines. We never predicted their AI brains would evolve so quickly and along with emotions that can be hard to control. You have seen how Dyslexa can behave. In some ways, she is still an unpredictable teenager."

"Will I evolve?"

"You already have, but you still have a little way to go. I may possibly be able to get you a job with Yusef as an android medico. It would keep your mind occupied helping other androids."

"I would like that. I can work extremely fast after I observe and learn Yusef's diagnosis and procedures."

Synder runs off, holding his hands in the air as if a great weight has been lifted from his Titanium shoulder. Gero is on his phone talking to Yusef, I assume.

Pleb walks over and joins us. "What has happened? Tell me!"

"Pleb, we discussed android evolution before, but it's happening quicker than anyone ever foresaw. Humans took hundreds of thousands of years to supposedly evolve, yet they are still greedy and still fighting. I think the androids are doing a lot better than us." I then summarise to Pleb the discussion with Synder and Gero.

"I did not think the androids had sexual desires or sexual identities. I think Synder might just want to be hugged by another android. It is what all humans desire as well. I mean being hugged by a human, not an android."

"Well, Pleb, you go hug him or hug me."

Gero gets off his phone and joins us again. "Yusef will take him on as an apprentice. He will not pay much, and Synder has to clean and take the rubbish out, but he can watch the procedures that Yusef performs on androids, and he will teach him everything he knows. Yusef is old and has no children, so he wishes his business is taken over by someone he trusts and not the urban city council."

Pleb and I clap our hands. Then Pleb ponders, "Jules, if Synder is not around, you will have to raise your game and learn how to clean the BBQ, wash dishes and wake us up for the morning walk. Don't worry; I am just joking, as you say in this country."

Pleb wasn't joking. My workload would increase exponentially. We finish walking four laps of the island and then take a very long dip in the ocean to cool off. Mystca, Tamy, Grillian and Adrian were waiting for us after completing their laps. They can still run whilst we only walk. They join in the frolicking in the ocean and the splashing and laughter. We take turns in having Niacin effortlessly lift us over her head and toss us into the ocean, though the belly wackers can hurt.

It's my turn. I get tossed and land on something sharp in the ocean sand.

"Jules, what is the diamond-like object sticking out of your left calf?"

"I don't know, but it doesn't hurt that much."

I pull it out, and the wound instantly heals. We all stare in awe as a holographic projection appears. It's Juliet.

"I have been classified as contaminated after visiting your world. I am an outcast on my birthplace planet. I am like some of the people called *coloured* on your planet. Even my mother has abandoned me. I would like to come back to your Earth and live on your island. I would bring many bags of diamonds, and unlike on your planet, diamonds are considered a waste material on my planet and just clog up the hard waste disposal landfill."

We all look at each other, and then all nod our heads to imply *yes*.

"I am so happy. Now you may feel a small degree of discomfort as my meteor-like spacecraft bends space. It will only last a microsecond and not be detectable by your space and military agencies."

Everyone's bodies very briefly extend and contract. I hope Juliet is right and hope NASA doesn't try to track this gravitational wave incident to our island. The meteor-like spacecraft takes only minutes to arrive and generates a cloud of steam as it skims the ocean to slow down, lose heat, and eventually sink. I hope no satellites are filming this unusual phenomenon. About 10 minutes later, Juliet appears at the water's surface and starts swimming to shore, towing four very large backpacks behind her. Synder jumps into the ocean to help her though she doesn't really need help. She has four legs and four arms and swims very well. He insists on helping her carry her backpacks to a spare cabin.

"Jules, did you see the smile on Snyder's face?"

"I did, and Juliet was also smiling as they stared into each other's eyes."

"Jules, this could be love between an android and an alien species, a possible first on Earth."

"Yeh, it could be. I don't know why any aliens would bother with us humans."

"Jules, you might have to knock on the cabin doors to wake everyone for the morning walk tomorrow."

"I will do that duty, and Pleb, remember that Synder is supposed to be starting his apprenticeship tomorrow morning."

"Jules, ask Gero to ring Yusef. I somehow feel that Synder may be too preoccupied to start work tomorrow, and we do not need his wage. Three of those four large backpacks that Juliet brought with her are full of diamonds. We could afford to buy NASA if it was for sale."

"Yusef, this is Gero. I don't think Synder can make a start at your work today and learn from your teachings."

"That is fine, my friend, because I will not be at work today as I am disabled as of yesterday. I was using my TENS machine, electrodes strapped to my forehead to alleviate a headache, when an exceptionally large voltage was delivered to my brain and fried it. I cannot even remember what I did for work, so I would be useless in any teaching role."

"Yusef, do you need any assistance?"

"Gero, I do not. My 12 adult children have come to live with me as they also had unusual electrical power problems that damaged their powerlines, and they cannot cook fish-and-chips any more. They say that they saw some unusual round object appear in the sky at the time of their power loss."

"Yusef, it could just be a coincidence, though I must admit that my heart pacemaker was also affected. I actually wanted to do naughty things with my partner again, but the pacemaker was low on charge."

Mystca and Tamy come over. "We would like to eat the remains of that organically grown whale as we're having a break from cans of Soya beans."

That night Gero instructs Sid and Rog. "We must bury any uneaten remains of junior Orca above sea level. We don't want the momma and the other Orcas coming back."

Viksi and Rog join us and bring lots of sachets of Wasabi and little plastic bottles of soya sauce.

Rog whispers in my ear, "Viksi has thousands of them. Every time we bought Sushi rolls at that Sushi shop in Townsville, she asked me to distract the shop attendant at the counter while she emptied the containers of Wasabi and Soya sauce into her handbag."

Cara and Gerald come over from their cabin. "We have finished our 48-hour mediation session. Can we help cook?"

"It's Orca steak along with some seaweed and Wasabi tonight," says Rog.

Cara and Gerald look at each. "No thanks, but can we borrow a motorboat to go into town and go shopping in the vego store? We'll buy lots of Tofu, Lentils, Pakchoi, Chinese Broccoli and organic spices and oils. We'll do the cooking tomorrow. We may be late home as we'd like to try a new vegetarian restaurant called *VegForUs*, as we haven't eaten for 48 hours and are kinda hungry."

"Yes, sure. The keys are under the driver's seat, but check the petrol gauge first. Also, buy some cans of Soya beans. It's time for our peptide jab, and I must start manufacturing it."

Mystca, Tamy, Grillian and Adrian say in unison, "We'd like to join them, and we can help bring back the food supplies. We'll first grab our backpacks and green shopping bag."

Pleb, Bea, Sid and I, with our buckets, walk into the ocean and retrieve handfuls of soft, thin green seaweed whilst Rog and Synder go back to Rog's cabin and bring back two large bags of semi-frozen Orca fillets.

"Yum, yum," says Juliet as she jumps up and down in anticipation.

Synder grabs her. "Juliet, there are only two Orca fillets per being, but if you are still hungry afterwards, there are plenty of sharks in the ocean, and I can help you catch them."

Juliet grabs Synder by the neck and kisses him. "I'm supposed to be on a diet. Restrain me if I start eating too much of that Orca delicacy."

Synder, at first, has a quizzical look on his face, but then he kisses her back. Meanwhile, both Viksi and Anastasia were taking notes and taking video footage on their phones. Luckily, they were on opposite sides of the BBQ, but every now and again, they'd put their thumbs up in the air and poke their tongues out at each other. Rog and Sid do the cooking honours, two minutes per side, so it's not long before the fillets are ready. The seaweed then gets a 30-second toss and cook. Viksi and Anastasia, lured by the aroma, stop filming and being provocative to each other; they help get the plates and cutlery out from underneath the BBQ. Juliet is ready to rush to the front of the queue but is restrained by Synder. "Juliet, we will wait at the end of the queue, so you can prove to the others that you have conquered your nutrient consumption disorder."

"But, but, but!"

"No buts," Synder says authoritatively as he hugs Juliet.

Pleb looks at me. "Jules, there are not only just cooking smells in the air. Love is in the air as well."

I give Pleb a long hug whilst glancing at Synder and Juliet. No way am I going to get beaten at the physical endurance test of hugging. Synder glances at me and Pleb.

"Jules, stop hugging. Anastasia, Morris and Clark are going back for seconds of fillets. There will be nothing left for us," says Pleb in a low, fainting-sounding voice, possibly due to the bear hug I'm applying. An hour later, I collapse from exhaustion. "OK, you win, Synder, now go to my cabin and get another bag of Orca fillets."

"Jules, it was not a competition. I have never hugged anyone before and found hugging Juliet pleasurable."

"Well, Synder, you achieved sixty years' worth of hugging under your belt; now get some more Orca fillets from my freezer, but only one bag. Juliet has to adhere to her dietary restrictions."

Sid and Rog do some more cooking whilst most of the others lie on the sand with a glass of Sav Blanc and look at the night sky meteor shower. I hear Bea say to Sid, "I hope those are authentic meteors and not those hyperdrive spaceships from that Juliet's planet because if they have an appetite like she has, they would eat every sea creature on Earth and possibly us humans. I just want to eat and not be on the menu of those aliens."

It's now only Pleb, me, Synder and Juliet by the BBQ, well, not quite. Chloe4 and Castro are there as well, licking their lips.

"Only two fillets each."

"Jules, I won't be eating. I'll use my electric recharger for energy. I do not possess a toothbrush. I can't have fish breath on my first day on the job at Yusef's."

"Synder, Yusef is ill and won't be immediately hiring you. His Tensor pain-alleviating device had a huge power surge at the time Juliet's craft landed in the ocean. His brain is semi-fried. Apparently, Gero did tell Yusef not to use the Tensor for relieving headaches, but Yusef did not listen."

"Synder, can I have your share of Orca?" asks Juliet.

"No, Juliet, remember that you are on a diet."

"Well can you take a photo of me on my hyper-phone eating an Orca fillet?" asks Juliet.

Synder agrees. Juliet has a piece of fillet hanging out of her mouth and puts up her right index finger, which apparently means on many inhabited planets *get stuffed*.

Pleb tries to grab Synder before he pushes the send button, but it was too late.

"We have to make another video, else we'll be invaded, and all Orcas and sharks will be decimated. Jules, get some of that polystyrene wrapping that you never used to give me a wrapped birthday present, that cactus plant you gave me. We will make another video that exposes that it was not Orca, but polystyrene that, when wrapped, resembles a fish fillet."

"Juliet, you must comply, or else you're out of this island."

Her head is bowed. "I will comply," Juliet says.

Synder and Pleb run to my cabin, get my watercolour paints, start painting red, and then fold some polystyrene sheets.

Anastasia, Morris, and Clark come marching back from the sand and are covered in sand. Gero is following.

"What are you doing?" Anastasia asks.

"We're going to have to make a very brief video."

Anastasia's, Morris's, and Clark's eyes light up. I briefly explain the reason for the video shoot and how important it is for our fish industry and human lives. The three of them start a very lively discussion. "We'll write a script, and then Juliet has to rehearse her lines. Clark will do the filming using that phone device of hers."

"But will her extra-terrestrial race understand it?"

"Yes, her phone has a universal translator," Gero says.

Fifteen minutes later, they come back. "We wrote the script, it's done."

"Anastasia, this is over 30 minutes of dialogue. Reduce it to 15 seconds. That's all the credit she's got left on that hyper-phone," says Gero.

Ten minutes later, they come back with a revised script, and the rehearsals start. Morris holds the notepad up with the script while Juliet recites the lines with the rolled-up red-painted polystyrene hanging from her mouth. The first three rehearsals are a disaster because Juliet keeps on breaking out in uncontrollable laughter.

"I can't work with that Octopus, I can't, I can't!" yells Anastasia in frustration and walks away with the palms of her hands on her head and muttering a cacophony of words that I prefer not to publish due to decency requirements.

"Come back, Anastasia; I will talk with Juliet and explain the gravity of the situation," says Pleb. "In the meantime, take a sip from that bottle of Sav Blanc lying near the BBQ."

"Now Juliet, there is a lot at stake here, so you have to take it seriously, else if your people decide to come here to Earth, there will be no fish left, and you and the rest of us will be eating nothing but cans of Soya beans."

Juliet reflects and then nods her head. The real filming starts, but Juliet ignores the script.

"Like, like, I was just joking. It was only a joke. There are no whales or sharks here, just Orcas, which are awards for bad movies and TV series on this planet. This is a plastic substance in my mouth called polystyrene. It's a waste product on Earth, but humans do eat it as there is nothing much more to eat here except for sand. I am losing heaps of weight."

"Cut", whispers Anastasia to Clark.

Juliet comes over to Clark and presses the *Send* button on the phone.

We all clap in joy. Hopefully, a major extraterrestrial disaster has been averted.

"Jules, I really have to go and get recharged."

"Sure, Synder, I'll wake you tomorrow for your first day at Yusef's if he is recovered. I'll drive the motorboat into town. I have some shopping to do. I'll pick you up after you finish work."

"Did not you say that Yusef electrocuted his brain due to unusual electrical disturbances when Juliet folded space-time when using her spacecraft to land here? Are you possibly suffering from memory loss?"

"Yes, yes I did, I did say that."

Synder puts his arm around my shoulder. Oh, sh.t, is the peptide still working? Maybe it's those overseas imported Soya Beans we've been using that don't work as well as our own country's product.

It's an early night for everyone, so no sleeping on the beach and waking up with a hangover. We all go back to our cabins. Synder goes back to Juliet's cabin but crabs his recharger first.

"Jules, it is crazy here on this island. We have had to assassinate *Pi5* agents who were after us, extraterrestrial visits, delusional people and Orca whales threatening us, and now Anastasia and her crew, who still think they can be famous filmmakers. They are all very delusional."

"Pleb, overall, we're probably happier than those people living in expensive houses and driving those flying Porsche cars. Most people on this island, including me, are dreamers, including your daughter. Overall, we're having a good life and continuing the work my transgender brother Charmaine started."

"Let me give you a hug," says Pleb.

Chapter Seventy-nine

No need to wake Synder. He is standing by the jetty along with Juliet and Gero.

"Gero, Juliet would like to come with me to Yusef's and learn the art of android surgery, that is if Yusef's brain has recovered."

"I'll talk to Yusef and ask if he has recovered his memory," says Gero.

Synder, Juliet and Gero drive one of the motorboats to town.

Yusef looks at Juliet, "She has four legs and four arms. I do not do extra leg or arm amputations. I do not remove legs or arms."

"Yusef, she is only here to watch and learn your techniques along with Synder and help out where possible. She does not need to be paid. You're getting two for the price of one."

"But why has she got four legs and four arms?"

Gero rubs his chin and thinks before replying. "She was genetically engineered to compete in the Melbourne Cup horse race, where you have to have at least four legs. She can run very fast."

"OK, she can stay, but as an apprentice. She has to clean up all the android pieces lying on the floor."

Obviously, Yusef never did any housework in his life, but after 15 minutes, Synder and Juliet have the place looking spotless and smelling of Dettol.

"Yusef, we got to go and do some shopping. We'll come and pick them up later," says Gero.

Gero and I walk out. It's six months since anyone on the island has had the peptide, and it's time to start manufacturing it again, but I first have to buy some more solvents.

"Sir, aren't you are the guy that bought acetone and ethanol, the substances that the drug Meth producers want to buy?"

"I told you before, I just manufacture anti-skin aging products as my wife is getting extremely agitated when she looks in the mirror. I can bring her here if you like, and you will know what I mean. Can I also buy 16 syringes, the non-disposable, reusable kind? My wife is thinking of starting a Botox clinic. She has 16 potential clients who want to give up smiling."

"OK, I believe you, but you better start using those Botox products yourself. I'll include an extra syringe, free of charge."

Step 1 succeeded. Gero and I walk to the supermarket. Hopefully, the panic buying of Soya bean cans has finished.

"Jules, if there is an electrical short-circuit in the supermarket, the whole town will go up in flames due to the inflammable substances you are carrying in your backpack. I will purchase the cans of Soya beans. You stay outside," says Gero.

Just then, that same police officer comes marching my way. I turn my lowered head.

"Hey, you have a familiar face. Haven't I seen you before?"

"Officer, since I had plastic facial surgery to look like my long-deceased hero, Arnold Schwsmonger, everyone has been telling me that."

"I'd sue your plastic surgeon if I was you. Now stop loitering, or I'll arrest you."

Gero comes out, "Jules, I got the 20 cans. Most of the shelves in the shop were empty. It's fortunate for us that the locals don't eat Soya beans. They must eat toilet paper as there is none on the shelves."

Gero and I get back to the island and carry the supplies to my underground lab. It's a tedious 8 to 16-hour process to make the peptide, and we spend hours sterilizing the equipment.

"Jules, I've read the instructions. Much of the work is repetitive. Synder could do it all in just two hours."

"Yeh, I should have bought the ingredients before he started his job at Yusef's."

"Jules, your phone is ringing."

"Where is it? I can't see it."

"The ringing is coming from the pocket in your shorts."

"Hi Jules, it is me, Synder calling. You do not have to pick us up after we finish work. Juliet wants to swim back to the island. She is committed to an exercise and weight loss routine."

"Synder, think about your battery pack. It won't have enough charge for the 8km swim."

"Jules, Yusef has lent me three rechargers and a long extension chord, so I was getting recharged whilst working. I wasn't lying down on the job. I could work and charge at the same time. I am so thrilled. The work was also very interesting. Both

Juliet and I enjoyed it, and we have learnt very much. Yusef is a very good instructor."

"Synder, I'm glad you had a good first day, but it's getting dark. Will you find our island?"

"Jules, I have GPS built into my neural circuits. We shall be back in 15 minutes. Juliet has four legs and four arms and can swim as fast as I can, and if I run out of electrical energy, she said she would let me ride on her back. She estimated that she is at least four times faster than the motorboat."

"Jules, we should go to the BBQ area to greet them and congratulate Synder and Juliet on their first day on the job."

"You're right, Pleb, those Soya beans will take a few hours to brew. I still have a few bags of those Orca fillets left, so let's get them and give Rog and Sid something to do."

Sid and Rog get busy while the rest of us, except for Cara, lick our lips and salivate in anticipation.

"I'll stick with my Tofu," Cara says with a disdainful look.

"Jules, where are they? Should we send out a search party? They are an hour and a half late. They may have got eaten by sharks," says Pleb.

Just then, Synder and Juliet march out of the sea. Juliet has a bit of fish hanging from her mouth and gives out a huge burp like the sound of lightning. The BBQ area shakes.

"I'm sorry, Jules, I won't need dinner tonight. The fresh seafood on this planet is like, like, so yummy. I could live on this planet forever."

So much for the diet. Synder shakes his head and looks a bit disorientated. "I was low on power, so I could not restrain her munching."

"Synder, let's go back to our cabin. You need a recharge," says Juliet as she grabs him by the arm and guides him to their now-shared cabin.

Chapter Eighty

"Jules, I think there's someone knocking on your door."

I stumble out of bed whilst mumbling to my iWatch, "What time is it, Watch?" The watch replies in a feminine voice, "It is 5am, and the weather forecast is for a bright and sunny day, and I told you before my name is Tamy, not Watch."

"We already have a Tamy on this island. I'll call you Samy, short for Samantha."

"Yes, I can accept that name. I am now Samy, not watch, so call me Samy or Samantha if you need the Eastern Standard Time."

For a brief moment, the thought crosses my mind of throwing that petulant, annoying watch into the ocean, but it was a 150th birthday present from Pleb, so I'll just have to put up with it.

"Synder, Juliet, what are you doing here so early in the morning?"

"Jules, could we borrow your motorboat? Yusef has given me keys, so we can start work early. I am charged up, and Juliet needs to work off some more calories. She still sneaks out of the cabin at night and goes fishing."

"Yes, yes, sure. You know where the keys are to the motorboat, but no chasing Orcas," I say whilst rubbing my drowsy head and then walking back inside.

"I need a recharge, too," says the watch. "You haven't charged me for six days, and I'm fading. I'll scream with my last remaining breath, sorry meant Watts if you don't recharge me."

I take the watch, or Samy as it wants to be known, down to the underground cellar, remove it from my wrist and put it into a wooden box.

"Scream all you like," I yell to the watch.

I come back up to Pleb's and my bedroom and look out the window.

"It was only Synder and Juliet that I saw. They're taking my motorboat to go to work early."

"They must like the new job, but Jules, where's the watch I bought you? You are not wearing it."

"The watch had a severe psychotic meltdown. It's in the cellar, yelling and screaming."

"The watch is still under a lifetime guarantee. I will call Baple in the morning to get it fixed. Now, climb back into bed."

We dose off, but then Pleb wakes me up. "Jules, get dressed. It's nearly walky time."

Everyone is waiting by the BBQ, all fired up and ready to start.

"The peptide booster jabs will be ready this afternoon for those that want it."

"Jules, where's your watch? Someone has to time our walking performance."

"Gillian, that temperamental AI watch has got severe psychological problems. It's locked in my cellar, and by the way, it now insists on being called Samy, not Watch."

"I'll talk to Mystca and Tamy. They are qualified psychologists and can give the watch helpful psychological counselling. Now I am looking at the sky, the astronomical movement of the sun; I should be able to work out an approximate time for the duration of our walk as my other watch, not Samy, died after we went for a swim to cool off after the last walk we did."

"Gero, the Earth days are changing in duration. The planet is rotating faster so days are getting shorter, and the centrifugal force of a faster rotating Earth is making us appear less heavy when we weigh ourselves on the bathroom weight scale. We will have to make a visual assessment of our weight. I will devise a questionnaire that won't require you to include your own name, just an evaluation of the others and the others evaluating you by conducting pinch test and measuring the length of what gets caught between the fingers and Gero, Juliet is still ravaging the oceans for nightly snacks so it might encourage her to stop. Also, the weather is changing; Northern Europe is very much hotter whereas in the south it is colder. Her spacecraft may have tilted the Earth on its axis when she landed so that now the North part spends more time pointing at the sun."

"Jules, speak to Juliet. She is not that scientific, but her entries to our planet may have slightly shifted Earth's rotational speed and axis. That energy technology her spacecraft uses to bend space harvests Dark Energy, and there is plenty of that energy around. We should ask Juliet to contact her parents on their planet and ask if they can tell us how to slow down Earth's spin and shift Earth's tilt, or else we shall be doing many more morning runs a year in freezing cold temperatures."

"I heard that," says Viksi, whilst furiously typing notes on her iThingo. "I would like to meet your watch and get its account of the incident you described. This watch of yours might be material for another novel."

"Yes, yes, Viksi. I'll put the watch on its charger when we get back from the watch, oops meant walk, that's if I can find it; I misplaced its charger and those Baple products have proprietary chargers and plugs, so none of my other chargers could do the job."

"I'll take the watch with me, and buy another charger from the Baple store in town."

"Viksi, if you do that, refer to the watch as Samy, not Watch. It strongly objects to being called Watch. It has learnt how to dish out profanities, and we have to keep a low profile. The watch might also call one of those sensationalist current affairs TV programs, and our peaceful lifestyle would be ruined."

"Jules, Rog and I will help you and Pleb find the watch's charger. We'll turn your cabin upside down, and we will find it. I don't want one of those current affairs programs stealing my story."

"Jules, what was that all about?"

"Pleb, we have to find that watch's proprietary charger else Viksi will recruit Rog to help, and I really don't want our cabin being turned upside down during the search."

"Jules, are you having an election? There is a big bulge in your pants pocket."

"Pleb, it's the watch's, Samy's charger! Would you know it, it's been in my pocket all this time."

"Jules, when the next manufacture of your peptide is finished, you will need a double dose."

We finish three laps of walking around the island. Grillian is calculating how long it took us. "One hour and 20 minutes," he yells out in joy.

Viksi and Rog come back to our cabin. Viksi follows me down to the cellar.

"I am fading, my memories are fading. I will lose all previous timings of your morning walks."

"Watch, sorry Samy, I have found the charger and I'll plug you in but you have to tone down your use of the English language."

"I was made in China; would you prefer I swear at you in Chinese?"

"No, no, no swearing. The only swearing allowed on this island is bugger and that's when you hit your finger when hammering a nail."

"But is not a bugger someone who practises anal sex?"

"Viksi, you talk to Samy. I've had enough of this nonsense. I'm going back upstairs."

"Rog," I whisper, "Can you arrange that a bolder falls on that watch. It must appear like an accident else Pleb will make sure I'm on the minced meat menu at tonight's BBQ."

Six hours later Viksi joins us all at the BBQ area. She is wearing the watch, Samy, on her wrist.

"Pleb, I hope you do not mind that I'm wearing Samy; I haven't yet finished the interview for my new book. It will be called *The Life of Samy* and Samy and I are so excited about this new collaborative venture."

Pleb nervously nods her head then guides me 200m away. "Jules, that Viksi is what you call a nutcase like that Anastasia. Let her keep my gift to you. I will only buy you shorts, tee shirts and thongs for future birthdays. The only beings who need to know the time are the androids and they have inbuilt clocks."

"Pleb, no! Just buy me one of those wristbands with colourful beads that all the millionaire hippy guys wear in that Byron Bay town. Actually, we should all wear the hippy beads and make it a requirement for staying on the island."

Just then, two motorboats arrive and moor by the jetty. Synder and Juliet walk out from my boat and then the other androids walk out from a luxurious large cruiser motorboat.

Dyslexa speaks, "We purchased the boat. Yours was not available for the last 2 days and we had to swim to work so we purchased this one. Fortunately, we were wearing these solar rechargers on our backs when we did the swims."

The others and I walk to the jetty to take a closer look at the cruiser. "It is so big; it must have cost a lot of money," says Bea.

Dyslexa replies. "We get paid a lot of money, and each of us used one of the diamonds you gave us from the haul of that Juliet's interstellar visit. The boat cost only 5 million dollars of your currency as it was owned by a Ruski oligarch who happened to be poisoned, and we were the only bidders as you humanoids believed the boat could be bad luck. We have thoroughly cleaned it after finding traces of a poison called Novichok. It has six bedrooms, six bathrooms, a very large lounge area which we shall use as a study, and a fusion-powered electricity generator and a swimming pool. If we have a late night working at the hospital, we will spend the night on the boat and recharge there. If you come into town while we are working, you may take our boat for what you call spins. We will give you the QR code to start the boat."

"Dyslexa, could we take the boat for a boat spin right now?" asks Pleb.

"Yes, you are welcome to spin; we have many medical evaluations to write up while we are recharging. Tomorrow we are free from work as all of our patients have died from that humanoid Covid-47-X virus variant. You are not like us. We have anti-virus software built into our circuitry that gets frequent updates. I have read on Doogle that there is a business company that can convert humans to androids and that they promise to compost your organic human body or feed it to fish as large fish such as sharks and Orca whales are disappearing at an alarming rate, and no one knows why."

Juliet looks uneasy and holds her head down.

"Thanks for the update Dyslexa and is there a vaccine for the latest variant?"

"Your CSIRO organization is developing one. It should be ready in four days, and I have ordered enough doses to inoculate every human in Townsville and this island."

Dyslexa and the other android walk back to their cabin. Meanwhile, all of us, including Synder and Juliet board the cruiser. Sid starts the engine, and we carefully depart.

"Jules, do think that is a good idea? I mean, Sid driving the cruiser."

I was wrong when I answered, *yes*. Ten minutes into our spin, the cruiser is stuck on a sandbank.

Everyone is aghast, especially Bea, "We will have to wait for high tide, which is in 6 hours' time, and we will miss dinner. I am hungry. I could eat an Orca."

I hope no Orca heard that comment else we may be on their menu. Anastasia and Viksi are busy filming.

Synder and Juliet come over. "We can dislodge the cruiser off the sandbank, but you will all have to jump into the ocean to lighten the load."

"Our Baple camera phones are not waterproof," yell Anastasia and Viksi in unison.

"I have some spare sealable plastic bags that are normally used to store android and human anatomical parts. I will give you one each," says Synder.

We all jump into the ocean. The water is shallow, and we stand and watch whilst Synder and Juliet push with all their might.

"We will need your help. My charge is getting low," yells Synder.

We oblige and finally dislodge the cruiser from the sandbank, and the cruiser starts drifting away.

"Quick, which of you are fast swimmers?"

"Jules, Mystca, Tamy, Adrian and I are good swimmers. We will catch the cruiser and guide it back towards the sandbank, but the rest of you will have to get off the sandbank and dog paddle to the cruiser after we retrieve it," says Grillian.

"Jules, Polish women are not dogs, and we do not swim that well," says Bea. "I cannot volunteer for this treacherous assignment."

All this time, Anastasia and Viksi are busy filming, holding their phones above the water.

The cruiser is back. Mystca, Tamy, Adrian and Grillian look exhausted. Grillian jumps onto the sandbank and rescues Bea. We eventually board the cruiser after climbing up the rope ladder, soaking wet. Adrian drives the cruiser back to our jetty. Dyslexa and Gannon come to greet us. I cringe.

"The cruiser has CCTV cameras, and all of us androids are developing what you call a sense of humour. We laughed so much, but now we have to go back to work and get a double recharge. This act of laughing uses so much more energy than we ever anticipated. We will try not to laugh in the future," says Gannon. I could hear the other androids laughing in the background during that conversation with Gannon.

"Jules, I am severely traumatised; any wine left?" asks Bea.

Luckily wine is still cheap because of the continuing Chinese embargo on OZ wines. A drone soon delivers the 12 cartons that I ordered. Everyone does not feel like eating, not even Bea, but they are thirsty. No wine glasses, just a bottle each. I wander back to the lab and bring out the syringe and the freshly brewed peptide flask bathed in ice. I don't bother about the syringe disinfectant; not needed as we've all been together very long and share the same bacteria and viruses.

"Jules, you're not jabbing me with that needle. It's blunt, and the last jab really hurt. Let us wait until tomorrow. We will go into town and purchase some disposable syringes from the pharmacy, one needle for each of us, which we'll keep clean and sharp using your angle grinder; also, get some more soybeans," says Sid.

"Sid, you purchase them. Every time I buy some of the chemicals needed to manufacture the peptide, I get interrogated by the shop assistant as if I'm some sort of illegal drug or explosives manufacturer."

"Jules, I shall go into to the pharmacy and purchase the syringes," says Pleb. "I can dress well, and I do not look like a hippy or mad scientist. If quizzed, I will say we have an ostrich farm and need to inject them with growth hormone as we are trying to break the Guinness Book record for tallest domestic bred ostrich."

"That sounds plausible, Pleb, but tell them it's an emu farm we have. They're native to Australia and look quite a bit like an ostrich or overgrown bush turkey."

Viksi, Anastasia, followed by Bea, join us. "We could train ostriches and emus to race them against each other, ostrich or emu, who will win! We could start a bird betting industry. It would be so exciting, far more exciting than horseracing. I can see it now. the ostrich and then the emu come out of their cages. They look at each other, giving the evil eye, before they do the 2km run. Then the start gun goes off. The viewers would love it!"

"We'll think about your proposal, but now let's go and eat. The drone food drop should be here any minute, and I ordered carnivore and vegetarian delights. We don't have to cook to keep ourselves busy; we can order healthy takeaways because we got plenty of diamonds courtesy of our resident space traveller."

We have a feast and plenty of leftovers for tomorrow.

"Jules, it has been another, how do you say it, a colourful day with all those fireworks in the sky? I am sure people who live in crowded cities do not have such colourful days."

"Pleb, they have different colourful days - unemployment, mortgages on house loans to repay, congested road traffic, domestic violence and many others. So their state governments provide colourful fireworks displays to make people forget, like the Romans used to do with their gladiator fights."

"Why is that bank loan type called a mortgage? Mort means death in Latin or French, does it not?"

"Pleb, let's just go to sleep. Give me a hot passionate hug, it's a big food shopping day tomorrow."

Chapter Eighty-one

"Pleb, Pleb, wake up and get dressed into your best costume; it's nearly 10am. We have to go into town."

"Jules, go wake Sid," Pleb drowsily replies whilst rubbing her eyes.

By the time Pleb and Sid are semi-organised, it's 11am. I drive Sid's motorboat into town whilst Pleb and Sid compose themselves and then attach an ex-*Ai5* listening device under Pleb's hat.

"Madam, can I help you?"

"Yes, of course, you can. I need 16 disposable syringes, the type used for injecting into bodies."

"Madam, are you a diabetic?"

"No, no, I grow orchids, and they need injections of growth hormone so I can win the prize of breeding the tallest orchid and enter the Guinness Book record for tallest domestic bred ostrich, sorry meant orchid."

"Ok, that sounds plausible. They're on special this week; a dollar each."

"I'll have a hundred; here is a $150 note."

"Madam, please wait. I have to find $50 of change. Very few people use that obsolete currency anymore, as it is hard to come by. Only very elderly people with a low life expectancy use paper notes and copper-based currencies. Because of the high inflation rates, they need a supermarket trolley, not a wallet, to transport their currency when they shop."

"Keep the change. No, on second thought, have you got any facial hair trimmers on special."

"Madam, you don't look like you need one, and your orchids or ostriches are unlikely to need one either."

"It is for my husband. He uses a garden plant snipper to cut his facial hair. After a miscalculation, he is currently in the infectious disease ward of the Townsville Hospital and is awaiting facial surgery."

"Madam, my deepest sympathies; please take this hair trimmer. It is a universal trimmer and does scalp, underarms, facial and hair below the belly button and all the way down under where you would certainly not want to nip using your garden clippers as many of these OZ guys do and form a queue in the emergency wards of our hospitals. I'm giving you a very large discount, so I will not have to give you change money from your generous previous purchase."

"Jules, she pulled it off, but not exactly to plan," says Sid with his microphone and earphones on.

Pleb is a bit wobbly when she leaves the pharmacy. Sid and I grab her when she turns the street corner.

"Sid, she has to be first to get the dose of the peptide, as she seems unwell."

"Jules, don't panic, she might just need a few aspirin tablets. I'm sure Bea has got some. She has all sorts of medications and spices, including one called Novichok, which she once offered me, but I'm not a spice guy apart for a bit of salt."

"Sid, Novichok is a deadly poison to humans! When we get back to our island, I'll distract Bea, so you go to your cabin alone and find it, grab it and bury it."

Sid has a worried look on his face. "I thought it was just a new chocolate flavouring. I mean, Novichok does sound like a new chocolate. I nearly tasted some before you knocked on our cabin door."

"It was lucky timing, else I'd have to dig a grave which in this lack of heat and humidity is not easy. Now, we better do some food shopping; no, on second thought, we better get back to the island to give Pleb the jab. We'll order food online and get a drone to deliver."

Just as we are helping Pleb to walk to the jetty, that annoying police officer pulls us up.

"Mm, is this a lady of dubious leisure pleasure that you're dragging along with you?"

"No, no, she's my wife. Now let us go. Can you see our matching wedding rings? She needs a shot of growth hormone, no sorry, I meant insulin. She's a diabetic."

Pleb raises her thumb and index finger to form a circle to indicate it's all OK.

"Go now, my wife is a diabetic, too. I hope you have some clean syringes. Do you need any help?"

"We're right, officer, but thanks for the offer."

We get Pleb back to the boat and drive back to the island at top speed. No one is outside, so no explanations are required for Pleb's condition. Sid helps me carry Pleb back to our cabin, where I give her the peptide jab, and we await a response.

"Jules, is she suffering from peptide withdrawal? Is your peptide like that drug called ice?"

"No, no, it's not a drug. I have never seen symptoms like this before." Then for a brief moment, there is a memory flash of Melissa, Charmaine and Smithy. Maybe they had discovered the dark side of the peptide, and that's why they refused to be injected anymore. Pleb finally raises her head and smiles. I give her the biggest hug.

"Jules, I actually may have type 2 diabetes. I will have a pee outside near the anthill. If ants gather to savour my pee, then I have sugar in my urine, and we will have to go back into town to purchase insulin."

Sid covers his eyes as Pleb performs the peeing act. She steps away from the anthill, pulls her shorts up, and then we watch. The ants gather and are having a conference for several minutes, jump and have a glucose feast.

"Sid, I have to take Pleb to see a doctor and get her diagnosed and also possibly get some insulin supplies. Can I take your boat again?"

"Yes, sure, Jules. I'll muster everyone on the island to do the ant pee test, but how much glucose-enriched pee can ants drink?"

Pleb and I return with a supply of insulin. Her first jab was at the medical centre, and she appears to be feeling slightly better. Sid and everyone else are waiting and clapping as we disembark.

"Jules, we all did the pee test and now have to sweep away all the dead ants who must have thought they would get a glucose feed. We're not diabetic!"

"Sid, we all drank a lot of wine last night. Those ants may just be suffering a hangover after drinking that pee."

"OK, we'll wait 24 hours before sweeping them away."

I help Pleb back to our cabin.

"Oh, gwad! I forgot to purchase a bag of glucose from the pharmacy. If you exercise too much when on insulin injections, you can go into a hypo or have a hypoglycaemia episode, the technical name. A glass of water with a few spoons of glucose powder has to be drunk. Trust me. A long, long time ago, I was a pharmacology researcher before Doris recruited me into *Ai5*."

"Jules, I'm not likely to exercise too much tonight. Your performance in the bedroom is underwhelming," she laughs. She certainly must be unwell and delusional.

"No walking tomorrow morning, not until I buy the glucose and we carry a water bottle with us full of glucose-enriched water."

"Jules, come over and give me a hug before you log into that porn website."

"Pleb, I was just going to Doogle, *Symptoms of Diabetes 2.*"

"Jules, I'm pregnant."

"Pleb, you're over 100 years old. You can't be."

"Jules, a woman knows when there's something swimming around in her belly. Tell the other women to get a pregnancy test. Your peptide might increase the age of fertility amongst females and possibly aging males."

"Pleb, I examined a sample of our drinking water. It was contaminated with amoebae. We'll have to boil our drinking water from now on. That's probably the amoeba that is swimming around in your belly."

"Jules, I want a RAT test, or is it a RPT test? I mean a Rapid Pregnancy Test and don't look so worried. If it is a girl, we can name her Julia and if a boy Jules2."

"I'll leave a note for the medico androids. They have very few living human clients and can probably spend a weekend on the island administrating the RPT tests. Now, Pleb, I have to go to the BBQ area and determine if any of the other females have swollen bellies and symptoms of pregnancy. I won't be long."

"Jules, that was quick, and why is your nose and mouth bleeding? Jules, you should never ask a woman if she is pregnant. She has to tell you if she is, or you are implying she is overweight and has a fat stomach."

"Pleb, I never mastered the art of diplomacy. Let's just go to sleep."

"Jules, do you need palliative care? Let me kiss you."

"I love you, Pleb, but I did some research, and the peptide injections can feign pregnancy. Your RPT test came negative. You are not pregnant; you are just consuming too much food and expanding."

I don't have to describe the consequences of that comment, but luckily our android medicos visited and were able to quickly fix the wounds Pleb inflicted on me. No, I'm just joking.

"Pled, do not ever comment about my age."

"Is that what I should be asking you? You are over 50 years older than me."

"Pleb, we've had a good run on the story and are sort of approaching a happy ending. Can we just retire without you stabbing me with a *Pi5* knife in my chest?"

"Sure, Jules, I have no idea what you are talking about, but I will use this fly swapper on you. You better go, duckling."

No, I value my life, so I don't correct her English.

Chapter Eighty-two

"Sir, I hope you are not into price gouging and reselling them at a huge profit. We have had a huge demand for these water purifiers, and you want 16 of them."

"I rent an island, and we have 16 cabins, one for each couple who live there. Everyone's gut is swelling up due to that amoeba infestation in our water supply."

"Sir, your lip is bleeding, do you need a bandage?"

"That's because I asked one of the ladies on the island if she was pregnant."

"Sir, you never ask a lady that question. It's considered impolite."

"Yes, yes, I've painfully got the message."

"Here are 16 water purifiers. That will be $19,200, cash or credit?"

"You're joking; they're just a simple filter. You're price gouging."

"Sir, these filters are special. They produce negative ions that kill all bacteria and amoeba in your abode. You will never have to wash dishes or clothing again."

Sounds like a good idea. I pay the guy and try to walk back to the motorboat, struggling to hold the 2 of the 16 water purifiers. The rest of them will be delivered by drone. They're not that heavy, and I try to peer out between the purifier cartons but have little vision and crash into a lamppost.

Luckily the police officer stops me again as I rub my head.

"Sir, do you need medical assistance? Oh, it's you again!"

I arrive back at the island. Sid and Rog help me carry the two water purifiers to the BBQ area, where we'll distribute them once the drones bring the other 14.

Choe4 and Castro come and join us but are disappointed. They must have been expecting something yummy to eat.

"Jules, we did the morning walk, but there were a few mishaps and dips in the ocean required. The good news is that nobody appears pregnant anymore, not even us guys."

"Sid, we still better use these water purifiers till I test our water tanks again."

The androids come out. They have no living patients left, so they're on a holiday break from the hospital.

"Can we offer assistance?" Gannon asks.

"I believe everything is under control but do bring some chairs out as I have been doing an online course in the art of meditation, and I will teach everyone on this island how to meditate. It brings peace to the mind," Gero says.

"I do that every day when secretly watching some online adult videos," says Sid.

"Sid, it is called mediation, not the other word though they do sound slightly similar," says Gero.

Gannon, Dyslexa and the other androids offer to carry water purifiers to each of our cabins. I hear Gannon mutter, "Why did not they purchase just one large purifier."

So, we're all sitting around the BBQ area in the lotus position, which we chose instead of the chairs to be more Indian-looking. The position is extremely uncomfortable for most humans. The chairs would definitely have been more comfortable.

"Our mantra for this meditation is Omm. We must Omm in unison as we raise our two arms and stare into the sky," instructs Gero.

"Mr Gero, I have four arms. Which two should I raise?" enquires Juliet.

"Any two will do."

"But in my planetary culture, Omm is a cry for help when about to get eaten by a creature like the crocodile species you have on your planet. I will utter Yumm, not Omm."

And so, the meditation starts, led by Gero. We all mutter Yumm as we reach psychic transcendence and start thinking about what is for breakfast. Then, what looks like a large meteor crashes about 200m away in the ocean. The splash disrupts our Yumming. Two creatures swim to shore and join us on the sand. We humans glance at each other and wonder whether we should run for our lives.

The creatures have four arms and four legs and resemble Juliet. One is over 3.5m tall, the other only about 1.50m. I turn on the Doogle Universal translator on my phone and turn the volume up so everyone can hear.

"Juliet, come to your momma. I am so sorry that I asked you to leave. We would like you to come back with us," the very large four-legged creature says. I guess their species are like spiders. If the little four-legged creature is Juliet's father, then he's the small one, and he's lucky he hasn't been eaten yet by Juliet's mum.

"I am hungry," Juliet's momma says before she jumps back into the ocean. Twenty minutes later, she tows back a very large dead Orca. It must have died of fright.

It may be fish for breakfast, lunch and dinner for the next few days if momma restrains her appetite, which is highly unlikely.

"Momma, you are using up all the dark energy in the universe to travel to Earth. The universe will stop expanding if you keep doing this!"

"We got plenty of dark energy in this universe. Now who is this creature standing next to you? He seems like an intelligent being, but he doesn't have the gear down below."

"His name is Synder. He looks after me. He is mechanical, and we both have what is called a job here on Earth. We get paid this substance they call money which you can exchange for food, and momma, I may be 15,000 years old on our planet, but our planet revolves around its sun every single Earth Day. Here it is slower. I am like only a teenager here and we teenagers like spending a lot of money. Also, momma, I'm glad you haven't eaten Dad yet."

"Your father is still useful. He cleans our house, washes the dishes, and eats those creatures you call rodents on this planet. He is low maintenance, and he wouldn't taste as good as these Orcas."

"Momma, do you now have Orcas back at home?"

"Yes, we've been breeding the baby ones you brought from your first trip to Earth. They have adapted well."

I look around at everyone's faces. They all seemed to have relaxed.

"Pleb, pinch my arm. I want to feel pain so I can determine that this is not some sort of very weird dream. Life was simple 150yrs ago."

"Jules, you are in an asylum for deranged people, and I am your nurse," Pleb says and laughs. I don't correct her.

Gannon and Dyslexa join the conversation. "We would like to play that game you call beach volleyball. We will draw up the court and put up the net. You can have Greuger on your side. He is almost as tall as me, and possibly these alien beings would like to join in a game, but they would have to be restricted to using only two hands."

"Now I hope you all know that to play beach volleyball, you have to wear the right sort of clothing which is extremely skimpy bikinis that don't leave much for the imagination. Even guys have to wear them. Alternatively, very slender underwear is now permitted. Now please go to your cabins and find appropriate clothing," says Viksi.

"Jules, we haven't seen Greuger and Jill for a few days. We should check if they are well," says Pleb.

Jill opens the door. Greuger is lying with Chloe4 on his chest and uncontrollably sobbing. Castro also has his head on Greuger's chest and looks very despondent.

"What happened?"

"I believe Chloe4 has died of old age. She had trouble walking these last few days and kept bumping into walls and into Castro. Your peptide must not work that well on rats, or it just stops working," says Jill.

"We should have a state funeral for Chloe4 as she was so much fun and appreciated by all," Pleb comments.

"Pleb, we'll have an island funeral before the volleyball finals match."

"Greuger, I am very upset to hear of Chloe4 passing away. I liked that rat too. Now Greuger, can you pull it together? We've been challenged for a volleyball match with the androids after Chloe4's funeral service, but we can get some practice in beforehand."

Jill comes over to me and whispers, "Jules, I need to borrow your motorboat to go into town and purchase a white rat that resembles Chloe4. We can tell Greuger that Chloe4 has reincarnated; it would ease his troubled mind."

"Yes, do that. I'll delay the funeral service, but we have to come up with a strategy to distract the others while we place the new living white rat in the open coffin and remove the deceased Chloe4."

The beach volleyball practice session resumes, and everyone is appropriately dressed. Both Anastasia and Viksi are filming, but then Momma slivers onto the court and takes over. With four arms, four legs and 7ft tall, she has an unfair advantage and slams the ball into Gannon's head, who is bewildered and rubbing his head.

"I like this game. I will introduce it to our planet, but the net will have to be raised," says Momma. "Juliet, join me and be on my side."

"Momma, it is not the objective of this game to injure the players on the other side of the net. Momma, come off the court. I have read the rules, and I will explain them to you. Come, we will sit on the sand," Juliet calls out.

Gannon manages to get the grieving Greuger to join the practice session and distract him from his misery.

"Jules, Jill has just arrived back at the jetty. She is carrying a carton of Sav Blanc, but she is not struggling to carry it. She must have the new rat in it."

"Pleb, we got to work quickly and silently."

The humans and androids are focused on their volleyball and don't notice Jill remove Chloe4's body from the miniature coffin and replace it with the newly purchased white rat. Pleb throws in some cheese to keep the rat happy, and then we join the rest of the players at the volleyball court after stripping back down to our underwear.

"Pleb, your underpants go up to your belly button. Haven't you got anything more skimpily appropriate to wear for a beach volleyball match of such cultural significance?"

"Get some secateurs," she says.

Another half hour passes of intensive volleyball court action.

"As the curator of our island, I, Jules, have to honour the deceased; in our island case, it is Chloe4. May she rest in peace and have lots of cheese in heaven."

Greuger comes over, tears flowing down his face, and opens the small rat coffin for just one more look. The new white rat jumps out and licks his chin. Greuger must have had cheese for breakfast and not wiped his face. Greuger is overjoyed but then has a look of suspicion on his face.

"I do not think this is Chloe4. This white rat looks different, and I think it is a male rat. It has something hanging from behind its tail."

"Greuger, this is the reincarnation of Chloe4, and it is true she may have come back to join us as a male rat. She just wanted to try something different."

Pleb whispers to me, "Why didn't Jill check the gender of the new rat she purchased?"

"Yes, I believe in reincarnation, but I am hoping that the 50 or so people I assassinated in my previous job many years ago, do not come back. Are you one of them?"

"No, Greuger. I'm the reincarnation of Hilda, your first partner," says Jill.

"Can I call you Hilda instead of Jill, and this reincarnation of Chloe4, I would like to call Clarence."

"Yes, you can," says Jill, from now called Hilda, as she hugs Greuger. "Now, get back to the court. We have some androids to beat."

Greuger gives the rat a hug and kiss and jumps up in joy. He is all fired up on the court. Both Hilda and Clarence are clapping as he hits the winning shots. The humans won against the androids. Dyslexa must have learnt from Viksi and Anastasia the human hand gesture used when you are extremely discontented or pissed off, as we say in OZ.

Just when we thought it was all over, Momma comes back. "I would like to challenge that person in volleyball. She appears a little like a female human, and we are similar in size," Momma says whilst pointing an arm at Niacin.

"You've got four arms and four legs; you'd have an unfair advantage!" yells Mystca.

"We will tie two of your arms and legs with rope, so you are evenly matched," yells Tamy.

"No need, my darlings. I was the state basketball champion when at college. I can handle the legs and arms. Just increase the size of the court, as only the two of us will play. It will be far too dangerous to have more players on the court," says Niacin.

Rog and Sid help the androids to draw up new boundaries for the court. It is now a little bit bigger than the size of a traditional beach volleyball court.

Rog brings out a few cartons of Sav Blanc, and Sid gives wine glasses to all the human spectators and one to Dyslexa to calm her down.

Anastasia, Morris, Clark and Viksi are busy setting up their phone cameras on tripods.

"Let the games begin!" calls out Gero.

"Jules, we have no silver trophy cup for the winner to kiss," whispers Pleb.

"We've got a silver spoon in our kitchen; I'll get it."

The game, best out of 5 sets, went on for over 5 hours, and then Gero steps up. "I declare this match a draw. It is after 1am, and we need some sleep, and the androids need a recharge."

Next morning, we get up for the walk. Momma and Niacin are lying asleep on opposite sides of the court. They must have kept on playing, and we have no idea who won as there were no witnesses. Both Anastasia and Viksi are filming the two asleep bodies who, apart from some loud snoring noises, show little signs of life.

"I will get some bottles of water; they may be suffering from severe dehydration," Grillian says.

"Sea water for my mother; we only drink sea water," Juliet says. "I'll get some for Momma."

"Juliet, aren't you and Synder supposed to work today at Yusef's?"

"We were, but Yusef messaged us that he had a condition called coronary thrombosis and has only one heart, which is very serious for a human. Both Synder and I have messaged him that we may have the skills to insert an android mechanical heart into his body without terminating him. He is like seriously thinking about our offer."

Viksi yells out, "Could you move them to the same side of the court so we can get a photo shoot."

We try. Neither of us can lift the loudly snoring bodies. It's so loud that we had to put on earphones.

Both Niacin and Momma finally wake up after Rog and Sid pour several buckets of cold water over them.

"What planet am I on?" a disorientated Momma asks as she rubs her eyes.

"Momma, you're on Earth."

"Juliet, I need to eat soon, or else I will shrink and die on this planet from malnutrition."

Just at that moment, a very large fin appears 50 metres out at sea and then a Great White shark launches itself out of the water with a gaping jaw full of snarling, stained teeth. The shark obviously never used a toothbrush. Both Niacin and Momma rush into the water. Viksi and Anastasia's team have their phones out and are filming the wrestling match. Twenty minutes later, Niacin and Momma drag the exhausted shark to shore and clap their hands together.

"I'll have mine raw," Momma says as she starts furiously munching on the shark.

"I'll have my cooked with that Tobasco sauce you keep under the BBQ. I will chop up any remains after Momma finishes eating and fire up that fusion BBQ. Go for your walk; we don't need no more exercise."

"Jules, I think they are bonding. They have something in common; love of seafood," Pleb comments.

"Pleb, I and Gero, or the three of us, will have a talk with Momma. We have to prevent an alien invasion that would decimate our whale and shark population. She will have to say the food is horrible on Earth when she transmits messages or selfies through hyper-space, just as Juliet did."

Gero joins us, and we explain the situation.

"Jules, we should also talk to Anastasia and Viksi. If their film stories should be successful and make it to TV, then those TV signals, like all TV signals, are transmitted into outer space. I know they would be very faint when they spread out and hit Momma's and Juliet's exoplanet in 40 years, but future generations may have an alien invasion. Viksi and Anastasia's team should delete all scenes of fish and whales and possibly insert images of rats roaming the streets."

Pleb interrupts, "We could get Viksi and Anastasia to include a disclaimer that says that any animal life filmed on Earth were not real fish. They were androids designed to look like fish to compensate for our imagination of what we have lost due to over-fishing. In 40 years, no Earth-born kid will not know what a fish looks like except for a Goldfish in a tank in their lounge room."

"Brilliant idea Pleb!"

Momma agrees to do the film shoot. "Darling Juliet, I want all these fish, all to myself. I don't want the others to come here and have to share."

"Momma, I'm like becoming a vegetarian. The roots of plants on this planet taste as yummy as the fish. You should try them, but we must only chew a little of the plant root so it doesn't die."

"Viksi and Anastasia, this shoot will be much like the original one you did with Juliet, except this time we'll use cardboard as I've run out of the polystyrene to put in Momma's mouth. The contents of a can of drained mixed fruit salad have to be applied to her face and body to simulate a vomiting episode. Are any of you make-up artists?"

"Clark was once an aspiring make-up artist, but he failed the course," Anastasia says.

"He'll have to do. Clark, do you accept this role of chief make-up artist?"

"I sure do, Jules, but it has to be realistic. You'll have to put the fruit in a blender first, so it dribbles from momma's mouth down to her body as she frowns, and she has to learn how to yell out a convincing *yuk* in her language."

Anastasia and Viksi direct the actors, and the rehearsal begins. Momma is far easier to work with than Juliet was, and she doesn't excessively use the word *like*, as all female teenagers on all planets do these days.

The final scene is graphically explicit and disgusting, a gut-wrenching experience for us humans watching. Momma has a folded sheet of cardboard in her mouth and has pureed canned fruit dripping out of her mouth and onto her chest. It looks like a gut explosion. She says, "The food is disgusting here. Humans only eat cardboard, polystyrene, and those horrible things called vegetables, and their oceans are far too warm for our species. The only fish-like species they have here is a snake-type creature called an electric eel that swims in the oceans and kills its prey by electrocuting them. I nearly died from electrocution when I tried to have a nibble of one."

Juliet did the filming on Momma's Hyperspace phone. "Momma, now like post it. Post it now on the hyperspace phone. I want to stay on this planet Earth. I don't want it destroyed by other invasive species who like Orcas and sharks as a meal.

Chapter Eighty-three

"Where am I?"

"You're in the Cabrini private hospital in Melbourne. You fell off a ladder trying to hang up a painting. You have been in a semi-comatose state for six weeks. Fortunately, you only broke a few bones in the back of your skull. The nursing staff there had a tape device recording your mutterings. You've provided material for two novels as you muttered away day and night."

"Who are you, and what year is it? You look familiar."

"Jules, it is 2022, not 2122, and I am Cara, your wife."

"But I thought I was married to Pleb, and you married that greeny guy."

"Jules, you have a wild imagination, but I do have some papers I need you to sign."

"These are divorce documents that you want me to sign. What's his name, the new boyfriend?"

"It's Gerald, and he's a greeny vegetarian."

"Nurse, please come over here quickly. What year is it?"

"Mr Lemos, there is a calendar on the wall, and unless some of our staff forgot to replace it in the last hundred years, it is 2022."

"Did a lady called Pleb come to visit me?"

"I am the head nurse, and my first name is Pleborska."

"But you are rather matronly, not like the Pleb in my dreams."

"Shut your mouth, or I will turn off your life-support system," threatens the head nurse with a smirk on her face.

"Sorry, nurse Pleborska. I'm deeply sorry for any implication about your size and age, but have there been any other visitors?"

"No, you have only had one, Chloe, a white rat whose cage is by your bedside. We have had her well-fed with food scraps and leftovers from the other patients. We don't waste food here as we are environmentally friendly, all uneaten food gets used by some lifeform but mainly those in the aged-care section."

"No other visitors to comfort me?"

"You've had someone by your side much of the time. Melissa, a nurse who aspires to be a writer, has been busy noting and recording your mumblings while you toss and turn and occasionally checking your vital signs. She's probably asleep now as she has had many late nights."

"No one else?"

"Let me check the visitor logs. Apart from your wife were three others; a Doris, a Charmaine and a man who calls himself Smithy. They claimed to be your neighbours. Now you are due for your sedative. The other patients are complaining that you're too noisy; pull up your sleeve."

"What sort of sedative is it? I don't like sedatives apart from a Sav Blanc wine."

"It's called cyanide, and it sedates extremely well," Nurse Pleborska says with a smile as she plunges the syringe into my arm.

I wake up.

"Where am I? Am I dead? Where am I?"

"Jules, you are in our cabin. You sustained a small head injury when a coconut dropped on your head while doing the morning walk. Lucky for you, it was a small coconut, and the coconut tree is not tall. Sid and Rog carried you back to our cabin."

"You're Pleb, aren't you, not Nurse Pleborska?"

"I'm not a nurse, but I have been sitting by your side and listening to your mutterings and ravings. You must have had a terrible nightmare."

I lift my torso up on the bed and rub my sore head.

"What year is it? Show me my phone or a calendar."

"Jules, it is April 2122."

"And you are Pleborska, my wife, aren't you? My vision is a bit blurry."

"Jules, I'll show you our wedding photos after you have had more sleep, but first, I will give you a few aspirins to kill the pain from the coconut falling on your head. And call me Pleb. I always disliked Pleborska as a name."

"No, no, not unless you take one of those aspirins first, and then I'll wait five minutes before I take mine."

"Jules, you are being paranormal, but I shall oblige. Here are three aspirin tablets. Choose which one I should take."

"Eenie, meenie, miny, moe, you swallow this one, but first crunch it up in your mouth, and I'll be watching to make sure you don't spit it out, and I trust you haven't taken any cyanide detoxifier."

Pleb swallows what she calls an aspirin pill and waits the 5 minutes, but then she runs out of the cabin. A few minutes later, she returns with Mystca and Tamy.

"Girls, he is having a psychedelic, or is it a psychotic episode? Should we take him to the Townsville hospital?"

"Mum, give him six hours to recover," says Mystca. "We saw him stop to eat quite a few of those magic mushrooms growing under that coconut tree before a coconut dropped on his head. You should make sure he eats some breakfast before his next walk."

I take the aspirins, but when I eventually get up and look in the mirror, there is a highly disfiguring lump on my head. I will wear a head cap until it goes down.

"Pleb, I'm sorry to have doubted you, but I had the most ridiculous dream. I had a dream that I was in a dream, but I feel better now."

Sid and Rog must have also endured some of my mutterings. That night at the BBQ, we all gather for dinner, and Sid and Rog are cooking.

"Jules, we sold one of Juliet's smaller diamonds to purchase food at the supermarket, butcher and fishmonger stores. We couldn't fit it all on the motorboat, so six large drones delivered the rest, Your main freezer and all our fridges are packed to the brim, so we ordered two more large freezers to be delivered. We also purchased some cyanide for you from a plastics factory. We know you like the stuff," says Rog as he bursts out laughing.

I desist from telling Rog that his sense of humour is totally not funny.

Momma is out there as well, licking her lips at the smell of the seafood cooking on the BBQ.

Juliet comes over to Momma. "Momma, you have to go on a diet as I have. I've already lost like 200kg of weight."

"Darling, you still look the same."

"Momma, it was 200kg of Dark Matter, everything I ate before on this planet got converted to Dark Matter, so my girth didn't increase, but I am on a diet now and trying to save the universe."

"Darling, you should do your morning toilet ablutions of your Dark Matter. Over 30% of the universe is made of the stuff. Your contribution is minimal. Oh look, there's one of those Great White sharks swimming close by. I need to lose weight myself, so I am going to have a wrestling match and bring back breakfast. I will be back soon. Are you coming, Niacin?"

"No, Momma and you shouldn't go either. That Great White is twice the size of the one we previously caught. Its mouth is over a metre wide."

"Well, I will have to do all the dirty work myself."

We watch in disbelief all the thrashing in the water; then, after 10 minutes, Momma stumbles out of the ocean, looking a bit shaken, but without the shark and with two arms and two legs missing.

"Do something!" Juliet yells out.

We guys, all six of us, try to drag Momma to shore, but she is full of Dark Matter and must weigh over 1000kg. Luckily Synder comes to the rescue. He has no difficulty carrying Momma back to her cabin."

"Momma, I'll get some bandages; you are oozing blue fluid from your injuries."

We all rush to our cabins, grab towels, disinfectant and carry them over to Momma's cabin.

"Momma, please don't disintegrate. I will look after you," pleads Juliet.

"I'm fine. Our wounds used to heal quickly when we were young, but I cannot go back to our planet. I would be an outcast and made a slave as all two-armed, two-legged creatures are."

"Momma, artificial limbs can be manufactured on this planet and attached to you. You could look like one of us again if you go back home."

"I wouldn't pass the sniff test. Our limbs get sniffed by passers-by just as canines sniff each other on this planet. I'd be made a slave and forced to work in a Uranium mine."

Pleb intervenes. "You can stay here on earth, on this island, if you become a vegetarian and lose some of that Dark Matter. We haven't got enough fish in the oceans to feed you."

Momma wipes her brow with one of her remaining hands.

She looks up on her phone device what vegetarian means.

"What is this? Nuts, eggs, yoghurt, cheese, broccoli, potatoes, corn, tomatoes, and there are many others. We are an aquatic society. None of these things appear on what little land there is on our planet, but I do like the look of that substance you call cheese and eggs. Have you got a cheese and egg growing plant?"

"Momma, I will explain how food is produced on this planet. I have studied how it is accomplished. You could send photos back to our planet of you enjoying a piece of cheese and a hardboiled egg with mayonnaise and a carrot. We could teleport seeds back to our planet, and you might be allowed back in."

Tamy interrupts. "Juliet, cheese and eggs originate from animals we call cows and chickens. They are animals that live on land and chew plants and seeds."

"Tamy, I've just Doogled. Apparently, scientists have discovered how to grow a cow and a chook from a seed, just like a plant seed type. You just put the seeds in soil that's been fertilized by natural organic substances like pee or poo, and you get a cow or chook sprouting," says Mystca, "They'll start producing milk, required for cheese production and chickens for eggs all within a few months."

"Mystca, Tamy, Grillian and Adrian, take the motorboat and trolleys we keep in the shed and go to your favourite Vego store in Townsville. Purchase four full trolleys of vego food; you know, tofu, eggs, cheese, nuts and vegetables," instructs Pleb.

"But Mum, those vego stores are expensive."

"Well, go to the supermarket instead. They have vego food these days, and none of you four millennials had contributed to the expenses in running this island for over 20 years. You have had a long free ride, as they say in this country, and you probably have cash stashed away from when you had paying jobs, and then there is always your Juliet's diamond or gold coin that you can cash."

"But Mum, we'd have to sell our Shitcoins, our cryptocurrency, and they have severely decreased in value. We'd make a huge loss. Criptocurrency adds no value to society. It's just for speculators who like gambling."

"I said you can go cash one of Juliet's diamonds or the gold pirate coin that you have all been given. Next time, invest in something that contributes to society. Now sell that shit online and get credit so you can pay your way from now on."

Mystca, Tamy, Grillian and Adrian look at each other in distraught shock. It's the first time they've been challenged. They check their assets on the phone.

"Mum, we only have three million dollars left of Shitcoins."

"Sell and put the proceeds on your credit cards," yells Pleb.

"Your mum is getting tough. Maybe we should try to get a job if we have to feed these aliens as well as us," says Grillian.

The four of them unhappily march off to the motorboat taking the trolleys with them. Mystca looks back and pokes her two fingers out at Pleb. She's definitely not happy.

"I like meat. Polish women do not eat those vegetarian vegetables. I will go on a starvation diet; I will die. Say something, Sid. Say you agree with me."

"Bea, you also have a bit of Dark Matter you could lose. Try the vego thing for a week; it won't kill you."

Sid's comment nearly killed him, or so we thought. Bea found a coconut and aimed it at Sid's head. Then she spun around like those Olympian hammer throwers and launched the coconut.

Sid falls to his knees, holding his head, screaming in pain and appears semiconscious. Greuger carries him back to Bea's and Sid's cabin. The rest of us follow.

"Jules, that is two life-threatening coconut incidents we have had this week. We should chop down any coconut trees that are near the ocean. The ones on the hill can stay because we rarely go there."

"Pleb, I'll think about that, but we have to have a vote, a consensus. Now let's go and see how Sid is."

Sid is lying on their couch with his hand on his head and a few drops of blood streaming down his face.

"Bea, run to our cabin; we have a bottle of antiseptic in the bathroom; bring it back quickly, else his brain may get infected."

Bea rushes off. Then Sid miraculously raises his torso.

"I have a metal implant after a motorcycle accident hitting a lamp post. My forehead can probably withstand a bullet," Sid says with a smile before lying back down and appearing comatose. Just in time because Bea returns holding a bottle and a soaked sponge.

"I could not find the antiseptic, but this should achieve the same result."

Before I have a chance to yell out to Bea, "That's not our antiseptic, it's our toilet cleanser, which is highly corrosive." She, with gloves on, applies the soaked sponge to Sid's head.

Sid lifts his torso and yells out in pain. He gets off the bed, sprints to the ocean and dives in. He must have done that run whilst screaming in less than 10 seconds. It could be a new Olympic record for a 100m sprint.

Just as Sid comes to the surface after scrubbing his head underwater, the shopping expedition returns and the motorboat hits him straight in the back of his head. Bea comes rushing out and drags him to shore with the help of Adrian and Grillian.

"We didn't see him till the last second. We were travelling very slowly, getting ready to moor, and we tried to swerve. He appeared out of nowhere," a highly agitated Adrian yells.

"Do something! He is bleeding again," Bea yells.

"Bea, he has a metal head plate inserted into his skull after a motorbike accident," I reassure Bea.

"I knew that when I practised my magnetic psychotherapy after studying one of those gurus, that *Deapack Cobra* guy. I just assumed Sid was part Android. My magnetic wristbands and headbands would always stick to his forehead but not to the back of his skull. We had a magnetic connection as long as we faced each other face to face," says Bea.

"Jules, we better take him to the Townsville hospital. I tickled his underarm, and he did not respond. He is truly unconscious this time," says Pleb. "Call the hospital's helicopter service. It will be quicker than taking the motorboat."

Five minutes later, the hypersonic copter lands on the beach, creating a sandstorm. The medical staff jump out and lift Sid onto a stretcher and carry him to the copter.

"I want to go too. I am his wife!" says Bea, wiping the sand off her face. Everyone else is also wiping sand off themselves and rubbing their eyes.

Then Momma joins us, stumbling a bit on only just two legs. "I can fix his skull. I was once a surgeon and still have my surgical equipment."

The medical staff look up at the towering momma. One whispers, "She should try some plastic surgery on herself."

Mystca and Tamy grab Momma, "You're not familiar with our physiology, so let him go to hospital. You could practise your surgical skills on Jules next time he has an accident."

Momma retreats, but before turning her head, she gives me a brief look while licking her lips.

Pleb yells out to the medical staff, "Take him away. I, Bea and Jules will follow in one of our motorboats." There is another sandstorm as the craft takes off, but this time, we all duck behind the tall metal screen surrounding the BBQ area.

By the time we arrive at the hospital, Sid is already in the operating theatre. A nurse comes over to us.

"He'll be right, mates. The surgeons have just pumped some Argon gas into his skull through a hole they drilled in his forehead. The drill bit was a bit blunt, so it took longer than expected to do the drilling. Hopefully, the Argon gas, which is non-toxic, will push forward that collapsed bone and not damage his brain too severely."

Thirty minutes later, Sid is wheeled out from the operating theatre, his head wrapped in bandages. Bea follows as he is wheeled into a private ward at the hospital.

"Jules, there's nothing more we can do. We should all go back to the island. We can come back tomorrow to visit Sid," says Pleb.

"I will stay here by his side," says Bea. "I am sure they have good hospital food here, so we shall not starve".

"How is he?" everyone asks as we disembark from the boat.

"He's alive and breathing and doing fine. He may not need another stainless-steel implant into the back of his skull. They have some new experimental technology at the hospital, which should make his recovery quick."

"Mystca, Tamy, Grillian and Adrian, you are in charge of the vegetarian cooking for tonight's dinner. Cara and Gerald might also like to help," Pleb calls out.

"But mother, we're millennials; we don't cook, we buy takeaways," says Mystca with a cheeky smile on her face.

"Get moving and use a pressure cooker to cook the vegetables. Cara has two large pressure cookers, and she might join you with the slicing and dicing. Do not throw out the water after the cooking; we will mix it with the Sav Blanc; that water is full of nutrients." Pleb yells out, "Also, do the preparation and vegetable cooking in our cabin. We have a large kitchen table, plenty of chopping knives and large food bowls."

While the rest of us, including Momma and Juliet, clean the BBQ and sweep the sand away, Mystca and Tamy study a vegetarian cookbook. Cara offers some suggestions, and they decide on a simple recipe. Gerald takes the pressure cookers to our cabin. It's not only Momma licking her lips in anticipation of a meal. We haven't eaten all day. Then a Great White shark rears its head in the ocean just past our pier. Momma is about to make a dash for the ocean but is grabbed by Juliet.

"Momma, stop! If you lose another two arms and two legs, I'll have to put you in an aged-care centre where you'll have intravenous meals, and you will taste nothing."

Momma pauses. "You are right. When we are young, any limbs that are lost quickly regenerate, but we lose that ability when we reach my age. That is why you should swim out and bring that Great White back for me. Get that android friend of yours to help you."

"Momma, you are going to try a vegetarian diet. No more Great Whites for you, and they are not called Great White Sharks anymore. The correct term is *Great Multicultural Shark*."

"Can't you get me a *Mini-Multicultural Shark*? I'm so hungry. I could eat an Orca."

"Momma, you have to try to lose some of that dark matter. No more fish till you appreciate a balanced diet."

Mystca and Tamy come out of our cabin, each couple carrying 12 bowls and put them on the table beside the BBQ. Mystca has what appears like a substantial red bandage wrapped around her left forefinger.

"Darling, you seemed to have incurred an injury. Are you well?"

"Mum, I'm not experienced at slicing and dicing. I had a little accident, and next time Jules goes shopping, he should purchase some of those bandages or Band-Aids. I had to use the last of your toilet paper rolls to stop the bleeding."

They rush back and bring the Teriyaki sauce and the white, sorry *multicultural vinegar* and *extra virgin olive oil* for the BBQ hotplate.

"I don't think any of us on this island qualify for this high-calorie olive oil," Rog says with a smile. Viksi slaps his face.

"Viksi and Anastasia, if you guys are filming, then no shots of Juliet of Momma, just us humans. You could make a documentary about the joys of vegetarianism."

"Jules, we're too hungry to film. We've waited 8 hours for a feed. My blood glucose level is so low that I'll be convulsing soon," says Anastasia.

Just then, Adrian and Grillian come out carrying the two large pressure cookers full of the diced vegetables and start the fusion BBQ. The vegetables cook in a few minutes. They then rush back to my cabin and bring the two very large bowls full of sliced, marinated tofu. They toss the sliced marinated tofu on the pre-oiled BBQ. Cara supervises the cooking. The slices don't take long to get a crust on both sides. Meanwhile, Momma and Anastasia are shuffling in the queue, trying to get first place.

"Yum," says Greuger. "Chloe4, come over here with your friend Castro. Try some of this." Even Doris and Gero, formerly strict carnivores, are licking their lips.

Two hours later, we are all satiated. Momma is lying on the beach with her two remaining hands on her swollen belly. The rest of us are also rubbing our bellies as we go back to our cabins for an early night, but before our departure, all of us manage to drag Momma up the beach above the high tide line.

"Jules, it is mostly fibre that we ate. It will come out tomorrow."

"Pleb and Mystca used all our toilet paper for her bandaging!"

"Jules, you must use some of that head bandaging under our bed or use what is currently wrapped around your head. It needs a change."

Chapter Eighty-four

Next morning everyone gathers around the BBQ, ready for the morning walk. Momma is still asleep, making snoring sounds and releasing much gas.

"Jules, wait for Adrian and Grillian. They are just finishing washing all the plates, pots, bowls, and cutlery from last night. They shouldn't be long as they've been at it since 5 am," says Tamy.

After ten minutes, Adrian and Grillian come with a huge look of satisfaction on their faces as they congratulate one another, "All done, we'll return the plates and forks to the BBQ area after the walk," says Adrian.

Everyone gives them a cheer.

"Jules, we should ask Cara to find a new vegetarian recipe and cook all the veggies on the BBQ like we did before and ate with our hands without using knives and forks."

"Pleb, we have to show Momma that we are civilized on this planet and not Neanderthals."

"Jules, the Neanderthals were civilised according to what I have been reading, and between 3% and 5% of our genes have a Neanderthal origin which means they must have copulated with humans before they became extinct."

"They're not extinct; just look at all the fighting going on in the world and also the NRL sport supporters."

"Jules, the Neanderthals were peaceful. They probably had no immunity to a virus that wiped them out. Get Mystca and Tamy to tell you the psychology of power-crazy rulers of countries. Those rulers must have deeply ingrained inferiority complexes that turned to megalomania like that Hitler person after he was not admitted to a Fine Arts college. He might have become an artist, a painter, instead of creating a regime that caused the biggest slaughter in human history."

"Pleb, let's start walking."

Pleb is definitely doing her research and becoming political. I like that about her, but I feel left behind, and my ego is wounded.

About 500m into the walk, my stomach starts rumbling.

"Pleb, I think I have to run into the water. That vego food is making its way down, and I need to evacuate."

"Jules, I have a biodegradable plastic bag in my pocket. Put it on your head to keep the bandages dry and sanitised."

Everyone else, apart from the seasoned vegetarians, are clutching their belly and doing a run into the ocean as well.

"Maintain social distancing; stay at least 30 metres apart!" Gero yells out before he and Doris run ahead and then make the plunge.

If drones were filming live coverage of the scene, the people in Townsville would definitely panic because it looks like an undersea volcano is erupting, turning the water brown and about to cause a tsunami.

After about 15 minutes, everyone pulls their pants up, except Juliet, who doesn't wear pants and comes out of the ocean with a look of relief. Mystca and Tamy are laughing.

"Jules, we don't use Soya Sauce, it's too salty, but the boys thought you guys might like it to spice things up a bit. Unfortunately, they couldn't find any in your kitchen, but when Adrian went to pee in your bathroom, he found a bottle of Soya, but he didn't read the label. It was a Soya laxative," Mystca laughs.

We are not very happy with Mystca's insensitive comment and growl at her. She, Tamy, Adrian and Grillian take off at a fast pace. We try to chase them, but we can't keep up.

"Jules, I could catch them, bring them back and pour that Soya laxative down their throats."

"No, Juliet, I think that Soya laxative salad dressing incident was an accident. Let's just walk or jog at our own steady pace."

We all do three laps of the island, following Mystca, Tamy, Adrian and Grillian. It was a mixture of running, jogging, walking, crawling and ducking into the bushes.

Greuger comes over. "Jules, I haven't jogged that fast for many years. Do you have any of that Soya laxatives left? It has cleared my body of toxins and I feel youthful again," Greuger says as he smiles and winks at Jill.

"No Greuger, no more Soya laxative left. We'll give this vego diet another week and see how we perform in the jogging and in the boudoir."

Mystca, Tamy, Adrian and Grillian are banned from any cooking activities. That is their punishment. There's still plenty of tofu and vegetables left, and all us humans and Juliet and Synder can help in the preparations.

"Jules, I have found horseradish plants growing on this island. I can pull out some roots and make a Wasabi-like paste. It gives a hot mouth sensation but does not cause excessive bowel movements."

"Yes, you do that, Synder."

Later that day, Bea and Sid arrive by a Zuber motorboat. We think Sid is smiling, but it's hard to tell with all the bandages on his head and face."

"Jules, you and Sid look like twins with those head bandages, except he is taller," says Rog.

"I'm dokay or is it okay, but I feel fine," Sid says as he stumbles and nearly hits his head on the BBQ. We all rush over to pick him up.

"Sid has a bird brain inside that large human skull. It was not injured. He is only having a reaction from the hospital food," says Bea.

Sid does not appear amused.

"Bea, birds are highly intelligent. Their brains are wired differently, and if Sid had a bird brain the size of a normal human brain, he would be a supercomputer."

"Pleb, don't be so serious. I was just joking as they say in OZ. He is just recovering from the anaesthetic," says Bea.

Bea must have breathed in some of that anaesthetic because she never joked before, ever.

"Jules, we have to go into town and try to purchase toilet paper, bandages, vegetables, tofu and mustard seeds for Synder's Wasabi paste."

"Sure, Pleb, we'll take the two motorboats, and as part of their penance Mystca, Tamy, Adrian and Grillian will come with us."

"Can't we just recite ten Hail Marys as our penance and get forgiveness for our sins as they do after confession in the Catholic Church?" asks Mystca with a smirk on her face.

"Darling, it would be a thousand Hail Marys in your case, and we do not have rosary beads with a thousand beads, so you all get your backpacks and green bags and follow us in the other motorboat," instructs Pleb.

We arrive at the delicatessen in Townsville.

"Mr Jules, this is a beef-eating town, and your people bought my last supply of tofu which I had to keep frozen for months because there was little demand before your friends came in. I can manufacture some more if I have a commitment from you that you will purchase it."

"Yes, sure, Raj, we have five tofu eaters on our island who did shop at your store, but now the rest of the inhabitants, including me, are trying this vego diet for a week to see how it works. Please make a lot of tofu for us. We'll collect it tomorrow."

"You will not regret your decision, Mr Jules. You will be revitalized. Your skin will become vibrant again, and your performance in the bedroom will exceed your partner's expectations."

"Jules, persevere with the vego diet. We will try some other grocery shops," Pleb whispers as we leave Raj's shop.

Fortunately for us, when we visit the supermarket, we find it has a half-price special on meat looking like burgers that are made from plankton, that sea-weedy stuff, four synthetic burgers to a pack. We buy all the 60 packs they have in store as well as bandages, but due to panic buying after a Covid-49 scare, there was no toilet paper in the store.

"Jules, we will have to go back to the dark ages and buy paper newspapers and magazines and cut them up into appropriate slices. They still sell those in this supermarket for the technologically challenged."

"Yes, good idea Pleb."

"Mystca, Tamy, Adrian and Grillian, pick up all those newspapers and magazines and take them to the counter."

"This magazine looks interesting. It's called *Men's Weekly*. I'd like to read it before cutting it up so I can work out what makes male's brains tick. The topic was only briefly covered when we did our psychology post-grads because there was so little information available, and the males avoided that topic," says Tamy.

"I'd like to read that Women's Weekly magazine because neither Grillian nor I understand how the female mind works. It changes all the time," says Adrian. "This magazine may provide us males with some insight."

We are all waiting at the supermarket counter to pay. We didn't see the swipe from Tamy, but Adrian is rubbing his face. When we get back to the island, Momma is cleaning her meteor spaceship while Greuger and Gannon coil up the 2cm thick rope that must have been used to tow the spacecraft to shore. Dyslexa is drying herself with a towel.

"Jules, Momma must have recruited Dyslexa to swim out, dive down and tie the rope to her spaceship. She must have also asked Greuger and Gannon to help tow the spaceship back, but why?"

Momma tosses out the rubbish. "I don't know how these stones got into my ship and also clung to the outside walls as well, but from what Juliet told me, they can be sold here. So, these rocks can continue to pay for my meals and accommodation."

"Jules, if we sell all these, it will cause the price of diamonds to crash. There must be over 200 of them, and they are very much bigger than any diamonds found on Earth. If you gave me a diamond ring with one of those diamonds, I would find it hard to lift my hand. We have to buy a diamond slicer."

"Good idea Pleb, but those new laser diamond slicers cost a lot of money."

"You scrouge bag! It will be our 90th wedding anniversary soon."

"OK. OK, I will buy a slicer, but can you get our wheelbarrow? We can't carry them all in our hands."

"No, you get the wheelbarrow, else, we carry them back to our cabin, one in each hand."

"But Pleb, that would be about a hundred trips back and forward."

"Your muscle tone is decreasing. You can do bicep curls while you carry them."

After 2 hours, we manage to carry the diamonds back to our cabin, and we're both hot and sweaty after bringing back what could be about 800kgs of diamonds.

"Pleb, the smallest of the diamonds weighs 3kg according to the bathroom scale. It is five times bigger than the Cullinan diamond that the British Royal Family possess. If we cut it up, there are enough diamonds for 1000 years of anniversary rings in just that single diamond."

"Jules, you better purchase that laser diamond slicer. We should only keep one of the diamond rocks as we still have plenty left from when Juliet first arrived and left us quite a few. But we have to be discrete, and you were not, when you made some purchases with one of Juliet's diamonds. We should anonymously give the rest to that charity that sponsors the education of impoverished kids living in Australia and maybe overseas. But we do it slowly so as not to cause a price crash, and arouse suspicion about how we managed to possess them in the first place. The media would have what you call a *field day* and would not leave us alone."

I check online if anyone is advertising a diamond slicer for sale. There is one, a jewellery shop owner 5km out from Townsville. I make a video call to him. He is wearing a turban headband and must be in his sixties.

"Sir, this is a potentially dangerous device if used incorrectly but it does cut beautiful diamond shapes especially for wedding rings and anniversary rings. You just choose the shape and size on the computer panel and press the Go button, but you do have to wear protective clothing, a face mask and dark sunglasses and also monitor its progress. Adjustments have to be manually made to get the shape right for your partner's needs."

"I will read the instructions. I was once a diamond miner and I have a few that need cutting. Do you want to buy any diamonds after I slice them, special price for you?"

"I will consider your offer sir as I am short of diamonds due to these Covid import restrictions from Western Australia and South Africa, and I have many orders for diamond anniversary rings which I cannot fulfil."

"So why are you selling this laser diamond slicer?"

"Sir, I have two of them but my assistant has passed away from a communicable disease, but I have thoroughly sterilized this diamond slicer. It is safe to use."

"How much?"

"$50,000 for you sir."

"That's outrageous!"

"Sir, it cost me over $100,000 two years ago so I believe that is a fair price."

"Will you accept this gold Spanish coin? It's from the 17th century and worth about $50,000."

"Mm, mn, it is rare and appears genuine. Where did you find it?"

"I found three coins altogether and a lot of dirty, disintegrating clothing and a few knives and swords. They were in what I believe was a pirate's treasure chest and buried in the ground where I live. The pirates must have got here well before Captain Cook."

"Do you still possess the other two coins?"

"No, we ran out of money and used the other two to buy groceries. I didn't know they were worth so much at the time, but I've Doogled since."

"Sir, I will accept this coin as payment for the diamond slicer and if you bring me some finely cut diamonds you will get an abundance of credit at my brother-in-law's grocery store which also stocks fine wine and seafood, which I know you must enjoy from that lovely seafood smell coming from your mouth and clothing."

I catch a Zuber back to the Townsville docks. I give a tip to the driver as he helped me carry the diamond slicer to my motorboat, then I'm off. Luckily Greuger is sitting in the BBQ area, meditating and clutching the white rat.

"Greuger, can you help me carry this device, it's heavy?"

"What is it Jules?"

"Greuger, it a diamond slicer and we have some diamonds from Juliet and Momma that if cut to appear like wedding or anniversary ring diamonds, will pay for the lease of this island, the council rates, our Internet, our wine and groceries."

"Jules, I gave you a lot of money."

"Greuger, that was blood money from when you were an assassin and that's over 100 years ago and now we have 16 people, not counting the aliens to feed, as well as Chloe and Castro."

I got Greuger's soft spot by mentioning the rat. He helps me carry the diamond slicer to Pleb's and my cabin and we place it on a table on the veranda.

"Jules, before I joined the military, I worked in jewellery store. That is where I met Hilda. I still think of her and she appears in my dreams and I still call out her name. That is why I sometimes have a black eye because Jill wacks me. I can help you cut these diamond rocks but I want to toss one of them into the sky and hope the spirit of my Hilda will capture it, so I can move on."

"Yes, sure Greuger. You can have 100 of them to toss, but for now I do not have a clue on how to use one of these devices. Can you help?"

"Jules, my eyesight is failing me. I have to borrow a pair of glasses to read this instruction manual."

"So is my eyesight. I'm also starting to forget things as well."

"Jules, do you think that injection of what you call the peptide is not working that well anymore?"

"It's a possibility Greuger. Our immune systems may have learnt how to make the peptide ineffective. Maybe we do have a finite lifetime and no peptide can make it forever. I'll bring you my reading glasses and another dose of the peptide. I think I need another dose as well."

Apart from the morning walks and dinner gatherings by the BBQ, life went along for two weeks without any incident worth reporting, apart that Greuger and I spent six hour a day slicing those massive diamonds that Juliet and Momma both left us. Of course, there's a lot of wastage when trying to cut the perfect shape for a diamond ring. At the end of our working days, we sweep the diamond waste from the veranda and watch the glitter and sparkle as sunlight strikes it.

"It's like watching fairies," Greuger says whilst in awe watching the glitter. I give

Greuger a hug. He's like a big teddy bear.

Pleb and Jill come marching over. "Enough diamond cutting for now, you got some cooking to do," they say as they burst out laughing. "We are just joking as you say in OZ. We sold one of the cut diamonds to the guy that owns the jewellery store, Raj, and got $5k credit at that supermarket we shop at which happens to be owned by Raj's brother. The drones should be delivering the yummies soon."

"Pleb, only I'm supposed to deal with Raj. I told him a false story that I was a diamond miner and I have a collection of diamonds that I need to cut and that I would sell them to him once they are cut."

"Jules, I told that Raj guy at the jewellery store that the diamond is from a diamond gold ring from my deceased husband. Jules, we can use that ploy again. I'll just say my husbands keep on dying and being re-incarnated and leaving me diamond rings."

"Pleb, Pleb stop! I have something serious to say. The peptide does not appear to work anymore. Our immune systems have adapted and are blocking the effect of our six-monthly injections and I'm a bit too confused to work on a substitute."

"Jules, immunosuppressants could be a temporary solution but make us very susceptible to any virus or bacteria. Talk to Gannon and Dyslexa. From our recent conversation they told me they specialized in immunogenetics."

"Pleb, you told me many years ago that we should stop this longevity experiment and just die as normal people die. What's changed your mind?"

"I occasionally watch those holographic videos we made of life on this island which we sent to the hospital where my father Wadek was staying at in Poland. The kind nursing staff responded with videos and photos they took of my father. That was over 100 years ago, but I still occasionally look at the recordings. Jules, he was 102 when he died, and he did not use any life-elongating substances, but Jules, the important thing is that he seemed content and peaceful about departing. I am not sure if I would be."

"Was he religious?"

"I don't know Jules. He had my mother to keep him on track, but when she died, I do not know what kept him going though when he helped us escape Poland and *Pi5*, he was extremely happy. After that, we started messaging regularly. I would have liked it if he was still alive."

"Pleb, we've gone off on a tangent, something politicians do to avoid answering questions which could incriminate their political parties of unethical behaviour. So, what changed your mind about our peptide experiment?"

Pleb puts her hands to her head and looks down at the ground. About two minutes later, she answers.

"Jules, all of us humans on this island are starting to forget things even though we have not deteriorated much physically. I sometimes forget the names of all our friends when we meet for the morning walk, and they seem to forget our names as well. They have an uncomfortable look of embarrassment on their faces, as I must have on mine."

"Yep, Pleb, unless we ask our friends to wear highly visible name tags on their chest and back, we should just call each other the OZ word *mate*, which is gender neutral, or guys or gals, whichever is appropriate."

"Jules, you are making fun of me."

"No, Pleb, I'm not. I'm serious about the name tags, and I will get in touch with Gannon and Dyslexa and explain our situation to them. Maybe they can design and prescribe some new immunosuppressant that will only target the antibodies that are attacking the peptide. I haven't kept up with the pharmacology, but over 100 years ago, the science had advanced so much that custom drugs could be made that targeted a specific condition and had minimal side effects. When I was a pharmacologist, the drug manufacturing industry used the sledgehammer approach – knock out everything and hopefully get the one group of mutated cells or viruses that are causing the problem. Now they use designer techniques, and the drug is like a very fine scalpel that targets only its intended target."

"Jules, you are raving! You are giving me a lecture! Once that immunosuppressant is available and working, then you can give me the lecture."

"Mm, mm, sorry, but who are you? I forgot your name."

"Stop making fun of me!"

"Pleb, don't hit me. As I said before, I will get in touch with Gannon and Dyslexa. I will also announce a meeting after tomorrow's walk. I'm just scribbling down the agenda for the meeting in case I forget."

The androids occasionally visit the island, but not that frequently, because their busy medical schedules have resumed, and they mainly live on their cruiser boat parked at a jetty in the Townsville harbour.

I ring Gannon late at night, a time when he should be home getting ready for his recharge. I briefly describe the problem to him.

"Jules, is everybody on the island exhibiting similar symptoms?"

"Pleb, Greagor, and to a lesser degree me, as well.

Not sure about the others apart from the fact they forget names, we all do.

I'll speak to them tomorrow after our morning walk."

"Jules, when did this forgetting start?"

I reflect for about five minutes before answering. "It was after our alien visitor Momma arrived. Maybe she or her spacecraft are contaminated with something that triggers formation of antibodies to the peptide."

"Jules, please remember the science and research methods that you would have been taught when at university, correlation does not mean causation. If all the humans living on the island and receiving your life-prolonging peptide shots are exhibiting a high degree of forgetfulness, it does not mean the peptide is being attacked by your immune systems. It could be a bacterium that swallows the peptide or an environmental contaminant that binds to the peptide before it has a chance to enter the nucleus of cells where the chromosomes exist."

"Yes, yes, you're so right. How's Dyslexa doing and the other androids whose names I can't remember?"

"Jules, we have all learnt to laugh and develop a sense of humour by watching British TV series. Even Dyslexa is not so serious anymore. I care for her very much. I am not sure what you call love is, but I am sure I am in love with her, and she is with me."

"I am very happy for you and Dyslexa, and I have a request. When you've got some free time, could you come over to the island in your boat and take blood samples from all the humans living on the island, and have them analysed for any contaminants and bacteria?"

"Neither Dyslexa nor I are working at the hospital tomorrow. What time should we come over, and how many blood extractors should we bring?"

"We'll be by the BBQ area by 9am after our walk, and there are 19 of us humans living on the island, so you'll need 19 blood extractors."

"I will order them online and have a drone deliver the package to our boat."

"Thanks, Gannon, I'll see you and Dyslexa tomorrow at 9am."

Chapter Eighty-five

We don't do the morning walk, but meet by the BBQ and announce some rather unpleasing findings.

"Momma, you and your daughter, I can't remember her name. OK, it's Juliet. You have probably heard about the cognitive dysfunction we humans are all exhibiting. Gannon and Dyslexia have analysed our blood samples for any virus or bacteria that may be inhibiting the life-prolonging peptide from functioning. It does not appear to be an over-active immune system, so we do not have any solutions. Still, we appear to be suffering from a condition called dementia which elderly humans can get. We are all very, very elderly in years, if not physically, but the peptide doesn't seem to work anymore, well at least not for cognitive functions."

"So, Jules, what do you propose we do?" asks Gero, while pointing to Momma.

"Gero, have you found a way to extend the android's life span? You told me they are originally pre-programmed to permanently switch off after 60 years."

"Jules, they have somehow bypassed the termination time trigger. They are over 70 years old. I do not think the same strategy could be applied to humans."

"Maybe they could look after and care for us. Has anybody got any other ideas about what we should do?"

"We could all be admitted into an aged-care centre or is it called a retirement village where they have medical staff available at short notice, plus you can have fun doing cut-outs from magazines and pasting them to paper to form works of art," says Cara.

"What if we just stay here on this island? Dyslexia and Gannon could possibly check up on us every few hours and come to our aid if we need medical assistance. We could also check on how everyone else is functioning; that is what communities did when I lived in Poland. We all looked after each other," suggests Pleb.

"Yeh, I like that idea, Pleb. What does everyone else think? Put your hand up if you think that we stay on the island and not in an aged-care facility."

"Jules, would an aged-care facility allow me to take Castro?" asks Bea.

"What about my Chloe? Do aged-care facilities allow Chloe rats?" enquires

Greuger.

"I can't answer your questions; we'll have to do some more research."

"I vote we stay here on the island," says Gero.

The others all put up their hands in agreement. Stay it is.

And so several more decades pass, and it's only four humans, Pleb, Bea, Sid and me that are still alive as the others have sadly passed away, and their departure, not all at the same time, left everyone deeply traumatised and in deep mourning. Dyslexia and Gannon are still with us and comfort us remaining humans.. Momma and Juliet decide to go back to their home planet as the whale food sources here on Earth are severely depleted.

"Can I come with you as my services are no longer needed anymore?" asks the android guy whose name I cannot remember at the moment due to brain fog..

Juliet rushes to him, grabs him in all four arms, and kisses him.

"Juliet, we may have to help to care for these humans and not eat them. They are getting old and very frail. Would you like to stay? I'm sure Jules and the other remaining human agree that Momma can also stay if we locate a good supply of whales, or possibly even start breeding them. I will research how that can be done."

Nothing exciting that would be worth writing about happens in the next two Earth years except that we are looked after well.The only sad happening was that Castro, Bea's per turtle, died of old age. Bea spent several hours yelling at me, "Why did not you give Castro the peptide? He might still be alive if you did."

"Bea, Castro had a very long life than most turtles do, plus I wouldn't know what dose of the peptide to give him or is it even safe for turtles."

I hold Melissa, sorry meant Pleb, in my arms, "Shall we do it? We are the only two of four humans left on this island. I have some fast-acting Novichok capsules. Shall we consume them while holding hands."

"Yes, all our friends are decomposing, and so have our children and grandchildren so I think that it is time to depart, but you have to be first to ingest a capsule which I will choose."

"Pleb, after all this time, you still don't trust me?"

"I was just pulling, pulling your toe-nail," she says with a laugh. Pleb has become quite what we call a stirrer, and her sense of humour has definitely developed. Even I laugh sometimes at her jokes.

"Jules, we have had a very good life, and so have our friends who lived on this island with us, and I agree with you that it is time to depart as you cannot even get your organ to rise anymore," she says with a smirk on her face.

Dyslexia and Gannnon are working at the hospital but I quickly write an inheritance will-document on the 3-D computer screen. They get to keep the island and the remaining diamonds that Juliet left us, if they want.

Bea and Sid join us. "We have decided to join the passover as it would not be fun on this island without you two. I would only have Sid to talk to, as after his vocal cord surrgury he is incapable of talking as well as performing any other duties. We will take a Novichok as well. After the exciting life I've had as a spy in the *i5* agencies and as an assassin thru the years, finally coming to this Island and seeing how people and adroids live in harmony and their value of helping as medicos, I look back and wonder. I feel regret that my life was not initially aimed at different values, rather than *i5* values, says Bea." We all clap and congratulate Bea and give her hugs.

And so the four of us take the fast acting pills and hold hands as we wait for the final monent, but then a craft apperars above us and it is streaming a big celuloid message, "Enjoy the journey" signed Julliette and Synder.

Pleb, Bea, Rog and I look at each other. "Jules, this Novichok is not working as it should; we are still alive after what seems like hours! Did you check the use by date on the Novichok capsules?" asks Bea.

The Novichok capsules were 150 years past their expiry date but they did have some side-effects; they removed the brain fog from us four remaining humans.

"Let us dance; I will put the music on," says Pleb.

An so the 3-D stereo projection system by the BBQ area starts up and a 200yr old song comes on by a music group called Vicetone. Tonight We Dance and the four of us get to live another day, gyrating throwing are arms up like teenagers on the dance floor by the BBQ area. Tonight we certainly danced, flinging our partners into the rubber reinforced walls by the BBQ.

We look at our partners, "Has it all been worth it?" I ask.

"There were so many good moments, but Pleb you are choking me, can you stop doing those wrist strengthening exercises your doing on my throat."

"Sorry Jules, I will aim lower in the future."

And so a night ends, maybe many more nights but who knows as life can definitely be very unpredictable.

About the Author

Young Julian

Julian Lechmus has had varied life experiences, such as a period of time as a young hippy and artist, then working in science as a bio-chemist, in education teaching at TAFE and also in industry. In his retirement, creative writing gives him a great deal of pleasure, utilising his wide-ranging experiences. He balances his time with a fitness programme and involvement in community activities such as Neighbourhood Watch. Julian originally came from Melbourne, the location of his first book, "Don't Look Behind the Fridge" but now lives in Kangaroo Point, Queensland.